Praise for Gabriele Wills's first novel,

A Place To Call Home

"**A Place To Call Home** is a gripping and fascinating saga about an Irish family's immigration to Canada and the building and founding of the [*fictional*] Ontario town called Launston Mills. Wills masterfully traces the development of the town, told through the eyes of Irish immigrant, Rowena, and her son, Keir. The historical facts were flawlessly researched, but rather than it reading like a series of facts, Wills peopled the book with vivid and very real characters whose experiences captivate the reader. .... an exceptionally well-told story. ... **A Place To Call Home** offers a delightful glimpse into Canada's past, told through characters who come to life and jump off the page. Very well done." - *Writer's Digest* Magazine

The following are excerpts from readers' comments.
You can see more at
www.mindshadows.com/publishing/place/comments.htm

"Thank you for writing this important book, which I enjoyed immensely.... Apart from the story line, which I believe carries the narrative brilliantly, I was fascinated by the wide spectrum of characterization."

"Absolutely wonderful! **A Place To Call Home** is so vivid, descriptive and intriguing...I couldn't put it down! You made me feel like I was part of the story from beginning to end. The characters are so real, their lives so intense that it stirred emotion. You intertwine fact and fiction in such an interesting way...so insightful."

"I am not much of a book reader, but your fictional chronology of a pioneering family felt so real to me that I read the entire book in about 2 days."

"I was immersed in your descriptive and vivid writing style, which flowed so magically."

"You have a very special gift of relating historical events in a wonderfully interesting manner."

"I found the book to be a fascinating and insightful story about family relationships, romance, and 'roughing it' in Upper Canada. It was a wonderful read!"

"I could go on and on about how much I've enjoyed getting to know the characters, how I've become involved in their struggles, and tremendously impressed by their courage as well as moved by their human frailties."

"The fiction interwoven with your detailed research kept me reading chapter through chapter, only stopping when I had to!!!"

"Your book... is a superb story start to finish."

"The characters and the story itself were so compelling, I was reluctant to put the book down once I started to read it!"

"I really loved and related to your **A Place To Call Home**. I have read it twice and got much enjoyment out of both reads."

"When I wasn't reading the book, I was thinking about it."

"I have just finished reading it for the third time.... Like long-time friends, a good book teaches one something through every reading!"

A Place To Call Home

is available online and at select stores, which are listed on the following website:
www.mindshadows.com/publishing/place

Moon Hall

To Claudia,
All the best!

Gabriele

A Novel by

Gabriele Wills

Cover photo by Melanie Wills

National Library of Canada Cataloguing in Publication

Wills, Gabriele, 1951-
    Moon Hall / Gabriele Wills. -- 1st ed.

ISBN 0-9732780-1-3

    I. Title.

PS8595.I576M66 2004   C813'.6
C2004-906085-6

First edition
Published by Mindshadows
http://www.mindshadows.com
Printed and bound in Canada

Author's Notes

Todmorden and Kintyre will not be found on any map of Ontario, but are representative of the unique character of Ottawa Valley towns and villages. Although this is a work of fiction, a few historical personages do mingle with the fictional characters. Great care was taken in the research to provide the reader with an accurate account of our social history.

I'm deeply grateful to all those who took the time to send me their comments about my first novel, *A Place To Call Home*. There is no greater compliment to a writer than to hear – repeatedly – "I couldn't put the book down!"

Once again I'm indebted to Dorothy Lumley for her astute editorial contributions, to my daughter, Melanie, for creating the artistic cover photograph, and to my husband, John, for helping me deal with the vagaries of computers!

This book is dedicated to my husband, John, in fond remembrance of our Ottawa and Valley years!

Prologue:

November 19, 1879

Violet McAllister slid her diary into the secret compartment of the desk and shut it in. Her life, cloistered in darkness, concealed. She could appreciate the irony of it.

She ran her hand over the smooth wood, which, cleverly constructed, gave no clue to the hollow that served as a crypt for her words. She wedged the key into the crack at the back of the drawer. From habit, for there was no purpose for it now. She might as well toss it away. And yet, might it not pose a puzzle to someone? Would anyone even care to speculate on this little key or be intrigued enough to search for its mate?

Once she was gone, did it really matter who discovered the dreadful secrets of her life?

She lined up the letters on her desk, more tidy than she had ever cared to be. One to her solicitor brother-in-law and one to the vicar. She stared at the third for a long time and suddenly snatched it up and tossed it into the fire. She watched the flames taste the paper and then devour it. It was better that way. Let him have no regrets.

Now there was only one thing left to do before Dr. Townsend arrived.

She had given Betsy the afternoon off and the Skuces wouldn't be back today. So the house was silent, save for the ticking of the grandfather clock in the hall. Violet's boots clicked loudly on the polished hardwood floors. The noise was intrusive, shattering her fragile calm.

She let out a howl of rage and despair. Who was there to hear after all? But it did nothing to lessen her anguish.

She stepped out into the sombre November afternoon, under a sky swollen with the first snow of winter. She glanced about her beloved domain once more. But the gardens she had so lovingly tended resembled a graveyard, and the wooded ravine, the blackened bones of summer. Beyond, the barren patchwork fields stretched across the windswept valley to the distant hills.

She couldn't find the beauty in it anymore. It was the blackness in her mind seeping out, encompassing all.

It had already smothered the goodness in her, leaving her with nothing but festering hatred and bitterness and anger. Soon it would destroy everything she touched. She couldn't allow herself to sink to that. Above all she feared madness.

Violet strode through the ice-crisped meadow grass to the orchard, unaware of the biting wind. She knelt beside a wooden cross and whispered, "I'll be with you soon, Tristan." The thought gave her comfort. It would be such a relief to be a spirit unencumbered by all this earthly pain.

The first wet flakes of snow were falling as she retraced her steps. She stopped outside the carriage house, staring down toward the secret garden. She could just glimpse the half-naked Pan through the winter-bare trees. He looked absurd in his cocky brazenness, defying even the winter storms. She marched down to her once-favourite spot.

He mocked her, this stone god. *Foolish mortal!* He had witnessed moments of great joy, and of deep despair. And he had merely laughed. With a mighty heave, she toppled him from the plinth, but he thudded unharmed to the earth. *Foolish mortal!*

She ran to the carriage house, her face wet with tears and melting flakes of snow. Inside, she took a sturdy rope off the hook and slung it over a beam.

Chapter 1

June 1, 1980

Dear Fran,

Have you ever wanted to live in a Norman Rockwell painting? If so, then you may well envy me, because I'm living on the edge of one!

When I left Nigel, I had to leave Toronto as well. And I couldn't stay with Mom and Dad! Oh, a few weeks were alright, but I need my own space, away from Mom's overly solicitous mothering. She even wanted to cancel her visit to you because she thought I needed her to look after me!

Of course she and Dad will be upset at my buying this house while they are away. Dad likes to be consulted, and Mom will think it's too far away (about a 4 hour drive from Launston Mills). But I already love it here. I wish you weren't on the other side of the world just now! How can I wait another year and a half to show you my treasure? Tell that brother of mine that I'm still annoyed that he took that job in Australia!

And tell the girls that I miss them. I so enjoyed my visit in January!

And maybe getting away from Nigel then helped me to overcome my inertia and make a decision.

Of course, Mom thinks I'm giving up too easily. She thinks that I should try to work things out with Nigel, that relationships shouldn't be discarded as carelessly as old clothes. I think she is secretly relieved that we never married, for now there won't be the shame of divorce. But of course, she hated my living "in sin" with him, too, didn't she?

Do you know why I finally left Nigel? Because he called me a literary harlot! "You have a marvellous style," he said, "but your plots are tripe - pure, unadulterated garbage. I can't understand why you prostitute your talent like that."

I riposted with my opinion of literary critics. "And you are nothing but a parasite!" I told him. "Feeding off the glory of others. Ingesting, digesting, and then spewing out your own brand of trash. I wonder if you've ever had an original thought or opinion. I will write my 'Great Canadian Novel'! But it will be in spite of you, not because of you."

How ridiculous it all sounds when I put the facts down on paper. Who else but you would believe that a long-standing relationship could be destroyed by literary criticism?

But it was a bitter quarrel. I'm afraid there was much said between us that was unforgivable, each of us striking at the very credibility of the other. Even your level-headed intervention could not have saved us this time, Fran. You know that I haven't been happy lately anyway, so this was just the impetus - or excuse - I needed.

I wonder if I ever truly loved him, or whether I was just impressed by his seeming intellectual superiority.

Remember how we (and all his other students!) used to drool over him? An English prof who looked like a cross between Byron and Paul McCartney. I don't think I ever quite reconciled my romantic notion of him with the real man. Maybe I've always been a bit disillusioned.

Anyway, I felt restless after Mom and Dad left. I wanted to find a place for myself - not in Launston Mills, which makes me feel as if I never left high school. (Horrors!) But I didn't really know what I was looking for. I spent weeks driving aimlessly, becoming more and more disheartened. I was just about ready to go back to England (to write my Great Canadian Novel?) when I found it - this quaint little village. The sun was dappling the broad expanse of lawns through a canopy of tender, spring-green leaves, and warming the mellowed Victorian brick and stone and clapboard houses. There was the old general store, proclaiming itself as such. Not a supermarket or a Mac's Milk to be seen. There (for God's sake!) was a real, live, working blacksmith! And, would you believe, two churches? There was the ruin of an old stone mill, weathered smooth, the boulders moss-encrusted. There was the tumbledown railway station, its tracks overgrown, but still evoking images of a gentler time. I felt that, if I were to listen long enough, I would hear the ghostly whistles of those long-ago trains.

Yes, I know that you think I'm a hopeless romantic. (Nigel once told me I was living my life vicariously through my own fictional characters. Bastard!) But I'm not romanticizing. It really is a most charming and tranquil place. The countryside is reminiscent of the Sussex Downs - or perhaps Thomas Hardy country. Perhaps I have found my Wessex. Rolling hills, scattered farms and woodlands.

My own house sits on a rise above a laconic stream. How this magnificent piece of Canadiana could have stood empty for two years is beyond my comprehension. It's called "Moon Hall" - isn't that wonderfully evocative?

Built circa 1840 by the well-to-do millowner, its stone walls are nearly three feet thick. It has a parlour (I daren't call it a living room), a dining room, one other room (back parlour? morning room?), and a library complete with bookcases. Above are four oversized bedrooms and a modern bathroom. The kitchen is in its own wing - a beautiful monster of a kitchen with a cavernous fireplace and a brick bake oven built into the wall next to it! A couple of rooms off the kitchen must once have been a pantry and scullery, but now serve as laundry room and storage area. A narrow staircase leads up to three small bedrooms that must have housed the servants. These quarters have no access to the second floor of the house, and since I don't need seven bedrooms (or servants), I can close up that section. There's a three-bay drive-shed - also of stone - stretching out behind the kitchen. The house is on three acres, and is two miles from the village. And best of all, it cost me no more than a townhouse in the city! Incredible!

If you haven't yet sensed it, Fran, I want you to know that I am absurdly happy! I moved in only yesterday....

Kit paused to glance around the library. "Moved in" was hardly the most appropriate phrase, she thought. It suggested a tractor-trailer depositing crates and cartons and roomsful of furniture. All she had brought were her clothes, boxes of books, and a few paintings and knick-knacks. Everything else had belonged to Nigel.

That was indicative of their relationship, she thought. Indicative of the way that Nigel had dominated her life. Had she really been with him for seven years?

The morning sun struggled through the grime of the tall, deepset windows, and skidded across the newly-polished mahogany desk. Kit caressed the smooth surface, feeling a childlike thrill of joy at its ownership. It had been a bargain! She suspected that, had it been possible to remove this enormous desk without actually chopping it into pieces, it would long since have gone to the auction block. Surely the room had been built around it!

She had also bought the scarred refectory table in the kitchen, along with its mismatched antique chairs, an old couch in the parlour, and the surprisingly modern appliances

Kit gazed at the bookcases, the shelves barely visible through the ochre patina of accumulated dust and tobacco smoke on the glass doors. Her books (quite a collection, she had thought) would barely fill a tenth of them.

How it must have looked once! Row upon row of leather-bound volumes, most of them so new that their spines cracked when they were opened. The mill owner sitting at this desk, going over his accounts, puffing on his pipe. In the background, barely discernible through the heavy doors, the sound of children playing, the swish of silken skirts, the aroma of baking bread....

She was getting carried away again, her mind forever drifting off to conjure up lost times as if reliving old memories. But none of her own memories dwelt here. Not yet.

And all that was here now was the dust, decades of it. She sighed. It would take her weeks to clean this place. Weeks before she could get down to her novel.

Kit resumed writing her letter.

After I've made this place habitable, I'll start on my novel - I should write MY NOVEL. You know, the one Nigel has been hounding me to write ever since we met.

Would she be writing this book for Nigel? No, no, no! Wasn't it what she had always wanted to do? A serious work of fiction, not the Gothic genre that seemed to have become her forte.

I know that I can write it here. I could never have done it under Nigel's tutelage.

And she never would have. It was strange how perverse she was when she was with him, she suddenly realized. She had revelled in playing the anti-intellectual. Perhaps that had been her only defence.

A knock on the door saved her from further reflection. She stepped into the spacious entrance hall, but saw no one through the etched glass of the sidelights. Another knock seemed to emerge from the kitchen. Kit hastened to that wing.

For a brief moment she thought, "Nigel!" and then realized that he had no idea of her whereabouts. Anyway, Nigel would saunter in as though he owned the place and were just late in arriving. *Interesting house. Don't think much of the decor, darling. But I suppose we could do something with it.*

A picture of his townhouse flashed into her mind. Close to the university, in a once-fashionable district that had in recent years seen a much-needed revitalization, it was as schizophrenic as Nigel himself. The exterior was a beautifully and painstakingly restored Victorian brick rowhouse. Inside, nary a vestige of its former self remained. It was an ultra-modern statement in black and white, in open spaces, in chrome and vinyl and mirrors. It was sleek, characterless, and sterile. Nigel's particular favourite was the attic party room, a huge open space lit with skylights, and boasting a spectacular sound system, a well-stocked bar, low, yielding couches, and lots of seductive pillows for people to lounge on, arranged in convenient "conversation" areas.

Kit shook herself out of her reverie. Two women, clad in what she immediately thought of as their Sunday best, greeted her when she opened the kitchen door.

"How do you do?" the elder of the two said. "I'm Jean McGrath. This is my daughter-in-law, Mary. We're your nearest neighbours. The farm over there." She indicated the place less than a quarter of a mile down the road.

The two women were about as different physically as was possible. Mary was short and curvy, running to pudginess - voluptuous compared to her mother-in-law's tall, rake-thin angularity. Jean's somewhat craggy features gave her a canny look, and hinted at a strong personality. Kit imagined that Mary, all smiles and dimples, was easily dominated by her mother-in-law.

"I'm Kit Spencer, and I'm delighted to meet you. Won't you come in?"

"We're on our way to church, and thought we'd just stop by to welcome you to the neighbourhood."

Both women cast quick, appraising glances into the room.

"We know how busy you must be, this being your first day and all," Jean said. "So, well, we thought you might like to join us for dinner."

"Thank you, I'd love to!"

"Fine. Dinner's at one. Well, we'd best be on our way."

"I'll see you then." Kit said awkwardly.

She watched the car roar to life, back out the driveway, and disappear down the road toward the village.

Kit poured herself another cup of coffee. The coffee maker, dishes, pots and pans, cutlery - all were new. It was sad, really, how little she had to show for her 30 years, what few possessions to which she could attach memories.

Perhaps it was just as well that everything had been Nigel's. At least she had nothing to remind her constantly of him.

A resounding thunk on the door startled her. Another welcoming committee?

A small, spare woman, dressed in what was surely a catalogue sales special, greeted her. Her chinless face gave undue prominence to her sharp snout of a nose, reminding Kit of a mole.

"Gidday! Myrtle Skuce. This here's my daughter, Bonnie."

The girl seemed to be about fourteen. She wore tight, faded jeans ending above the ankles, and a sloppy grey sweater, the elbows mended with ragged stitches of a different shade. Her dirty-blonde hair hung in greasy strands about a remarkably fine-featured face, creamy white skin, and lovely, but doleful, brown eyes.

Kit introduced herself and invited them in.

"What a grand kitchen this is!"

"Coffee?"

"Well, I wouldn't say no." Myrtle slid onto one of the chairs, and, with a sharp jerk of her head, motioned to Bonnie, who was wandering about. The girl obediently took a seat next to her mother.

"Always liked this house," Myrtle said, as Kit placed steaming mugs of coffee on the table. "Mind you, it must be a bugger to keep clean. Now you'll be interested to hear that my husband's great grandparents once ran this here house. Jeremiah Skuce was the head gardener and his wife, Margaret, was the housekeeper and cook. They were so highly thought of that they were remembered in two of the family's wills! Interesting times, they were, as you'll no doubt hear." Myrtle looked slyly at Kit, as if she were bursting to reveal a shocking secret.

"Really?" Kit prompted, always interested in gossip, which she considered grist for the writer's mill.

"Sure, the McAllisters were queer people. Especially that Violet - she was the last of them to live here. A real character, she was. But enough said for now! There are some things a young girl like you doesn't want to know about. Not when you're living here alone."

Kit wondered how the woman could possibly have known that. Had someone watched her move in?

"Big house for just one person," Myrtle persisted. "No husband, eh?"

"No."

Well, whenever you get lonesome now, you just give me a ring."

"That's very kind of you, Myrtle. So, you live around here?" Kit thought it a ridiculous thing to say. She could see only two other houses from here, the McGrath farm, toward the village, and a farm in the other direction. "Around here" in country idiom could be miles away.

"That's right. Just down the road. Can't see it from here, of course. Next past the Bryce farm. Jeremiah built it with his inheritance from old McAllister, over 100 years ago that was. And this here place is even older, but it's stood up pretty well. Mind you, I wouldn't be surprised if there wasn't a few things to be put to rights. These old houses, you know. Always something wants fixing. If there's any repairs to be done, you can't do better'n my Wayne. He can fix about anything, he's that handy. And he'll charge you a fair price, mind. Not like some plumber or carpenter as you'd have to get from the town. Charge you extra, they do, to drive the twelve miles out here."

The nearest town was Kintyre, with a population of 5000.

"Is Wayne your husband?"

"Nope. One of my sons. The oldest. About your age, I reckon."

"How many children do you have?"

"Eleven. And all of them can turn a hand to something! There's Billy, just seventeen he is, but he can take any motor apart and put it to rights. Why, even the youngest lad, he's nine, could cut the grass for you, or chop some firewood. If you don't want to be bothered doing it yourself.

"But I can't says how I regret being past my childbearing years now. Why, I just had to stand downwind of Jack and I'd be knocked up." She laughed at what seemed to be an oft-quoted joke. "So... what brings you out this way?"

Kit had been wondering how to answer that inevitable question.

"I wanted to get away from the city, to have some peace and quiet." Since that sounded rather rude, she quickly amended it by adding, "I'm a writer."

"That a fact?" Myrtle's sharp, black eyebrows rose a fraction of an inch. "Can't say's I seen your name now."

There it was, that feeling of embarrassment, that conditioned rush of blood to her cheeks. Nigel had done that to her, had made her feel that acknowledging her work was like... like admitting to masturbation. Damn him!

She said, "I write under a pseudonym. Victoria Penn."

Myrtle's eyebrows, had they not been so securely anchored to her face, would surely have taken wing. "Well don't that beat all! Eh, Bonnie? Why, didn't we just finish your last book the other week? And a grand tale it was, I don't mind saying. Well... don't that beat all!"

The awe on the woman's face, the sudden silence, brought a new rush of embarrassment. Kit had never done publicity tours, and thus had met few people who had ever praised her work. Even in her hometown she was still just a local girl who had a successful career, not unlike other people's successful kids who were doctors or lawyers or professors or company presidents.

Nigel and his friends thought her novels frivolous, and viewed her as some sort of exploiter of the human condition.

Pure escapist pulp. The words still rang in her head. *You're capable of better work.*

I enjoy writing them, and people enjoy reading them, judging by the sales. Nigel had never complained about the money the books earned. Never thought of it as tainted as her work.

There's enough of that trash on the market. Too much. You have to write something that reflects the real world, something that will make people think, evaluate their lives. Instead, you pander to the human condition. If women can escape into one of your novels for even a little while, they'll have that much less incentive to climb out of their own mediocrity.

How those sweeping, arrogant generalizations infuriated her! Listening to Nigel, one would think that he was of some different breed from the "people" that he championed. But Kit could never argue with him. His arrogance would bring her to such a boil that she could no longer think logically or debate coherently.

Nigel was always cool. Analytical. Nothing roused him to a passion. It was as though he truly cared for nothing.

Yet he had cared enough for her once, hadn't he?

"I loved it, " Bonnie said quietly.

"Now here's one of your biggest fans. Spends half her time reading, and the other half, mooning about, thinking herself one of them grand ladies she reads about."

Those words hit a vulnerable spot. Was that what Nigel had meant? Creating false hopes in a world of illusion?

"When her sisters were fifteen, they were out working, waitressing at the Wild Horse Inn. They looked eighteen, sure enough, and nobody thought different. Brought in good money they did too. But this one here now, I reckon she takes after me more. Never had nothing up front or on behind, to speak of. Nothing for a man to get his hands on." She laughed and looked at Kit with a smirk, as if they shared some dirty joke.

Kit was beginning to find this woman's vulgarity offensive. She had hidden her surprise at the coarse language, and her disapproval of it being used in the presence of the girl - though

Bonnie was probably accustomed to it. Kit had not wanted to judge her new neighbours too quickly. Yet the woman was like some noisome odor that Kit would be heartily glad to be rid of.

"I reckon you'll be mighty busy with your writing then. Now Bonnie here, she's right good at cleaning. Never mind what I said about her mooning, 'cause she knows right enough if she don't do a job good she'll get a hiding."

Kit felt sympathetic toward the girl, who sat mutely beside her mother. There was about her an air of fatalism and a tragic beauty. Kit could already imagine her as the heroine of her next Gothic novel - a love-child, farmed out to an old harridan, who doesn't discover her true identity, her noble heritage, until almost the last chapter... There she was, romanticizing again. For this girl there would be no such easy escape.

"I'm sure there won't be any need for that, Myrtle." To Bonnie she said, "Would you like a job cleaning this house?"

"Oh yes, Miss Penn!"

"It's Spencer, but do call me Kit. Once this place has had a thorough cleaning, it shouldn't take more than a few hours a week to keep it in shape. I shan't be using much of it, actually. Well, then I'll see you after school tomorrow, Bonnie," Kit said, rising, hoping that the Skuce woman would take the hint and leave.

"Why, the girl could start right away if you like...."

"Tomorrow will be soon enough, thank you, Myrtle. It was so kind of you to drop by."

"Well, I'm right proud to have made your acquaintance." Myrtle clasped Kit's hand in a hearty shake. It was a thin, skeletal hand, rough and dry, but warm. Kit suddenly felt there was a certain poignancy about Myrtle Skuce. She had no idea what sort of life this woman had, but she was certain it had not been an easy one. And Kit felt contrite. Who was she to judge Myrtle and to patronize her?

That was the way Nigel would have behaved.

"Do come again, won't you?"

"I'd be right pleased to, and that's a fact. Now you remember... anything at all you want done, you just give us a ring."

When they had gone, Kit had less than an hour to ready herself. As she was showering, she recalled Myrtle's enigmatic hint of some mystery to do with... was it Violet McAllister? She had been so surprised that Myrtle had known she lived here alone, that the woman's allusion had not even registered in her consciousness. But now Kit was intrigued. Maybe the McGraths would be more forthcoming with the "Mystery of Moon Hall"!

Not since she had lived at home had Kit had Sunday dinner in the middle of the day. Nigel liked to sleep late on Sundays and then lounge around the attic room in his pajamas, drinking cups of strong, black coffee, and listening to old records. He liked making love to her there, with the sun streaming in to warm their nakedness amid the haphazard tumble of cushions. Jokingly, he had once said that that was his religion, that others could sit primly on the hard church pews and extol the glories of God, if that's how they wished to waste a Sunday morning, but that he couldn't think of a better way to celebrate life. Afterwards, they'd inevitably meet his friends for brunch somewhere, and the day would drift into oblivion.

But Sundays still first conjured up thoughts of morning church service with her parents and brother, Richard, followed by the traditional dinner fare - roast beef, Yorkshire pudding, roasted potatoes, crisp vegetables, and a fruit pie. And when they had been old enough, she and Richard had partaken of the pre-dinner sherry, and the burgundy with the meal. For her parents, there had been the post-prandial rest before the substantial late-afternoon "tea" with all kinds of cakes and biscuits.

How stiflingly Victorian! Nigel had said to her after the first time he had shared their Sunday. And yet, she was certain that that had been part of her appeal for him. He, with his fascination for Victoriana, seemed to have both a longing for and revulsion of that era. If she had met him socially first, she would never have imagined him a professor of Victorian literature, but he had been an excellent teacher. And that was how they had met....

Kit was looking forward to sharing what appeared to her to be a traditional kind of Sunday with her new neighbours. Not wanting to go empty-handed, she decided that a bottle of red wine would be appropriate, and was glad she had brought a stock of her favourite wines along.

It was a glorious day - warm, sunny, fresh-scented. With the wind at her back, there was only a slight but not repulsive odour from the cows that grazed in the pasture across the road from her. They were probably the McGraths' cows.

At the bottom of the drive she turned to survey, with an intense pride of ownership, her domain. What a charming, dignified house it was. The smoky stone was tinged with blue and pink, giving it a warm glow in the sunshine. It was two storeys tall, with a gothic-arched window in a peaked gable above the entrance. The heavy, panelled front door was surrounded by elegant sidelights and elliptical transom. Across the symmetrical front stretched a veranda - in surprisingly good repair - which wandered around the corner to the kitchen wing.

To the right lay an overgrown orchard, the tangled apple trees bedecked like June brides with halos of delicate white blossoms. That sight brought mouth-watering anticipation of a bountiful harvest of apples. (What would she do with so many? Set up a road-side stand?)

About two hundred feet behind the house the land dropped sharply into a wooded ravine through which a shallow stream trickled. Beyond this belt of trees, a patchwork of fields undulated toward distant hills. Dotted about the valley were miniature farms, their silos glistening in the sun. It all seemed like some delightful child's toy. And Kit was the delighted child.

To the left of the house lay sparsely-treed grounds separated from the meadow beyond by a stone wall. There must once have been lovely formal gardens surrounding the house, judging by the rampant shrubbery, much of it in bloom, the carefully spaced but overgrown evergreens, the shoots of unknown perennials, the tired clumps of daffodils. How easy it was to picture pruned, orderly shrubs, spade-edged perennial borders, ladies in silk gowns gliding across velvet lawns.

Kit felt a sudden urge to tackle that rank garden, to dig her hands into the rich black soil, to plant seeds that would burst into glorious midsummer flowers. Perhaps she would even grow vegetables. Wouldn't that be something? To eat fresh produce from your own backyard? The idea so enchanted and excited her that she was determined to begin tomorrow.

Kit hurried down the road, or tried to. Her high-heeled shoes did not allow for sure footing or an easy gait on the rough gravel. She would have to add a pair of sensible dress shoes to her list of necessary purchases.

A narrow wooden bridge spanned the creek, which curved around the house and outbuildings of the McGrath farm. The streambed here was just a shallow depression, no longer a ravine as it was behind her own house. Kit crossed it and turned up the long laneway.

The large, red-brick house ahead of her was in the vernacular style so typical of Ontario farmhouses. As Kit approached, she noticed that there was no walkway to the front door. Shrubs grew thickly around the porch, and, although not exactly overgrown, they lent an air of disuse to this entrance. Had it been boarded up, it could not have looked less welcoming.

Recalling that her visitors had come to her kitchen door, she thought it prudent to do likewise. So she continued along the drive. Here, sunny beds of spring flowers edged the house. A picnic table stood nearby, under a towering elm. Beside it, an old dog lazed in the sun. He cocked an eye at the intruder, grumbled, and let out a sharp bark. His duty done, he laid his head back down on his paw and closed his eyes contentedly.

A well-trudged path led to the back door, standing open in the afternoon sun. Kit almost breathed a sigh of relief, and then felt rather ridiculously proud of herself for having so effortlessly learned her first lesson in country living - no one used the front door.

The screen door was flung open before she had a chance to knock, and Mary, her cheeks bright pink, her blonde curls bouncing, ushered her into the kitchen. There was a curious look on Mary's smiling face, a sort of feverish excitement.

"Is it true?" she asked. "Are you really Victoria Penn?"

Jean, stirring a sauce at the stove, said, "Goodness sakes, Mary! We haven't even welcomed Kit into our home, and here you are, pestering her with questions!"

But Kit barely heard the good-natured reprimand. "How did you find that out?"

Jean said matter-of-factly, "Myrtle Skuce was at your place an hour ago, isn't that so? Well, then, I expect there isn't a soul in the village hasn't heard that we have a famous writer in our midst." Jean seemed amused at Kit's surprise.

"I'm flattered that you've even heard of me."

"We've read all your books, Mary and I. Wouldn't miss one of your novels now, would we, Mary? Then we pass them on at the Women's Institute, so I don't think you'll find too many hereabouts who haven't heard of you, and, I might add, enjoy your work."

"You're embarrassing the hell outa the poor girl, Jean," a gruff male voice said.

Kit had hitherto been too stunned to notice the other occupants of the room. She turned toward the long wooden table where three men sat before mugs of frothy ale.

Jean said, "My husband, Duncan. My sons, Stuart and Alan."

Although seated, Duncan did not look as though he would reach his wife's formidable height. He was stocky and grizzled, with a tanned hide and powerful hands that looked proportionally too large for his body.

Stuart's rugged handsomeness rather surprised Kit. And yet, as she looked more closely, she could see that he had his mother's height and her large dark eyes and glossy black hair, his father's muscularity and sensitive mouth (which was all but hidden amid the coarse silver stubble on Duncan's face and distorted by the pipe that dangled first from one corner of his mouth and then the other).

Alan, however, had not inherited the same pleasing configuration of features. He looked like a caricature of his older brother, with a comical face and a lopsided grin.

Duncan said, "Sit yourself down, girl. Alan, get the lady a drink. What'll you have? Beer? Rye and coke? Gin?"

Kit declined. "Nothing at the moment, thanks. Oh, I brought a bottle of wine for you."

"Mighty kind of you," Duncan said, shifting his pipe from one corner of his mouth to the other.

Mary took it from her. "How lovely. I'll put it in the freezer."

"That's not necessary," Kit said, realizing that wine was not a customary drink in this household.

"No problem," Mary replied. "Then it'll be nice and cold by the time dinner is ready."

"But red wine is served at room temperature, Mary," Stuart said. "Isn't that so, Miss Spencer?"

Kit thought she could detect a note of contempt in that challenge, and wondered why. How would poor Mary feel at having her ignorance of wine etiquette exposed, particularly in front of someone whom she professed to admire. (Although Kit could not associate herself with that person.)

She felt a sudden surge of anger at this man. Calmly she asked, "Is your beer cold?"

"Yes."

"An Englishman wouldn't consider drinking cold ale. Says it destroys the flavour of the brew. And I'm sure that a Frenchman doesn't chill his red wine. But there's nothing to say that you can't. I suppose it's all a matter of what you yourself prefer." Now her eyes challenged him, but he looked away. She'd made an enemy, she thought, incredulous.

Mary said lightly, "Well, then we'll have our wine like the French do."

Duncan shifted the pipe again. All his comments seemed to be prefaced by this gesture. "Not for me, thanks, Mary. I'll stick to my usual."

Which turned out to be several glasses of rye and coke. The others politely tried a glass of wine, served in water tumblers. Mary had attempted to hide a grimace after her first taste, but seemed to be enjoying it more as the level in her glass dropped. Jean hardly touched hers. Alan soon gave up, and helped himself to another beer. Only Stuart seemed to be savouring it.

He eyed her over the rim of his glass as if to say, "So far we're equal. What else do you have to prove?"

But Kit ignored him. The others were providing her with interesting insights into the area, the neighbours, the services provided by the town, the history of the village and of their own family.

The first McGrath had arrived here nearly a century and a half ago. All this land had been wilderness - dense, primitive forest. His ancestors had hacked out a clearing, and built their first home with the massive timbers, Duncan told her proudly. The old log cabin still stood, if she'd care to see it after dinner.

The next house had been clapboard, the part that now served as kitchen, and as the family had grown and prospered, so had the house, which - after two more additions - now had two sitting rooms, a dining room, a study, and five bedrooms.

The dining room, in which they now sat, was a lovely, airy room with a high ceiling and tall, lace-edged windows. The patterned wallpaper was old and faded, but suited the 19th century atmosphere of the room.

An enormous walnut dining table and matching china cabinet and buffet table must have been the pride of some ancestor. They had been lovingly polished and cared for over the years, so that the wood had a warm patina. The table was covered with a crisp white linen cloth, and laid with fine old china - some pieces slightly cracked or chipped - and heavy sterling silver cutlery engraved with an ornate *M* on the handles. A vase of fresh flowers added a touch of colour to the table.

The room - indeed, the house - had that pleasant old wood smell that Moon Hall had, with just a hint of lemon furniture polish, overlaid with the delectable aroma of the dinner spread before them.

"We'll be like three little peas rattling about in this great old pod once Stu and Mary move out," Jean said. "You'll have noticed the house they're building themselves, just down the road a ways."

That rather nondescript shell of a bungalow.

"Not that I can blame them for wanting a place of their own," Jean said, echoing Kit's own thoughts. "They've been married - what is it now? - eight years?"

Before his mother or his wife could say anything more about his domestic arrangements, Stuart asked, "Do you know anything about the history of Moon Hall?"

Kit told him what little she knew, and they all added tidbits of local lore.

"McAllister was a large, powerful man. Could carry a hundredweight sack of flour on each shoulder as easily as..."

"... He had eight women in his care. Seven daughters to marry off...."

"And he killed his wife, trying to get a son. She gave him one too, but the baby didn't live longer than she did, poor soul..."

"Strangely, he never married again. So the McAllister name died out, though there must be plenty of his descendants around, what with all those daughters of his having families. Mind you, they all moved away - Ottawa, Montreal, Toronto."

"All except for Violet," Stuart said.

Did she imagine the moment of strained silence, Kit wondered, before Mary hastily informed her, "All his daughters were named after plants - Rose, Iris, Daisy, Hazel, Lily, Heather."

"And Violet, of course," Stuart reiterated.

Jean started to change the subject, but Kit interrupted her. "And what happened to Violet?" she asked Stuart, who seemed as eager to talk about her as the rest of his family was reticent. "Myrtle Skuce has already intrigued me with references to her."

"She never married. So she stayed on, all alone in that big house. She'd been in love with a local lad, a ne'er-do-well, her father had claimed. McAllister had refused to let her see him again, and sent the lad away with money in his pocket and a flea in his ear. When the lad came back for a visit years later, he was a rich and successful man - had made it big in the brewing business. And he'd brought along his glamorous wife. Violet had always claimed he'd be back for her. She'd waited all those years. But he'd as good as forgotten her. So she hanged herself. But some think she lives there still."

Stuart had delivered that last line so off-handedly that it had been robbed of melodrama.

"Oh, good. Then she can keep me company," Kit quipped.

The others laughed nervously. Alan said, "You asshole, Stu. What do you want to go and spook Kit for?"

"I'm only telling her what she'd hear from anyone else," Stuart said in innocent surprise. "In fact, I'm surprised that Myrtle Skuce didn't already blurt it out. She's usually the town crier around here. Anyway, Kit didn't strike me as being skittish. City folk have to put up with real threatening situations all the time. The ghost of a harmless old crackpot won't disturb her sleep, I'm sure."

Kit wasn't so sure, but she wasn't about to let Stuart see that his words had disturbed her. But what bothered her most at this moment was his blatant antagonism toward her. She had never been so swiftly and totally rejected by anyone before. It both puzzled and intrigued her.

"Was she a crackpot? Violet?" Kit asked.

Jean answered, "Eccentric, they say. She used to wear trousers, and men's frock coats. Actually, she was a good friend of Hugh and Ruth McGrath, Duncan's great-grandparents. Violet and Ruth used to paint together. We have one of Violet's paintings here. I'll show you after dinner."

"Were there any other interesting characters who lived in Moon Hall?" Kit asked.

Alan said, "You should have seen the people who owned the house before you. They came from Toronto, too. Figured they could do their own thing here, which happened to be running around in the nude." The others had already broken into laughter as they remembered, and anticipated the end of the story. "The woman used to sunbathe on the back lawn, and either didn't know we could see her when we were working in the fields, or didn't care."

Mary interrupted him. "You used to spend more time in those fields than necessary, if I recall."

"With binoculars," Stuart added.

Alan shrugged nonchalantly amid the laughter. "Well, they used to wander around the house stark-naked, too, only they got caught out a few times with people coming to the door, and being able to see them rush past the windows to get a coat or something on. Must have frozen their butts off. They didn't last through the first winter."

"They did a lot of work to the old place, though," Jean said. "Saved it from ruin, I'd say. I'll bet they put more money into fixing it up than they spent to buy it in the first place. And then they just up and left."

"Maybe they couldn't get along with Violet," Stuart said.

Alan shot his brother an angry look, and Mary looked embarrassed.

As if following his own thoughts, and unaware of the strained silence, Duncan said, "Yup, it's a real zoo here these days, if you ask me." He pushed his chair back from his empty plate and lit his pipe. "Wait till you meet them God-damn hippies from the next concession."

"Hippies?"

"There's a commune just behind the Bryce farm," Jean explained. "They've been there nigh on eight years now, don't you reckon, Duncan?"

"Too God-damn long for my liking," he replied.

"Pop doesn't like them because they've proved him wrong," Alan explained with a grin. "He said they'd never make a go of farming, but they've been so successful that they're putting us to shame."

"And who'd they run to for advice?" Duncan asked rhetorically. "Us, that's who. If we hadn't helped them out, they wouldn't have lasted a God-damn year!" The pipe shuffled back and forth in his mouth as if both corners were unsuitable.

"They're no bother to anyone," Jean said placatingly. "They keep themselves to themselves, and don't cause any trouble, which is more than can be said of some folk."

Duncan grudgingly admitted Jean was right, and it seemed to Kit that he would have been well pleased if these "hippies" did cause trouble and live up to his red-neck ideas. She could hardly wait to hear his opinion of women, ethnic minorities, and homosexuals, to name just a few. And if he kept guzzling those whiskies, she soon would.

"My family's been on this land a hundred and forty years," Duncan said. "It burns me up to see the young 'uns leaving for the cities. Making better lives for themselves, so they claim." He snorted in derision. "What could be better than working the land, I ask you? Land that's been worked by your family for generations. It's your legacy - that's what I always tell my lads. Our eldest now, he took off for the bright lights. An accountant he is now, and he has more money than he knows what to do with. Doesn't seem to miss the land. Hardly ever comes to see us. But I've got the other two lads with me. Not like that poor old bugger, Bryce. His son left him alone with a woman and an idiot, and him a God-damn cripple since his accident. His farm's almost as old as this one, and now it's crumbling away around him. That daughter of his keeps selling off bits of land to pay the bills, and soon there'll be nothing left. Poor, God-damn bugger!"

This had been spoken as a soliloquy. Duncan yawned and announced, "I'm going for my lie-down. Alan, show the lady the log cabin before she leaves." To Kit he said, "You let us know if there's anything you can't handle. And don't be shy to ask for help."

She thanked him, and took it to mean that she had been accepted into this rural community.

Stuart excused himself, saying he had accounts to do. Kit thanked Jean and Mary for the truly delicious meal - baked ham, scalloped potatoes, and apple pie with whipped cream - and offered to help wash up. But the women were adamant in their refusal. They told her coffee would be waiting for her when she and Alan returned from visiting the cabin.

Once they were outside, Alan said, "I feel like I should apologize for my brother. But then, if he wants to act like an asshole, why should I care?"

Kit smiled. "He does seem to have taken a dislike to me."

"He's a moody bugger," Alan said dismissively. "I think he was behaving so badly just because Mary's so starry-eyed about you. Can't stand the thought that there's someone other than himself that his wife worships."

They were ambling up the lane, past the enormous wooden barn on the streambank. "May I see inside?" Kit asked.

"If you want," Alan said with a mystified shrug, as if he couldn't imagine why anyone would care to. "Best be careful. You're not exactly dressed for mucking about in barns." His glance took in her expensive silk dress and flimsy, leather shoes. "Watch where you step."

It was dingy inside. Sunlight ·squeezed through the gaps between the boards of the walls, and spotlighted the dust that hung suspended in the heavy, hay and animal-scented air. It looked misty, like a stage set behind a scrim. A loft stretched across half the length of the barn, creating eerie shadows beneath.

Kit looked up toward the rafters. "Did Violet really hang herself?"

"Yup. In the carriage house."

A shiver crept up Kit's spine. "And what about the alleged ghost? How did that superstition get started?"

Alan grinned at her with his endearing, crooked smile. "Got you worried, has it?"

"Just curious. Of course I don't believe in ghosts!"

"Good thing, I'd say - a young woman all alone in that big old house," he teased. "You know how these things get started. Someone dies in a house - especially in such a grisly way - and pretty soon people start seeing things. Particularly when a place is empty."

"Has the house stood empty for long?"

"Empty more than occupied, since I was a kid. So when you have some locals seeing lights moving about, they're more likely to think of ghosts than burglars or kids messing around, trying to scare themselves. Doesn't every kid have a 'haunted' house in the neighbourhood, where he can go to test his courage?"

"I take it that you were one of those kids once."

"Camped out by myself one night, on a dare from Stu and Cam - that's my oldest brother, Cameron. You know, the accountant. I knew the silly buggers would try to scare me, so I was prepared when they showed up at midnight - the witching hour - rattling chains, and howling like sick cats. Since that didn't work, they tied me to that old desk and left me in the dark half the night. I was eleven then. Stu was 14, and Cam, 16."

"How cruel! And dangerous." Kit wondered where Jean had been when all this was going on.

"That was nothing," Alan said, implying that he had suffered much worse under his brothers' bullying. "Seen enough of the barn? We have some milkers, chickens, a few turkeys - Thanksgiving and Christmas dinners, they'll be...."

Kit interrupted, "Then I have no wish to meet them, thank you."

Alan laughed. "I suppose you're one of those city folk that thinks your meat comes from a package and your milk, from a plastic bag."

"Let's just say I don't like to be reminded of their origins."

"Squeamish, eh?"

"Very."

"We have a lot of steak-on-the-hoof here. Your place is almost surrounded by our cattle."

"I refuse to think of them as walking roasts."

"Stu sees them as walking dollar signs."

"You mean he has no feeling for the animals?"

"He hates this place altogether," Alan said, as they stepped back into the sunshine and the light, breathable air.

"Then why does he stay?"

"You heard Pop at dinner. It's a speech we've heard a million times over the years. Stu feels it's his duty to stay. So he stays, and blames Pop for making his life miserable. The only way he can cope with it is by turning himself into a businessman. He's even computerizing now - has one of those new-fangled little machines."

"And what about you?"

Alan understood her. "I guess I've always loved this place. Never thought of myself as anything but a farmer."

"Then why doesn't your father let Stuart go?"

"We'd have to hire help. Anyway, Pop's worried that he'll have no dynasty. He doesn't think I'll ever settle down and have a wife and family. Thinks I'm irresponsible, anyway. Mary's miscarried three times already, and although things don't look promising there, Pop hasn't given up hope. I guess we're Pop's insurance policy. One of us will eventually have a son, he reckons, and Pop wants to tie the kid to the land as soon as he can."

Alan laughed. "You should see Cam's kids when they visit. You'd never know they came from generations of farmers. They complain about the stink and the bugs, and won't help with the chores. Just want to watch TV, and then grumble that we don't have cable and they can't get all their favourite programs. And one of the girls once said she wouldn't eat her Christmas dinner unless it was a store-bought turkey, not one of those nasty, dirty beasts that run around in the barn." Alan shook his head. "It nearly kills Pop."

There had seemed to be no bitterness in Alan's revelation of his father's assessment of him as "irresponsible". But Kit thought that he must surely resent that, as well as his father's choice of Stuart as heir to all this.

"All this" included the old log cabin that they had now reached. It stood on the edge of the outbuildings, near a stand of trees behind which the land sloped upward into rock-studded hills. Its days as a shelter for people, and later, animals, were long past. The roof was caving in, most of the chinking between the logs had fallen out, and the entire structure listed badly to one side. Surrounded by unmown grass half as tall as the cabin, it seemed as if it were sinking into the earth. From whence it had once come.

"Pop always wanted to preserve this old place, but never had the money to spare. Stu wants to bulldoze it down. Says it harbours varmints, and poses a danger to the children, though I don't reckon they've ever cared to go near it anyway. When we were kids, we always played here. It was our fort."

"What would you do with it?"

"Leave it as it is. I kinda like ruins," Alan said with a grin. "Anyway, it seems like a fitting end for it to just moulder away, like the folk that used to call it home. Their graves aren't far from here."

Kit smiled at him. "You have a poetic soul."

"Jeez! Makes me sound like a God-damn pansy! Maybe I'd better keep my mouth shut around you. Next thing I know, you'll be putting me in one of your books!"

"Aren't you conceited to think I might write about you," Kit said with a laugh.

"Sure! Wouldn't I make an interesting villain or something?"

"Hardly a villain, I'd say."

"But never a hero, eh?" Before she could respond, he said, "The coffee'll be ready. We'd best get back, or Mum'll have us paired up, ready for the altar. In case you haven't noticed, Kit, everyone around here knows everyone else's business. And what they don't know, they invent."

As they strolled back to the house, Alan asked, "What's Kit short for?"

"Kathryn. But no one ever calls me that - just my mother when she's annoyed with me."

Nigel had called her Kat. It felt good to be in possession of her usual nickname again.

"Coffee" included a selection of cakes, which reminded Kit of her family's Sunday teas. She enjoyed sitting in the parlour with its antique furniture that the family had accumulated over the generations. (They'd never think to buy something like that, for a very modern reclining easychair sat in front of the TV, and next to Grandma Ruth's sofa, complete with antimacassars. She was certain that all impractical or worn things had been relegated to the attic, or even the dump.)

Nigel would think it a horrible, fascinating clutter of the paraphernalia of people's lives. He much preferred his paraphernalia new and unfettered by association with anyone else's past. Perhaps it was because he judged people by their possessions that Nigel was so careful in choosing his own. And why his own were so cold and impersonal.

But this room had warmth and comfort and charm. The pictures on the walls were photographs of family groups, past and present, and some watercolours that Grandma Ruth had painted.

And there was the painting by Violet McAllister. Kit was astonished by the skill and artistry evident in the watercolour. It was a pastoral, summer scene depicting men haying in the fields.

Jean explained, "That's Hugh and his brothers. Violet must have painted this from the edge of the ravine."

No faces were visible, but one man in particular stood proud and strong. A man of the land. Was it Hugh? He was so beautifully and sensitively rendered that surely the artist had more than merely a neighbourly interest in him. Or was she romanticizing again? Anyway, her "ghost" was really beginning to fascinate her.

Kit noticed a violet painted in the bottom right-hand corner, rather than a signature, but no date.

"Violet bequeathed this painting to Hugh," Jean said. "And they do say that he was devastated by her suicide. They'd known each other since they were children."

"Do you think they had some sort of... romantic attachment?"

"The McGraths would never admit it, of course," Jean confided. "But you see it, too, don't you? The way she painted him? I'd be surprised if there hadn't been something between them."

It wasn't until she saw the men, dressed in their work clothes, heading for the barn that Kit realized how late it was. And it wasn't until she was home that she realized how relaxing the afternoon had been.

Kit spent the rest of the day unpacking. When she had finished, she poured herself a stiff drink, and wandered about the rooms, mentally furnishing them. From the back parlour she watched a brilliant, lingering sunset over the valley. And for a long time she stood in the darkening room watching the colours fade, and the sky deepen to indigo.

It wasn't until she was in bed that she remembered Violet McAllister. But her exhaustion prevented any sinister thoughts, and she soon slept.

Chapter 2

It all began with a lie. So perhaps I am responsible after all.

I am consumed by such rage and pain and shame! And fear. But I can tell no one, so you, dear diary, must bear the burden of these secrets.

My joy of last summer only increases my despair. I still recall when I first thought myself in love with Neil.

Of course I have known him since we were both children. We met at the village school, where my sisters and I attended daily classes until we were twelve, at which time each of us in turn was sent off to the Ladies' Academy in Kingston. Last summer I had just graduated from there, and how delighted I was to be truly home at Moon Hall again!

I had sometimes seen Neil during my summer holidays. He and Hugh McGrath have been best of friends for years, and so Neil often came to the McGrath farm. Although they are three years older than I, they occasionally allowed me to play with them. I've never cared much for the feminine pursuits that occupy my sisters so contentedly. So when I could sneak away, the boys would take me along to their fishing hole, or we'd race across the meadows, bareback, on our ponies. Neil would help out on the farm, and I sometimes watched the boys haying in the hot fields from the cool shadows of the ravine, where I like to sit and sketch.

When Neil finished school, he started working at Harrigan's General Store, running errands, stocking shelves, making deliveries, and doing whatever needed to be done - once, even painting the building. He has always been a hard worker, and expected to learn the business well, so that one day he might manage his own business. All this he told me, as well as his dreams of the future. I thought Father would approve of such initiative, and perhaps even offer Neil a position at the mill. How mistaken I was!

Neil delivered our weekly order from Harrigans, and although I often saw him, I rarely had the opportunity to speak more than a greeting to him. But one day in late June, a wheel broke on his wagon just as he pulled into our rutted drive. I was working in the garden, where I love to "meddle", as Jeremiah

Skuce calls it. (Jeremiah, our handyman-gardener-groom, takes a proprietorial attitude to the gardens, although it seems to me that he has no real talent or love for them. Not as I have. Perhaps he is jealous!)

Anyway, I talked to Neil about old times while he fixed the wheel. (He seems able to do anything!) When he had finished, I took him to the pump so that he could wash his hands. Mine, also begrimed with dirt, I rinsed in the cold, gushing water. Neil suddenly grasped my dripping hand, studied it for a moment, and said, "You have beautiful hands, Violet." His touch sent a thrill through me. And when our eyes met, it was as if we were instantly drawn together. "And you're the only girl I know who would use them to dig in the garden!" he added as he - reluctantly, it seemed - released my hand.

"Do you remember how we used to run along the stepping stones in the creek?" he asked me.

"Slipping into the water more often than not!' I replied, recalling well that refreshing game on hot summer days.

"Do you go to the ravine much these days?" His eyes probed mine. His words were entirely innocent for those who might overhear them, but his intense stare questioned and invited, challenged and promised. As if he had physically touched me, his look sent a shiver of anticipation into the very core of my being.

"There's no place more refreshing around here on a hot summer's day. Or evening," I replied casually.

Just then Mrs. Skuce, our cook, came out onto the back porch with a bowl of peas which she intended to shell. I know that she considers herself to be *in loco parentis* since I have no mother and my older sisters are all married now, and mistresses of their own domains. I suspect that Mrs. Skuce had noticed me talking to Neil, and figured I needed a chaperone.

She sat herself down in the wicker rocking chair and poured the pods into the apron that made an ample nest across her lap. "How's your mother then, Cornelius?" she asked.

"Same as always, Mrs. Skuce," Neil replied. "You yourself are looking well, if I may say so."

"I've no cause to complain," she replied with obvious amusement at his flattery.

"Well, I'd best be on my way," Neil said. As he turned away from Mrs. Skuce, he gave me a wink and a smile.

When he had gone, I sat down on the porch step and helped Mrs. Skuce with the peas. I enjoy working with the produce from our vegetable garden, as well as the flowers. Every few days I make new floral arrangements for the hall, and the drawing and dining rooms.

"He's a charmer, that Cornelius," Mrs. Skuce said without looking at me. "He's made many a heart flutter, I can tell you! But I'll warrant he'll be a heartbreaker."

I said nothing, for Mrs. Skuce never needed any prompting. I know that, as a lady, I should never listen to servants' gossip, but I'm fascinated by what I learn, not only about others, but about the speaker's ideas and attitudes.

After a moment, she continued. "Of course, he's not a suitable catch for any girl, coming from such a questionable background. Maude claims he's the son of her first husband. Wed only two weeks they were, when he was killed in a brawl in Ottawa. So she claims. But there's many a woman thinks herself wed - without the benefit of clergy - to any man who shares her bed. Delaney was his name. Brendan Delaney, if memory serves. No one knows if Maude was ever legally wed to Jacob Spenlowe either. He only stayed long enough to father another child on her and then left her to raise the two children.

"I have to hand it to her, she hasn't had an easy life, and has worked hard to keep the children decently clothed and fed. Mind you, things must be easier now that Cornelius and Theodora are both working. What names those children have! You'd think Maude expected them to become important people. I'm sure I've never heard of ordinary folks giving their children such fanciful names!"

I laughed at that. To me, "Cornelius" is too staid and stuffy a name for Neil, whereas "Neil" makes him sound dashing and handsome and daring. Which he is. I know that Mrs. Skuce's Christian name is Margaret, which is surely a most sensible and appropriate moniker for her.

I couldn't resist asking, "How do you know all this, about Maude Spenlowe?"

"She told us herself about her so-called husbands, but my cousin's wife knew her somewhat in Ottawa, and she it was who figured that Maude had never properly married either of them. In fact, my cousin tells me that there was more than one man hanging around Maude at the time, who could have fathered Cornelius. There are some women who are so naive about how children are conceived!" She shook her head.

Since such things were never mentioned, I was not surprised. No one had explained the mechanics of procreation to me either, and I felt annoyingly ignorant. Having noticed the local animals mate, I had my suspicions, but was still puzzled as to how this behaviour translated to humans. It was treated as a dark and sinister secret, yet could hardly be so bad since children were constantly being born. But it would do no good to point this out to Mrs. Skuce.

"And how did Maude come to be here, in Todmorden?" I asked.

"Jacob Spenlowe brought her. Cornelius was just a babe in arms, and Theodora not yet conceived. Jacob worked for your father at the mill for a year or two, and then just disappeared one day. He had a winning way with him, though soon everyone knew him to be irresponsible and selfish. Maude's been better off without him, I'd say."

It was a perfect summer day. I still remember the smell of the peas as I released them from their pods. Bees hummed and hovered about the nearby flowers. The sun poured its yellow warmth over everything, including Jeremiah, who had stopped digging weeds to wipe his brow and ease his back. He gazed longingly at the cool shade where we sat so comfortably.

I know what prompted Mrs. Skuce's next words, though she had said them often enough before. "I don't know why your father has never married again. It's not right that there's no woman in this house to see to you girls."

She was afraid that I would fall under Neil's spell, and there would be no one to stop it happening. I suppressed a grin as I said, "But, Mrs. Skuce, my sisters are all properly married to most excellent and suitable men!"

She nodded, but eyed me sternly as she said, "And it's my hope that I can say the same about you one day. You've never been like your sisters, more's the pity. Such notions you have! You should have been a boy, I think."

"Would that I were!" I replied with delight. "I can think of nothing more exciting than being allowed to participate in the world of men. Just think, Mrs. Skuce. I could manage the mill, or become a doctor or a lawyer or even Prime Minister!"

"Heaven help us!" she guffawed. "How be you get back down to earth and go fetch some mint? There's nothing like fresh mint on these sweet peas."

Thus dismissed, I stepped gaily to the herb garden to do her bidding.

That evening after supper, I went down to the ravine. Father had never taken much notice where we girls were, so long as we didn't wander too far or make mischief. Since Nanny left, when I was eight and my older sisters were supposed to supervise me, I've had lots of freedom, and everyone knows I prefer to spend my time out of doors. I'm happier perched in a tree than seated in a drawing room. Anyway, Father works in his library every evening, so there is nothing for me to do but amuse myself.

Neil came, as I knew he would. He worked late at the store, so it was sunset when he arrived, but we had some precious time together. We met almost daily after that. Only on rain-drenched, stormy nights could I find no reasonable way of escaping from the house.

What bliss those times were! We talked of our thoughts and feelings and plans more openly than we had ever spoken them to anyone.

Neil was committed to improving his family's fortunes. He worked hard to refine his skills and augment his knowledge. I thought his ambitions laudable, and was determined to help him succeed.

He held my hand as he told me his dreams, absently stroking my fingers as if he delighted in the shape and feel of them. Did he realize what fires he stoked within me with his gentle caress?

My lips were as eager as his when they met.

But one day Father caught us kissing in the ravine. He was furious. His sharp words pelted us like rocks. His brows drew together into a black line, as if underscoring his disapproval. A muscle in his cheek twitched as he gritted his teeth. Tall and powerful, he is a forbidding man at the best of times, but terrifying in his anger. I thought he would strike us both with his clenched fists.

I told Father there had been nothing between us but a chaste kiss to seal our bargain. How proud I was of Neil as he stood up to Father and announced that he loved me and wished us to wed!

I thought lightning would shoot from Father's narrowed eyes and thunder rumble from his gaping mouth. But his words came out in a tight, threatening voice. "You presumptuous scoundrel! You dare to seduce my daughter!? You think I would give her to an errand boy, the bastard son of a scrubbing woman? Begone before I take my stick to you!"

With that he grabbed my arm and dragged me away from my beloved. I shrieked in protest but Father shook me and commanded, "Comport yourself like a lady, Violet, or I shall yet box your ears!"

How I pleaded with Father to allow me to marry Neil! I told him that my heart would surely break if he denied us. I cajoled and begged and wept and bargained. But nothing moved Father. He might have been carved from stone.

I contrived to see Neil again, passing him a brief note when I went into Harrigan's later that week. Father had not yet curtailed my riding alone, so we met on the old logging road up on the ridge.

What ecstasy to be in Neil's arms again! We swore our undying love to each other. I said I would run away with him, should he but say the word. Shamefaced, he told me he had no money for us to elope. I scoffed at our need for money when we had so much love to sustain us. But he shook his head and smiled indulgently, telling me I had not the least idea what it was like to live in poverty, telling me he would never subject me to such hardship and degradation.

Would I wait for him, he asked. He had some schemes in hand to make money, and as soon as there was enough for a good start somewhere else - far from here - we would run away. I swore that I would wait for him an eternity if necessary, but hoped it would surely not be so long. It was agony not to spend every waking moment with him!

How he laughed! It made my heart sing to see him so merry. And so determined.

Perhaps Father started to suspect my duplicity thereafter. Perhaps I looked too contented as I hugged my secret to my breast. Had I learned then to hide my feelings - as I have now - perhaps all would have been different.

First Father forbade me to ride out without a chaperone, so it became virtually impossible to meet Neil unobserved. And then, one rainy August day, Father told me that Neil had left town. He almost gloated as he said, "You should have heeded me, Violet. I told you that the boy was a scoundrel. He was merely after the wealth and power he thought would be his if he married you. We must always be on guard for fortune hunters."

"I don't believe you!" I protested.

He smiled with self-satisfaction. "But I can assure you, it is true. Every man has a price, you see. I know you are headstrong, Violet, and I suspect you've been disobeying me with secret trysts. I decided to rid us of the problem permanently, so you will no longer be tempted to wickedness and disobedience."

For a horrible moment I thought Father must have killed Neil. But then he said, "I made the boy an offer. He would leave town, never to return, never to see you again or write to you. In exchange for a financial consideration. Of course he took it. He's no fool. It was more money than most men would make in a year, let alone see at one time." Calmly he buttered his bread as he said, "So you see, my dear, that you were not so much loved as coveted."

How I hated him then! Sitting there so smugly, so pleased that he had been proven right. And not a thought to how devastated I felt. I could not believe that Neil would desert me!

I wanted to lash out at him in my anger, to wound him the way he had wounded me. So I said, "And what will happen if I am with child?"

It was impossible, of course. My relationship with Neil had been entirely innocent, and I knew enough to realize that babies are not made by kissing.

Father went deathly pale, and I feared for a moment that his heart, which had been troubling him, had stopped completely. But still I hurt and still I persisted. "Would it not be better to let me marry Neil and preserve the family from scandal?"

He slapped me so hard across the face that I tasted blood. "You little slut! You whoring little vixen! I shall send you to your aunt in England. If you are with child, she will see that it is discreetly dealt with. If not, you will be sent to a finishing school and taught to behave like a lady!"

With that he stormed from the room. Shocked at what my spiteful lie had precipitated, I sat in the empty dining room in disbelief. But it occurred to me that Father's decision had not been made in that instant. Surely he had already planned to send me away, perhaps to keep me from running after Neil. Which is what I intended to do that very night.

It was midnight when I sneaked down the shadowy hallways and tiptoed from the house. Fortunately, the rain had stopped, and there was a half-moon to light the way. I dared not take my horse, for fear the sound of hoofbeats in the quiet night would awaken Father, whose widow was open to the breezes. So determined was I, that the darkness held no terror for me. I practically ran the two miles to the village.

The Spenlowes lived in a tumbledown cabin next to the railroad tracks. It was not until I saw it, sitting there in utter darkness, that I wondered what to do. Dare I knock? If Neil were there, would he be prepared to leave with me that instant? But I feared the truth of Father's words - that Neil had left already. I expect Father would not have told me of his devilish bargain until Neil was safely away. So what would I say to his mother? Would she tell me where he had gone? Would she even know? Was I prepared to be humiliated? Might she not be angry with me for being the cause of Neil's leaving town?

I stood there for a long time, gazing at the sleeping house, my feet rooted to the ground. Lost in indecision, wretched, I didn't hear the horse until it was almost beside me.

"Neil's gone, Violet. He left on the afternoon train," a voice said gently.

And while my heart froze at the words, I was grateful for the compassion in his voice. It was Hugh McGrath. He was twenty then, and already courting Ruth. Her father's extensive holdings are closer to town than to Todmorden. It was a long ride, and Hugh must have been on his way home from there. All this I thought in an instant as I stood, crumpled, sucked dry inside.

"Neil asked me to tell you that he would return for you some day. Come and I'll give you a ride home," Hugh said. He mounted me before him on his horse and walked the beast sedately through the empty streets and down the sweet-meadowed lane to home. I was grateful for his uncritical silence and the strong arms that held me firm and warm, for now I noticed the chill in the night air and I shivered with cold and emotion.

How was it possible to be so miserable and yet so excited at the same time? Neil had not sold out to Father! He would use that money to make a start somewhere else, and then he would come for me! I had known in my heart that he wouldn't forsake me!

I bade Hugh drop me at his laneway so that I could walk the rest of the way. But he escorted me safely to my door. I could see his sympathetic smile as the moonlight touched his face, and realized that in him I had a true friend. That welcome thought penetrated even my befuddled senses.

Less than a week later I was on my way to England with my sister Rose as chaperone. Of course I told her about Neil - but not the lie I had told Father - and she was appalled that I would stoop to consider anyone as low as Neil Spenlowe as a suitor. Father did well when he chose her to be my gaoler! Married to an ambitious senior civil servant, Rose is socially adept, with influential acquaintances, including the Governor-General and his wife, and managed to introduce me to everyone of consequence aboard ship. Not one of the young men interested me!

Annoyed by my "recalcitrant behaviour", she was only too glad to give me into my aunt's custody and return to Ottawa.

Aunt Caroline, my mother's sister, was quite kind to me, although she did seem to watch me with apprehension. Goodness knows what Father had written to her! But I did enjoy finding out more about my mother, whom I barely remember. I was, after all, only four when she died. Finishing school was boring, and seemed to me hardly useful training for life in Todmorden. Aunt Caroline had hopes that I might accept one of the many suitable young men to whom she introduced me, but my heart had room for no one but Neil.

And yet, how I wish I had stayed with her in England!

This nightmare, from which I cannot escape, started barely a month after my return.

Chapter 3

... *So you see, Fran, I've already met some interesting characters - perhaps in more than one sense of the word - and I've only been here a day. I'm looking forward to what today will bring!*

But I should finish this letter and mail it to you before it turns into a manuscript!

If Nigel should write to you or call you, don't tell him where I am, alright? It's not that I'm afraid he might persuade me to return to him. It's just that I want some peace. No hassles, no guilt trips, no verbal flagellation. I just want to get on with this new life of mine. And so far it feels great!

Love to Richard and my darling nieces! And, of course, to Mom and Dad. I hope they're not driving you to distraction. Dad is undoubtedly restless and wants to putter around fixing things, and Mom will be afraid that she's not doing enough to help out. They really make such uncomfortable guests, because they don't let you pamper them! It's so different when they're playing the hosts, isn't it? Tell Dad there's lots for him to tackle around Moon Hall!

Kit finished her letter to her sister-in-law and best friend, along with her third cup of coffee. It was still early, she realized with surprise. Only 8:00 AM , and she felt as if she'd been up for hours. The twittering birds had awakened her at dawn, and the room had been so bright that she couldn't get back to sleep. She had yet to buy drapes for the windows - at least they might help to keep the morning at bay for a while.

But she supposed the farmers and their families had been up and working for hours already, and would consider her terribly decadent for wanting to stay in bed until eight.

She and Nigel had never been early risers. Whenever he awakened early, he would begin a long and exquisitely slow lovemaking....

Kit sealed her letter, and pounded on the stamps with her clenched fist. As if she were imprisoning her memories of Nigel in that letter.

She drove into the town of Kintyre, a dozen miles away, and first visited the bank, where she arranged to have her accounts transferred. Then she shopped for furniture, delighting the salesman by taking several entire suites of room settings. She had to stock her house with all kinds of things from towels to spices. After an unmemorable lunch in a small restaurant, she went to the library, where she took out a membership and half a dozen books on gardening. Before she left, she was curious to see if they carried her books. And delighted to know that they did.

The trunk and the back seat of her BMW were piled with packages by the time she drove home. It was already mid-afternoon when she pulled into the carriage house. (She couldn't think of it as anything so prosaic as a garage.)

It was on her third trip to the car to unload that she noticed a movement in the dark recesses of that long building. Unbidden, an image flashed into her mind. A woman in a long silk dress over a multitude of petticoats. Her booted feet dangling at eye level. Slowly rotating, like a marionette. Violet McAllister.

"Is anyone there?" she called out.

A laugh echoed back to her. An eerie, maniacal laugh. And a moment later a giant of a man stepped out of the shadows.

Kit shrieked.

He had a crazy, leering grin on his face, and chuckled like a child caught being naughty. His short, black hair stuck up wildly, as if he tugged on it constantly. Slowly he shuffled toward her.

Kit backed away. She screamed again as a hand clasped her arm from behind.

"Sorry I frightened you," a woman's voice said, close to her ear, and Kit spun around to see a friendly, smiling face. "That's Arnie Bryce." To the man she said, "Came to meet your new neighbour, did you, Arnie?"

He nodded enthusiastically.

"You didn't mean to frighten her, now, did you? Of course not. But you do have to be careful not to sneak up on people."

He looked crestfallen, like a chastised three year old.

"Promise you won't do it again. Come on, Arnie."

He suddenly grinned, a gap-toothed, idiotic grin. "OK." And he bounded off toward the ravine in a stiff-kneed gait.

"He's really quite harmless," the woman said.

"He doesn't look harmless," Kit replied, as they both watched him disappear into the trees.

"I grant you that the sight of a six and a half foot simpleton built like a lumberjack, looming out of the shadows could be a heart-stopping sight. I was terrified of him at first, too. But he literally can't bring himself to hurt a fly. He seems to have an affinity for creatures. We call him the 'gentle giant'. And I'm Liz Meekin, by the way. One of your neighbours."

She was an attractive woman in her early thirties, dressed like one of the flower-children of a decade earlier - in a peasant blouse, ankle-length granny-print skirt, and flat sandals. Her brown hair was scraped back from her unadorned face, and hung almost to her waist in a braid.

"I've never been so glad to meet anyone before! I'm Kit Spencer."

"Alias Victoria Penn."

Not to be outdone, Kit replied, "And you must be one of the 'hippies' from the commune."

"'God-damn hippies', you mean."

"How did you know?" Kit asked, genuinely surprised.

"Everything's damned in this valley, I've learned. Especially unconventional outsiders."

They both laughed, and felt remarkably at ease with one another.

"Will you come in for a cup of tea?" Kit asked.

"I'd love to. Here, let me give you a hand with those packages."

"Is Arnie Bryce in the habit of sneaking up on people then?" Kit asked as they entered the kitchen. "I don't think I could handle having him spring out at me from the shrubbery whenever it takes his fancy."

"Arnie likes to watch. And usually he does watch from the bushes. But it's not like him to approach strangers as he did you today. I'll bet he was snooping around while you were gone. You must have surprised him in the carriage house."

"I don't like the idea of being spied upon. He seems to move awfully quietly for a man his size."

"I used to think I could feel his eyes on me whenever I was out working in the yard, and it gave me the creeps. But there was always a houseful of people, so I never let it worry me. Oh! Not that Arnie would ever sneak into your house. I didn't mean to imply that. Just that I can understand your apprehension - you being all alone in this...." Liz shook her head and laughed. "Now I really have been thoughtless."

"Don't worry about it," Kit assured her. "I've already been informed about the ghost of Violet McAllister."

"You're doing well for your second day then. Just think of how much you'll know about us by the end of the week!"

"Well, I'm curious to hear all about this commune of yours," Kit said as she poured the tea, and offered biscuits.

"There's not that much to tell, really. There was a group of us at university who got rather disillusioned with the status quo, in our final years, so we decided to 'drop out' of society. We wanted to become self-sufficient. We wanted to live off the land, without fouling the environment with chemicals. We wanted to shun the artificial values society was imposing on us. We wanted our life's work to be more than a scramble for the almighty dollar.

"Drew Caldwell was a law student. He came from a long line of lawyers and judges and politicians, so he'd only gone into law because it was expected of him. He bought the farm with some money that he'd inherited from his grandfather, and we all moved in. More than half of the original group is still there, but things have changed a bit during the last eight years." Liz chuckled. "Business is actually so good that we're becoming quite successful. And I have to admit that not one of us regrets that. We're no longer so idealistic as we were a decade ago."

"And what career did you give up for this?" Kit asked.

"I was an English major. Kevin, my partner, was a med student. I suppose I might have gone on to do a Masters, but I didn't have any career goals. Most of us didn't really know what we wanted to do with our lives. Just what we didn't want, which was to be like our parents - boringly middle class. Yet we've managed to become quite comfortably middle class in spite of everything. Oh, I know the locals think we're weird, but that's mostly because of our appearance, and our not living in conventional family units. None of us got married either, and 'living together' is still considered a sin in these parts. I'm sure you'll hear tales of orgies, and drugs, and God knows what else."

"I was an English major, too. Just a couple of years behind you, I guess."

They talked about their university days for a while, and Liz seemed quite nostalgic. She said, "You know, I didn't really feel I'd been alive until I went to university. It was there that I made my best friends. And it was there that I really developed my love for literature. One of the best profs I had was Nigel Trent. Do you know him?"

Kit burst into laughter. "Even in the Biblical sense. You'll have to excuse me, Liz. I'm really not insane. I've been living with Nigel for the past seven years. But I left him two months ago. Well - in body, anyway. The spirit takes longer to clue in."

"I'm sorry, Kit."

"Don't be. We were bad for each other. You're quite right - he is an excellent teacher. I made the mistake of becoming infatuated with him. And when he asked me to go to Oxford with him one summer as his research assistant, I was thoroughly hooked."

"But it couldn't have been all bad," Liz said. "There wasn't a girl in class who didn't dream of jumping into bed with him."

"Don't I know it!" Nigel was considered devastatingly handsome by the undergrads, and fair game too. She had to give him credit for not allowing all those swooning females to further inflate his ego. Mostly he dismissed them as silly schoolgirls, and was impervious to their fluttering eyelashes and coy smiles. It was only when beauty enriched a formidable intellect that he took any notice. Amazing to think that he had once considered her in that light. How disappointed he had become in her.

Kit said, "You're right, of course. Those early years were bliss. But let's talk about something else. I'm not ready to analyze Nigel yet. What sorts of things do you do on the farm?"

"Well, we all help out with the chores and the housekeeping, but we're becoming such a well-run operation that I have lots of free time. So Mandy Downes and I do a variety of crafts, and sell them at craft and gift shops throughout the district. It brings in quite a bit of money." Liz chuckled. "And I'm beginning to sound like a capitalist. Although I do have to admit, I enjoy being able to earn money with my handiwork. It makes me feel as though I could be independent."

With a puzzled frown, Liz said, "I've never admitted to anyone that I'd sometimes like to be free of this way of life. But Kevin would never leave. He likes being part of a closed society. Sometimes it feels as though we're still at university. Sometimes I think that all we've done is tried to stop ourselves from growing up - and away from each another. And sometimes I think I'm just talking rot! Look, I really must dash. I just came by to invite you to dinner. We figured Friday, to give you some time to settle in. At seven."

"Great. I'm looking forward to meeting everyone. How do I get there?"

"Well, you could follow the creek. It runs right alongside our farm. It's about half a mile that way." She pointed in the opposite direction from the McGrath farm. "And if you don't fancy walking - or returning in the dark - you take this road north to the first intersection, turn left, and we're the second house on the left side. Mole End Farm."

"Ah, fans of *Wind in the Willows*! How delightful. I'm glad you didn't call it Walden something or, God forbid, Shangri-La."

"Well, we're on the riverbank, and there are willows...."

"I hope you don't call this place Toad Hall, though," Kit said.

"The thought had occurred to us."

As Kit walked her to the door, Liz said, "By the way, I almost forgot to tell you how much I enjoy your novels. I'm both a mystery and history buff, and your Gothics are top notch. You obviously spend a lot of time researching your material."

She had started the first novel that summer in England with Nigel. They had travelled all over the country, spending weekends in ancient inns that could have conjured up tales from the most unimaginative person. "Yes, I did, and I had a lot of fun doing it. You know, I've just discovered my biggest fan club is right here! Thanks, Liz."

Kit was delighted to have made a new friend. A friend of her own, not one of Nigel's. As she unwrapped her parcels, she wondered idly what the other "hippies" were like.

It wasn't long after four o'clock that there was a knock on the door, and Kit remembered that Bonnie Skuce was coming to clean the house.

"Am I glad to see you!" Kit said. "I've got what seems to me to be a month's worth of groceries spread out on the kitchen table, and just realized that the cupboards need to be cleaned out before I can put things away. So why don't you start by helping me with that?"

The girl worked quickly and efficiently, Kit was pleased to note. But she spoke little. Questions about her family elicited only monosyllabic responses.

Finally Bonnie said, "There've been mice."

"How do you know?"

"The droppings." Bonnie showed her.

"Yuck! Is that what that smell is? I thought it was damp rot, or mildew, or something. So what do I do about the mice?"

"Find the holes and plug them. Mice won't come in till the fall. From the fields. Look, there's a hole there. My brother could fix things for you. Should I tell him?"

"Yes, I suppose you'd better."

They worked in silence for a while, and then Kit said, "What do you think of the people at the commune."

"They're alright, I guess. Pa hates their guts though, so I never get to see them much."

"Why does your father hate them?"

She shrugged, not in ignorance, but as if she couldn't understand why. "Says they're into drugs and kinky sex. He even thinks they grow marijuana between their rows of corn. One night Wayne - that's my oldest brother - he and some friends snuck into the hippies' fields just to check. Though I reckon Wayne don't know what marijuana looks like." Her smile transformed her face.

"They've been buying up the Bryce farm, bit by bit, and that gets Pa's goat, too. Says the bloody communists are trying to take over the world, even Todmorden."

Kit laughed. "Do you know anything about the history of the village?"

"There was an inn at the four corners for years, but it wasn't until The McAllister built his mill that people came. Todmorden was a thriving village once, so they say. When the railroads came in. But it's been slowly dying for the last hundred years."

"You're interested in history, I think."

Bonnie shrugged. "Sure. Specially the way you write it. I kinda climb into one of your books. Like I'm the heroine, or something. You gonna write a book about Todmorden?"

"Perhaps."

It wasn't until later that evening, when Kit had poured her customary nightcap, that she thought about those words. What was she going to write? What would this long-awaited novel explore?

She could think of nothing. In time, once she settled in, something would come.

Kit picked up one of the gardening books she had borrowed from the library, and began to read it. As the night deepened, she found herself constantly looking toward the large windows of the library. She could see nothing in them except the reflection of herself and the room against the blackness beyond.

And what did you expect to see, she chided herself. *A face? Arnie Bryce?*

The thought sent a chill through her.

She put down her book, which she hadn't been able to concentrate on, and turned off the lights, thinking it preferable to being spotlighted. Exposed.

But she hadn't anticipated the blackness of the moonless night. There was no illumination from street lamps or neighbouring houses - the McGraths' house was a mere pinpoint of light in the distance. There were no high-rises or bank towers to act as beacons. No car headlights, no traffic lights, no glittering marquees to pour their brightness into the night.

On the horizon to the east was a smudge of grey, where the town lay. Otherwise the darkness had no depth or form.

Ubiquitous, it engulfed her. It was suffocating, like a heavy, blinding smoke. Like death.

Kit turned the lights back on, and poured herself another drink. She recalled what Alan McGrath had told her, about being tied to this desk by his brothers and left in the dark half the night. She wondered if that night had been as black as this one, and shuddered. Children could be unbelievably callous and cruel. In fact, it was her theory that psychopaths and other perverts were just uncivilized and unsocialized, overgrown - and therefore dangerous - children. That was why she couldn't quite believe that Arnie Bryce was as harmless as Liz said. Could he gauge his own strength or sublimate his anger? She certainly wouldn't want to be near him if he were to throw a tantrum! She remembered Arnie's vacant gaze, as if something not quite human dwelt behind those watery blue eyes.

When she went to bed a short while later, she left the upstairs hall light on. She could think of nothing more frightening than waking in the night and feeling disconnected from her surroundings. Enshrouded. Tomorrow she would buy nightlights and flashlights.

And drapes. In the city, they had been needed to keep out the light - as well as the prying eyes of neighbours. Here, they would keep out the darkness, too. And the eyes.

Chapter 4

Practically the first thing that I did when I returned from England was to visit the McGraths.

Father has never had any objections to my spending time at their house or even mucking about in their barn. He himself comes from what he refers to as "good, honest farming stock" - by which he means that his father had a successful and substantial farm in Scotland, which now belongs to his eldest brother. So Father has respect for neighbours like the McGraths, who manage to scrape a decent living out of the rocky soil.

I found Hugh in the barn, and offered to help him milk the cows. There was admiration in his eyes when he looked at me. "You've grown into quite the lady, Violet," he said. "Are you sure you want to risk that gown?"

"Pooh!" I retorted. "It's merely a dress! My aunt does have impeccable taste in fashion, but I'm damned if I'm going to become a clotheshorse and stop having fun!"

He laughed at that and said, "I'm glad that you haven't changed too much."

Not in the least embarrassed, I went on to tell him that I detested wearing those fashionable but absurd crinolines and suffocating corsets, and thus, never did at home. I had persuaded the dressmaker in London to sew my gowns so that neither was required beneath them. My aunt had been appalled, but I had explained to her that one couldn't climb a tree or dig in the garden in those restrictive garments.

I asked Hugh to give me news about the village, which he did, and finally I inquired if he'd had word from Neil.

"No. He sent for his mother and sister in the spring. They packed, left the key to the cabin for the landlord, and got on the train, with hardly a word to anyone."

I must have looked as stricken as I felt. So sure had I been that Neil would have gotten a message to me. Sent for me! Hugh said, "I'll tell you as soon as ever I do hear anything, alright?"

I thanked him, and asked if he was still courting Ruth.

"Me and half the county!" he said with a laugh.

Plunking myself down on a bale of hay, I suggested, "Well, if you're in love with her, why don't you just come right out and ask her to marry you?"

"If I had your courage and boldness, Violet, I most certainly would," he said with a glimmer of amusement in his eyes.

I scoffed at that disclaimer. "You have plenty of both! Tell me an excuse I might believe."

"I can't see her living on a farm so far from town," he replied seriously. "And she has plenty of admirers from Kintyre. One fellow's a lawyer, and bound to make a good life for her in town."

"But I'll bet he's not the handsome devil you are, Hugh," I said honestly. He was an attractive and virile man, I realized. No longer a boy. I blushed, for it suddenly seemed inappropriate for me to talk to him as candidly as I had.

After leaving Hugh, I was surprised to find myself no longer so enthralled with Neil. It seemed that for the past year I had woven a fantasy about him, imbuing him with noble qualities that he didn't seem to possess. He had become a prince, ready to battle dragons - or fathers - for his lady-love. But it seemed that he was but a pauper with dreams that Father's money could fulfill more readily than my devotion. Perhaps Father had been right about him after all.

But as soon as Father alluded to that, I was on the defensive.

How can I ever forget that fateful night?

August can be fickle - oppressively hot and humid or prematurely cool. This was a sweltering night when everything was damp, and even darkness brought no relief from the stagnant heat. Perhaps tempers are more volatile on such nights.

When Father said to me, "Your Aunt Caroline writes that you rejected the attentions of many a suitor," I replied, "I love only one man, Father, as you well know. No one else will do," even though the armour of my particular knight seemed already too tarnished to me by then.

"Don't be ridiculous, Violet!" Father scoffed. "We must find you a suitable husband soon. There is nothing else a woman can do but be a wife and mother."

Perhaps if I hadn't goaded him and persisted in my lie, things would have turned out differently. But I was still angry at being treated as a chattel, to be bought and sold and bargained over at the whim of men. Saucily, flippantly, I said, "And who would have me, Father? Am I not a tainted woman?"

He blanched at that as if he'd had some horrible realization. Then he stared at me strangely, as if he had only just noticed me and found me a curious and repugnant creature. But he said not another word on the subject.

And I thought nothing more about it.

Since it was a hot night, I lay uncovered in my bed in my gossamer lawn nightgown. The tumescent moon spilled its silvery light through the open window, but no breath of wind intruded.

I don't know how long I had slept when I was suddenly awakened. I felt the air upon my naked skin and something heavy bearing down upon me. In a panic I tried to rise, but was shoved down. In the moon-bright darkness I saw Father looming over me. I tried to squirm out from under him, but he is strong, even when the worse for drink - as he was then.

My nightgown had already been shoved up under my chin, so I lay there, naked and powerless.

"You are useless now. Damaged goods. Fit for nothing decent," he intoned. "Whores must be punished!"

"No! There was never anything between Neil and me! It was a lie, Father!"

"You are no daughter of mine, Jezebel! Behold the instrument of chastisement," he said, lifting his own nightgown to reveal his manhood, absurdly swollen and rigid.

My scream of protest was choked off by pain as he ripped into me "Fucking trollop!" he cursed, as he again plunged into me. "Whore of Babylon! Jezebel! Poxy whore!" Each foul exhortation was accompanied by a punishing thrust.

He climbed off me quickly, as though I were somehow poisonous. He pulled down my nightdress, wiped himself upon it - oblivious to the blood, the evidence of my innocence, which was visible even in the moonlight - and said, "You disgust me!" before he staggered out of my room.

How can I begin to tell you, dear diary, of my feelings then? I could hardly breathe for the horror of it all. My face was wet with tears of pain and humiliation. I felt soiled and debased. And shocked.

Surely I had been plunged into a nightmare! Surely this agonizing violation was against the laws of God and man!

How could my father, who had always been protective and fair-minded and righteous, have so abused and betrayed me? Was what I had lied about so wicked that it warranted such severe and brutal punishment?

Although indulgent, Father had never been outwardly affectionate to us girls, thinking us a "silly brood of hens". But he had always done what he thought right and best for us; this I had believed without doubt. And certainly now that my sisters had married so well, he rather considered them and their husbands with pride and his grandchildren, with great joy. He was a man who was respected and admired not only in the village, but also in Canada's major cities, where he had influential friends. How could such an honorable man have done such a despicable thing to his own daughter?

If I did not have the evidence of my pain to bear witness, I would have thought myself dreaming. Or mad.

Then I had the presence of mind to wonder if my broken cries had awakened Betsy. The wall between this floor and the servants quarters - where Betsy alone slept these days - is stout and soundproof, and she often claimed she slept like the dead. Thank goodness the Skuces live in their own house down the road, for I'm certain that nothing would get by Mrs. Skuce.

But no one must discover what vile act had taken place here this night! I cleaned myself up as best I could, using my nightgown to wipe away the blood and filth. The smell of it nauseated me. Then I slipped on a dress and stole from the house. I ran down to the ravine, where I buried the fouled garment under a rock. Then, lifting up my dress, I waded into the shallow stream, and sat down, trying to cleanse myself in the sweet, cool water.

The water was soothing. But still I felt defiled. Tonight, the father I had loved and admired had died, I realized. And there, in that peaceful, gentle place, caressed by the trickling stream, I wept until I was empty inside.

Although I usually rise early, for I love the mornings, I could not face him at breakfast. I stayed in my room until he had left for the mill. All the while I looked about for evidence of the previous night's debauchery. No one would miss my nightgown, for a woman from the village came in weekly to wash and iron, and so neither Betsy nor, of course, Mrs. Skuce had anything to do with my clothes. Unlike Aunt Caroline, I had no personal maid to dress me and pamper me. Nor did I choose to!

After I straightened the sheets, the bed looked no different from usual, I was sure. Betsy would notice nothing out of the ordinary when she made up my room. But to me that smell still lingered. I could hardly wait to escape.

Of course I couldn't avoid him at dinner. It was with great trepidation that I entered the dining room, where we always ate our meals, even though there were only the two of us now, lost at either end of the long table. I couldn't look at him at first, but when I finally did, in surprise at his question, I saw nothing there that acknowledged what had happened between us last night. No guilt or shame or regret. I recognized only that the warmth I had always found when he regarded me was no longer there. As if I were a stranger to him.

My sister Rose had written to say that she was having a reception at the end of the month, and would we attend? This was the news that had startled me. Partly because it seemed so sane and ordinary, and partly because he had spoken to me as if it were any other day.

Of course we would never mention the previous night. How could we put voice to what had happened? It was unthinkable!

So we carried on a normal conversation. How convenient the rituals and etiquette of society! They at least gave one something to cling to.

Yes, of course I wanted to go! Anything to escape from here! And Rose's soirees were popular and fun. One met the cream of Ottawa society there - what little there was.

Montrealers and Torontonians scoff at Ottawa's self-importance as Canada's capital city. They recall that, not so many years ago, Ottawa had been a brawling, backwoods lumbering town. (Some maintain it is still!) It would never have become much more than that had Queen Victoria herself not named it the capital city of the new Dominion.

But to me, it is an intriguing place where, daily, important decisions are made. By men, of course. And the Viceregal presence of Governor-General Lord Lisgar and his wife make it even more glamorous a city than its rivals.

Before he returned to the mill, Father asked me to write to Rose and accept her invitation.

By supper time, I had thought that perhaps life could return to a semblance of normality.

The Skuces always leave for home after Mrs. Skuce finishes preparing supper. In summer, it is usually a cold collation with plenty of fresh vegetables from our garden. Betsy lays it out and removes the dishes later, but otherwise, has the evening off.

The house seemed much quieter and more solemn then, even though it was early evening and still light outside when we ate.

I realized that, as the youngest child, I was the only one who had spent any significant time alone with Father. I was ten when Heather went off to the Academy. For two years I had been the only one to keep him company at meals. Sometimes he read documents or newspapers, but always he expressed his opinions, becoming especially effusive after several glasses of good wine. And so, I was used to stretches of silence interspersed with interesting insights into the worlds of business and politics. It all sounded so exciting that I often cursed the restrictions put upon me as a female.

But this time I could hardly wait to escape. As soon as I could I went out to the orchard and sat in the arms of my favourite apple tree as I watched the bleeding sun stain the clouds over the valley.

I locked myself into my room that night. Even so, I did not sleep well. At one time I heard the doorknob turn and lay tensely in bed, wondering if the door might fly open and Father stand there in a rage. I thought I heard a muttered curse and then quiet footsteps go away.

The next night I discovered that the key to my bedroom door had gone, and that was when I hid myself outside and my nighttime vigils began.

If anyone has noticed me, they must think me a madwoman, or a wraith haunting the grounds. Sometimes I feel that I am both. I escape from the house whenever possible, hiding in the branches of trees or in the depths of the ravine until long, long after all the lights go out. Then I wander in the garden or sit in the gazebo watching the stars move across the heavens, listening to the sounds of the night creatures - the cries of nighthawks and whip-poor-wills, the rustling of skunks and raccoons, the scurrying of mice and moles. And I feel as if I have turned into a night creature myself.

I don't go inside until nearly dawn, and sleep until noon, feeling truly safe only after I hear him leave the house. I know not what the servants think, only that Mrs. Skuce complains of my skipping breakfast and not rising until such an "ungodly" hour.

Let them think me foolish or spoiled or contrary. Just don't let them know the truth! To have anyone else know would make it all too horrifyingly real. This way, I can almost believe that it never truly happened, but was the product of my fevered mind.

Last night the moon was full, and I turned my face gratefully to its benign light. I beseeched God to help me, for I know that I cannot keep up this evasion. When it rains, what shall I do? Or when the snows come?

So lost in thought and misery was I that I jumped and nearly screamed when I sensed a presence behind me and a man's voice said quietly, "Violet?"

I spun around to find Hugh there. My face, thankfully, was in shadow, but his was bathed by the moon, and I saw concern and puzzlement etched there. He said, "So you are the ghost. I've noticed you a few nights now, when I've been out late to the barn. At first I thought my eyes were playing tricks, but then I wondered if someone was trespassing or causing mischief. Is something wrong?"

Yes, I wanted to scream. *The universe has turned upside down. I'm living in hell. I have no safe haven. And I'm terrified.*

Instead, I said, "I cannot sleep. I have demons that visit me in the night. I don't know what to do anymore."

I had my arms wrapped tightly about me as though I needed to physically hold onto myself to keep from flying apart. It was such a relief to share even this evasive truth that I felt hot tears coursing down my cheeks, and couldn't suppress a sob. I was about to turn away from him, but he drew me into his arms and cuddled me like a wounded child.

I wept and wept, as if the tears were poison that needed to be purged from me. All the while Hugh held me and stroked my hair.

When I was once more calm, he said, "Is it Neil who distresses you so?"

Neil, because of whom I had told a lie. An insidious lie that was to destroy me. Neil, who had taken Father's money and left without a goodbye. Neil, who had never once in the past year written, or contrived to pass a message to me. "Neil preferred my father's money to me. He could have saved me," I cried in an anguished voice.

"Then let me help you, Violet," Hugh said with such tenderness that I looked at him. He brushed strands of hair away from my wet cheeks.

How surprised I was by the warm affection in his eyes! Neil had always been so wrapped up in himself and his dreams that I had felt like a privileged and welcome spectator in his presence. But Hugh seemed enthralled with me. I saw myself reflected in his eyes, as though he could feel my pain and understand my grief.

We had gone far beyond our childhood friendship now.

I closed my eyes for one brief moment to allow myself the luxury of speculating about what might have been. To be so loved and cherished, as Hugh's eyes promised I would be, would have been paradise.

But it could never be. I was defiled. I was tainted. I was damaged goods, fit for marriage to no decent man. And because it was my own father who had debauched me, I felt more debased than if I had given myself in love to Neil. What bitter irony that my lie should have become so twistedly, grotesquely real.

Sadly, I rested my head against his shoulder. "Promise me you'll always be my friend, Hugh."

I dared not look at him to divine his thoughts, but he held me close and laid his face against my head as he said, "I promise you that and more."

"There can be no more," I replied brokenly.

"Anything is possible."

"I wish to God that were true!" I said, pulling away from him. "But you don't know! You can never know! Everything is ruined! No, don't ask me any more," I cautioned as he began to protest. I was afraid I would break down completely, overcome by the many emotions that were tearing me apart inside. I felt like hurling myself from a rooftop or throwing myself into a river - anything to end the fear and loathing, the hate and guilt, and now this yearning and despair.

"Please leave me now. I... thank you for coming here tonight, Hugh."

I gave him a quick kiss on the cheek in gratitude, but before I could move away, he pulled me into his arms and placed his lips on mine, gently at first, and then more insistently. I groaned at the sheer sweetness of it, which travelled through me to that secret place that throbbed now as if to remind me of my disgrace.

"No!" I cried, pulling away from him. "For both our sakes that must never happen again!" I ran from him then, toward the house, but hid myself on the back veranda until I was sure he was gone.

And then suddenly he was there - the demon of my nightmares. "So, you gratify men even here, at my home!" he accused as he dragged me into the carriage house. He forced me to the ground, kneeling between my legs.

I wanted to scream, to shout for Hugh, who could not yet be far down the road. But I couldn't bear him to know my shame or witness this degradation.

I fought, punching and writhing, but as ineffectually as a moth battering against a window pane. Throwing back my skirt,

he tore my knickers off as if they were made of paper. Then he
drove into me so deeply that I thought I would be torn asunder.

And perhaps I was, for a part of me watched this monster
with cold detachment. And bitter, vindictive hatred.

Still raw and bruised from his previous assault, I nearly
fainted with the agony of his brutality. I bit my lip to keep from
crying out, and yet I whimpered.

"It was a whore like you who gave me the pox," he said as
he rose. "Made me unfit to marry again, to have sons. A dirty, pox-
ridden whore! And one day the world will know of your sin, for the
pox will eat away at you, body and soul, so that your disease will
be evidence of your wickedness and God's just punishment. And
you won't escape my punishments either, whore!"

He left me lying there, on the hard-packed dirt of the shed.
I turned onto my side and curled up as I wept silently.

I don't understand his words about the pox, but they
terrify me. What manner of disease does he have? I know of
nothing but his heart condition. Surely his are the words and
actions of a madman!

And what if I become with child? I swear I will cut the
abomination from my belly with a knife.

I found little solace in the ravine that night. With the light
of dawn I began to write this to you, dear diary, to purge myself of
some of the intense and destructive emotions that possess me.

I shall catch the noon train to Kintyre. Heather won't mind
my turning up unannounced. I shall tell her - tell all my sisters -
that I had missed them so during my year abroad and that only a
special visit to each will satisfy me. I intend to stay at least a week
with each of my sisters. That means I won't return here until well
into autumn.

Before I go I shall need to finance my travels. Father does
not realize that I discovered the secret compartment in his desk,
where he hides cash. I feel no compunction in taking it all. Let him
accuse me of robbing him! He has stolen so much more from me in
coin that can never be repaid.

Chapter 5

Fortunately, it was nearly morning by the time the storm broke and the electricity went off. The rain was hurled against the window by terrific gusts of wind. Lightning sliced through the dusky room; thunder rumbled through the ancient floorboards. Kit snuggled deeper into the blankets, as if drawing a shell about herself. She almost expected to see the ghostly hand of Catherine Earnshaw clawing at the window, begging to be let in from the storm....

She decided it was silly to stay in bed, frightening herself with unforgettable scenes from *Wuthering Heights*, and got up. The gloomy grey morning was about as bright as it was going to get anyway.

The hall window overlooked the valley, and Kit stopped to watch the storm. Boiling black thunderheads rolled toward her from the west. Lightning forked down to the earth, uncomfortably close to little farmhouses. A fierce wind whipped the trees and snapped branches. It was an awesome spectacle.

Kit went into the bathroom and flicked the light switch, forgetting that the electricity was still off. But she was surprised when the water stopped running as she was washing her face.

Until she remembered that her water came from a well, and had to be pumped up with an electric pump. Damnation!

Another lesson in country living she told herself, and resolved to keep some water in the tub at all times for washing and flushing the toilet, and drinking water in the fridge. Now, if only she could figure out how to make a cup of coffee, she'd be all set to weather any blackout. Perhaps she should stock up on firewood for the kitchen fireplace. Winter mornings would certainly be more pleasant with a cheery blaze in the hearth.

The electricity was soon restored, and Kit was able to face the day properly groomed and with a pot of coffee at her elbow.

It was reassuring when the Bell service man arrived a little while later, and installed jacks throughout the house and hooked up her telephone line. A lifeline.

Kit's first phone call was to a drapery store in town that advertised "at home service". The saleswoman came later that morning, just after Kit's new furniture arrived, and it didn't take Kit long to choose fabrics that matched the furniture as well as the character of the house, and that appealed to her simple tastes. The woman promised to have them ready in two weeks.

Kit wondered how she would get through the next fourteen evenings.

There was a moon that night, brilliant, white-gold against the black sky, much brighter than it ever appeared in the city. As indeed were the millions of stars, most of which weren't ever visible on a city night. Stark black shadows of trees stretched across a silvered lawn.

It was as though everything was more intense in the country - storms, darkness, brightness. Fear.

But Kit could see no lurking figures in the bushes or sinister faces in the moonlight, and she chided herself for her foolishness. Nor had she seen any sign of the ghost of Violet McAllister. She sat down in the cozy new armchair in the library and made note of all the things she hoped to accomplish by the end of the week.

By Friday she had done most of them, including purchasing seeds for her vegetable garden. She had already finished reading the gardening books that she had borrowed from the library, and now felt competent enough to begin working on the garden. Acting upon the advice in the books, she had drawn a sketch of her proposed garden - how many rows were to be given to corn, beans, zucchini, onions, and carrots, and the spacing of the rows and plants. She had purchased tomato and cucumber plants and seed potatoes from a nursery, but she had yet to prepare a bed.

And that was no easy chore, she realized, after digging up a few forksful of weedy turf. The soil was clay and rocks. Boulders, sometimes. She'd need lots of manure. Perhaps she should order a load of topsoil. Probably she should start a compost pile.

After more than an hour of hard digging, Kit had made little progress. Taking to heart what she had read in the books, she was digging to a depth of eighteen inches or more. The pile of rocks and weeds and sod was far larger than the prepared area. And already she was sweating and aching and gritty. Some damned biting flies kept circling her head, buzzing and nipping when she wasn't swatting at them. So clods of dirt clung to her where her flailing hands had tried to ward them off.

"Deer flies are attracted to dark colours, particularly jeans, I've found," a voice said from behind her.

Kit swung around. Stuart McGrath was leaning against the stone wall that separated them. He wore no shirt, and the sun gleamed off his tanned, muscular torso which was covered in a film of sweat. There was a hint of a smile on his face.

Amusement at her predicament, Kit thought sourly. She was really in no mood to spar with him at the moment.

"I'll keep that in mind," she said.

She continued digging, but felt his eyes upon her, judging and critical. She expected him to tell her that what she was doing was all wrong, so that when he spoke again, she tensed at his words.

"How large do you intend to make the garden?"

"Thirty feet by twenty," she replied, suddenly realizing the enormity of the task.

"That's pretty ambitious."

She could feel him smirking, but refused to look at him.

"I'll send Alan round with the plough later. It'll save you a lot of work."

And then he walked away.

Kit drove the garden fork into the ground as if she were hurling it after him. What was he doing in that field anyway, besides spying on her? The arrogance of the man! He hadn't even waited for her to agree!

Or to thank him.

Filthy and dishevelled and still angry, Kit was quite out of sorts when there was a knock on her front door a few minutes later. Having abandonned her fruitless labours, she was just going upstairs to immerse herself in a soothing bath. For a moment, she didn't even think it unusual that her visitors announced themselves at the front door.

Two elderly people greeted her with practiced smiles. "How do you do? Cleo and Everett Pugh. We're neighbours," the woman said as she swept into the front hall.

"Kit Spencer. I'm pleased to meet you." Liar, she told herself. She wanted nothing more than to soak in the tub. She scrubbed her muddy hands on her jeans, and said, "Do come in. I'm afraid I've been gardening and..."

"Quite. Do run along and wash up, dear, and we'll make ourselves at home," Cleo said.

Kit pointed them toward the parlour, but Cleo had already scented it out and was heading toward it, with her husband trailing behind.

Kit joined them a few minutes later, having washed the worst of the dirt off her hands and face, and brushed off her jeans. They rejected her offer of coffee.

"What a charming little house this is," Cleo said. "I took the liberty of looking about a bit. Quite old, isn't it? We had an old house once in England - well, a country manor, actually. It had been built in the sixteenth century and been added on to every century since - you know, the kind of place with miles of corridors, acres of parkland, and tons of history. But there's really nothing like a brand new one. All the conveniences, efficient. They're always improving on the old, aren't they?"

Kit found herself taking an instant dislike to the woman. But if she thought that Everett was a hen-pecked husband, she was soon to be disillusioned.

"Bet you have mice," he said with glee. "You won't find any in our house. Nosiree."

"We moved here two years ago, when Rhett retired. He was in banking..."

"Supervised the building of the house myself..," Rhett said proudly.

"...Decided we should have a country estate..."

"...Pretty piece of country hereabouts..."

"...Of course, the house is small, but now that we're retired we don't entertain so much..."

"...We've lived all over the world - Geneva, Singapore..."

They both continued to talk at the same time. Kit didn't know which of them to listen to, and trying not to be rude to either, attempted to make the appropriate responses to both. She thought that surely they must realize that she couldn't give either of them her full attention. Surely they must realize that they were being extremely rude to one another, and unfair to her! But the two monologues continued.

Cleo was saying, "My father was a diplomat. I was born in Cairo. That's how I got the name Cleopatra..."

"...We only spend the summer months here. Have a condo in Florida..."

Kit soon tired of listening and of appearing interested. Neither of them seemed to care whether she did or not. She wondered what their life together must be like. Perhaps they never spoke to one another at home. Certainly they didn't seem to respect each other.

Or perhaps, when they left here, they would discuss her own rudeness in ignoring them.

As if prearranged, they both ceased chattering at the same instant. As she rose, Cleo said, "Well, you must come to lunch.

Tomorrow at 1:00. We're on the third concession line. Right next door to that commune."

Rhett said, "You'll have heard of it by now, I imagine. Really, some of these country folk are pretty queer."

"You're a writer, I hear," Cleo said. "Myrtle Skuce cleans for us, so we're never short on gossip. Can't say I've read your novels. I prefer more literary works myself."

"Still, it's nice to see new blood in our little community," Rhett said, as if smoothing over his wife's unkind inference.

"Until tomorrow then. Just a light luncheon. Nothing formal, dear."

Rhett held the door for his wife. Then they strolled down the walkway arm-in-arm to their mile-long Lincoln in the driveway. Kit burst into laughter when they had driven away, and then went for her bath.

The bathroom had been recently redecorated (by the nude Torontonians?) with a country calico wallpaper. The elaborate cornice and baseboard mouldings had been inexpertly stripped, but Kit liked the warm, honey-coloured maple, even if it was still flecked in places with pink paint. The wide pine boards of the floor had been sanded smooth and clean, and stencilled with a border of flowers and vines in the old-fashioned way.

The tub was one of those enormous old claw-footed ones. Kit was luxuriating amongst the bubbles, enjoying a very un-literary novel, when she heard a faint noise, like a far-off knock. She hated to get out of the tub, and hoped that whoever it was would go away.

But a moment later she heard someone calling, and then footsteps in the front hall. Damn! She'd forgotten to lock the doors!

"Just a minute!" she shouted, as she scrambled out of the tub, and climbed into her roomy terry bathrobe.

It wasn't until the shock of seeing the stranger at the bottom of the stairs that Kit realized what an awkward - and vulnerable - position she was in.

"Well, gidday to you," he said with a lecherous grin. "The door was open. Saw your car was here."

"Who are you?"

"Wayne Skuce. Ya told my sister, Bonnie, ya had some work for me. So here I am. An' glad to make yer acquaintance, I'm sure."

Again that leer.

"Kindly wait for me in the kitchen. I'll be down in a few minutes. You might check for mouse holes in the cupboards while you're waiting."

Standing casually with one foot on the lower stair and his elbow on the newell post, he stared at her assessingly up the long tunnel of the stairwell. As she stood there, barefoot, her wet hair hanging limply about her shoulders and clinging to her face, water dripping from her slick body beneath the robe that suddenly seemed insufficient to hide her nakedness, she felt like a mouse that had been spotted by a feral cat. A shudder ran down her spine as he hesitated. With a grin he turned and shuffled off toward the kitchen.

Kit waited to make sure he was there before going into her bedroom. She felt instinctively that Wayne Skuce was not a man to turn one's back on.

Wanting to hide beneath her most androgynous clothes, she dressed quickly in jeans and a long sloppy sweatshirt. But still she felt acutely uncomfortable, knowing that someone had so casually invaded her home. She almost expected Wayne Skuce to barge through her bedroom door.

It was with some relief, and a sense that she had regained control of her domain, that she found him doing exactly as she had bid.

"A couple here, alright. Won't take me no time at all to fix. Anythin' else ya want doin'?"

His smile revealed crooked and broken teeth. He was small and wiry like his mother. Weasely. His only attractive features were his eyes - large and soulful, like his sister's.

"Yes. I bought some chain locks for the doors. You can install them."

"If ya want. Though they do say them things ain't no good. If I was wantin' to break into yer house, and that was all that was stoppin' me, I'd have it tore off in no time."

In her present state of mind, Kit wondered if that was a threat. And she had thought that Arnie Bryce was the only one to worry about around here!

"Then you make sure you install them so they can't be torn off."

"Ya scared livin' here? Get lonely, eh? Specially nights, I bet."

"I'll be in the study. I trust you have all the tools you need?"

He grinned. "Sure do."

Kit left the room, glad to get away from that creep and his insufferable innuendoes. But then she felt restless, not knowing what he was up to, and wished she'd stayed to keep an eye on him. And yet, unless she had engaged him in friendly conversation, it would not have been a very neighbourly thing to do. And she did not think she could hold any sort of reasonable conversation with Wayne Skuce.

Half an hour later he walked into the study and said, "All done."

"That was fast," Kit replied, already feeling relieved at his imminent departure.

"Nothin' to it. That'll be twenty bucks."

"Twenty?"

"That's what I charge for an hour, and minimum one hour for a job."

Kit didn't believe it for a moment. His large cow eyes challenged her.

As she reached for her wallet, she said, "Your mother said you worked cheaply."

"Ma oughta keep her mouth shut sometimes."

Kit extracted a twenty dollar bill. "Perhaps I'd better inspect what I'm paying for first."

He shrugged. "Suit yerself."

She tugged on each of the three locks - the front entrance and the two doors off the kitchen - and they seemed sturdy enough. Wayne showed her where he had nailed bits of wood over the mouse holes in the cupboards.

When he took the money from her, he said, "This house needs a lota repairs. Soffits, for instance. I seen rotten boards and even some holes. Ya'll get 'coons and bats movin' into the attic if ya don't see to that. We could make a deal for big jobs like that. Say fifteen an hour. Or a few bucks less."

"I'll keep that in mind," Kit said, and wondered why she didn't have the courage to tell him to get lost and never darken her threshold again.

That's what Nigel would have done. No. Nigel would never have hired him in the first place. He only dealt with professionals.

Wayne grinned at her and then left.

Kit leafed through the yellow pages of her telephone book, found a contractor, and asked him to come out next week to give her an estimate for repairs to the house.

She decided that she would have him put spotlights at the back kitchen entrance that led into the carriage house - lights that would eliminate the darkness in that chilly, eerie building. Where Violet McAllister had hanged herself, and Arnie Bryce liked to hide.

When there was a knock on the door a short while later, Kit was tempted to put up the chain before opening the door a crack to find out who was there. But it was the middle of the day, and really - was she going to start over-reacting to everything? Did she think that Wayne was back with an axe?

It was Alan McGrath.

"You seem almost relieved to see me," he said.

"I am! Wayne Skuce was here not long ago, and I found him an extremely unpleasant character."

Alan snorted. "Wayne! He's such a big asshole that I'm surprised he hasn't disappeared up his own backside yet. What was he doing here?"

"Myrtle had convinced me to hire him for some repairs. But never again!"

"I'll bet he gypped you, too. Listen, I'd be happy to help you with little things. Don't have time for any big jobs just now. Anyway, I've got the tractor here. Stu told me you were hand-digging a garden. Jeez, it'd take you a week or more at that rate!"

"Your brother smirked enough about it this morning."

"Stu thinks you won't last the summer here."

"Does he indeed? Then I'll have to prove him wrong, won't I?"

"Sure hope so. It'd be good to see him eat humble pie for a change. Anyway, you've livened up the neighbourhood. Everybody's talking about you these days."

"God forbid!" They had reached the tractor, and Kit showed him where she wanted to have her vegetable plot.

"I don't think you should start with such an ambitious size," Alan told her. "There's a helluva lot of weeding and hoeing to do. How about half the size - fifteen by twenty? You might even find that a bit much the first year."

She liked his implication that this was just the beginning of her life here, that next year there would be another garden.

"Take my word for it. I know what I'm talking about. What do you plan to do with all the produce anyway? Preserve it? You could feed a dozen people for a year on a plot this size."

"Alright, you've convinced me," she said with a laugh.

It took him less than ten minutes to plough up the garden. "I'll be back later this evening with the tiller to chop up the soil a bit finer."

"I won't be here tonight."

"I'll do it anyway. Then you can start your planting tomorrow."

"Thanks, Alan. I really appreciate this."

"No problem. Let me know if there's anything else I can do."

"You could give me some advice right now. I want to hire someone to cut the grass. Any suggestions?"

"The youngest Skuce lad, Byron, he could do it for you. Or Arnie Bryce. He's none too bright, but he's capable of simple chores, and does what he's told."

"Some choice!"

"Byron's OK. Not like Wayne. Well, not yet, anyway. He does a few lawns around here, and even has an old ride-on mower."

"And when is the garbage collected?"

Alan let out a hoot of laughter. "You collect it yourself and take it to the dump. That's about eight miles down the second line."

"You mean, for all the taxes I pay here, I don't get water or sewers or a paved road or sidewalks or even garbage collection?"

"You got it!"

"Do they plough the road in winter?"

"When they get around to it."

"So where's this dump again?"

"Listen, I go every Saturday morning anyway. I'd be happy to take your garbage as well. Just leave it in a bin in the carriage house - not outside, or the skunks and 'coons'll get into it."

"I am grateful, Alan."

"Don't mention it. Don't neighbours help each other out in the city?"

"I didn't even know my neighbours! Well... only to say hello."

Nigel had said they had nothing in common with their neighbours. The stock broker talked about nothing but his new boat, and the insurance agent, about the sports car he was going to buy, Nigel had complained that evening she had invited them for drinks on the patio.

When Alan had left, Kit collected the boxes and cartons and all the other detritus of moving, and stacked them in the carriage house. Then she went to ready herself for her dinner at the commune, having first made sure that all the doors were locked. Because of her interrupted bath, she jumped into the shower to wash her hair.

Her shoulder-length blonde hair was permed into an easy care wash-and-wear style, which needed only to be picked at with a hair rake and left to dry. She had never been one to fuss over her appearance, and yet managed to look both elegant and appealing with little effort. So Nigel had told her.

He had loved running his hands through her soft, wavy hair. For a moment she felt a sharp physical longing for him.

She would not think of Nigel tonight, and hoped that no one would mention him. And yet, amongst people who had once been his students, she would feel closer to him than she had since she'd left the city. And someone was bound to mention him. Ironically, Nigel was someone that they had in common.

Kit passed only the Bryce farm before she reached the third concession line. At the corner sat a dilapidated little clapboard house, badly in need of paint and repairs. A few bits of old gingerbread trim clung defiantly to a second floor gable window and dangled from the veranda eaves. The veranda itself looked as though it was about to collapse into a heap of rotten lumber. An assortment of rusty and battered vehicles was scattered about the yard amongst old appliances, tires, odds and ends of machinery, and every imaginable sort of rubbish. There was no lawn to speak of, only patches of weeds amidst hard-packed dirt.

It wasn't until Kit saw Bonnie Skuce emerge from the house, followed by Wayne, that she realized it was the Skuce home. Bonnie looked at her, but did not acknowledge Kit's wave. As if she were too ashamed to be seen there.

Kit's shock gave way to wry amusement. The Skuce house was not a good advertisement for a handyman, a gardener, or a maid! (Kit was convinced that the inside would prove even more insalubrious.)

It was only a quarter mile along the third concession to the stream. And that two-storey, pillared, southern-mansion clone of a house on the eastern bank of it must be the Pugh's place, she realized. There was not a tree within a hundred yards of it, so that it sprawled large and white and ostentatious, and somehow ridiculous, in a patch of carefully-tended lawn bordered by fields of sprouting corn.

The large stone farmhouse on the opposite bank blended in much better with its surroundings. A few tall shade trees on the front lawn did not detract from its size, but did help to soften the outlines.

Kit was amused to see that there was actually a sign proclaiming it to be "Mole End Farm". She pulled into the drive, and headed toward the other vehicles near the outbuildings. She was surprised to see a Porsche, a beautifully restored Triumph TR6, a van, and a new Volvo station wagon among the fleet of cars. These people were obviously not living a minimalist lifestyle.

The house had a large modern addition tacked onto the back, and it was from a door there that Liz stepped out to greet her.

Kit wondered fleetingly if Liz's long flowered skirts were the same ones she had dropped out of society in all those years ago. But the style suited her, and this evening she wore her waist-length hair loose, making her look nearly a decade younger.

Liz ushered her into what was obviously a kitchen-cum-lounge. An enormous pine table dominated the room, with a dozen cushioned, cozy chairs set invitingly around it. Sofas and easy chairs were arranged about coffee tables piled with newspapers and magazines. A stone fireplace set into one wall promised toasty winter evenings. An island counter partially divided this section from the kitchen, itself a spacious area, well-stocked with appliances and utensils, and from which a most delicious aroma wafted. The room was lit with skylights and wall-sized windows that overlooked the valley - although from a slightly different perspective than Kit's vistas.

The people who had lounged about reading newspapers or chatting rose to greet her, and Liz introduced her. Kit wondered how she would keep them all sorted out.

Kevin Fenwick - Liz's companion, she recalled - and Drew Caldwell, the ex-law student who technically owned this place, and Mandy Downes, who made crafts along with Liz.

Erick Jansen in his chef's hat and apron was obviously the cook. Pete Sage, who had been strumming his guitar, was introduced as the resident minstrel, Teresa Kelleher as the farm's business manager, and Leighton Pearse as the man who sang arias to the cows.

Dianna Webb owned an art gallery and craft shop in town, but still lived on the farm. "...Well, we see her once or twice a week, anyway," Liz said. "She has this new 'friend' in town. And Nick Radcliffe has pretty well deserted us. He lives in the city now, and comes for weekends sometimes. For old times. And this is one of his city friends, Cindy...."

But Nick Radcliffe didn't supply her last name, and Kit wondered if he knew it. Nick did indeed look as though he had left the simple life behind. His clothes looked expensively casual, and Kit was certain that the Porsche in the parking lot was his. He was a handsome man, with a lean, athletic build, piercing blue eyes, and expertly-cut, collar-length dark hair. His "friend", Cindy, was a Barby doll of a creature - all legs and hair, and at least a decade younger than he. She looked somewhat spaced out, and gave Kit the strong impression that she was a bit of fluff that had clung to Nick at a bar the night before.

"It's my country retreat," Nick said. "Where else could I get such gourmet meals as Erick whips up, and such witty company as my best friends provide?"

"The best of both worlds, eh, Nick?" Pete Sage said. "A ridiculously well-paid desk job, and quiet, inexpensive weekends in the country. I'll bet you tell them that it's your country estate, the way they brag about their cottages in Muskoka." Pete sounded inordinately bitter. Or was he jealous, Kit wondered.

But Nick took no offence. He laughed and said. "You know I'm not above giving myself airs, Pete. And I've enjoyed many a weekend at those Muskoka cottages. In fact, you know what's missing here is a lake. Or how be you put in a pool? And maybe a hot tub and sauna while you're at it."

"Right on!" Cindy said.

Kit realized that Nick was baiting Pete. There were obviously undercurrents here that she would know nothing about. Pete said acidly, "You're beginning to sound like my fucking brother, Nick. Can't talk about anything but his amazing success, his expensive cars, his monster home, his prestigious cottage, and his Club Med holidays!"

"Hey, old buddy," Nick said, "It wasn't me who brought all that up. But I'm sure Kit doesn't want to hear about your brother just now. She's just met a whole baseball team of new people and is probably wondering how to keep us all straight. And could undoubtedly use an aperitif before one of Erick's exquisite Boeuf Bourguignonnes."

Kit returned his smile, and accepted a sherry from the tray that Kevin Fenwick was passing around.

Pete Sage took a drink, and turned away angrily from Nick. Kit felt a twinge of sympathy for him. With his long hair and round granny glasses, Pete reminded her of John Lennon during the twilight of the Beatle years. *LET IT BE.* Was it envy of Nick's lifestyle that angered him, or that Nick had abandonned the philosophy that they had once shared? Perhaps Pete was tempted to abandon it as well.

"We all think it's wonderful that you've moved into the neighbourhood, Kit," Mandy Downes said. "And to think that you trod the same halls as we did... It's almost like meeting old friends!" Mandy seemed to bubble with enthusiasm when she talked, as though genuinely pleased, which served to make a newcomer feel at ease. Mandy was a pretty, bouncy brunette with a merry gleam in her eyes. "When Liz told us you were a writer, I just had to read some of your books. What riveting tales! I think it's a shame that Gothics are regarded as 'women's novels'. It's those covers that are responsible, I think. Voluptuous women fleeing from castles on stormy nights pursued by darkly handsome men on horseback."

"Are you telling me that I should read one?" Drew Caldwell asked Mandy as he sat down beside her. That they were a couple was obvious by the tender amusement in his eyes.

"Certainly! Kit has written clever mysteries with a romantic twist. And I'll bet there's not much Kit doesn't know about 19th century England. You just might learn something, guys, if you stopped being influenced by stereotypes."

Kit said, "Thank you, Mandy. What a welcome!"

They gathered around the table, and helped themselves to the mountains of delicious food. Kit was pleasantly surprised to find that it was indeed a gourmet meal, as fine as any to be had in a pricey Toronto restaurant. She congratulated the cook, Erick Jansen, who, she was told, had once been an engineering student, but loved nothing better than to create masterpieces in the kitchen.

Several fine wines, courtesy of Nick Radcliffe, were consumed with relish, and helped to loosen tongues.

"So, have you met many of our charming neighbours yet, Kit?" Dianna Webb asked. Dianna's short, dark, carefully tousled hair was decorated with a beaded headband, which matched an elaborate beaded necklace, bracelet, and anklet. Her designer gypsy-style clothes were new, and worn to lend her a bohemian air, Kit suspected.

"So far, I've had dinner with the McGraths, been spooked by Arnie Bryce, been ripped-off by Wayne Skuce - but ably assisted by his sister Bonnie - and been entertained by the vaudeville team of Cleo and Rhett Pugh! In fact, they've invited me to lunch tomorrow."

"That should prove an interesting experience," Liz said with amusement.

"They're a couple of strange old birds," Teresa Kelleher said.

"Aged Yuppies," Pete Sage mumbled. He'd had far more wine than anyone, and, although his speech was not slurred, he was well on his way to being drunk. No one paid him much attention.

Teresa continued. "They do nothing but complain about the smell from our animals, the flies from our barns, and the dandelion seeds from our lawns. We don't believe in polluting everything with chemicals, and we've gotten use to the dandelions. In fact, Kevin uses the plants for various things, including dandelion wine."

Kevin asked, "And how are you managing by yourself, Kit?" At narrowed glances from the women, he smiled and said, "No offence, Kit. I was just going to offer our help, but I'll send the women over, since they're so keen on being liberated from traditional female roles."

Kevin seemed a shy and gentle person behind his horn-rimmed spectacles. He had a trim beard, and his long sandy hair was tied into a tail at the nape of his neck. He reminded Kit of popular pictures of Jesus Christ.

"I'm just putting in a garden, so any advice on growing vegetables would be welcome," Kit said. Kevin just happened to be an ardent horticulturalist, and the rest of the meal was spent discussing organic gardening and the farm. They regaled her with amusing stories of their early tribulations and of their thrilling successes.

Over coffee and liqueurs, Kevin talked Kit into planting herbs in her garden as well.

"Kevin knows the medicinal properties of a lot of plants," Liz told her, "and we make infusions and tisanes and concoctions of many of them for ourselves and the animals."

"I heard that you grow marijuana, and that there've been spies in your fields seeking it out," Kit said with a grin.

"Ha! That must be the Skuces," Leighton Pearse said. Leighton struck Kit as a genuine hippie, with his wild red mane and scraggly beard, his oft-patched jeans, old tie-dye T-shirt, and bare feet. He truly seemed not to care about his appearance, although, beneath the neglect, he appeared to be a handsome man.

"I'm trying to decide if I should hire the youngest boy - Byron is it? - to cut the grass for me," Kit said. "Do you suppose he's reliable?"

"He and Bonnie are probably the best of the bunch," Drew said.

"Of an otherwise rotten bunch," Teresa amended.

Leighton said, "Well, if you'll excuse me, I'm off to listen to some opera. I'm sure we'll see a lot of each other, Kit. And if you're a lover of classical music, you can come to the National Arts Centre with me some time for a symphony or an opera. *Boheme* starts next week."

As he left the room, Liz explained, "Leighton's turned the attic into his private domain, complete with quadraphonic sound. Music is like a drug to him. If he doesn't get his daily hit of opera - particularly Maria Callas - then he's unbearable to live with."

"Did he study music?"

"No. Theoretical physics. He'd almost finished his Ph.D. when he decided to chuck it all."

Mandy said, "It's his one love in life - music. The only thing he ever spends his money on. He travels all over the world to see operas - New York to the Met, Vienna, La Scala. Just for weekends. And he has thousands of records in his collection - every version of every opera that he can get hold of."

Nick Radcliffe, lounging on one of the sofas with a brandy snifter held carelessly in one hand and the sinuous Cindy leaning sleepily (or drunkenly) against him, said to Kit, "I'll bet you've never met anyone as unpretentious and down-to-earth as Leighton. And he's honest to the point of rudeness sometimes."

Kit sensed that Nick and Leighton were close friends. Certainly Nick seemed to have great admiration for Leighton, which somewhat surprised her. Nick, the apparent Yuppie, was perhaps not such a turncoat as Pete Sage thought.

Pete rose unsteadily to his feet. "Off to work on my novel. Like you to read it some time, Kit. Maybe you know a publisher... All the ones I've tried have rejected it, the bloody fools. Be a best seller one day. That'll show them. 'Scuse me."

No one spoke while Pete negotiated his way out of the room, but many eyes followed his progress. And on most of the faces there was pity or sadness. Only Dianna looked disgusted.

When he was gone she said, "How much longer are we going to put up with his drunkenness? It's revolting watching a person wallow in self-pity the way Pete does."

There was an uncharacteristic frown on Mandy's face. Somewhat sharply she said, "He's not usually this bad, Dianna. He needs time to get over Jackie, and he needs to feel he's not a failure - what with Jackie leaving and his book being rejected time after time, and then there's that ultra-successful brother of his that his mother keeps writing to him about. He needs our support more than ever just now, not our vilification."

"So speaks the psychologist," Dianna said nastily. "And wasn't Jackie right about that so-called book of his? I've never read such crap! What did Jackie call it? A 'vomiting onto paper of Pete's rage and envy'?"

Liz explained to Kit, "Jackie Beauchamp lived with Pete for nearly a decade. She made rather a success at pottery - you might have read about her in some magazines. All kinds of shops carry her wares now. She decided to move out last year, back to the Maritimes."

"And is Pete's novel really so bad?" Kit asked.

"It is rather - how shall I put it? - iconoclastic and highly personal."

"Bullshit!" Dianna said. "It's a plotless, whining diatribe."

Drew said, "I equate it with modern art."

"Oh, it's as bad as that, is it?" Kit asked, much to the amusement of the others - except for Dianna.

She said, "Another philistine! Well, I'm off early tomorrow for the weekend. Fraser is taking me to Toronto. For a bit of culture. So I'm going to pack. Nice meeting you, Kit, even if you have no appreciation of fine art. Come into my shop sometime."

"I'll do that."

Liz showed Kit around the original part of the farmhouse. There was a TV room, a well-stocked library and reading room, an office - Teresa Kelleher's domain - three bathrooms, eight bedrooms, and of course, Leighton Pearse's attic quarters. Music poured down from there, flowing down the walls and beams and floorboards and into the very core of one's being. Kit recognized it as the mad scene from *Lucia di Lammermoor*.

Liz and Kevin walked her to the car when she left a short while later. She felt a pang of loneliness and envy, seeing them standing with their arms about each other's waists, waving goodbye to her. They were silhouetted against the bright picture windows of the kitchen, which exuded warmth and companionship.

The loneliness became more acute when Kit pulled into the carriage house a few minutes later. She hated to turn off the car lights, for the one weak bulb just outside the door did little to dispel the darkness. She fumbled with her keys, nearly dropping them, but finally managed to unlock the door.

She had left the kitchen lights burning, but the room was empty and cheerless compared to the place she had just left. She felt like running back there and asking if she could stay the night. Or going off to the city.

If only Nigel were here. Nigel would like Mole End Farm and its fascinating inhabitants, too.

Chapter 6

October 31, 1871 :

During my two month absence I schemed to end my victimization. I even considered murdering him.

Heather was delighted to see me that August day, if somewhat surprised at my precipitous arrival. She glowed with health and excitement, for she was in the early stages of her first pregnancy.

I almost wept with the sanity and normality of her home and her warm and loving welcome. I could never let her, or any of them, know what a monstrous act had occurred. I fear that somehow I am to blame, and that they would regard me with contempt and disgust. I dread to lose their love as well.

So I tried to be my usual outspoken, vivacious self. It has helped me to heal somewhat, to make important decisions and to face my destiny.

I considered poisoning him. I know that his heart medicine contains digitalis, which comes from the foxglove plant, of which we have an abundance growing in our gardens at Moon Hall. But I wondered how one would administer it - as crushed leaves added to some food, or as liquid steeped from the leaves or root, added to his whisky? Was it bitter? Would he notice? How much was needed to make the dose fatal? Could a doctor easily detect such an overdose?

I thought to tackle Heather's husband, Gordon Forrester, on the subject - for he is a doctor - but could think of no reasonable way to elicit answers to those crucial questions.

Besides, I had an even more pressing problem to consult him about.

I waited until I could catch him alone, since I could never broach the subject in front of Heather, and I suspected that Gordon would not discuss it in her presence either.

But all my family - even my brothers-in-law - know me to be slightly outrageous, and would not think my curiosity odd.

So I cornered Gordon in his study one afternoon while Heather was resting in her room. I pretended I had come seeking a book, and indeed, I had been snooping into his medical texts whenever opportunity presented itself. I pulled one of these off the shelves now, and idly flipped through it.

Gordon took it from me, saying, "Not suitable reading for young women. I fear you would find it most tedious."

"Oh, I doubt that! I'm fascinated by all manner of knowledge, including medical. Perhaps you can satisfy my curiosity on a puzzling subject, Gordon."

"Certainly, if I can."

"I overhead Father talking with someone about an acquaintance who has the pox. I've heard the word, of course, but am unfamiliar with this disease."

Gordon looked startled and even embarrassed, so that I felt slightly guilty for raising the subject. But I had to know!

"Of course you are, Violet, and always will be! It is not a disease of polite society or virtuous women. You need have no fears about it."

"But it sounds most horrible! They spoke of it eating away at the victim, body and soul." I shuddered to repeat those words.

"You mustn't distress yourself, Violet! It is a disease of women of loose morals - God's punishment, perhaps, for a life of sin."

I had to play dumb. "So how could this man have contracted it?"

Gordon seemed reluctant to answer. "He must have consorted with such women. It is generally spread by physical intimacy. Now do not persist in questioning me about this inappropriate topic."

"But I must have my curiosity satisfied! You know, I have been thinking that I might study medicine. Like Dr. Emily Stowe." It wasn't a complete lie, although I had soon decided that I didn't have the stomach for it.

"Heaven forbid! You?"

"Well, you need not laugh quite so heartily!" I retorted, stung by his mirth. "I'm fascinated by diseases and medicines. And I think myself strong enough to withstand the ridicule of male students and doctors, and clever enough to learn as much as they!"

"No doubt! But even you, my dear Violet, would be appalled at the horrors that a doctor has to witness."

"Such as the pox?"

"Precisely. Syphilis is a most insidious, deceitful, and contagious disease. It can lie dormant and flare up with a vengeance up to twenty or even thirty years after infection. Initially it can seem quite mild, with painless sores and rashes, headaches and fevers. But it can also cause supporating ulcerations, and horrible lesions both inside the body and out, destroying livers, hearts, muscles, even minds. It can eat away noses, eyes, mouths, and bones...You look quite shocked, Violet. I knew I should not have told you!"

He helped me into a chair - for indeed my legs were weak - and poured me a medicinal measure of brandy. "I didn't mean to be squeamish," I explained. "It's just so appalling to think of this happening to someone of Father's - and perhaps our - acquaintance." Or to me! God forbid!

"There are some medicines that, carefully administered, might be of benefit. But I'm not convinced that these are cures. I've seen cases of degenerative madness in syphilitics many years after their cures."

"You said that virtuous women would never get it, but what if a husband is not faithful and contracts it from ... another woman?"

"There's always that risk, certainly. But as soon as the husband is diagnosed, he is told most adamantly that he must cease all intimate relations with his wife, for fear of infecting her and their offspring, who could be born deformed and mentally deficient. But I doubt that your future husband would stray, if that's what concerns you, Violet," Gordon said with renewed amusement. "I'm sure he'll have his hands full with you!"

"I may choose not to have a husband," I stated in truth, for of course I was now under sentence of this horrible death. "Perhaps I should become a doctor and help these unfortunate wretches!"

"Doctors can but patch up broken and diseased bodies as best they can. It would be preferable if we could stop it happening altogether."

"You're right, Gordon. Something should be done to encourage the women of the streets to lead more moral lives. Perhaps that is what I shall dedicate myself to!"

"I doubt you'll find many to reform in Todmorden." He chuckled. "Or even here in Kintyre."

"But plenty in the cities, I presume?"

"No doubt Ottawa would challenge you," he replied. "It's an unhealthy enough place, riddled with disease and vice and poverty."

"Then I shall have a good look around when I visit Lily and Rose," I said before I quit the study.

I was quivering when I reached the guest room, which I had claimed as my own for the time being. I lay down on the bed to contemplate what Gordon had told me.

Father must have had this disease for many years, possibly even before Mother died, otherwise he would have married again soon after her death, I was sure. Had Mother been infected, too, and had that somehow caused her and the child to die? Aside from what seemed to me his one madness, he showed no outward signs of the affliction. Had I overlooked other indications of his mental derangement?

Was it possible that he didn't even have the disease? But no, he would have made certain of the diagnosis before giving up his quest for a son. And Gordon had said that it could lie dormant. Was Father's weakened heart a result of it?

I felt corrupted. My skin crawled. Would that I could dispense with this shell of contaminated flesh!

Dare I ask Gordon for some medicine? I examined myself carefully in the mirror, but saw no signs of skin ulcers. Perhaps my symptoms wouldn't appear for years to come. Perhaps I didn't have it, I thought with hope, but then recalled that Gordon had said it was highly contagious. How could I have failed to contract it?

And it wasn't the sort of disease one could ask one's doctor - or brother-in-law - about. How would I explain my fear of having this sinful leprosy?

Perhaps it was better to die now, and save myself the anguish of the disease and of my shattered hopes. Never could I marry and have children of my own! Surely that was an excessive punishment for the telling of a lie! Why had even my Heavenly Father deserted me when my own earthly one had gone mad?

I thought of the Chaudiere Falls in Ottawa, which might swallow me up, or any number of riverside cliffs from which I could hurl myself. But all the while I knew I wanted to live. Even if I had to live alone, without the comforting companionship of an intimate, caring friend, which a loving husband must surely be, or the delight and support of children.

Perhaps I would dedicate myself to good works. Saving whores might be a start.

I stayed with the Forresters for two weeks. I can only wonder what they must have thought of me, for I was an emotional mess. Of course I kept up my spirits in their presence, perhaps too boisterously, for Heather asked if something troubled me. How I wish I could tell her! When I was alone, I mourned and raged. I still shiver with dread whenever I think of what fate awaits me.

Heather and I both love walking, and Kintyre is such a pleasant place to roam about. Many of its downtown commercial blocks and its fine homes - such as the Forresters' - were built by Scottish stonemasons after they had finished constructing the Rideau canal back in the thirties. It feels like a well-established, comfortable, and prosperous community, and I know from our daily outings that Heather is most contented there.

Gordon is a popular doctor. Not surprisingly, since he is both handsome and charming, as well as dedicated and competent. How I envy Heather her happiness!

My week with Rose was less enjoyable. She and Edwin live in an impressive mansion perched on the bluffs on Cliff Street, overlooking the Ottawa River, just west of Parliament Hill. They've named it Rosecliff, for obvious reasons.

Rose has always been rather domineering, thinking that the rest of us should obey her simply because she is the eldest. Because she is thirteen years older than I, she was almost finished at the Academy when Mother died. After that, Rose was home with us for three years until she married Edwin Whitaker and settled in the city of Quebec, which is where the government of the Province of Canada was seated at that time.

Rose had a wonderful time there, claiming it to be the most marvellous, vibrant, and exciting city in all of North America. No one was ever bored, for there were always plenty of dashing, red-coated soldiers to flatter the ladies, government balls and entertainments winter and summer. We visited her only twice during the five years she lived there.

So Rose and I don't really know each other well. I do know that she is now not so gay or carefree. She despises the provincial nature of Ottawa compared to the sophisticated, long-established Quebec, and bitterly resented moving there when the seat of government changed in 1865, a little over a year before Confederation.

Rose seems driven to earn a reputation as pre-eminent hostess in the city, to the point that it appears to me she no longer really enjoys the actual events, merely the impressions they make upon others.

This soiree was to be the first in the city following "society's" return from holidays, for no one who is anyone would stay in the blistering and wretched city during the summer. It is fashionable to travel to the cooler towns along the lower reaches of the St. Lawrence River, like Riviere du Loup or Tadoussac, or to St. Andrew's-by-the-Sea in New Brunswick, where some even maintain summer homes.

I suspect that the Whitakers could not afford to join the exodus this summer, so they spent two weeks with us at Moon Hall, two with Hazel in Kingston, but only a week with Iris at her riverside summer estate, "Seabreeze Cottage", which is perched between the mountains and the broad St. Lawrence, well east of Quebec. It seems that half of fashionable Montreal gravitates to that lovely wilderness for the summer, so there is no lack of suitable company!

Rose was annoyed by the brevity of her stay, but Iris had told her that so many guests were expected this summer that a week was all she could offer. Or course, Seabreeze Cottage can easily accommodate twenty guests, so I know that a week was all Iris could stand of Rose's company. My two eldest sisters have always tried to outdo each other, so they are close only in age. Iris, the prettiest and most conniving of us, contrived to marry into one of the country's wealthiest families who have interests in mining, shipping, lumbering, and railroads. Rose aspires to the exclusive society in which Iris moves, and is intensely jealous of her younger sister's wealth and success..

The Whitakers' new house is extravagantly embellished, a true showpiece - though it doesn't come close to matching Iris's mansion in Montreal's Westmount. I wonder if the Whitakers are not living beyond their means and that this is the cause of the tensions I sensed between Rose and Edwin during my stay. Building the house itself must have cost them a fortune. Although Edwin seems to appreciate her social efforts - for they are a boon to his career - he said facetiously that they needn't try to outdo the Governor-General.

They have five high-spirited children, who, understandably, try Rose's patience at times. My two oldest nephews, Edward, ten and Arthur, nine, frighten even me with their wild antics. They delighted in showing me how quickly they can scale the cliffs behind the house. My heart nearly stopped as I watched them scramble up and down the steep precipice that must be a hundred feet or more to the river's edge.

I spent some time wandering alone about the city, which really is a dirty, foul-smelling, and noisy place. Edwin complains about the bad drains - there is no proper sewer system - which seem to be constantly blocked and pollute the air with such putrid odours one can sometimes scarcely breathe. There is no water supply either, so water must be bought in large puncheons, filled from the river and of questionable quality!

The city looks raw and unfinished and at the same time, tumbledown, for there are many old shacks. Great piles of lumber and sawdust seem to grow everywhere, and the whining buzz of saws is the cacophonous music of the capital. There is nary a tree to soften the harsh skyline of rooftops or to give blessed shade from the scorching summer sun.

Pigs forage in the refuse scattered in the streets. Cows stray, rats scurry, flies and mosquitoes pester. A most insalubrious place! I wore only ankle-length skirts that wouldn't drag in the garbage and excrement and spittle that befoul the dusty streets.

So I can understand Rose's dislike of the city, especially after the civilized beauty of Quebec. I myself longed for the sweet-smelling country air of Moon Hall, spiced with the early autumn scents of windfall apples and haystacks.

Yet is there not promise of greatness to come for Canada's poor little capital?

The Parliament Buildings are magnificent, perched high atop the cliffs overlooking the wide and lovely river and the distant hills of Chelsea. My favourite place to stroll is a surprising jewel of a path which encircles Parliament Hill and is known as Lovers' Walk. Stone steps lead down into a lush woodland that covers the hillside. Here in the cool tranquility one can hear birdsong and find some refreshment for the soul. I'm told that Prime Minister Macdonald enjoys walking here, but as government was not in session then, I met few fellow strollers.

But I went elsewhere as well, into Lower Town and the poorer quarters.

I noticed women and children with thin limbs poking out from beneath too short rags. I don't know what whores look like, but if the pathetic creatures that I saw were these supposedly wicked, loose-moraled women, then I little wonder why they try to sell their bodies. It seems they have no other way of keeping their souls anchored to this earth.

Is that why these women sacrifice their virtue and risk disease? Perhaps virtue and morality don't count for much when one is starving or watching one's children starve.

More surprising, though, is to think that any man would lust after such pitiful wretches, and pay to have his need satisfied. I can hardly believe that Father, always so fastidious in his habits, would engage in intimate relations with such filthy creatures.

Perhaps whores were different. Perhaps they were ordinary looking women, like the housewives buying farm-fresh produce from the stalls in the By Ward Market. Or were they the flower sellers, or even those rather giddy and fashionable young women who jumped aboard the horse-drawn trolley? But then where was the evidence of their sins, the festering sores and corruption of the flesh?

More than once in my rambles I encountered drunken men. I know that drunkenness is a great problem in Ottawa - our own Prime Minister is a notorious boozer. But it appears to me that it is the weak and helpless who suffer most when men overindulge in cheap whiskey.

On one stinking, rubbish-strewn street of mean little dwellings, I was nearly bowled over by a young woman who could not have been older than I. She had come barrelling out of one of the rickety hovels and straight into me.

Unfortunately, that delay allowed her pursuer to catch her. He was a big brute of a fellow and she seemed small and frail in comparison. She winced as he gripped her arm. With surprising strength she fought him, kicking and scratching, as he slapped her hard across the face several times, cursing and shouting at her. She shrieked, and screamed abuse at him. Dogs were barking. Neighbours were coming out of their homes.

Probably I should have done nothing. But I felt my blood boil at this bully's ill-treatment of the girl.

I carried a walking stick - at Edwin's insistence - for there are many curs on the street only too ready to snarl and snap at one. There is always the danger of rabid animals as well.

So I swung the stick and fetched the fellow a blow across his back. He howled in rage and released the girl as he gasped for breath. Quick as a jack-rabbit, she bounded off down the street.

The bruiser stumbled and lurched toward me. I know I am tall for a woman, but this lout towered over me and seemed to have the iron muscles of a prize fighter. He was close enough for me to smell the stench of soured sweat and too much whiskey.

I kept my eyes fixed defiantly on his, but felt my heart threatening to jump out of my chest.

"Fuckin' bitch!" he hissed. "What the hell do you think you're doin'?"

He tore the walking stick from my hand and flourished it before my face. "You need to be taught a lesson, you stupid bitch!" He jabbed it at me, poking my arm as I, unwittingly, backed up.

"How dare you!" I demanded, angry as well as scared.

He whipped my thigh with the stick. It stung, but he hadn't swung it with full force. Yet.

And suddenly my retreat was halted. A hand on my arm pulled me aside, and the stick was snatched from my persecutor, who had been so intent upon intimidating me that he stopped in muddled surprise.

"Well, Jack, I see you're still picking on people smaller than you," my rescuer said. He had a beautifully melodious voice, which, unfortunately was not matched by his countenance. His intense, dark eyes were the best features on his chiselled, lean face.

Like a bull, Jack, grunted. "This be none of your business, Doc. That stupid bitch hit me!"

"Not without good reason, it seems," 'Doc' replied. "Go and cool off, man, before you get yourself into trouble. This lady might press charges against you, and you'll end up behind bars."

Jack spat a stream of brown tobacco juice onto the road in front of me. "Next time you get lost in the wrong neighbourhood, you'd best watch yourself, you interferin' bitch!" he said to me before turning and staggering back into his house.

A strong hand gripped my elbow just as I felt my knees would buckle beneath me with relief. "Can you walk?" my rescuer asked.

"Of course," I replied with dignity, though I was grateful for his support as we shuffled away.

His smile quite transformed his rather nondescript face. "Allow me to introduce myself... Daniel Haywood."

"Violet McAllister. Thank you for your timely intervention, Mr. Haywood. Or is it Doctor?" I asked, for I had noted his bag, and how the bully had called him "Doc" with a measure of respect.

"Call me Daniel if you like. I don't stand on formality. I was in the neighbourhood, tending to some children down with scarlet fever. I saw what you did. A very brave and foolish thing, if I may say so. I trust you are not injured?"

"Not at all," I replied, though I suspected I might well have a bruise or two.

"Allow me to buy you a cup of tea, Miss McAllister, for I think you have need of it."

"Thank you. I accept, " I said, for I still felt weak and jittery inside. It seemed neither awkward nor improper that Daniel Haywood should hold my arm as he escorted me along the three or four blocks to a restaurant. Of course, if Rose had seen me, she would have been mortified.

It was a relief to sit down in the small but relatively clean establishment. Despite the warmth of the day, Daniel Haywood ordered tea for us both. He seemed to be well known there.

"Well, Miss McAllister. What brought you into our neighbourhood?"

His eyes were probing and intelligent, and I realized that he did not suffer fools gladly. I wondered at his use of the possessive "our". Surely he himself did not live there?

"I am curious about different areas of the town. I've been wandering all over the city."

"Perhaps not a wise pursuit for an unprotected young lady," he said.

I felt I had been chastised, and was rather annoyed. "Surely women can walk the streets of our nation's capital unmolested!" I protested.

He smiled, and I marvelled at how attractive he suddenly seemed. I don't suppose he could ever be called handsome, but neither was he plain. A man who must surely have an interesting life to go with such a face.

"Most assuredly. If you keep to your own neighbourhood. But if you begin to interfere in rough areas where you don't belong..." He shrugged.

The tea and cakes came and he said, "Lots of sugar for you. Doctor's orders."

I complied. When the waitress had gone, I said, "Well, I couldn't just stand there and watch that brute beat that poor girl."

"I grant you it's not a pleasant sight, but 'that poor girl' is his wife and there is nothing anyone can legally do about his mistreatment of her. But she's a feisty woman, and often gives as good as she gets. Not long ago I had to treat him for a knife wound."

I sipped my tea, thinking how wrong it all sounded. How could there be no laws to protect women from such barbarians?

"But you mustn't trouble yourself about such things, Miss McAllister."

He didn't say it, but I could almost hear him thinking, "You go back to your nice, safe, sheltered haven and forget about all the misery and suffering in the rest of the world." How dare he presume to know anything about my life! Perhaps the tale I could tell would be even more shocking than anything he had yet encountered!

Indignantly, I said, "But I do trouble myself, Doctor! I deplore violence, especially against women and children. It should not be allowed!"

Again he smiled. "I agree with you. But since the law does not forbid it..."

"Then the law must be changed!"

"Quite so! Until then, there is little that you or I can do to change things."

"We shall see," I stated with conviction.

"Is your father a politician, Miss McAllister?"

"No. We live in the country, and I am visiting my sister, whose husband is in the civil service."

"Do you think that he might have political influence?"

"He has influential friends, but that was not my thought. Though of course I shall try to influence his friends, if ever I have the opportunity. But tell me, why does this woman stay with a man who beats her?"

He regarded me indulgently, as though I were a naive child. "Because she has nowhere else to go. There is little that women on their own can do to survive. Employers demand a certain standard of appearance, deportment, and skills even for servants. Abandonned women too often end up on the streets, selling their bodies simply to stay alive."

If he thought to shock me he soon realized that he had miscalculated. "That is what I thought." I said. "And so I've been wondering how to help these unfortunates. Would not a shelter, a temporary home of refuge, be of some benefit?"

"Undoubtedly. At least in the short term. But accepting charity from society ladies is a bitter pill for many of the indigent to swallow." He regarded me assessingly for a moment and said, "You don't strike me as the usual frivolous miss who has good intentions of aiding the poor, but little stomach for it."

I stared into his dark eyes and said, "I have a mission." What I didn't say was that by helping others, I might save myself from despair. I decided then that as soon as I had solved my own problem, I would set up a house of refuge for women.

"And you, Doctor. Do you earn your living by tending to the unfortunates of this city?" Judging by the cut of his frock coat, I thought that he must have a decent income that dedicated service to the poor would never provide.

He chuckled. "One would hardly call that a living! We must all be practical, Miss McAllister. I have quite a number of patients of the business and professional classes, since, all too often, I am paid little or nothing for attending to the unemployed, the crippled, the destitute, the dispossessed, the forgotten of the city. You see, I do know how to behave in polite company," he said with a grin.

I laughed, for I realized I had sounded challenging, and deserved the tease. I thanked Daniel Haywood for the tea, which had restored me. He pressed a calling card into my hand and said, "If ever you have need of my services, don't hesitate to call me."

I couldn't suppress a shudder, for I was reminded that I might indeed require his professional services some day. Somehow, it seems to me that he is a doctor I could trust with the truth. If necessary.

As is so often the case when one learns of something or someone new, it wasn't long before I heard of Daniel Haywood again.

I moved to Lily's more modest but comfortable house in Sandy Hill before Rose's soiree. Rose seemed so preoccupied with preparations that I did not wish to intrude, even though I had mostly amused myself anyway. Also, I wanted to be well away from her house before Father came. I thought that if he insisted upon my returning to Moon Hall with him, Rose would assuredly coerce me into obeying him. At least this way I would be under Lily's protection. And she would be more inclined to take my side.

Lily and Heather are my closest sisters, not only in age, but in affection and temperament. I consider them my very best friends. How lucky I am that both live so close to me!

Lily is married to Augustus Blake, a studious, thoughtful man who is a solicitor by occupation. By training and inclination he is a classical scholar with an endless curiosity about everything from art to engineering.

Lily is quite an accomplished pianist, and has started her own little chamber ensemble recruited from among her friends. They play only to amuse themselves, though Augustus threatens to hire them out for Rose's parties!

It was the evening before Rose's soiree that Augustus mentioned Jonathan Haywood. He was saying, "Of course, he's a brilliant barrister, and rumour has it that he'll be made a judge one day soon. He's still quite young for such an honour, deserved though it is."

"Does he have a brother who is a doctor?" I asked.

"I believe he does," Augustus answered.

"Do you know him?" Lily asked in surprise.

"I met him by chance one day," I replied casually, without meeting her eyes.

Lily shook her head and said, "I daren't ask how, for I may not want to know."

"Quite right," I replied with a grin.

"You might see him tomorrow, for he and his brother are undoubtedly invited to Rose's do."

I rather doubted it, for I thought Daniel Haywood might scorn the frivolity of society. Yet he was neither a martyr nor a fool, and would not ignore the good he might accomplish through influential acquaintances.

So I began to look forward to Rose's party with more enthusiasm.

But the first person I saw was Father. His brow furrowed when he noticed me, but I managed to avoid being alone with him. In the presence of others, I mentioned how lovely it was to visit each of my sisters, so that he knew of my plans and could not now deny them. I escaped from his loathsome presence as soon as I was able.

I had met many of the guests before. Neither the Governor-General nor the Prime Minister was expected to attend this time, so the gathering did lack some of the usual sparkle and importance. But Rose would undoubtedly have another soiree or a ball once "the season" really began.

I have to admit that I was rather disappointed when I didn't see Daniel Haywood there. Possibly he was busy attending to dying children while we drank champagne and gossiped.

I was introduced to his brother, Jonathan, who is a more dashing figure than Daniel. He has the same intensely intelligent eyes and lean physique, but with more gentle and pleasantly aligned features. He and Augustus seem to be good friends, who appreciate each other's company and are undoubtedly well suited intellectually.

Sipping my wine, I sauntered outside to the back terrace to watch the last rays of sun touch the mountains across the river. If one ignored the logs and sawdust hills in the foreground, it was quite a spectacular view. A few others strolled about the gardens, but I was content to be by myself for the moment.

"I was wondering if we might meet again, Miss McAllister."

I was delighted to hear his pleasing voice. I turned to face him. "Doctor Haywood! You must indeed know how to behave in polite society, for my sister is quite particular about whom she invites."

His eyebrows rose. "Your sister is Rose Whitaker? I see."

As he looked about him, I knew exactly what he saw. A family of wealth and privilege.

"Do you?" I challenged. "I find one can rarely judge by appearances."

He smiled. "How wise you are, Miss McAllister. May I join you?"

I smiled back. "But of course." He perched beside me on the balustrade that edged the terrace. "Did work delay you? I had guilty visions of you tending the dying while we indulged in frivolous chitchat."

"Even frivolous chitchat has its uses," he replied with amusement." I recommend it for the relief of daily stresses. But I was called out. Such is the lot of doctors!"

"You must meet my brother-in-law, Dr. Gordon Forrester, who lives in Kintyre, and is also here tonight. He says that Ottawa is the one place where his patients can't find him! They have even sought him at our house, which is a dozen miles from town."

"Well, I told no one where I would be this evening, so I intend to enjoy myself."

"You must know many of the people here."

"I do. Quite a few are friends as well as patients."

"Another brother-in-law of mine, Augustus Blake, seems well acquainted with your renowned brother."

"Augustus Blake! Quite an esteemed solicitor himself. I did not realize that you had such illustrious connections when we met the other day. I'm afraid I mistook you for a crusading bluestocking."

I suddenly realized how I must have appeared to him in my unfashionable gown. Tonight I wore the required crinolines and stays under my expensive mauve and green London-designed silk, and my hair was tidily up and curled. "Not a mistake I think," I responded somewhat archly.

"I am glad," he replied with a grin.

Gordon appeared and I made introductions, and soon left the two men to their conversation.

Iris and Reginald Thorndike had declined to attend the soiree, saying they had just returned from Seabreeze Cottage and needed time to settle back into Montreal. Since Iris has a house full of servants, one wonders what she could possibly mean, except as a poor excuse to stay away. Probably she would have come had

Lord and Lady Lisgar been expected. That was one trump card that Rose gleefully flourished in Iris's face - that the Viceregal couple belonged to Ottawa society.

Hazel and her husband, Tobias Templeton, who live in Kingston, had also begged off, but then we know that they eschew society, and never expect them to attend anything but weddings and funerals. Tobias is a professor at the university there, and both he and Hazel are more concerned with scholarly pursuits than social intercourse. I'm certain neither even knows how to make polite conversation. They seem to speak only when they have something profound to impart.

However, Daisy and her husband, Elliot Caldwell, had come up from Toronto. Elliot is from a well known legal family. His grandfather was a Chief Justice of Upper Canada, his father is a judge, and Elliot and his two brothers are all lawyers.

Both Elliot and Daisy are social creatures, intent upon their pleasures. Daisy has always seemed flighty and scatterbrained to me, but appears well suited to Elliot and the somewhat dizzying social life they lead. I wonder if they ever spend an evening at home.

Unfortunately, it seems that both are a little too fond of drink.

It was Elliot who was the most worrying. Before long he was disgustingly drunk. His speech was loud and slurred as he talked of Toronto's superiority to Ottawa, much to the dismay of guests and the mortification of Rose.

"You must stop teasing and acknowledge that the Queen had valid reasons for choosing Ottawa as the capital, Elliot," I said as I started to steer him away from an embarrassed group.

"Poppycock! Stuck a pin in the map while she was blindfolded, I heard!" Elliot guffawed.

Gordon and Daniel came to my aid as I tried to manhandle Elliot from the room. Since he wasn't completely legless yet, he was reluctant to leave.

"You're making a spectacle of yourself!" I hissed in his ear. "Come away, or Rose will never forgive you, and never invite you again!"

"The Caldwells are a more distinguished family than either the Whitakers or McAllisters," Elliot muttered with a pathetic attempt to stand on his dignity.

"Then you will have the sense and breeding to know how to preserve your good name!" I retorted.

We managed to get him upstairs to his bedroom. I fetched Daisy, who had herself become quite tipsy on champagne, and entreated her to look after her husband. She, too, was reluctant to leave the company, but I insisted.

As the three of us returned downstairs I said, "I fear Elliot emulates his hero, Sir John, a trifle too much."

"So it would seem. Unfortunately, our Prime Minister has been bodily carried from more than one party in his time," Daniel replied.

Gordon said he would talk to Elliot in the morning and urge him to practice restraint in his consumption of alcohol. I was glad that I wasn't going to be at Rosecliff's breakfast table the next morning. Rose would be angry and scathing in her complaints and accusations. Elliot would be cocky and unrepentant. Daisy would be silly; Heather and Gordon, embarrassed.

I danced with Daniel several times, surprised at his skill on the dancefloor. "You have many talents it seems, Doctor Haywood."

He must have read my thoughts, for he replied, "Despite my sympathy for the poor, I do not deny myself the pleasure of interesting company or lavish entertainments."

"But it must seem strange to you, who sees such misery and despair daily, to also see such extravagance and waste."

"That is the way of the world. I accepted long ago that there are the very rich and the very poor and all levels in between. I do what I can to help those who need it, no matter their position. However, my wealthy patients, whom I charge well, unknowingly support the charity cases."

"Of course!' I replied, delighted with the thought.

"And where you live, Miss McAllister, do you not see poverty?"

"Not desperate poverty," I said, thinking of the few poor, like the Spenlowes, whom I knew. I told him about the farming community that surrounded Moon Hall, and our village which existed mostly because of Father's mill.

"It sounds idyllic," Daniel said.

What irony! But I replied, "It can be. But there are no extravagant balls, merely a few rustic entertainments. There is no cultural activity and no society to speak of. One can feel quite isolated from the world at times."

"Then you can always visit us in Ottawa."

"Indeed, I shall."

There was a sumptuous supper laid out and more dancing, so guests lingered until after two in the morning.

In parting, Daniel said gallantly, "I hope you'll grace our city with your presence often, Miss McAllister."

"I plan to," I replied. "But not, perhaps, in the way you imagine."

"You intrigue me, Miss McAllister," he said, his eyes querying mine.

"Then I am well satisfied!" I replied with a smile, and refused to enlighten him.

Daniel has crept into my thoughts often. He is himself a most interesting and intriguing man. I think that he will approve of my plans, and perhaps even help me establish the refuge.

For the remainder of my stay with the Blakes, I scouted the city for a sight for my mission. (Wondering, at times, if I might encounter Daniel on his rounds, but I didn't.) I pondered the financial aspects of setting up and running such an institution. I queried Augustus on the laws concerning women and children and was appalled to discover exactly how powerless they (we!) are. We have no more rights than criminals and idiots!

And I realized that I am Father's chattel until such time as he gives me to another man. Such a thought is intolerable! It means that he could imprison me at Moon Hall. Or even throw me, penniless, into the street. Which might be preferable under the circumstances!

I had to find a solution to my problem before this hiatus was at an end. For one day soon I would have to return to Moon Hall.

Chapter 7

Lunch at the Pughs' was a farce.

They had it on the back patio - an extensive, interlocking stone patio with a fountain set in the middle, and funereal urns of flowers lining its perimeter. They sat in the shade of a colourful umbrella set into an oblong table. A silver ice bucket containing a bottle of white wine reposed beside Rhett, and they sipped the cool wine from Waterford glasses. The table was elegantly set with Wedgwood china and sterling silver cutlery. Condiments were displayed in silver dishes, covered with plastic wrap to keep off the bugs.

And that was the problem. The aptly named horse flies were buzzing about and landing on everything. They bothered Rhett inordinately. A rolled up magazine was flailed constantly about the table, heedless of the people and the dishes. Kit avoided being smacked in the face several times, and once just barely rescued her wine glass from certain destruction. Crushed fly carcasses unappetizingly peppered the table.

"Bloody flies!" Rhett expostulated. "Because of the bloody farms around here!"

"They really should be outlawed," Kit couldn't resist saying, but Rhett was too busy fighting flies to listen, and Cleo registered no surprise at the sarcasm.

She said, "It does rather spoil our *al fresco* meals! Such a shame that one has to put up with it. We both so enjoy sitting outdoors, communing with nature, so to speak, but the flies are a nuisance in the daytime, and the mosquitoes drive us indoors at night. We have a few of those bug lamps - you know, dear, the ones that attract the insects and then electrocute them - but even they are not a hundred percent efficient. That's why we're building a screened gazebo.

"And we've complained more than once to our neighbours about the shameful state they allow their lawns to get into - dandelions as thick as a carpet! It's little wonder we have a constant struggle to eradicate the weeds from our lawns. And Rhett takes such pride in his lawns. Well, Rhett, I think the barbeque is hot enough for you to start cooking the steakettes."

Cleo went into the kitchen to fetch the salads, refusing Kit's offer of help. Kit was glad to be left alone for a few minutes.

She hoped that Rhett would refrain from waging war on the flies during their meal, but in the meantime enjoyed her wine in peace.

But her heart sank when Rhett returned with a plateful of grilled hamburgers in one hand and a can of bug spray in the other. He set the plate on the table and then fogged the air as if trying to create a physical barrier against the flies. Although there was no wind, Kit could imagine the drift of tiny poisonous particles onto the plates and salads and burgers. Almost reflexively, she put her hand protectively over her glass. Cleo, noticing that gesture, said mildly, "Now Rhett, not so close to the food."

Kit did not do justice to the meal, and her appetite was further diminished when Rhett sprang up every few minutes and zapped a foolish intruder with a squirt of RAID. The contaminated flies would wriggle and writhe and slowly die amid the Wedgwood and Waterford and silver.

Kit watched Rhett's face when he delivered his deadly blows. There was a look of triumph and spite there that surprised her. Rhett got rather carried away with one particularly large and evasive bluebottle. Kit stopped even pretending to eat while the RAID can zigzagged in front of her face and hovered near her plate. Finally with a cry of "Got you, you bastard!", Rhett sprayed the victim right onto Cleo's plate.

She sat back and said, "I really wasn't very hungry. But I think we should refrain from eating out here until the gazebo is completed. Let's have our dessert indoors."

Kit admired her aplomb, and agreed wholeheartedly. Rhett mumbled something about refusing to be "driven out of my own back yard", and kept eating while the women cleared the table. But then he did follow them indoors.

Kit was much happier about eating the rather delicious cheesecake which Cleo served along with freshly brewed coffee in the ballroom-sized living room. That the Pughs were affluent was evident from their many and costly possessions. They had the newest and largest TV available, a satellite dish in the backyard, every conceivable appliance and labour-saving device, the thickest carpets and plushest furniture, and an amazing clutter of knick-knacks and souvenirs.

They also had an electronic alarm system.

"And I keep a gun in every room," said Rhett, pulling a handgun out of a drawer and flourishing it. "Burglars won't stand a chance here."

He would probably attack a burglar with the same destructive gusto as he tackled the flies, Kit thought. She asked, "And is your condo in Florida so well armed?"

"Hardly necessary there, in the middle of civilization," Rhett told her indulgently.

Kit thought it wouldn't be worth the effort of pointing out to Rhett that the crime rate was much higher in Palm Beach than in Todmorden.

"You'd do well to arm yourself," Rhett said. "A young woman, alone in an isolated country house. Just asking for trouble, that is. The stories one reads in the papers these days! It's weeks sometimes before anyone finds the bodies."

Kit excused herself, pleading work, as soon as she decently could. "You must come again sometime, dear," Cleo said. "We have lots of visits to make this summer, to friends all over the country, but we'll be home occasionally. I don't suppose you play bridge? We usually have two tables once a week when we're home. We have friends from town who join us, but sometimes we need a fourth at one of the tables, and it's such a scramble to find someone suitable at the last minute."

"I'm afraid I'm hopeless at cards," Kit said, neither untruthfully nor regretfully.

When she got home she made herself a peanut butter and jam sandwich, which she ate curled up on one of the deep windowsills in the library. Then she went out to tackle the garden once again.

True to his word, Alan McGrath had tilled the soil, even mixing in the bags of peatmoss and manure she had bought. All she had left to do was to rake the soil smooth and to plant the seeds. She didn't have much accomplished when she noticed Nick Radcliffe approaching her from the ravine.

"Hard at work, I see," he said. "I was taking a stroll along the creek, so I thought I'd stop by to say hello."

But those startling, icy-blue eyes said much more than that, and Kit was flattered by his interest. It had been a long time since she had assessed a man as a potential lover. Nick had... possibilities, she thought. But Kit was not one for casual relationships, and she was still too scorched by her years with Nigel to think of getting involved with anyone just yet.

"And where's your friend, Cindy?" she asked.

"Sunbathing. Amongst the cows. 'Friend' is hardly the appropriate label for her. I've only known her a few days - as I'm sure you suspected last night."

She smiled. "I think you don't even know her last name."

"You're right. I suppose you think I'm a bastard, too."

"Do the others?"

"Some."

"I imagine she's not the first girl you've brought with you on the weekends."

"Right again."

"Do these women act as buffers between your two worlds?"

He smiled. "Am I so transparent?"

"Sometimes it's easier for an outsider to notice things."

"Mind if I help?" he asked. As he worked beside her, planting seeds in the furrows she had scored, he said, "I haven't been able to leave the farm altogether, although I've tried to. I can't endure staying in the city longer than necessary, much as I enjoy my job and the amenities there. I suppose it comes down to missing my friends. They're like family, only better. Oh I know Pete resents me, but that's only a recent problem between us.

"Everything changed for me when Suzanne left - she and I were a couple for years. I suddenly felt I had to get away from here and become more self reliant or I'd smother. I think maybe that's how Pete feels, but he hasn't taken the next step. I went out and got myself a job - after I finished my Masters degree in Business Administration. All I had left to do was to type and hand in my thesis. A lot of us dropped out at the eleventh hour, as it were, of our degrees. Leighton's Ph.D. thesis is complete too. He uses it to prop up one of his speakers."

"You're fond of Leighton."

"He has a formidable intellect. I have great admiration for him, even though he makes me feel intellectually inferior. At university, when we had Scrabble tournaments, Leighton would read his physics books between turns, while the rest of us agonized over strategy, and he'd still win. Easily. Meanwhile, he'd learned another complex theory. He could have been a brilliant scientist.

"I'd say Leighton is the only one of us who fully subscribes to the ideology that brought us here in the first place. I'm sure he has no lingering regrets about not having completed his degree. I had. I suppose I couldn't get that inculcated materialism and ambition out of my soul. Drew has focussed his energies on the farm - that's why it's become so successful financially. And I doubt that it'll stop there. I expect he has plans for buying up other farms, and expanding into other areas. All those generations of breeding haven't been wasted on Drew. He just hasn't channeled it into the legal field like his ancestors.

"And the others all have an outlet - Dianna, her shop, Erick, his cooking, Teresa, her office work, Kevin, his plants and medicines, Mandy and Liz, their crafts. But Leighton wants nothing more than to listen to his music. And he does like the communal atmosphere - the company of trusted friends when you want it, solitude when you need that."

Nick straightened up, having finished another row, and said, "I still enjoy grubbing in the soil. And what about you, Kit? What brings you to the back of beyond?"

Kit was grateful to be spared answering by a shouted, "Oh, Nicky!" from the direction of the ravine. Cindy emerged from the shadow of the trees and wobbled toward them in her high-heeled sandals.

Totally ignoring Kit, she said, "Why didn't you tell me where you were going? Why'd you leave me alone with them?" She draped herself about his arm and looked up at him like a child pleading a favour. "I'm bored, Nicky. Let's get outa here."

Nick looked at Kit wryly over the top of Cindy's bleached head. Kit suppressed her amusement.

"I'll drive you back to the city," he said rather abruptly to Cindy.

She pressed her body seductively against his. "Great! I know where there's a party tonight. Let's go, Nicky. Come on!"

"I'll see you, Kit," Nick said.

"Thanks for your help, Nick."

Kit enjoyed working alone in the tranquility of the late afternoon. Bees droned past, birds hopped about nearby, eyeing her quizzically, perhaps ready to steal her seeds once her back was turned. There was an occasional bellow from a cow in the pasture across the road. From far off came the hollow sound of hammering, and Kit guessed that Stuart McGrath was working on his new bungalow.

Probably she should be thinking of making dinner, but she really wasn't hungry. Eating was something she did by inclination these days, not by a schedule. Besides, the evening was too beautiful to miss. The light was golden as it is only on these endless June evenings, with long gilded shadows creeping across the lawn. The sun was still warm on her back, and not a whiff of wind rippled the calm.

Kit had just finished watering her new garden and was surveying it with pride when she heard a noise behind her. The back of her neck prickled with fear at the heavy, quick panting. She swung around to see a massive dog the size of a pony staggering toward her. It was a wolfhound, badly injured perhaps, certainly starving, and frothing at the mouth.

Although Kit was not comfortable with dogs, particularly large ones, she was touched by the dog's plight. "You poor thing," she said softly, and started to go toward it.

"Don't move!" Stuart McGrath shouted, coming around the corner of the carriage house.

Before Kit realized what was happening, he raised a rifle to his shoulder. Her scream of "NO!" reverberated with the gunshot, and the animal fell, twitching, to the ground. A moment later it lay still.

Stupefied, Kit walked toward it, but Stuart was there before her. "Don't touch it!" he said.

She glared at him. "For God's sake, why did you shoot it?"

"Because it probably has rabies," he told her.

She shivered when she realized how close she had come to touching it - a dog, larger than she, that could easily have mauled her, and might very well have been mad.

"Come on," Stuart said, seeing her shocked expression. "I think you need a stiff drink. Alan and I will deal with this brute."

"He must have been a beautiful dog once," she said as he led her into the kitchen.

"Where's your whiskey?" he asked.

Kit pointed to one of the cupboards and then rubbed her arms, trying to restore warmth to her quaking limbs. She had moved the old couch from the parlour into the kitchen when the new furniture had arrived, and now collapsed onto it. Stuart poured her a large brandy.

After the first few sips melted the chill in her bones, Kit felt embarrassed. Stuart McGrath was the last person she wanted to apologize to but she said, "I'm sorry. I feel rather foolish."

He shrugged. "I wouldn't worry about it. Can I use your phone?"

When Stuart had called Alan to come and help, Kit asked, "Where did that dog come from? Does he belong to one of the neighbours?"

"No. People are always dropping off unwanted pets in the country. Either they delude themselves into thinking that farmers will take in the stray animals, or they think the animals can fend for themselves. Usually they starve. Sometimes, they get rabies. We've had lots of rabid foxes reported already this year. But you can't take chances with animals like these. It might just have been starving, but it had the symptoms of rabies. I noticed it earlier, when I was working on my house. By the time I was able to get my rifle, I thought I'd lost it."

"How can people be so cruel?" Kit said, thinking that this animal had once had a home and security, and had given all its love and trust to a human, who had finally betrayed it.

"People have an infinite capacity for cruelty." He said it as though he spoke from experience. Kit wondered if there was a passionate, sensitive soul smouldering beneath that tough exterior. Stuart McGrath was beginning to intrigue her.

Alan arrived, and Kit watched the men carefully bundle the huge beast in heavy plastic and toss it into the back of the truck.

Before they left, Alan said to her, "Get yourself a .22, Kit, and read up on rabies. Then forget your city-bred sentimentality. This won't be the last one of these you encounter, and it seems to me you were lucky that Stu got here when he did. Jeez, this is one hell of a creature to be faced with even if it hasn't got rabies."

"The thought had occurred to me," Kit said with a smile, touched by Alan's obvious concern for her. "It also occurred to me that I'm lucky he's such a good shot. I was only a few feet from the target."

Stuart said wryly, "I didn't realize I was such a good shot either."

Chapter 8

October 31, 1871 :

So I've come home on Halloween.

I know now that I am not with child, for which I am eternally grateful. And I have yet no skin eruptions to brand me a sinner. I am almost lulled into thinking that it is all a dreadful lie or a mistake. But Gordon called the pox insidious and deceitful, so I worry still.

I've missed my beloved autumn at Moon Hall. The trees are now bare, the gardens, dead. The icy breath of winter taunts us. Tomorrow will be November, a bleak and dreary month when autumn battles winter and loses.

I spent the afternoon writing my previous entry to you, dear diary. How lovely it was to relive those weeks away from this nightmare!

Father was in Kintyre today and did not come home for supper.

But when I heard him come in late this evening, I went downstairs to the drawing room and poured myself a brandy, which I swallowed in two fiery gulps, to give myself courage. Then I knocked upon the door of his library. "Come!" I heard him say.

He seemed surprised to see me, for, as children, we had never been allowed to disturb him in his sanctum, and so we'd ventured inside to seek a book only in Father's absence. He sat behind his desk which was spread with papers. Beside his hand was a crystal tumbler half-filled with whiskey.

"So. You've come back." He didn't say "home" "Well?" he inquired coldly, as if I were a bothersome servant.

I closed the door, so that Betsy would not hear, should she venture into the house from the kitchen. Then I faced him across the expanse of the desk.

"Have you come to return the money you stole?" he asked.

"No. That paltry sum can't even begin to repay your debt."

"So, you are a thief as well as everything else."

"I am what you have made me."

He frowned, but I forestalled his speaking. "Do you intend to rape me again tonight?" I stared at him, forcing him to confront my words, to end the silence that bound me to him as his victim.

He barely flinched. "Whores cannot be raped. Merely punished."

Now that the worst had been voiced, I gained courage. "But I am no whore, Father." I imbued that final word with sarcasm. "I was an innocent maiden until you defiled me."

"You lie! You vicious, poxy harlot!"

I glared at him angrily, leaning toward him over the desk as I said, "I lied to you about Neil to keep you from sending him away from me. But it was you who violated me and ruined me. It's you who's made me unfit to be a wife and mother. I buried my blood-stained nightgown in the ravine, but I could show you the evidence of my virginity."

His skin had gone grey. "A trick!" he said, but with fading conviction. "It could as well be evidence of your monthly courses!"

"But it isn't. And I think that you know it. You cannot admit to yourself that you violated me to satisfy your own diseased lust. What you have done to me is vile and sinful and criminal! You are a despicable creature! What if I should stand up in church and condemn you and your heinous crime - you, an elder, a hypocrite?"

"But you won't." It was an order.

"Oh, but I will - if ever you try to touch me again."

I saw his face suffuse with angry blood. "They'll say you're mad. No one will believe you!"

"The words will have been spoken. People will wonder. Some will believe. And if I am mad then you have made me so."

He rose from his chair and leaned intimidatingly toward me, his face almost purple with rage. "You are an immoral temptress, a brazen, cunning, lying bitch! I shall beat that indecency and sinfulness out of you yet!"

I drew out the knife that had lain heavily, but reassuringly, in the pocket of my skirt, and held it up before me. "If ever you come near me again, I shall use this," I said with icy control. "On you or on myself - I haven't decided which. Indeed, I care not which. Then one of us shall hang for murder."

His expression changed from anger to disbelief to pain in an instant. He doubled over as he crashed back down into his chair. He grasped his chest. "Pills," he whispered on a gasp as he tried to reach into his jacket. His face was contorted with anguish, and he seemed unable to breathe. "Pills!"

I distrusted him enough to wonder for a moment if it was a trick to get me within his reach. Even as I approached him, I expected him to suddenly pounce upon me. But he seemed frozen in agony. I fumbled inside his jacket pocket to locate the box. I closed my fingers tightly about it as I withdrew it. He reached wildly for it but I stepped back. There was panic in his look now. Fear.

But I felt no pity for him. No compassion, no love, no respect, no sorrow. He had destroyed all that when he had so vilely abused me, and willfully condemned me to a shameful, horrible death. I felt only relief that it might all be over soon. "I guess I shall see you in hell, Father," I said before I turned and left him there.

I closed the door quietly behind me, and then walked upstairs to his bedroom. Carefully I placed his medicine upon his dressing table. When I went back downstairs, I walked into the drawing room, where I poured myself a larger brandy this time, and sipped it slowly as I sat in an armchair and waited.

If he died, I would be liberated from terror. If he didn't, he will have learned to fear me, and thus, stay away from me. I did not think that he would accuse me to anyone. What would that gain him, for I should just reveal my reasons for wishing my father dead. He might try to have me incarcerated in a madhouse, but I doubted that Doctor Townsend or Gordon and my sisters would deem me mentally unbalanced.

It seemed to me an eternity that I sat there, dreading that the door might suddenly fly open and Father enter in a murderous rage. I still had the knife in my pocket, and envisioned all kinds of terrible scenarios, all of which turned the drawing room into a slaughterhouse.

Finally, when I heard the clock strike ten, I ventured back into the library. I approached him cautiously, still afraid he might spring at me like a mad dog. But then I could see the grey pallor of death upon his features.

I was shocked to think him truly dead. For a moment I stood there, feeling the blood drain from own face as I realized what I had done. Was I a murderer? Surely he might have died anyway.

But now I needed to act. I hastened into the kitchen, where I discreetly returned the knife to its drawer, and then called for Betsy as I rushed up the stairs behind the scullery to pound on her bedroom door.

"What is it, Miss Violet?" she asked sleepily.

"My father! I think he's dead! I must go for the doctor, Betsy."

"Dead?! Dear God!"

"You'd best get dressed, and I'll be back soon."

"Shall I go to the McGraths and ask them to fetch the doctor?" she inquired, though I know how she hates to go out into the dark night.

"No, Betsy. It will be faster if I ride. Make something hot to drink. I think we may all need it."

"Yes, Miss Violet," she called after me.

I grabbed my cloak and went out to the stable where I quickly saddled Moondancer. I didn't bother with a lantern since the moon was nearly full. Anyway, I know the road so well that every rock and hole is familiar.

The wind was bitter. The tears nearly froze to my cheeks. For yes, I was crying. Mourning the father I had once loved, but had lost all those weeks ago. Remembering the odd kindness he had done me, an affectionate smile, a complimentary word. By the time I arrived at Doctor Townsend's house, I must have appeared quite distraught, for his wife ushered me into the parlour and Dr. Townsend pressed another glass of brandy into my shaking hand. I confessed that I had already had one before starting out, thinking that they might well smell it on my breath.

How easily I embraced deception!

Dr. Townsend tied Moondancer to the back of his buggy and insisted that I ride with him, which I was glad to do, the effects of all the unaccustomed alcohol having quite gone to my head.

Back at Moon Hall, Betsy, now alert and dressed, clucked like a mother hen as she helped me consolingly into a chair by the kitchen fire. "There now, Miss Violet. You drink this hot tea. You look quite done in! Oh, what a tragedy! The poor master!" she said, wringing her hands.

"Do sit down, Betsy, and have some tea yourself."

Dr. Townsend joined us a few minutes later. "I'm afraid that you were right, Violet. He had a fatal heart attack this time. Strange that he wasn't carrying his pills."

"Would they have saved him?" I asked.

"Possibly. But in a massive coronary failure they might not have been able to act quickly enough. It was bound to happen sooner or later, Violet. And I had warned him to go easy on the whiskey, but I found half a tumblerful by his side." He shook his head. "I am sorry, my dear. I've seen to him for the moment, so there's no need for you to do anything further tonight. I'll send the undertaker around in the morning. You try to get some sleep, my dear, for these will be difficult days for you." He smiled, and I felt a fraud, accepting all this sympathy and concern.

And now I shall try to get some sleep, dear diary, for it is past one in the morning. The wind howls outside my window as though it were one of the wretched souls doomed to walk the earth this Halloween night, crying to gain admittance to my chamber.

Perhaps it is his hell-bound soul.

Chapter 9

Georgina Bryce was a large woman, built like a linebacker. There was a striking resemblance between her and Arnie. Though they stood stoop-shouldered, it did nothing to lessen the impact of their size. Arnie wore a wide-eyed look as though he were perpetually startled to find himself thrust into this puzzling world. Georgina hardly dared to raise her eyes from the ground, so intense was her shyness.

Arnie looked uncomfortable in his Sunday suit. Georgina looked ridiculous in a frothy, old-fashioned chiffon dress with a little flowered hat perched atop her badly-permed, frizzy brown hair. Kit hadn't seen a get-up like that since the early sixties.

They were standing in the garden, where Kit had been savouring a cup of coffee when their battered pickup truck had pulled into her driveway.

Georgina said, "Father says, could you come to tea?" She was twisting the handle of her purse between her large, powerful-looking hands - hands more used to birthing cows or wringing a chicken's neck, Kit thought, than holding a handbag. Georgina's nervous giggle was startlingly at odds with her largeness. "Figures he's the only one in the neighbourhood who hasn't met you yet. Father doesn't like to feel left out." She frowned. "He's... found things difficult since his accident. Doesn't get around easily."

She spoke in staccato bursts, with fidgety twitches of the lips and eyebrows. Her nervousness made Kit uncomfortable, but she said, "I'd be delighted to come to tea. I suppose I should have dropped by before, to introduce myself, but I've had a busy week settling in."

Georgina seemed to sigh with relief. "That's just what I told Father!"

Arnie picked up his sister's mood. He grinned. "Her's comin' to tea! Her's coming to tea!" he chanted, and would undoubtedly have kept repeating himself had not Georgina stopped him. Her gentle touch subdued his outburst. Kit smiled at the woman who was perhaps several years younger than she, but had a sort of middle-aged agelessness about her. In that awkward, unwieldy body there seemed to be a warmhearted soul.

When Kit saw her later that day, Georgina was more sensibly dressed in a skirt and blouse, but she was even more flustered than before. She bustled back and forth between kitchen and parlour with tea things, nearly upsetting a few precariously-placed ornaments.

"Look out, girl!" her father bellowed. "Ya damn near broke yer Ma's favourite vase!" To Kit he said, "Like a bull in a china shop, she is. No wonder there ain't been a man come to claim her." Loudly he added, "I said, no wonder she ain't never married."

Kit could see the blush creeping up Georgina's cheeks as she re-entered the room. "Now, Dad, you know you wouldn't want it any other way. What would you and Arnie do without me?"

"We'da had yer husband here to run the farm, that's what we woulda had!"

"I do the best I can - you know I do, Dad," Georgina said as she placed a cup of tea on the table beside him. Her smile was strained. "And Arnie is a great help."

George Bryce snorted. "Ha! An idiot and a woman running the farm!"

Arnie, busily stuffing his face with cupcakes, took no notice of the conversation. Georgina flushed a deeper shade of red. Kit tried to hide her dislike of the old man.

George Bryce must have been a formidable man in his time. Large, powerfully-built, with a neck like a bull and hands as broad as shovels, he must have dwarfed the rest of his family. Now he sat hunched over as though his bull neck could barely hold the weight of his bristly head, as though he were shrivelling up, curling inward like a dried leaf. Slowly imploding.

"Ya know how I like my tea!" he roared. "Fetch the whiskey, girl, and don't serve me any of that namby-pamby stuff!" He pushed his cup away irritably, making the liquid slop over the sides into the saucer.

Kit suspected that he'd already had more than enough.

"I thought you might like to join us in a regular tea today, Dad."

"Company manners, is it? Are ya teetotal then, young lady?" he asked Kit.

"Not at all. Although I don't care for a drink at the moment."

"Well, I sure as hell do! Don't put any of that piss-awful tea in it after all. Just give me the God-damn bottle!" He took a big swig from the tumblerful of rye he poured himself. "Christ, that's better. And don't look at me like a sick cow, girl. A man's got a right to drink in his own house. Jeez, what's a man work his butt off fer all his life if he can't enjoy a decent drink."

"Dad, please."

"Please what, my girl?" He drew himself up to his most indignant height. "Do ya see that, young lady? My daughter's embarrassed. Embarrassed that her crippled old dad likes a drink or two to warm his aching bones! Waddaya think of that, eh?"

Kit tried to ignore him, and was floundering for something to say to Georgina, but the old man wasn't about to lose his audience. If he always carried on like this, Kit doubted that there were many visitors.

"Damn shame, I call it. Ungrateful chit! No different from her brother really. Ya heard about our eldest, have ya, young lady? How he took off fer the city, cause farming weren't good enough fer him. Preferred to work in a God-damn grocery store, stocking shelves."

"But he's manager now, Dad."

"And too good to come see us! Thank God yer Ma was spared that. It woulda broke her heart. Now there was a decent woman. A real woman. She had this place running so smooth. Ya wouldn't find a speck of dirt in here in them days." Not like now, his gaze seemed to say as it travelled around the room. It seemed to Kit not so much that the room suffered from neglect as that it lacked the warmth and friendliness and comfort that the McGraths' place had exuded. "There was always the smell of something baking. None of this store-bought rubbish! And she'd be out helping with the animals. And three children to raise. And ya'd never hear her complain!"

Georgina no longer looked embarrassed. It was as if her worst fears had been realized, and she was no longer even nervous. Calmly she announced, "I'm going to show Kit around the farm."

"Show 'er what, fer God's sake? Empty fields? A few cows? Ya think on this, young lady - I farmed five hundred acres once. Did God-damn well! Now that she's taken over the farm, ya know what we got? Less than fifty acres left. Sold most of it to them God-damn hippies down the way."

"It was either that or lose the farm altogether," Georgina said.

"So ya said, so ya said. But if you'da done yer duty and got married, we mighta been able to save the lot. And don't tell me there wasn't a God-damn, fucking fella who wouldna jumped at owning all this land! But no, ya had to try and prove ya could do a man's job. And could ya? Ha? Shit! What did I ever do to deserve such a buncha useless, good-fer-nothin' kids?" George tossed off his third glassful of rye in one gulp.

The two women left the room. Both breathed more easily once they were outside. "I'm sorry you had to see him like that, Kit. But, then again, he's drunk most of the time now anyway. He'll be snoring on the couch in a few minutes, wake up in a foul temper later, and drink himself into oblivion again for the night."

"I hope you don't take what he says to heart. He's obviously bitter about what's happened to him, and probably misses your mother."

"You don't have to make excuses for him, Kit. I'm used to his abuse. He's never had much time for me, though, God knows, I've tried to be a help to him. As for my mother - he treated her no better than a servant. He's always had an inflated sense of himself - the Great Bryce, Lord of all he sees!"

"Why do you stay here?" Kit asked, as they walked toward the barn.

"I wanted to be a librarian, but Dad doesn't hold with women being 'overly educated'. He wouldn't allow me to go to university. I worked at the library in town for a while, just assisting, but I enjoyed it. Then Mother died. Dad took it hard, not having her to boss about. And then Jim, my older brother, left home. He and Dad never got on. Then Dad had his accident. Everything seemed to happen at once. What else could I do but stay here and take over?"

"You must feel as though you're sacrificing your life for your family."

"Sure, sometimes. But, God knows, I'm no martyr. I mean, what choice do I really have? I can't leave Dad and Arnie here alone. There's not enough money to hire a housekeeper and a farmhand. And if I weren't here, some government agency would step in and take Arnie away. Put him in some institution where he'd be miserable. He's never known anything but his home. There's no choice, you see. And I don't mind the farmwork. I've always enjoyed milking the cows. We don't make much money, but it's enough to keep us going. For the time being."

Kit was impressed that Georgina managed the cows, a brood of hens, and an enormous market-garden vegetable plot, to say nothing of all the maintenance that was necessary around the place. "I freeze and can a lot of the produce. The rest I sell at a market in town. We grow the best potatoes hereabouts, I don't mind saying, and our corn is deliciously sweet. The trick is to keep the raccoons from stealing it all."

"I don't know how you manage all this, and look after the household and your father as well."

She shrugged. "I like to keep busy."

"Well, you must need some time off occasionally. So come and see me."

Suddenly shy again, Georgina said, "You don't want to be bothered with me."

"My place gets pretty lonely sometimes," Kit said. "I'd enjoy your company."

Georgina's face lit with an eager smile. "Well, if you're sure. I'd like that!"

Later that evening, when Kit was trying to work in her library, she couldn't get the Bryces out of her mind. She resolved never to go near their place again, although she would welcome Georgina any time. But if the old man wanted a sounding board for his spite and foul-mouthed grievances, he'd have to find someone else. She wondered about his relationship with the rest of the neighbours. Surely he had old friends - the McGraths among them - who wouldn't have abandonned him in his misfortune. And what about Georgina? Had she no special friends - male or female?

Kit found herself growing angry, thinking of how George Bryce had been whittling away at his daughter's self-respect and confidence over the years. She was convinced the only words of praise that had ever crossed his lips would have been for others, as a wounding example to his own children.

In her anger, Kit pounded her fist on the edge of the desk, and for a moment she thought she had broken it. She looked in astonishment at the piece of moulding that was turned at a forty-five degree angle from the desktop. With a thrill, she realized that it was a secret compartment, the sort of place in which the master would have kept important papers hidden from the prying eyes of servants.

Kit did not really expect to find anything in it, but after convincing herself that neither spiders nor mice could have taken up residence, she carefully reached into the void. Her fingers touched something dry and rather brittle. Carefully she coaxed out a book - an old-fashioned diary.

She held it almost reverently in her hands. It was locked. Hardly able to contain her excitement, her fingers searched frantically through the compartment for a key, but there was none. Well, there was nothing for it but to break the lock.

It was a frustrating twenty minutes of prying with bobby pins, a knife, and screwdriver before the lock snapped. It was Violet McAllister's diary.

It all began with a lie. So perhaps I am responsible after all....

Kit poured herself a drink and curled up with the diary in one of her new armchairs in the back parlour. Only a smudge of sunset lingered on the horizon.

It was past two in the morning when Kit finished deciphering the closely-written text. She brushed tears from her cheeks, hardly able to believe that such a shocking and tragic story could be real.

And she felt angry for Violet's sake. Angry that she had been so vilely abused, and also that she had been misunderstood, not only by her peers, but also by history.

Syphilis. A disease that today was no more feared than a common cold. Like consumption and diphtheria, it was a scourge of the past, tamed by modern antibiotics. And Kit had to admit that she didn't really know anything about it.

To think that people lived in such dread of it, that a woman's life was so completely destroyed by it, was incredible.

Kit looked around the room as if searching for Violet's spirit. Surely a tremor of those intense emotions that had once been contained within these walls still lingered. But they seemed to have dissipated.

"Did you dream away your empty life in this bedroom, Violet?" Kit said when she went to bed. The sound of her own voice in the deep silence of the night startled her. It invited an answer, and Kit sighed with relief when none was forthcoming.

Chapter 10

November 15, 1871:

Moon Hall is mine!

I can hardly believe it! It is mine until I marry or die, at which time it is to be sold and the proceeds divided equally among us girls. Well, my sisters will have to wait a long time to get their share of Moon Hall and the five hundred acres that surround it, for, of course, I shall never marry.

I did not realize how much wealth Father had actually accumulated through his investments and ventures, but my sisters and I will soon be very well off, since the mill and other holdings are to be sold. I shall not want for anything. At least in the material sense.

Even Rose can breathe easier now and indulge in her extravagances. I wouldn't be surprised if she bought a "cottage" in one of the fashionable Quebec resort towns. Perhaps next door to Iris's Seabreeze!

The Skuces are overjoyed with their five hundred dollar legacy, which Father left them in gratitude for their fifteen years of service at Moon Hall. They plan to build a handsome little clapboard house next to their old log cabin. Their eldest, Peggy, and their youngest, Josiah, live with them still. Peggy has looked after their home and the younger children ever since she was twelve, at the time Mrs. Skuce took charge of our kitchen. Josiah does odd jobs for local farmers, but can't seem to settle to anything. The two other daughters are married and the eldest son works in the lumber camps.

Betsy was all a-dither with her fifty dollar bequest. I was afraid she might leave us to get married, for she is but five and twenty, but she has no followers and seems contented enough at Moon Hall.

I assured Betsy and the Skuces that I would not be selling Moon Hall - as several of my sisters expect me to!

Lily and Augustus are my legal guardians until I come of age (another three years) at which time I will have full and sole control of my inheritance. And my life. I was delightfully surprised that Father had appointed them, yet it shows that he was an astute businessman. Rose is quite miffed that she, as the eldest, wasn't named guardian, but Father must have been aware of her profligate spending. Iris and Reginald are too distant in miles as well as in attitude. Hazel and Tobias are hopeless outside their own little intellectual sphere, while Daisy and Elliot are too unreliable. Heather herself is only twenty, and, although Lily is not yet twenty-three, Augustus is nearly thirty and a wise and capable man.

They have allowed me to stay here at Moon Hall to my heart's content, knowing that the Skuces and Betsy will look after me well. I am to consider myself part of their household, and come and go as I please. Bless them for granting me such unbelievable freedom! Rose would never have allowed that! She thinks I should sell Moon Hall.... and do what? Live with Lily and Augustus or even one of my other sisters for the rest of my life? Much as I love them, I need my own space, and freedom to be my own mistress.

Of course, none of them realizes that I am also bound to this house by my guilty secret.

Even as I write this, I sit at his desk, in the chair where he died. But I feel no fear or revulsion. I am not fanciful or skittish. If Father's spirit wanders here, I care not, for he can no longer harm me. He frightened me much more in life than he ever could in death.

Perhaps I am thumbing my nose at him, for he would hate to see me invading his sanctuary, claiming as my own his beautiful desk, which he'd had specially built.

So I now have a safe place to hide you, dear diary, for no one must ever read these pages. Perhaps when I am no more than mouldering bones someone may find this, but then it will no longer matter, for we will all be long forgotten.

I will change some things to make this lovely room more to my liking - a new carpet and lighter drapes. I will fill the shelves with interesting books and give away - to Tobias probably - some of these dry and pedantic tomes. I will decorate the walls with my watercolours, for I have some very fine ones of Moon Hall and the area. There is one of which I am particularly fond, which depicts Hugh and his brothers haying in the field behind the ravine.

Hugh came to see me yesterday. Of course he and his family were at the funeral, but I had not spoken to him since. I received him in the back parlour, which is less formal than the drawing room.

He seemed uncomfortable, almost awkward, which is so unlike him. How often I've watched his sure and graceful movements as he slung hay bales onto the wagon, or cast a fishing line! But then I recalled that searing kiss at our last meeting, and I, too, felt somewhat disconcerted.

I offered him a whiskey, which he accepted, and poured myself a sherry.

Moon Hall can be permeated with such profound silence, especially on a winter's day. The kitchen wing is like a little world unto itself, and no noise or chatter intrudes into the main house. So Hugh and I faced each other across this sea of silence. His eyes questioned and assessed. Mine gave nothing away, though how difficult that was!

"We wondered if you planned to continue renting us the pastures and hayfields behind Moon Hall, or if you'd be interested in selling them to us," Hugh said.

"I would gladly sell them to you, Hugh, if I could. But it would require a consensus from my sisters. They - or rather, their husbands - might think that Moon Hall should be kept intact and sold as one parcel. I will ask them, though. And of course, I can continue to rent the fields to you."

He nodded as if he'd received his anticipated answer. Then he said, "What will you do now, Violet?"

"Stay here. It's my home. Although I do have projects I intend to pursue in Ottawa."

"Do you expect that Neil will come back now that your father can no longer stand in the way of your getting wed?"

I hadn't considered that at all. Of course it would make no difference if he did. But I realized what Hugh was leading up to. Too well I remembered - and yearned for - the promise of devotion in his eyes.

But it would be too painful for us both to let him speak the words I longed to hear, and then to reject his offer of love and marriage. It was so much easier to let him, and everyone else, go on believing a lie. "Neil said he would come back for me, didn't he? I once told him I would wait for him forever if necessary. And you know me, Hugh. I've always been stubborn." How odd that these truths maintained a falsehood.

The look in his eyes cut me to the bone. I wanted to shout out that Neil meant nothing to me, that yes I will marry, you, Hugh, if you truly want me! I could still remember the feel of his arms about me and his lips pressed to mine that night he comforted me. And I wanted to touch him, to hold him, to spend my life with him.

But I could only stand apart from him, allowing not even a glimpse of my true feelings in my determined, dismissive look.

And I felt as though something had been torn away inside me. I would have said it was my heart, though I felt that beating still. So it was my metaphorical heart that had been wrenched, root and flower, from my soul and left to wither and die.

Another legacy left me by my father.

Hugh knows me well, indeed, for he did not try to reason with me or to win me. He spoke no words of love or persuasion. He simply said, "You know where to find me, Violet, if ever you need anything."

After he left, I wept angry, bitter tears.

December 22, 1871:

Hugh and Ruth are to be married next summer.

Chapter 11

Kit dreamt of Violet. She drifted in and out of the rooms, obviously mistress of the house, but also its prisoner. Violet was faceless, although McAllister looked like a revitalized George Bryce, and the faithful Hugh resembled Stuart McGrath. They played out bits of Violet's life, distorted and disturbing.

And when Kit thought she had finished her dreams, she saw Violet standing at the foot of her bed, reaching toward her.

Kit woke with a thundering heart. She fumbled with the light switch, and it wasn't until the room was flooded with reassuring brightness, that she even dared to look toward the end of her bed. Of course there was nothing there. Not even a wardrobe that could loom darkly in the shadows of night.

Needing to hear her own voice, shaky though it was, Kit said, "Wow! Don't ever do that to me again, Violet!"

As she sat huddled in her bed, rationally reviewing her dreams, Kit realized that once again she had not seen Violet's face, even though she could recall every ruffle of her black dress, every fold and shimmer of the rich material.

Violet had been wearing black when she'd hanged herself.

Kit shivered and turned on her radio, softly, to dispel the gloom. Although she'd slept for only an hour, she knew that sleep would elude her. She picked up a novel - there was always a stack of new books on her bedside table - but her mind kept wandering back to the diary and the dreams. Even the '60s songs on the radio could not distract her; they seemed to emanate from another world.

She was alert to the slightest noise, but the deep silence was unnerving. It was as dense and suffocating as the country darkness could be. Even the crickets had stopped chirping, and the birds had not yet begun. The creak of a floorboard would have sounded like a pistol shot.

The noise of city traffic and sirens and late-night party-goers had made her feel safe and cozy inside her city womb. But here the silence could make one think that the rest of the world no longer existed. Like something out of the Twilight Zone

She would have liked a drink to steady her nerves, but didn't dare leave her bed. Even with the lights on, she couldn't face going downstairs through those large, echoing rooms. She soon gave up the pretense of reading, while she pondered Violet's poignant and disturbing life. Stepped into it, was more accurate - she had a facility for donning another's life. In that respect, Nigel had been right about her living her characters' lives.

She was getting drowsy by the time the song came on the radio. One of their songs. Vividly she remembered that night in the English West Country when Nigel had taken her to a delightfully charming, old-world inn redolent with history and romance. That song had come on the car radio when they had been returning to their hotel, replete with an expensive dinner, mellowed by fine wine and old brandy, happy and carefree and very much in love. And as she listened to Paul McCartney lamenting "Yesterday", she could not stop the tears.

It was dawn before she slept again, and nearly noon when she rose. She felt disgruntled and restless. So she was glad when her parents called to say they had returned safely from Australia and would arrive for a visit the following day. Preparing for them gave her something to do.

Her parents thought the setting lovely, and the house impressive, but were evidently not pleased that she was living there alone

"Do you feel quite... comfortable here, darling?" her mother asked. "It must get terribly lonely at times. And, goodness, if anything were to happen to you - suppose you fell down the stairs and broke your leg! - who would be around to help you?"

Knowing that this was one of the less frightening scenarios her mother had envisioned, Kit refrained from pointing out that she could still crawl to a phone, even if her leg were broken, and assured them both that she was perfectly content - and safe. But defending her choice of lifestyle served to bond her more closely with the house, dispelling her own doubts of the wisdom of staying. And with others there, she slept wonderfully well.

She didn't reveal her discovery of the diary to her parents. She had this absurd feeling that they might object to her staying in a place fraught with memories of such abominations. Her mother was likely to think that suicidal tendencies might be rampant within these walls, that they might be inhaled with the scent of aged wood.

Kit had the fanciful notion that Violet herself had decided Kit should be the one to find the diary and be entrusted with her secrets. Violet had become so real to her that Kit felt it would be a betrayal to reveal anything about Violet's life just yet. Perhaps this place really was getting to her! With a chuckle she decided that she would definitely leave when she started gazing into old mirrors and saw someone else staring back at her!

Her father did find lots of little things to mend, and her mother insisted upon cooking and making suggestions for decorating - once she'd accepted that she couldn't persuade Kit to move back home. Having felt somewhat forlorn at the thought that her entire family had been ten thousand or more miles away for the past two months, Kit was delighted to have her parents there. She enjoyed listening to tales of their adventures in Australia, and hearing news of her brother and his family. And, of course, there were dozens of pictures to admire. She took them to Ottawa for a few days, where they dined in French and Moroccan restaurants, shopped, and went to the theatre.

She promised to visit them soon - they'd be at the cottage for the summer - and then they were gone. And it was time for her to get back to work.

As she stepped out into the early evening sunshine, she startled a groundhog, feeding on the back lawn. It sat up on its hind legs, sniffing the air, and then dashed toward the ravine, where it disappeared down a burrow. Kit was delighted to think of the wildlife that shared her little domain - the squirrels and chipmunks and birds, and now the groundhog. She had already bought herself a book for identifying birds, since there were so many species here that she had never seen in the city.

Kit wandered around the orchard, looking for a cross or other marker, but found nothing. But she had more luck at the top of the ravine, where she discovered, amid the dense underbrush and towering trees, a crumbling stone bench enshrouded by a tangle of vines and a thicket of ferns. And she felt absurdly excited to have discovered Violet's secret garden. But there was no sign of Pan or even of the pedestal upon which he must have lounged.

Still, Kit felt another tangible connection with her fascinating predecessor. She wondered how difficult it would be to restore this wild area to a usable space. She also discovered the mostly overgrown flagstones that had once been the path to the bower.

But she would have to hire someone to do the work, for her own garden awaited her ministrations. Tender young shoots had appeared, and Kit hoped she wouldn't lose too many to insects. The weeds, however, were even more prolific than the vegetables, and already taller. After an hour of hoeing, she realized why Alan had advised her to make the plot smaller. Even so, it was looking formidable just now.

She spent part of the following day hoeing the garden, and weeding the flowerbeds. Then she drove to the nearest nursery and ordered bags of bark chips to mulch the beds. She was damned if she was going to spend the whole summer in maintenance. And she really did have to hire someone to cut the grass.

She asked Bonnie when she came to clean that afternoon if her brother Byron might be interested in doing it

"Sure. I'll tell him, if you like."

"The sooner the better. I have this feeling that if I were to sit and watch it long enough, I'd actually see it growing! I don't suppose I'll want it all cut though. I'll leave the old orchard to grow wild, and the back section, above the ravine." Where the groundhog's habitat was.

"We sometimes played in the orchard when we were kids, and there wasn't nobody living here."

Bonnie often revealed these little tidbits of her life, not so much to make conversation but as a little gift of fact. Having seen the environment in which she lived, Kit was intrigued to learn more about the girl, and so, when Bonnie had finished her work, Kit invited her to have a cup of coffee.

"Well, I should really be getting home."

"Do sit down for a few minutes. I can drive you back, if you like."

"Oh, no! I got my bike. Well, just for a few minutes won't hurt," Bonnie said with a conspiratorial grin.

"I was in Ottawa this week. Do you get there often?"

"Never been."

"It's a beautiful city." Kit had been going to say, "But it's so close, you really should go there sometime," when she realized that that might be as impossible for the girl as going to London or Paris. She told Bonnie about some of the attractions, and saw the girl's eyes light up with interest. Well, there was no harm in broadening her outlook somewhat, letting her know there was more to the world than Todmorden and Kintyre.

"Do you have a boyfriend?"

"Me?" That incredulous question implied that no boy would ever date her. Her eyes seemed to say that the only thing she'd ever had from boys was rude comments and vulgar suggestions.

Considering the hovel that was Bonnie's home, Kit could imagine the cruel taunts of other children. Kit suspected that life couldn't be easy for Bonnie at home either. She felt pity for the girl, and resolved to help her somehow.

"I didn't have a boyfriend either when I was your age. I was in love with the Beatles. I suppose you have heard of them? My girlfriends and I would sit around and listen to their records, drool over their photographs, and daydream about meeting them." Kit suspected that Bonnie had no close female friends either, and so refrained from asking.

They heard a noisy car pull into the driveway, and Bonnie started as if she'd been caught doing something illegal. "That sounds like Wayne's car. His muffler fell off yesterday."

Both Bonnie and Kit jumped up. Kit had no wish to have Wayne Skuce in her house again. He was nearly at the door when they stepped outside. "Hey, what's been keepin' ya?" he said to Bonnie. "Pa says the lady should let him know if yer to be workin' longer hours."

"We were just having a little chat over a cup of coffee," Kit told him. She didn't believe for a minute that Wayne was here just to fetch Bonnie.

Wayne grinned, showing his ugly teeth. "That a fact then? Well, Bonnie has chores at home that need doin', and she spends too much time dawdlin' as it is."

Judging by the look of their place, Kit wondered if any of the Skuces ever did anything there.

He looked around critically. "So, anythin' need doin' here? I might just be able to fit ya in later this week, if ya want me to start on them soffits."

"I've already hired a contractor to deal with that," Kit said boldly, determined not to be intimidated by the guy. She cursed herself for the nervous flutter in her stomach.

"That a fact?" Again that leering grin. "Give ya a good deal, did he?"

"I think so."

"I coulda gone one better, if ya'da asked. We don't take kindly hereabouts to them city folk comin' in and takin' our jobs. Stick together round here, we do. Help each other out. Know what I mean?"

The way he said it was almost a threat. Kit decided to make light of the situation. "I did give you the opportunity to work for me, but I can't afford your prices, Mr. Skuce."

Kit outstared him. Wayne said, "Next time ya let me know yer best quote, and I'll save ya a few more bucks."

"I'll keep that in mind," Kit said, barely keeping the sarcasm from her voice.

But Wayne sensed it and, with a derisive snort, said, "Be sure ya do that."

He put Bonnie's bicycle into the trunk, and they left with a roar. Gravel and dust spewed up from the tires and the exhaust belched smoke as the car screeched out of the drive.

It was odd to think that creepy Wayne was a descendent of that kind couple, Margaret and Jeremiah Skuce, who had cared for Violet, more like parents perhaps than servants. Bonnie was different, of course. A throwback, possibly.

The girl was even less forthcoming the following week, and when Kit questioned her about the bruise on her cheek, she said one of her brothers had chucked a shoe at another, and she had happened to get in the way. But Kit didn't believe her. To discover that Bonnie's father was a mean-fisted brute would not have surprised Kit at all.

Bonnie refused to stay for coffee this time, but Kit waylaid her with a parcel. She explained, "When I was unpacking my clothes I found a few things that didn't suit me anymore. The clothes are in great condition, and I thought they might fit you. If not, perhaps you could pass them on to the Salvation Army for me." It was a lie of course. The clothes were relatively new, and fit Kit just fine. She'd chosen a few casual outfits, probably too expensive for this simple country life, and better than anything the girl had ever owned.

Bonnie's eyes sparkled when she looked at them. "Oh, I couldn't take these! They're much too fine!"

"Then save them for a school dance. A new haircut and a new outfit can do wonders for a girl's morale! Now, not another word. They're yours."

"Thank you, Miss Penn... Spencer!"

"Kit."

Bonnie smiled. "Thanks, Kit."

Chapter 12

May 17, 1872:

The dreaded pox has manifested itself.

Early in January I had a sore throat which I took to be nothing more than a winter cold. When I started to feel unwell and feverish, I thought it was influenza. But I was horrified when I saw the rash spreading across my body.

Of course I didn't allow Mrs. Skuce to summon Dr. Townsend. Even when my knees and ankles became excruciatingly tender and swollen so that I could not bear the touch of the blankets upon them, I stifled my cries of pain and stoically told her I would soon be better. How could I have my shame exposed so soon? But when I became delirious with fever, she sent for him and for Lily.

I was quite ill for many weeks, the pain in my legs so intense that I was convinced my bones must indeed be rotting. Only the morphine that Dr. Townsend prescribed could give me respite from the agony.

I was terrified, too, for I did not know if this corruption would invade the rest of my body. And indeed, my fingers and wrists soon became inflamed - hot and red and swollen as if they had already been claimed by the hellish fires. But even more I feared that my face would become ravaged by the voracious pox, my nose and eyes eaten away.

Lily stayed with me and tended me, for I could not be moved. Augustus joined her on weekends, while Heather and Gordon came as often as they could. Heather had a little girl in late January, but it was a long time before I could see my new niece, Emily.

They all think I had rheumatic fever. But Gordon had once told me that syphilis was deceptive. Were not the symptoms the same as those he had described to me? Would a doctor not consider a different diagnosis if he knew of my exposure to the dreaded pox? Perhaps it will not be until the next flare-up that the truth will come out.

How dejected and frightened I was! I lay for weeks in my bed, unable to do anything but gaze out my frost-encrusted window to the white and silent world beyond. Lily read to me -

BLEAK HOUSE, which, rather than take my mind off my own troubles, actually made me feel more despondent.

While I was at my worst, Lily slept in her old bed, next to mine. Her nearness in the painful hours of the night was comforting. We talked of old times, when she and Heather and I had shared a carefree youth here. How often I was tempted to reveal my terrible secret to her, a secret that had become a fearful burden. But of course I couldn't.

When I began to improve, Lily moved across the hall into Hazel and Daisy's old room, where she and Augustus could have some privacy on the weekends. None of us even thought that they might occupy Father's room, which contains a large four-poster double bed. Perhaps because his stern presence still lingers there.

Dr. Townsend told me that my heart has been slightly impaired by the disease. I could have told him that the pox had long ago broken my heart, so what matter if it were the literal truth! So I am instructed to take things easy and not to strain or stress myself unduly. He told me if I am "sensible", I can yet hope to live a long and productive life. How little he knows me if he expects me to be sensible!

So I spent the winter as an invalid, silently bemoaning my fate, finding no energy to pull myself out of my melancholic lethargy.

Mrs. Skuce fussed over me and Lily, glad to have the extra company to appreciate her cooking.

Hugh's sister Kate came often to sit with me. She told me of village matters, and did cheer me up with her anecdotes. Kate and Heather, who were closest in age, had always been good friends, but Lily and I had often joined them for interesting outings, like berrying up on the ridge. Kate promised that we would go blueberry gathering again this summer.

Just the thought of the warm August sunshine bathing my aching body was comforting, for outside the icy hand of winter was reluctant to release the countryside from its tenacious grip. As Kate talked, I could almost smell the sweet and musty fragrances of the sun-baked ridge, and taste the tangy wild blueberries.

Hugh came to visit, too. The concern and sympathy in his eyes was almost as unbearable as my physical pains. He looked as if he wanted to snatch me up in his arms and give me his strength, curing me by sheer force of his will. Yet, he was afraid to come too close to me, for I was in obvious pain which was exacerbated by any movement or feather-light touch.

And though my spirit sang to see him, it was a bittersweet lament. Too soon he would belong to another.

So, even in my misery, I tried to recapture and cling to what we had once had - an easygoing friendship. I prompted him to reminisce about those long-ago times, and lay there, savouring the memories his mellow words evoked.

Slowly the attack abated, and I no longer felt myself to be in the death-grip of the devil. It took a while before my wasted body gained strength and I could walk again. My bones had not been eaten away! My legs were not twisted and useless, merely shaky at first.

And I was grateful that God had spared me from the worst ravages of the disease. This time.

I can walk in the garden now, but I'm not yet allowed to ride poor Moondancer, who, I'm sure, would love a good gallop. I've been supervising the gardens, much to Jeremiah's gruff delight. He doesn't know what to make of me when I'm not teasing and bullying him.

Like the flowers, I am reawakening. I seem to have spent the winter in a pain and drug-induced fog. But now that I see the leaves unfurling, and the spring flowers and shrubs in bloom, I feel strength and purpose blossoming within me.

The sun feels good upon my face, warm and healing. I wish it could penetrate into my bones and purge me of this cursed plague!

August 20 1872:

I am a coward.

I could not watch Hugh being married, so I contrived to be away. Gladly I accepted Lily's offer to stay with her and Augustus at a cottage they had rented in St. Andrew's-by-the-Sea for the month of July.

On the day my beloved was tied forever to another, I wandered restlessly along the seashore. I thought then that I might never return to Moon Hall. Perhaps it was best to start afresh somewhere far away from sad memories and old ghosts. I could do worse than stay in St. Andrew's, where the everchanging sea spoke to me.

But even there I could not escape from all I had known. A remarkable number of Ottawa's society summer there, and we were often invited to dine and to play cards with old acquaintances. Dr. Charles Tupper, one of the most renowned "Fathers" of Confederation and an important member of Macdonald's government, invited us to a luncheon at his cottage, where we dined *al fresco* in the lovely grounds with distant views of the sea. Dr. Tupper is a flamboyant and energetic man in whom I see the emerging character of our capital city. He made me realize that I cannot escape merely by staying away.

That night I could not sleep, so I slipped outside and watched the moon's reflection on the rising tide. I wondered if Hugh was gazing at the same cool and indifferent moon. He was closer to me then, I thought with perverse logic, for he and Ruth would have arrived at Quebec, where they planned to spend their honeymoon. But had he been next door, he still would have been forever out of my reach.

And so it is, dear diary, for now I am home and I see Hugh stacking the August cutting of hay. And though my soul cries out to him, it is best that he cannot hear.

I had to go and welcome Ruth. I had known her at the Ladies' Academy, where she had been a year ahead of me. And I like her. She is lively and pretty and interested in everything. Which makes it so much harder, for I cannot hate her.

How warmly she greeted me!

"I trust you had a beneficial stay at the seaside, Violet," she said. "I'm sure it's been a difficult time for you, but I am so glad that you're not leaving Moon Hall! But I do think it brave and unconventional of you to stay out here all alone. Just like you, Violet! Never mind, you have us nearby, and are always welcome here."

Kate, said, "Violet is almost like family, Ruth, and knows that our door is always open."

I think Kate finds Ruth's proprietorial air a bit hard to get used to. Kate has been in charge of the household since her mother died, five years ago. As Hugh's wife, Ruth now has the right to consider herself the mistress of the house. It must be a difficult situation for them both - Kate not willing to relinquish her position and be relegated to the role of spinster sister, and Ruth wanting to assert herself in her new home.

"I must thank you again for the lovely wedding gift, Violet," Ruth said. "You have exquisite taste!"

I had given them a set of silver cutlery to serve a dozen, each piece engraved with an *M*.

After she had poured tea for us, Ruth said, "Now do tell me what you think of our plans to add on to the house." She spoke of a new wing that would comprise a double parlour and an office, with extra bedrooms above. "That way this present parlour and the dining room can be made into one spacious dining area."

The money must be coming from her dowry, hence Ruth's involvement in the project. I suspect it will make her feel more as if it is her home as well.

I saw Hugh coming in from the barn as I was leaving. My heart caught in my throat. How handsome he is with his hair windblown and his face bronzed by the sun!

"You're looking well, Violet," he said. Was there just a tinge of sadness and regret in his smile? Or am I projecting my own wishful thoughts upon his countenance?

"A month by the sea can be most invigorating," I replied inanely. And then there seemed nothing else to say, for there was too much that could never be spoken.

"How did Jeremiah manage in your absence?" Hugh asked. "The gardens are never so fine as when you're tending them yourself."

"Jeremiah doesn't really see the point of growing flowers, since they can't be eaten. Hugh, I've just had a thought. There's no reason for me to keep Moonshadow." Father's horse and my Moondancer were both out of Moonbeam, which had been Mother's mare. "I'm sure Jeremiah isn't finding it easy to exercise the poor beast, on top of all his other summer chores. Would you like to buy her? I'm certain my sisters won't object to a nominal price, since I know you'll look after her well. She and Moondancer could still graze together in the south field."

"Ruth loves to ride, and none of our nags are spirited enough for her. I think she'd like Moonshadow."

He couldn't know how those words hurt me. I was practically offering father's horse for nothing, imagining Hugh riding her. Giving me - stupidly, I know - another tenuous link to my beloved.

Of course Hugh is right, and I am foolish. So I've decided that to stay here, pining for something I can never have, is ridiculous. It is time for me to take charge of my life and immerse myself in some worthwhile work!

Chapter 13

Kit sat in the leafy coolness of the ravine. The blistering heat of the day had permeated the dank, thick, stone walls of her house, and this was the only spot that offered any relief. Yet even here the air was still and sultry. She thought how delicious it would be to strip off her shorts and skimpy top, and slide into the cool, shallow stream.

But even here in this secluded grove she was not assured of privacy. The thought of suddenly encountering Arnie Bryce had made her reticent, until now, of coming here at all. But she was damned if she was going to let a probably irrational fear deprive her of the enjoyment of this spot.

The snapping of a twig behind her made her spin around, but she could see no one. Just a few birds and a squirrel, and the creek meandering for a short distance and then twisting out of sight.

Kit was perched on the trunk of a tree that had conveniently fallen across the gully, providing a rough bench just the right height for dangling one's feet in the water. On her lap was her sketchbook, forgotten in her musings, on which she had tried to capture the broken boughs and dipping tendrils. She had a very minor talent for watercolours, and usually little time to pursue her hobby.

She returned her gaze to the sun-washed field where Alan and Stuart McGrath were loading baled hay onto a wagon. She seemed mesmerized by their rhythmic movements, the flexing of their hard, naked muscles, the glossiness of their sweat-drenched bodies. The scene was an eerie echo of Violet's painting of Hugh and his brothers haying.

They were close to the ravine now and, knowing that they were unaware of her presence, Kit felt like a peeping Tom (or was it a Jill?). That their half-naked bodies could stir such desire in her made her squirm.

When they abandonned their labours a few minutes later and slithered down the bank toward her, she blushed hotly, certain that her thoughts lingered still in the shadows like a wraith.

Stuart saw her first, and checked his headlong dash to the water. She didn't know that it was the way she sat, with one shapely leg arched up on the log, and the other still dangling sensuously into the stream, her bare skin flushed with heat and embarrassment, that caused his startled expression.

Alan noticed her a moment later and paused in splashing his face and chest. He made no effort to conceal his admiration. "Well, well, well. A wood nymph, methinks."

She laughed at his comical expression, and the tension was broken. The men cupped the clear water in their hands and doused their heads until they were dripping wet.

"I suppose if I tell you you're in danger of getting sun stroke, working out in that heat, you'll just laugh at me," Kit said.

"Sure, if there's one thing we farmers can't stomach," Alan said in an exaggerated Ottawa Valley dialect, "it's them God-damn city folk coming here and telling us how to God-damn do things." It was quite a passable imitation of his father, Kit thought. In his normal voice, Alan added, "Of course, since it's neighbourly advice - and concern - we'll forgive you this time, Kit."

"I suppose next you're going to tell me that you're a breed apart, impervious to the afflictions we city slickers suffer."

"Couldn't have said it better myself," Alan replied with his lopsided grin. He pulled two tins of beer from the water. "Sorry I haven't one to offer you, Kit, but I didn't count on company when I put them there this morning."

"Thanks, but I can't drink beer in the heat of the day anyway. It just makes me sleepy." But Kit thought it a delightful idea. And to have all this - these acres of sun and trees and golden fields - as one's work space was enchanting. "Do you often do this sort of thing? Use the creek as a cooler, I mean."

"Sure, whenever we plan to be working in the fields adjoining the creek. There's nothing like an icy beer on a day like today."

"Unless you happen to be British," Stuart said.

Kit didn't know whether he was referring to her long-ago challenge with sarcasm or wry amusement. The latter, she decided, seeing his smile, and wondered if a truce had just been called. "Of course, the Brits don't usually have to contend with this kind of sweltering heat, either," she said. "Even the pop's warm and unrefreshing there."

"You been there a lot?" Alan asked, as he straddled a log and sat down.

"My books are all set there, so I've been going over once a year to research an area. I feel at home there."

A strange look flitted across Stuart's face, but Kit couldn't identify it. Could it have been envy? Longing? Did he really want to escape from all this, as Alan had suggested? Kit felt a stirring of pity for him.

As she watched the water drip from the tips of his tousled, dark curls, Kit felt herself stirred in another way as well. She could feel her nipples harden beneath her silky top and cursed the flimsy material that hid so little.

What was wrong with her today? Her body seemed to yearn for a man's touch. She had even begun to dream of Nigel lately, and had awakened more than once to find herself tingling with anticipation. It was time to get herself under control.

She lowered her other leg into the water and savoured its cool caress.

"Going over this year?" Alan asked.

Disoriented by her wayward thoughts, Kit didn't know what he was referring to at first. "To England, you mean? Perhaps not this year. My current book is almost finished, and I plan a Canadian setting for the next one." Although no idea had as yet crystallized.

"*Murder in Todmorden?*"

She laughed. "*Suicide at Moon Hall*, perhaps. I've become rather intrigued by Violet McAllister. What else can you tell me about her?"

"You should talk to Mum about that. She was on the historical society years ago, and there isn't much local lore she doesn't know."

"I'll do that."

"Violet been haunting you?" Alan asked with a grin.

"You might say that. It's hard not to think of her, living in that house. She's such an integral part of its personality." She told them about the diary, but revealed nothing about Violet's life. It was actually rather bizarre that through Violet's eyes, Kit knew more about the McGrath ancestors - Hugh, Ruth, and Kate - than they did. If Violet's memory had been accurate, Kit knew the very words these long-dead people had spoken. Maybe one day she would show the McGraths the book. But not yet.

"Strange to think that the old desk has kept her secret all those years," Alan said. "Guess she wanted you to find it, Kit."

"I do think of her as a sympathetic spirit." But there were nights when she couldn't keep the horror-movie images from her over-active mind. That was when she left all the lights blazing and hoped that the electricity wouldn't go off.

The men finished their beers. "Well, better get back to work on my tan," Alan said. "Don't be a stranger, Kit." They splashed themselves once more and left.

Kit found her leafy arbour curiously empty. Not as it had been before they had come, when she had delighted in the solitude. But as if they had taken something essential away with them.

She picked up her sketchbook, but found she couldn't concentrate on another picture. The heat made her languid.

She was startled by a rustling, and this time when she turned around, she saw Nick Radcliffe coming toward her. It had been a month since she had last seen him, and she felt a thrill of pleasure at his warm smile.

"You remind me of *The Lady of Shalott*," he said.

His allusion startled her. She felt another disconcerting link with Violet, who had compared herself to that poetic character. Even that incident last month with the rabid dog had a perverse connection to the past.

Kit said, "I hope not. Didn't she lie down in a boat and drift downstream, dying of a broken heart or a curse or something equally romantic? That sort of thing definitely went out in the sixties."

He laughed. "Actually, I was thinking of the setting:
On either side the river lie
Long fields of barley and of rye,
That clothe the wold and meet the sky;
And through the field the road runs by..."

"*To many-towered Camelot*? Mole End Farm, I suppose?" Kit interjected.

"*...And the silent isle imbowers / The Lady of Shalott*," Nick said as he sat down on the bank.

"Not much of an isle, this," she laughed, referring to her perch. "I never expected a stock broker to quote poetry to me."

"I did take a liberal arts degree before I went into business. Nigel Trent was one of my profs." He gave her a sidelong glance, and seemed relieved when she laughed.

"He seems to be quite famous around here!"

"Well, I have come bearing greetings and a dinner invitation. Erick's creating something superb as usual - Beef Wellington, I think. I trust you have no other engagements?"

"I shall have to consult my social calendar, but I venture to say that this evening is free." She looked away from him as she said, "And did the sinuous Cindy accompany you this time?"

He suppressed a grin. "I'm here alone."

She avoided his eyes so that she wouldn't have to acknowledge the message she felt sure he was trying to send. She floundered like an awkward schoolgirl who couldn't even handle a flirtation. And right now she was completely at a loss for words.

"So how's the garden coming along?"

"Not well," she replied with enthusiasm, glad he had changed the subject. "Something keeps feasting on the new shoots. I've put up a chicken wire fence, but it's still getting in and I can't find any holes under the fence."

"May I have a look?"

"Sure. And come see what I discovered." She led him to the secret garden, which had been cleared by a landscape contractor from town. "This was Violet McAllister's favourite spot."

Nick looked at her in surprise, and she laughed. "No, I'm not psychic! I found Violet's diary, and she wrote very eloquently and precisely about many aspects of her life. She was an avid gardener, and this was her special place. There was a statue of Pan here once, but I guess it disappeared long ago."

"Maybe one of the neighbours has it, bought at an auction perhaps, after Violet's death."

"I suppose that is possible."

"It must be an interesting diary."

"Fascinating. But I haven't actually decided what I'm going to do with it yet."

The meadow grass and weeds and wildflowers that Kit had let grow unchecked at the back of the property were nearly waist high. "I suppose I should do something about this," she said with a sweep of her arm as they wandered up to toward the vegetable plot. She felt a sharp stinging on the back of her hand. "Ouch!"

"What's wrong?"

She couldn't see an insect bite, but there was a deep burning sensation. "I don't know. Something must have stung me."

"Stinging nettles," said Nick, spying the culprits. "You've just been injected with acid."

"Sounds awful! What's the prognosis?" Kit asked, rubbing the whitened, puckering flesh.

Nick bent down and broke off a piece of a large leaf. "Without this magic antidote," he said, gently rubbing the crushed leaf on her hand, "you could expect the pain to last half an hour or more. But this should do the trick."

Already she could feel the fire abate. "Magic indeed! What is it?"

"Burdock. Strangely enough, it always seems to grow near the nettles, as though the plants exist in some bizarre symbiosis."

It was like a seductive caress, his one hand firmly holding hers, the other moving rhythmically, soothingly over the afflicted area. It sent a shiver of desire through her.

"And where did you learn about that?" Kit asked as she reluctantly withdrew her hand from his.

"We had numerous encounters with nettles when we first came. I remember one day when we were clearing an area, Mandy grabbed a handful of them. She had blisters all over her palm. But it was Alan McGrath who told us about the 'dock leaves. Anyway, I suggest you have that stand of nettles cleared. And take a good look at the plant."

"Don't worry, I'll recognize it next time. Thanks, Nick."

He smiled at her. "Glad I could help. You know, I'd forgotten what a dab hand I was at country living. It's like a different world. A different lifetime."

He seemed to be recalling happy times, and Kit felt strangely sad that she couldn't share those memories. "How long ago did you leave?"

"Four years." He shook himself out of his reverie. "Now let's go solve the garden mystery."

The garden was baking in the sun. Heat waves quivered above it. The shrill buzz of a cicada pierced the thick air, and then there was silence, as though even the birds and insects had succumbed to lethargy. Across the road, the McGraths' cattle lay in the shade, an occasional swish of a tail the only movement. Kit could see the McGraths' tractor pulling the heavily-laden hay wagon toward the farm.

It was odd to think how alone she and Nick were at that moment. Kit became aware of her body and of Nick's nearness, but vehemently pushed aside thoughts of lovemaking on the lawn.

"Well, what do you think?" she asked moving away from him.

"The zucchini's doing well - which is no surprise. But six hills? What are you going to do with them all?"

"Prolific, are they?"

"You won't be able to give them away fast enough. Especially around here. Anyway, I see what you mean about the rest. It's most likely a groundhog."

"What, that cute little guy that eats the grass?"

"That 'cute little guy' is probably an entire family of them - watch for them at dusk and early in the morning when they feed.

You've only noticed one at a time, I'll bet. And carrot greens and bean sprouts are much tastier than grass."

"Well what can I do about him...them?"

"Get yourself a .22."

"And shoot them?"

"It's them or you," he said melodramatically. Seriously he added, "They are vermin. The farmers hate them. Cattle can break legs in the burrow holes."

"Well, I'm not killing anything just to save a few vegetables! And I'm surprised you would even suggest it."

"We felt the same way at first, believe me - especially the girls. We tried trapping the groundhogs, and letting them go in the wild, but they usually end up in someone else's field. That practice is definitely frowned upon around here. Farmers can't afford to be sentimental."

"Well I can."

"Have I disillusioned you?"

Her anger dissipated in the wake of his perceptive question. "A bit, I suppose. I thought of your group as living in harmony with all creatures."

"Don't forget what we breed the cattle for - beef Wellington and suchlike. We're not vegetarians. But sure, we consider ourselves environmentalists of a sort. We compost our kitchen waste, recycle what we can, cull our woodlots to maximize new growth, and plant trees wherever feasible. But we haven't stopped driving cars or using electricity."

Curious how he had suddenly become one of them again. "And do you practice all those things in the city?"

He laughed. "It's a hard habit to break - thinking of myself as one of the group."

It had also broken the spell, and Kit had no qualms about asking him in for a drink. He accepted readily, and when they both had tall, frosty glasses of lemonade, Kit showed him around the house. Despite the sumptuous furnishings in the two sitting rooms, they ended up in the library - Nick in the armchair, and Kit in the window seat. How natural it seemed for him to be there.

Violet had said the same thing about another man once. Kit really was beginning to feel haunted by her!

Nick was fascinated by the house. "I admire your fortitude in living here by yourself. It must get lonely."

"And frightening," she admitted. "But I figured I owed it to myself. I went from home to residence to Nigel's place, and never had a chance to live alone. There are times when I love this place, and wouldn't want to be anywhere else."

He smiled. "It is a rather lovable place." Nick looked at the shelves of books. "I read a couple of your novels."

"Did you?" Kit asked in surprise.

"I enjoyed them. In fact, I was damned impressed!" He looked at her as if he couldn't fathom her.

"Nigel thought I was wasting my talent on trash." She said it almost as a challenge. She wanted him to refute Nigel's opinion, to deny Nigel's importance.

"English profs aren't the best judges of popular fiction. You have to be dead or eccentric to impress academics."

"He had me convinced."

"Then it really was time for you to be on your own. Well, I should get back. Why don't you walk down along the ravine, and I'll walk you back later? It's going to be a warm night."

"I'd like that."

When Nick had left, Kit immersed herself in a deep, cool bath, and an hour later she was on her way to the commune.

She had never been along the creek this far, and found it a delightful walk. She did keep a wary eye out for Arnie, but even as she skirted the Bryce farm, she saw no sign of him. Still, she wouldn't want to go this way by herself at night. Variations of *Murder in the Ravine* were becoming all too frequent these days. Then with a laugh, she thought that Rhett Pugh would be proud of her paranoia.

The ravine disappeared near Mole End Farm. There, the tree-lined creek became just a dip in the lawn - but an extremely pleasant one. White wicker chairs had been set up at its edge, beneath the dangling willow fronds. The grass, newly-mown, was fresh-scented. From a distance, it struck Kit as the setting for an Edwardian tea party, lacking only white-gowned ladies with broad-brimmed bonnets and gentlemen in straw boaters.

But the people lounging about on the chairs and on the lawn sipping cool white wine were anything but Edwardians. And they were amused by her fanciful description.

Kit said, "All you need here now is a tennis court."

"Which reminds me of that Monty Python sketch..." Nick began.

"*Tennis Anyone?*" several of them shouted.

"We...I laughed tears when I first saw that," Kit admitted.

A hilarious discussion of their favourite Monty Python programs ensued. Only Teresa Kelleher did not join in. "I find their brand of humour slap-stick and juvenile," she declared.

Pete Sage said, "We all know you dislike the English, Teresa. You'd be an active member of the IRA if you lived in Ireland, wouldn't you?"

Kit instinctively felt that Teresa would make a good terrorist. If she unleashed that fiery mane of hair that she had so primly restrained, and if her freckled face were animated by some passion, she could look quite the thundering Valkyrie. And yet, that cold, analytical look was perhaps even more conducive to terrorism.

"At least I have principles," Teresa said.

"Meaning I haven't, eh?" Pete said sourly.

Let's not squabble," Mandy Downes said. Deftly she manipulated the conversation so that neither Pete nor Teresa could argue without making a scene. Kit admired her skill, and realized that there was steel behind Mandy's frothy exterior. Mandy would have made a wonderful dowager duchess (and might still, in one of Kit's novels).

"I've discovered something interesting about your family, Drew," Kit said. "One of Violet McAllister's sisters was married to Elliot Caldwell of the famous Toronto legal family."

"Your joking!" Mandy said.

"Not at all. It must be some relation of yours, Drew. Elliot had a brother named Andrew - your great-great grandfather?"

Drew was stunned. "Probably, but I'm not even sure! How did you discover that?"

"Oh, the ghost of Moon Hall told me," Kit said with a grin, and then explained about finding the diary. But she didn't reveal more than the little that pertained to the Caldwells.

"It's uncanny," Drew said. "I doubt if anyone in my family even knows that. But it'll be in the family records somewhere. I'll ask my parents about it."

"I'm curious to discover what happened to the boys," Kit said. "Will you let me know?"

"Sure."

"I think I'd like to meet this ghost of yours," Liz said.

"I'll introduce you one day. She's quite a lady!" Kit said.

"Now you're tempting us, with no intention of satisfying our curiosity," Leighton accused.

"I'm just ensuring that I'll get plenty of invitations to dinner here!" Kit quipped.

The dinner was, as Nick had predicted, superb.

Dianna Webb wasn't there - Liz said that she was pretty well living with her new friend, and rarely stayed at the farm now. "She needs to keep a *pied-a-terre*, just to make her feel independent."

"Just another sign of our disintegration," Pete said, pushing his half-finished meal away. "People keep deserting. Not only this place, but the principles" - he looked at Teresa as he stressed the word - "that brought us here. Shit, look at Nick - a shining example of capitalist greed." He got up, poured himself a generous measure of brandy from the sideboard, and lit a cigarette.

Nick did not seem dismayed by Pete's accusation. Drew Caldwell said, "We're not doing too badly ourselves."

Pete turned on him. "No you're not, are you? Commune this may be in name, but legally it all belongs to you, doesn't it, Drew?"

"Now, Pete," Mandy said. "This place will always belong to all of us - those who choose to stay."

"I don't want to feel like a fucking hired hand all my life!" Pete shouted. He splashed some more brandy into his glass, and then with one final invective - "Shit!" - he left the room.

Leighton Pearse broke the awkward silence. "I think Pete's on the verge of a breakdown."

"What can we do to help?" Liz asked with concern.

"It might be best for him if he left," Nick suggested.

"Bullshit!" Teresa said. "You can't solve anything by running away, Nick."

He grinned at her. "It solved all my problems, Teresa."

"Sure! That's why you keep coming back," she replied nastily.

"I thought you'd be flattered by my visits, not resentful."

Erick Jansen interjected. "None of you is doing justice to the meal."

"You're absolutely right," Mandy said. "Tempers do get a bit frayed in this heat."

A more equable tone was established, but the former gaiety was gone. Still, they lingered in friendly conversation over coffee and liqueurs, and watched a spectacular sunset - thanks to the explosion of Mount St. Helens a couple of months earlier, which had spewed tons of ash into the atmosphere.

All the while, music from the late sixties and early seventies had been playing in the background.

Kit, feeling pleasantly mellow, was humming something nostalgic when she and Nick left. Nick brought a flashlight, but the moon was nearly full, so he didn't use it. He took her hand and cautioned, "Watch your step." It felt good, his warm hand caressing hers, steadying her as they picked their way across boulders and logs.

Although it was a beautiful starry night, they couldn't linger to enjoy it - the mosquitoes were ferocious. "One of the drawbacks of country life," Nick said when they approached her house. "Evening strolls are only for the hardy and foolhardy. I'd forgotten how bad it could be."

"Shall I drive you back?" she teased.

"No."

But he was expecting to be invited in. How could she have been so naive not to anticipate this? Lightly she said, "But you will stay to compare bites over a drink?"

He seemed to sense her nervousness, and pulled her into his arms. His kiss was gentle at first, tender and melting, and then more probing, insistent. Breathlessly she pulled away from him. She put her fingers to his searching lips. "Nick, I'm not one for casual relations... And I'm still too bruised by those years with Nigel for a more permanent one... I need time to get my head together."

He let her go. "Sure."

She wondered if he was angry or hurt. Did he think she had been leading him on? Stupidly she wanted to ask if they could still be friends. She needed him as a friend.

Shades of Violet again.

"I'll take a raincheck on that drink," he said. "Goodnight, Kit."

She felt bereft when he had gone. The memory of his arms around her made her shiver with desire. It would have been so easy to fall into bed with him, she thought as she poured herself a drink. And to fall in love with him.

And then what? Nick appeared to be something of a womanizer. She overcame her regret and longing through indignation. Did he think of her only as an easy lay? Was sex all he was interested in? Did he think she was just another Cindy? And when her anger was spent, she ached for his presence.

Remembering his first words to her that afternoon, Kit pulled an anthology of verse from her shelves and found Tennyson's *Lady of Shalott*.

It seemed curiously appropriate.

> *There she weaves by night and day*
> *A magic web with colours gay.*
> *She has heard a whisper say,*
> *A curse is on her if she stay*
> *To look down to Camelot.*

Was that prophetic? And did Nick consider himself to be Sir Lancelot, who compels the lonely, untouchable Lady of Shalott to abandon her mirrored shadows of life and confront reality? Trouble was, the lady couldn't handle it.

And she couldn't handle Nick, not if he merely wanted a fling.

Kit slept badly, dreaming of Nigel turning into Nick, of herself floating down the stream - now a river - in a sinking boat, past the commune where they all watched but no one moved to help her. And Nick turned away.

It was too hot to sleep anyway; everything felt damp - the bedsheets, her nightgown, the air. Every pore of her skin oozed moisture. She was up early, and spent a long morning half-expecting - and hoping - that Nick would come to see her, and that they could resume their friendship.

But he didn't, and by noon she was quite bad-tempered with the heat and frustration. She was damned if she was going to sit around waiting for Nick to grace her with his presence. There were more pleasant places to be during a heat wave than here.

Quickly she packed a bag, locked the house, and set out on the long drive to the family cottage.

Chapter 14

September 27, 1872:

How glad I am to be back home for a few days! I was determined not to miss autumn at Moon Hall this year, but I have taken on a rather big project which is more important than indulging my own romantic whims.

Still, Moondancer and I had an exhilarating ride across the ridge, beneath the stunning canopy of multicoloured leaves. The countryside has a radiant glow. The air is fresh and clean and scented with that evocative fragrance of dry leaves and the rich, earthiness of sun-warmed, newly-ploughed fields.

How different from the stench of Ottawa!

I have seen more squalor this time, and it is heartbreaking. I was unaware that we are in an economic depression. I've discovered that most of the mills are laying off workers, who can now find no paying jobs to maintain their families through the coming winter. Already Rose complains of pilferers raiding her wood pile, but who can blame the poor wretches, who need to keep their families warm and fed during our harsh and unforgiving winters.

I have found a building to serve as my "House of Refuge for Women". It is a former shop in the area of the By Ward Market. The three storey building is only a decade old, and constructed of stone. I have workmen there now, building rooms upstairs so that we will have several dormitories. This way we can separate the women with children, single women, pregnant women (whether single or not!), and elderly women, giving each group a bit of privacy yet allowing companionship with others like them. That, at least, is my theory, so we shall see what happens in practice.

Daniel is both amused and impressed by my efforts. I think he didn't really believe I would do anything once I realized the scope of the task. But I have discovered that I have a talent for organizing and getting things done.

I consulted Daniel about the location and asked for his input. I had no compunction about calling upon him unchaperoned. (Poor Lily never knows where I am!) He seemed only slightly surprised to see me alone at his door. He has consulting rooms above a bookstore on Rideau Street, with his own apartments above those. So he is only a few blocks from the Refuge.

"I hope you are here as a friend rather than patient, Miss McAllister," he said as he showed me in.

"I am quite well, thank you, Dr. Haywood," I said truthfully. I don't heed Dr. Townsend's edicts that I should behave as a fragile, injured creature. I feel hale and hearty, and I'm damned if I'm going to spend useless days lounging on sofas. "I have come seeking your advice on another matter."

"By all means."

I followed him up to the third floor. His sitting room was strewn with books and papers, but he has some very fine pieces of furniture and comfortable appointments. On a table at one end of the room were all kinds of flasks, bottles, spirit lamps, and a microscope - undoubtedly his dining table given over to some scientific experiments. Still, it has the homey feel of a busy man contented with life. I accepted the wine he offered and then told him of my intentions.

"Will you look at the building with me, to see if it suits? I need to know if I have overlooked anything that might become a health problem. I'll have to build some more privies, of course. I plan to have a couple of small rooms next to the kitchen to serve as bath chambers. We'll have to make sure certain standards of hygiene are observed or any disease could spread quickly, am I right?"

"Indeed you are! How many women and children do you intend to accommodate?"

"I think this building could manage fifty, perhaps more."

"And how do you intend to feed them and probably clothe them? Surely not from your own pocket?"

"I am not so wealthy, Dr. Haywood! But my sister Lily has already started canvassing her friends for support. She is a most charmingly persuasive person. Even Rose has been coaxed into holding a charity tea." Although Rose is appalled at my plans. It wasn't until I threatened to enlist as a patron our new Governor-General's wife, the Countess of Dufferin, that Rose, not to be outdone, acquiesced. "I have been thinking that the women could earn their stay at the Refuge. Perhaps we could take in washing. That way, they wouldn't feel it was charity. But nor do I want it to seem like a Dickensian workhouse!"

"But an admirable scheme, I think," Daniel said thoughtfully. "Perhaps if they were to see it as a co-operative venture, with some women cooking, others cleaning, and some, as you say, doing washing then they would feel more comfortable taking shelter there. But how do you propose to administer this? Surely you don't intend to live there yourself and take charge?"

"Not at all. I think it best if I stayed behind the scenes as much as possible. But I do have someone in mind to be matron. Rose recently fired her cook, Mrs. Carruthers, whom she found slightly tipsy one day. Marjorie Carruthers is a widow who has always struck me as a strong and capable women who was wasted in my sister's employ. I think she could be an army sergeant! In any case, I have tracked her down and put my proposal to her. She herself, dismissed without a reference, is poorly placed, although she did manage to find a part-time position in a rather seedy hotel."

"Do you consider her reliable? Being matron would be a big responsibility and I daresay, not a job for the fainthearted. Women running away from abusive men will undoubtedly come, with their husbands, possibly drunk and belligerent, not far behind them."

"Marjorie Carruthers doesn't have a drinking problem. She says she just gets a bit maudlin at times, and that day Rose had been somewhat tyrannical, so Marjorie had indulged in one too many glasses of cooking sherry. But she is a large, raw-boned woman who is not easily intimidated, I think. And she understands how precarious is the situation of women who have no man to support them. I have also asked her to recruit a woman capable of being her second-in-command. Her choice of person will be revealing. She knows this has not gone beyond the speculation stage yet."

"You are determined to do this then?"

"Indeed I am!"

"I'm impressed, Miss McAllister."

"Do please stop calling me Miss McAllister. *Violet* will do, and I intend to call you Daniel, for I have another favour to ask of you, and I would prefer to do it as a friend."

He grinned. "Certainly, Violet."

"Will you be our medical adviser, Daniel? There will be some funds available..."

"You must allow me to help as my own contribution to this worthy venture. Come, let us drink a toast. You are a most remarkable woman, Violet!"

How glad I was that he didn't call me a "girl", which would have detracted from the compliment. Although I am only nineteen, I no longer feel like a mere girl.

So Daniel came to see the building with me, and approved of my renovations.

I have won the laundry contracts for a couple of small hotels and boarding houses. Lily and Rose have managed to raise just over four hundred dollars so far, which I have discovered is the average working man's yearly wage!

Rose thinks me quite mad. She is afraid that my association with "unfortunate" and "fallen" women will lower her own standing in society. I tried to point out that good Christian women were always establishing orphanages and other ways of dispensing their charity to the needy, and that this was no different. Rose must have told Iris, who wrote to me that I must never forget my place in society, and that charity, while all very well, was best doled out from a discreet distance. What she means is that one can salve one's conscience by giving money and needn't have any contact with those who must need take it. She suggested that I indulge more in the social life of Ottawa so that I might find a suitable husband!

Knowing how absurdly wealthy the Thorndikes are, I wrote a cleverly worded reply to Iris, telling her how moved I am by the plight of the poor, especially the women and children who are too often the victims of bad men or unlucky circumstances. How appalling that such poverty and want should exist in Canada's capital! What must the aristocratic Dufferins think of our poor little capital now that they have arrived to take charge of Rideau Hall and all the responsibilities of the governor-generalcy? Might they not think that we Canadians are unconcerned about our fellow humans and intent merely upon ravaging the forests to put more profits into the bulging pockets of the wealthy? What about the age-old principle of *noblesse oblige*? After all, Ottawa, although the hub of political power, is still a lumbering centre, which has fallen on hard times.

How Daniel laughed when I told him this, and showed him the thousand dollar cheque that Iris sent in reply! Of course, she could have easily sent ten times that and it would be no more than dress money to her, yet I am grateful, and intend to keep pestering her for yearly contributions.

The building itself I bought with my own money - with Augustus's blessing, of course - so these donations will be spent on furnishings and supplies, and the remainder will be invested. With the interest, and the income from the laundry contracts as well, we might have enough to avoid having to dip into the capital again for some time. Lily has promised me she will keep soliciting funds, and I have every intention of recruiting Lady Dufferin's patronage once I become acquainted with her.

The Dufferins are in Toronto at the moment, and Ottawa has seen little of them as yet, since they spent the summer in Quebec and Tadoussac. But reports of their frequent entertainments and their lavish hospitality has reached the capital, so all are looking forward to their settling in at Rideau Hall - especially Rose. It has to be admitted that the Lisgars were dull company, but such is not the reputation of the Dufferins!

So things are well underway for me to open the Refuge next month - luckily, before the desperate cold sets in. Daniel will let patients know about it and word will quickly spread, he assures me.

Now that all is so near completion, I am a bit apprehensive, wondering if I've forgotten anything crucial. Fifty or more lives may depend upon my having planned carefully enough. Have I estimated the consumption of fuel properly and put in a large enough store of wood and coal? Have I taken proper fire precautions?

Marjorie Carruthers helped me to estimate the pantry supplies, and she has determined the menus, varying them daily, but sticking with filling stews and soups - nothing too rich, she assured me, since many of the desperately poor are not used to such diets. That will surely not give great scope to her culinary skills, but she knows best in these matters and will undoubtedly be too busy with other things to do more than supervise the kitchen anyway.

She has chosen her "lieutenant" wisely, and thus increased my respect for her judgement. Lise Gauthier is a small but rather fierce woman who is kindness itself. She is a widow with six grown children, and has now embraced this cause as if it were her own mission. And fortunately, she is French-Canadian, and thus will give us some credibility with the French community as well as the English.

Lise seemed surprised at my youth, judging me to be all of twenty-four! Because I am tall and do not possess the beauty of Iris or Lily, I have often been taken to be older than my years. I did not disillusion Lise, for I wondered if she would even take me seriously if I were to tell her my true age.

But it set me to thinking, and I decided that the Refuge needed a Board of Governors. It sounds so much more impressive and official to have a "Board of Governors" running the place rather than just me alone. I will be the Chairman of the Board, and I managed to inveigle Lily and Augustus, as well as Daniel, into becoming members. We will have meetings once a month, which I think will truly help me to make intelligent decisions. The thought that I am not completely alone in this venture has lessened the pressure somewhat.

Lily is somewhat more comfortable with the entire scheme now, for she has been concerned that the stress of it might affect my health. She takes Dr. Townsend's warnings more seriously than I, although I have assured her I am perfectly well and my heart, not so damaged that I must become an invalid! She has conceded to my stubbornness.

Daniel surprised me with a gift before I left the city. He found me at the Refuge, where I was going over arrangements with Marjorie and Lise. I was instructing the workmen on the construction of the two women's bedrooms. I had determined that they would sleep on the main floor and to share between their bedrooms, a private sitting room to which they could retreat. This way they would be separate from the rest of the women - for everyone needed their sanctuary - and at the same time, be readily available when necessary. They were rather pleased with the proposal, and we were laying out the dimensions of the rooms when Daniel came in.

"I thought I would find you here," he said to me. With a chuckle he added, "You look as though you've been lending the workmen a hand," as he brushed some dust from my cheek. Indeed, I was covered in sawdust, which was hard to avoid in the mess of construction. I had worn an old dress with a large apron over it, and a mob cap that I had borrowed from Lily's maid, so that I looked very much like a servant myself.

I introduced him to Marjorie and Lise as our doctor and a Governor. Marjorie said, "Your reputation precedes you, Doctor. You have many grateful patients around here, from what I can gather."

He acknowledged the accolade with a smile and said, "I expect we'll be seeing a lot of each other, ladies. My surgery is not far, so you must be sure to send for me when necessary."

"Now you must introduce me to this little fellow," I said to Daniel, squatting down to pet the puppy that he had on a lead.

"I don't know his name yet. That is for you to decide, Violet. He was given to me in payment for a treatment, but I thought that you might provide him with a better home out in your lovely countryside than I can here in the city, where I am rarely home in any case. Irish wolfhounds grow quite large, you know. He would not be happy cooped up in my rooms all day, nor might he be welcome on my rounds."

"He's adorable!" I exclaimed with delight. Father had never allowed us to have pets, deeming that animals were to be kept outdoors and then, only if useful. "What a friendly face he has! I shall be happy to give him a home. Thank you, Daniel!"

He handed me the lead, but I picked the little fellow up and was rewarded with a big lick across my dusty face. "I think I will call him Tristan. Didn't he have some place in Irish legend?"

"Didn't he come to a tragic end, along with Iseult?" Daniel said.

"Like Romeo and Juliet. But Tristan does seem an appropriately noble name for him."

"I'm sure he'll grow into it," Daniel laughed.

Needless to say, I fell in love with Tristan immediately. He has already become an inseparable companion, sleeping on my bed - usually across my feet - and following me everywhere.

Lily is as taken with him as I, which is fortunate, since she doesn't mind his presence in her house. (Rose, however, won't let him into her house anymore, claiming that he sheds filthy hair everywhere.)

When Lily said how thoughtful it was of Daniel to give me the dog, and that she would feel better about my being abroad at all hours with Tristan at my side (once he's fully grown), I realized that Daniel might have had that motive in mind. And I was deeply touched that he was concerned for me, and had so subtly arranged for me to have some protection.

Tristan lies on the rug beside me even now, his head between his large paws as he patiently waits for me to finish my scribbles. He looks forward to our rambles, and enjoys the gardens and orchard as much as I. Daniel could not have devised a more perfect gift for me than the love and friendship of a devoted and amiable creature like Tristan.

As soon as we came home to Moon Hall, I had to show him off to Hugh, for I knew he would appreciate what a fine animal Tristan is. That, at least, was my first thought. My second was to wonder if I could face the pain of seeing Hugh. But, of course, I could not long stay away from my closest neighbours and friends.

I keep trying to recapture my old brotherly feelings for Hugh, and have almost succeeded. It's as if I bleed a little inside whenever I see him.

He and Tristan took to each other right away, and I wonder if the dog is a good judge of character, or whether he has such a trusting, friendly nature that he will not be much of a guard-dog after all! But, of course, I love him just the way he is.

The McGraths invited me to attend the fall fair with them, but I declined, telling them I was expected back in Ottawa. They were all rather shocked when I revealed what I was doing there, but Kate said, "Well, if ever you need any help that I could give, let me know. It sounds like a worthwhile endeavour. I'm sure we don't often realize how well off we are."

Not to be outdone, Ruth insisted upon making a donation, which I graciously accepted. Then she invited me to go sketching with her tomorrow, which should be fun. I do enjoy my painting, and I remember now that Ruth is quite an accomplished watercolourist herself.

Since it was getting dark when I left, Hugh walked me home. (It's useless to protest that I'm perfectly safe, not frightened of the dark, and know the way blindfolded!) I knew before he spoke what he would say, for I could sense his disquiet.

"Violet, you must take care in that Refuge of yours. You're not accustomed to the ways of city women. You don't know the sorts of lives they've had, nor would you be familiar with the violence that some of them suffer at the hands of men."

Would I not? "I'm learning fast. I've seen some things on my walks through town. I'm not so naive, Hugh, nor easily shocked. But I am surprised that you might know of such things! When have you ever travelled farther than Kintyre?"

He laughed good-naturedly. "You're right, of course. You are more worldly than I am. I know only what I read in the papers. But you will take care?"

"Of course!" I was tempted to tell him about my encounter with Jack the Brute, but thought better of it. He'd only worry more. "I've been told that Tristan will be the size of a pony by the time he's fully grown, so I have a protector."

Chapter 15

Kit stayed at the cottage for nearly three weeks. She and Nigel had often been there for weekends, and sometimes Kit, Fran, and the girls had stayed on for a week or two while Richard and Nigel had returned to the city. But this was the longest time she had spent there in years. There was something rather comforting in allowing herself to be taken in hand, and freed from making even the simplest decision for a while.

Kit's father, now retired, had been a high school principal. Her mother had been a teacher once, too, but that had been before "the children came along" and she had devoted herself to motherhood and volunteer work. So, during her childhood, Kit had spent almost two months every summer at the cottage. It was like a second home.

She swam, played tennis at the country club, lay in the shade reading novels, and paddled a solitary canoe through the calm evening water - all things that she had done with Nigel, but also before Nigel, so that little vestige of him clung to these pleasures.

Nigel had liked visiting the cottage. It had appealed to the snob in him. It was, after all, less a cottage than a Victorian summer home in the prestigious Muskoka Lakes, once the playground of the rich, some of whom had arrived by private Pullman coach from Pittsburgh and beyond. Century-old mansions and lodges dotted the rugged shorelines, some in genteel shabbiness. But Muskoka was enjoying a revitalization - an influx of new money and young professionals with all the latest water toys - and becoming very much the "in" place to be.

But to Kit it had always been just the cottage that her grandfather had built, a rambling old place with acres of veranda, which her parents had often threatened to tear down and replace with something modern and practical. But of course they never would.

Kit tried not to think of Nick either. But she recalled Nick's saying that he spent weekends at friends' cottages in Muskoka, and it was not beyond the bounds of possibility that she might run into him at the country club. So when she attended the annual regatta there on the weekend, she scanned the crowd in hope for Nick, only to be disappointed.

Her mother tried once again to suggest that she and Nigel should "make up", hinting that marriage and children shouldn't be left too late. After all, she was getting on. Hedging her bets, her mother even introduced her to a few eligible men - wealthy young professionals who were divorced or in the process of.

That was when Kit realized that she had to go home.

During the four hour drive, her relaxed, holiday hedonism gradually gave way to worries about what she would find at Moon Hall. With a shock she realized that she hadn't even thought of telling Bonnie she would be away, or making arrangements for her garden to be tended. It would be hopelessly overgrown with weeds. At least the grass would be cut, since Byron was to do it once a week - but did the Skuces do things on credit?

To Kit's delight, the place showed no sign of neglect. She had been afraid that the house would seem too empty, but with all her things comfortably spread about, it was welcoming.

Most surprising was the garden - there was not a weed in sight. The corn had grown tall, zucchini were ready for picking, the tomatoes had been staked, and some of the beans had survived the ravages of the groundhogs. Kit wondered who had done all the work.

The phone rang while she was unpacking. Liz said, "So you're back! We were wondering what had happened to you." Liz gave an embarrassed chuckle. "Not that we expect you to tell us every time you go off somewhere, Kit. It's just that you didn't mention anything about going away when you were here for dinner, and Nick was surprised to find you gone the next day. And even more surprised that you hadn't returned by the following weekend. He...we thought...well... you are back to stay, aren't you?"

"Yes, of course I am. I was just visiting my parents at the cottage." Then it dawned on Kit exactly what Liz was trying not to say. "Did Nick think I'd gone back to Nigel?"

"The thought did cross his mind. Kit, I know it's none of my business, but..."

"Nick and I are just friends, Liz. But tell me, did one of you tend my garden while I was away?"

"No."

"Then I wonder who did. Anyway, thanks for your concern."

Kit had just hung up the phone when she heard a banging at the front door. That would be the Pughs, she thought with a groan, since they were the only ones to use the formal front entrance.

"There she is! Right as rain!" Cleo said to Rhett, stepping into the hall. Finally acknowledging Kit, she complained, "This is the third time we've been here this week."

"Just returned from the west coast and thought we'd check up on you," Rhett continued.

"And there you were - vanished!" Cleo stated.

"No one knew where you'd gone."

"Didn't even tell Bonnie Skuce you'd be away, so Myrtle told us. She thought that quite irresponsible of you, but Rhett thought that..."

"... damned suspicious. Thought you'd been done for."

"Of course, I told him that since your car was gone, you hadn't been murdered in your bed."

"But you could have been abducted along with your car. Wouldn't be the first time somebody'd been hijacked and murdered for their vehicle."

As Cleo sank into the sofa, she said, "And all a storm in a teacup! You really mustn't worry us like that, dear! I could use a dry sherry if you have one, while you tell us where you've been."

Kit couldn't take offence at their high-handed manner. Beneath their brash exterior, they were genuinely concerned, and Kit even found it rather touching that this childless old couple had taken her under their extravagant wing.

She produced the drinks, and told them about her sojourn at the cottage. Of course, the Pughs had numerous friends with cottages in Muskoka, so Kit was treated to stories of days past, and asked if she knew so-and-so. As it turned out, she had encountered a couple of them at the country club, which earned her a new status in the Pughs' eyes - knowing of an old friend made her practically one of the crowd.

When they had departed, Kit called Bonnie Skuce.

"She ain't here," Myrtle said. "Whatcha want her for?"

"It's Kit Spencer calling."

"Oh, yes." It was said with curiosity as well as a hint of censure.

"I just wanted to tell Bonnie how sorry I was that I didn't let her know I'd be away for a few weeks. It was rather a last minute decision."

"Oh, yes." This time there was expectation.

"Of course, I'll pay Bonnie for those three weeks."

"That seems only fair." Now Myrtle's tone became more friendly. "Will you be wanting her to come tomorrow? It's not her day, but she ain't got nothing else to do."

"That would be fine. You might tell Byron to come and get the money I owe him, too."

"I'll do that."

Kit was relieved when that was over, and then had a good laugh at the absurdity of it all. Her unexplained absence seemed to have disturbed rather a lot of people. So much for independence!

She changed from her shorts into a pair of casual cotton trousers and a roomy cotton-knit top, and decided to go for a stroll in her yard. It was a lovely, pastoral evening.

The perennials were doing splendidly, left to themselves, and Kit had been delighted to discover all the old-fashioned favourites like peonies, delphiniums, and irises, and self-seeders such as foxgloves and hollyhocks. The wildflowers fascinated her too, and she had already begun to identify them, checking them off in her wildflower guide with a little thrill of discovery.

She supposed she should have done some ruthless pruning of the shrubs, but rather liked the wild exuberance of the spireas and mockorange and snowballs. Lilacs had spread into a June-fragrant hedge along one part of the stone wall.

Apples were growing in her little orchard and, although she realized that judicious pruning was needed here to maximize the crop, there promised to be more fruit than she could ever need anyway.

As Kit rounded the corner of the carriage house, she collided with Arnie Bryce. She shrieked in surprise. Arnie looked startled too, and then his face split into a silly grin. He guffawed as he backed away from her.

Kit smiled warily at him. "Hello, Arnie." She noticed how large and thick his hands were. Like his father's. Giant paws.

Still he kept backing away, chortling. "Her's back. Her's back. Her's back...."

He turned and galloped toward the ravine.

Shaken, Kit sat down on the back veranda. She had been going to go down to the ravine herself - to recapture that afternoon with Nick and think about what Liz had told her - but it had once again become a sinister place. Damn Arnie Bryce for his spying and lurking!

Kit was still sitting on the back porch when Georgina Bryce arrived twenty minutes later. Kit could see Arnie hanging well back, not coming closer than the uncut meadow grass. With a shudder, Kit realized how easily even a man of Arnie's size could hide, were he to crouch down in the tall grass.

How quickly fear could shrink her world. If she kept up this nonsense she would soon confine herself to the house, and then one room. And then where? Her mind? Was this how madness began?

Georgina grinned shyly. "Arnie told me you were back, so I thought I'd best come over and explain." She looked nervously at Kit. "I set Arnie to weeding your garden. I hope you don't mind."

"Mind? I'm delighted!" And surprised. So Arnie Bryce had been tending her garden! "And I appreciate it more than I can say. I'd completely forgotten about the garden, I'm afraid, and I was sure I'd come back to a disaster."

Georgina seemed relieved. "That's exactly what I thought! When I heard you'd gone, I came to see if anyone was looking after things, you know... and... well, took it upon myself to intervene. I knew you were looking forward to your first crop, and I didn't want you to be disappointed."

"Well, I don't know how to thank you, Georgina. That was most thoughtful."

"Oh, don't mention it. I'm just glad that we could help. Arnie's good at weeding - he's meticulous, and can even tell the weed seedlings from the vegetable seedlings."

"Now do sit down and stay for a chat. Can I offer you a drink?"

"Well, I wouldn't say no." Georgina looked tremendously pleased. "I'll have a rye and ginger, if you have it."

"And what will Arnie have?"

"Oh, Coke. He just loves it. He'd drink nothing but, if I let him."

"Perhaps you could persuade him to join us then, while I get the drinks."

When she returned, Arnie was seated on the steps of the veranda with his great bear paws dangling between his knees. He grinned coyly at Kit as she handed him a tall glass of cola.

She said, "Thank you, Arnie, for the terrific job you did on my garden."

Georgina nudged him. "Welcome," he mumbled, looking down into his drink.

"I'd like to pay Arnie something for all his work."

"There's no need. He doesn't understand money anyway."

"Then something else perhaps? A present?"

"Well, he loves baubles - anything shiny. He collects things like a magpie, but goodness, there's not much of that sort of thing that gets lost around here."

Kit thought for a moment, and then jumped up. "I think I have just the thing!"

She returned a few minutes later with an enormous golden medallion in the shape of a snarling tiger's head, suspended from a heavy chain. It was a striking piece of costume jewelry that had once set off a slinky black dress, but Kit had never been fond of it. It had lain heavily against her chest. Nigel had bought it for her.

Arnie's eyes widened as she handed it to him. "This is for you."

He took it from her as if were a fragile flower. Then he burst into excited laughter, and rocked back and forth with the prize clutched in his hand.

"That was kind of you," Georgina said.

"Not at all! I've always detested that thing myself, but it seems right for Arnie."

He slipped it over his head - only just - and patted it happily.

They heard footsteps crunching up the drive and, a moment later, Alan McGrath appeared. "Good evening, ladies. Arnie, my old buddy, how're doing?"

They engaged in some ritual hand slapping that delighted Arnie, and then he proudly held out his medallion for inspection. Alan whistled appreciatively. "Struck gold this time, didn't you?"

"Her give it me. Her give it me."

"Well, you're a lucky lad then. Presents from ladies!" He gave Arnie a friendly pat on the back.

Kit was impressed with Alan's easy manner with the man. Judging by the look on Arnie's face, Alan was his hero.

Kit had not noticed Georgina's initial reaction to Alan's presence, but her cheeks were still suffused with colour. Well, well, so Alan was something of a hero to her, too.

He said, "We saw someone walking around here, and just wanted to make sure it was you, Kit, and not some vandals."

"Thanks," she said with a laugh. "I certainly appreciate the way all my neighbours have been keeping an eye on things."

Sensing her thoughts, Alan said with his quirky grin, "You sure as hell can't do anything secretive around here!"

"Then I won't even try! Can I get you a drink? Rye and something? Or a beer?"

"Can't fool me with rye if there's beer to be had! Sure."

As Kit went into the kitchen, she heard Alan asking Georgina about the farm, and as she returned, he was saying, "And how's your father?"

"Well, you know Dad. Sure, you've both seen him! And he's getting worse. I don't know what to do with him any more."

"I'll come by to visit him later this week. I guess we tend to forget how bored he must be, having been so active all his life. Jeez, I can't imagine myself crippled and shut up."

"He doesn't even want to go out to look over the stock anymore," Georgina said.

"It only reminds him of how things used to be, Georgie. He probably wonders what he's got to show for a lifetime of hard work. Couldn't even hold on to the farm his grandfather had carved out of the wilderness. It's the sort of thing my old man worries about all the time."

"I can sympathize with that," Kit said. "But that's no excuse for his treating people the way he does."

"What do you mean?" Alan asked.

"Being insulting and abusive..."

"Never mind," Georgina said, embarrassed.

"You mean he's worse?" Alan asked her.

"You know him. He never was one to keep his thoughts to himself," Georgina explained.

"You don't take it to heart, do you, Georgie?" Judging by the wistful look in her eyes, she certainly took Alan to heart. His kindness must be both heartbreaking and frustrating to her, Kit thought, since it was the attitude of a close friend, but promised nothing more. "Don't you go letting him upset you. And you just show him that you can run the farm. Now let me know when you want help with the haying. Well, I'm off! Thanks for the beer, Kit." There was some farewell hand slapping with Arnie, and then he left.

Kit figured it was the writer in her that made her so curious about people's lives and motivations. She could never resist probing. "I guess you and Alan grew up together."

"Yes. We're very distant cousins, you know."

Kit did know, thanks to Violet.

"Well, we all played together - the McGrath boys and my older brother and I. And sometimes the Skuces. The boys didn't always let me join in, but Alan often took pity on me. I guess, being the youngest, he knew what it was like to be left out. Actually, we played around here a lot, when the house was unoccupied.

"I'll never forget the time... No, maybe I'd better not say any more."

"Oh, come on! You can't possibly leave me dangling after an introduction like that."

"Well, it's not nice to say, but on the other hand it's hardly a secret. It's about Wayne Skuce. None of us liked him. Mom always told us we had to make allowances for his background - his father speaks with his fists, if you know what I mean. So I suppose it's little wonder that Wayne does the same. He's been in trouble with the law a few times, for assault, drunk driving, even suspicion of theft once. Anyway, he was a rotten kid, always goading or taunting, and spoiling everybody else's fun when he could. And he kept grudges. Nurtured them was more like it. And then sometime when you least expected it, he'd get you back.

"He had it in for me once - I can't even remember why now. Anyway, we'd built a sort of tree-house in the ravine, just downstream a bit. The other boys - my brother, Stu, and Cam - they'd come up to the house here to prowl around, and Alan and I were up in the tree-house. We've always had lots of barn cats, but, there was one kitten then that had taken a fancy to me, and I to it. It used to follow me around. Well, this particular day, it was playing near the bottom of the tree, chasing butterflies, I think, when Wayne came along. 'Hey Georgie-Porgie,' he called to me. 'Wanna play football?' And he gave the kitten such a vicious kick that it flew against a rock and cracked its skull. I screamed, and Alan was out of the tree in a flash and tearing across the field after Wayne. Alan felled him in no time and started beating him. Skinny runt though he always was, Wayne was wiry and slippery, and it was an almighty battle between the two of them. The other boys had heard me scream, and came running. If they hadn't pulled Alan and Wayne apart, I'm sure one of them would have been badly hurt. It probably would have been Alan, because he doesn't have the killer instinct that Wayne has."

"What a horrible thing for him to have done - killing your cat!"

Georgina nodded. "I was really upset. But Alan helped me through it. We gave the little creature a burial, and Alan even fashioned a cross for it. He's always been a good friend.

"...Well, we'd best get back. Dad gets into a real state if he wakes and finds himself alone."

With no one to fetch and carry, and bully, Kit thought.

She sat on the porch a little while longer after they had gone, watching the sunset. The blood-splattered horizon was fading to rust. A whip-poor-will chanted its lonely song. She could hear the echoing of Stuart's hammering as he worked on his bungalow. Somewhere else a dog barked.

Had Nick really thought she'd gone back to Nigel? And if so, did he care? More to the point, did she care what Nick thought?

And if the answers were all yes, what did that mean? Kit felt confused and dissatisfied. She didn't want her life complicated by a messy relationship with anyone just now. So maybe it was best to forget Nick entirely. That would be the sensible thing to do.

But there were times she didn't feel like being sensible. There were even times she felt like going back to Nigel.

What she really needed was to immerse herself in a new book, but no ideas had sprung to mind for her "Great Canadian Novel". And yet...

Violet McAllister haunted her still. Perhaps Violet needed her story told.

Kit could feel the frisson of excitement that usually preceded the birth of a new story. Random scenes flashed through her mind. They needed sifting, analyzing, and integrating, but she sensed there was enough meat there for a good feast.

Of course she needed to continue her work on her Gothic series of novels. Her fans - and publisher - expected at least one per year. But Kit always had two or three stories on the go, concentrating on one, but working on others when ideas struck her. This new book would be written under her own name, perhaps even in "collaboration" with Violet McAllister.

Kit only became aware of the plaintive cry as she rose to go indoors. It was coming from the carriage house. With thoughts of Violet so fresh in her mind, it was with some reluctance that Kit entered that place. She flicked on the new floodlights, and caught a movement in the corner.

"You poor little thing!" she cried, noticing the kitten cowering behind a garden fork.

Recalling Stuart McGrath's advice about stray animals, she hesitated for only an instant before approaching the frightened animal. He would shoot it without compunction, but she could neither kill it nor abandon it to die. And that skinny little creature would not last much longer without food. It looked to be no more than a few months old - hardly old enough to fend for itself.

It wasn't aggressive or frothing at the mouth; so Kit convinced herself it couldn't possibly have rabies. Damn it, she couldn't be paranoid about everything!

It eyed her warily, but sniffed her outstretched hand. Then it began to purr. Kit picked it up. "You poor little thing!" She stroked it gently, and its emaciated little body managed to produce an even louder rumble of pleasure. It had a mischievous little face and pearly grey hair with a white undercoat.

She took the kitten inside, and fed it a bowl of milk and a few morsels of canned tuna. While she watched it eat, she couldn't help but think of Georgina's story. It was not comforting to think that that vicious boy had probably turned into a vicious man - nor that he lived just down the road. Wayne Skuce was definitely a man to be avoided.

When the kitten had finished, she took it into the library with her and put it on her lap, where it proceeded to wash itself and then curl up to sleep. "I'm going to call you Oliver Twist, you little waif," she said. "Ollie for short."

And so she started jotting down notes on her new novel, with the kitten sleeping contentedly on her lap.

Chapter 16

October 31, 1872:

I had to be here for Halloween. I'm sitting at his desk, where he had sat that night, and I wait. If ever he intends to haunt me, it will surely be tonight.

Outside, the naked trees groan from the lashing of the wind.

I never draw curtains, for I like to feel that my world stretches beyond the four walls that shelter me. I don't fear the darkness beyond. Nor worry about peeping Toms, as Mrs. Skuce warns me I should! So, for a long time I sat in the window embrasure, looking out at the blustery night.

I recalled everything that happened here last year as if it had just taken place. And I examined once again my own culpability. Even if I didn't directly cause his death, I willed it. I took steps to prevent a possible recovery from the fatal attack. In the eyes of God, I must surely be guilty. But I wonder if God will judge me harshly. Surely I suffered my punishment before I ever enacted the crime. I know I suffer still.

Well, dear diary, the Refuge is keeping me busier than I had anticipated!

Surely it is a success, for already we have had to add beds to squeeze in more destitute souls. Even so, we are reluctant to turn anyone away, and many nights there are women and children sleeping on the floor of the common room and even the kitchen.

And although my idea was that the Refuge would be a temporary shelter, who has the heart to turn these unfortunates out into the bitter winter streets after a few weeks? Many are so pathetically grateful for food and shelter that they turn their hands eagerly to the various chores that we assign.

I asked them what they would have done had not the Refuge been here. Seek shelter in the gaol, some answered me, along with their children.

Their stories are heart-rending.

For example, there is Nancy Kelly. I was there the day she arrived. She came in tentatively, as if afraid that she might find a monster lurking behind the door. She carried but one carpetbag, and her dress and coat were grimy and wrinkled as if she had been sleeping on the muddy streets in them. She was rake-thin, which made the bulge of her stomach seem all the greater.

Marjorie was there first, to welcome her. Like an indulgent mother, she took the girl into the kitchen, where a bowl of soup and a slice of bread were put before her. And as the girl ate, Marjorie explained the rules of the house to her - everyone does her share of work, no men callers are allowed, everyone is expected to keep herself clean and neat, and visitors must make an effort to find other accommodations within a few weeks.

"We'll help you get home, if money's a problem," Marjorie told the girl.

Nancy's cold-reddened cheeks blanched. "Oh, no! I couldn't do that!" she cried. "My father would kill me!" Then she began sobbing.

I sat down opposite her and encouraged her to tell us what had happened.

She had been a maid in the home of wealthy and well-known local businessman, Horace Redding. Her employer had forced himself upon her, threatening her with dismissal if she did not co-operate. The abuse lasted for months, until she finally became pregnant. When her condition was detected by the wife, the poor girl was dismissed without a reference. Her family lives in a small village up the valley, and would never welcome her home in her shameful condition. For the past three weeks she had been sleeping wherever she could find a relatively warm spot - a stable or a sheltered doorway.

Nancy is barely seventeen. And she is not the only maidservant abused by employers. It makes me fume to think how vilely those men betray and mistreat the innocents who are under their supposed protection and control!

I was steaming when I told Lily, Augustus, and Daniel at our October meeting.

"How can such abuse go on unchecked?" I demanded. "Surely there must be a law against it!"

"If the girl can prove rape, there is," Augustus replied. "But rape is a capital offence, punishable by hanging. It is not an easy case to prove, especially against a prominent citizen. There are never witnesses, of course. The man will claim the girl is a deceitful slut who got pregnant by a follower and is trying to incriminate him. Or even that she is a loose-moraled temptress who seduced him. So the girl will be the one blamed for her own misfortune, and be even more discredited in the public eye. None of them ever dares risk a charge like that. Sometimes a father claims seduction, and tries to sue for damages, but again, it's the man's word against the girl's...."

"And who's going to believe a poor servant girl?" I finished rhetorically. "It's villainous! And Horace Redding continues to play the magnanimous, respectable citizen, devoted family man, pious churchgoer! Despicable, contemptible hypocrite!"

They all regarded me oddly. I hadn't realized how enraged I was. My fists were clenched, my cheeks burned, my hair almost stood on end. I thought I would explode with the anger. Of course, they didn't realize that I was remembering father as well.

"Do calm down, Violet," Lily said anxiously. "Or I'll have to take Dr. Townsend's warnings more seriously and keep you confined to the house."

"What's the problem?" Daniel asked Lily rather than me.

Somewhat miffed, I replied, "Absolutely nothing! I will not be mollycoddled!"

As if I hadn't spoken, Lily explained, "She had rheumatic fever last winter and has only just recovered her strength. Dr. Townsend said that her heart has been affected by the illness, and she should not be putting so much stress upon herself."

Daniel eyed me sternly. "You will do no one any good if you don't take care of yourself. We Governors could pass a motion restricting your direct involvement with the Refuge."

"You wouldn't dare!" I countered, engaging my eyes in battle with his.

"Don't tempt me." Still our eyes held, neither willing to concede defeat. "You must take it easy or I'll have you confined to bed or to sedate needlepoint in the parlour."

Finally I laughed. "That would kill me for sure! This is mutiny, you know! If I'd known you three were going to become subversive, I would never have set up the Board!"

I saw Daniel's gaze soften as he realized that he had won. "You should spend no more than a few hours at the Refuge at any one time..."

"I promise to get lots of rest and stop getting upset at every sad tale I hear," I said. Then I grinned slyly. "But I for one am not going to let that blackguard, Horace Redding, get away with his crime unscathed."

"Violet. What are you plotting?" Lily asked reticently. "Nothing outrageous, I hope?"

"Oh, nothing but a few choice words in his ear next time I meet him at a party."

"Be careful what you say, Violet," Augustus cautioned. "You could be charged with slander."

"You can trust me to be discreet," I assured them.

Lily and Augustus looked far from assured, but Daniel did his best to suppress a grin.

But there are so many sad tales that tug at one's heart. Old women who are unwanted and sometimes abused by their grown children. Penniless widows who have no means of supporting themselves. Women and children abandonned by husbands and fathers.

It frightens me to think of how helpless and dependent most women are. How lucky was I that Father - the devil take him! - left me enough wealth to live my life comfortably, without becoming a burden to my sisters.

But there are too many women out there who are at the mercy of others.

Tristan and I go to the Refuge for a few hours every day that I'm in the city. I spend about half of every week there, but then I must get back here, to my own home. I need the time at Moon Hall to reassert my independence, and my absences from Lily's keep our relationship from becoming strained.

It is now past midnight, but no ghostly hand has touched my shoulder. No voice from the grave has whispered in my ear. There is only the soughing of the wind, the ticking of the hall clock, and Tristan's sleepy snuffles. And so, to bed!

November 16, 1872:

When I was last home, Kate came to tell me that she was getting married to Angus Bryce next summer. She didn't seem over the moon as I would have been had I been about to marry my beloved. And I can understand why. Oh, Angus is a nice enough fellow - quiet, hardworking, serious. Plodding. Humourless. There's nothing about him to excite the romantic imagination of anyone. Kate is much more quick-witted and spirited than he. She has a fun-loving nature that has had little opportunity to express itself. And now it might be stifled forever.

Is she marrying Angus because she sees no other prospects in her life? Has Ruth already wrested control from Kate? Does Kate believe that eventually being mistress of the Bryce farm is better than living under Ruth's control? The useful but unwanted, unappreciated, and powerless spinster.

Of course, Angus has been waiting for Kate for years. Her excuse has always been that she was needed at home to look after her father and brothers. But I'm still surprised that Kate is marrying him. Is there not another young man in the area who can set her pulse racing?

I suppose I did have a bit of a devious plot in hand when I invited Kate, nay insisted that she spend a week or so in Ottawa with me. Kate was actually quite excited by the proposal. I wrote to Lily, who not only approved, but said she would arrange a small dinner party in honour of our guest.

Although I'm used to the two and a half hour train ride to Ottawa, it was the beginning of a great adventure for Kate, who had never been farther than Kintyre. I was determined to give her a memorable holiday.

In Ottawa, she marvelled at the shops, the grand houses, the many streets, and thousands of people. She was awe-struck by the parliament buildings and their commanding setting above the river. And she was disturbed by the shanties and poverty and filth. Of course, she insisted upon seeing the Refuge, but we didn't linger there.

"That's a wonderful thing you've done, Violet," she said earnestly as we left it. "There are so many women who are not as lucky as you or me."

I almost asked her then if she loved Angus, but thought it best not to pry. Kate had made her decision, not without much thought, I'm sure. Who was I to tell her she was wrong to settle for the dour and steady Angus?

We explored and shopped, paddled a canoe up the canal to Dow's Lake and back (despite the cool weather!), and took a steamer excursion down to Montreal for the day. But most exciting was our visit to the new Viceregal incumbents at Rideau Hall. Lady Dufferin has her "At Homes" on Monday afternoons. So Rose, Lily, Kate, and I called upon the Governor-General's wife, along with scores of other curious citizens.

The road out to Rideau Hall is appallingly rutted and potholed. Lily said, "I can understand why Lady Dufferin often walks into town! It's been reported that she wears sensible clothes and thick boots."

"A woman after my own heart!" I said.

"She's a true aristocrat," Rose informed us, for she had met Lady Dufferin the previous week. Until then she'd been rather miffed that both Iris in Montreal and Daisy in Toronto had already attended balls given by the Dufferins in those cities, while she had not even clapped eyes upon them yet. "You can see it in her bearing, and the ease with which she talks to people. And yet she does not consider herself above Ottawa society."

Rose can be such a snob! I replied, "That's fortunate, since she has to live here. Maybe she'll liven things up a bit."

"Just don't you bore her with talk of your Refuge," Rose commanded. She managed to imbue the last two words with contempt.

"Of course I shall do no such thing. I doubt if I am ever a bore, Rose. And I'll warrant that Lady D will become a champion of my cause."

"Lady D!" Rose scoffed at my nickname. I suspect that she was trying to think of ways of keeping me muzzled in Her Excellency's presence, for Rose knows that telling me to shut up is tantamount to a dare.

Rideau Hall keeps growing. Now it is sprouting an enormous wing, which we discovered is to become a ballroom. Rose's eyes were gleaming in anticipation of all the lavish entertainments she would attend there.

There was quite a crush of people present that afternoon. We were announced by an aide-de-camp who happens to be Lady D's brother. She is indeed a lively, interested, and gracious lady.

"Have you really been camping? Sleeping in a tent?" one Ottawa matron asked her in disbelief.

"Indeed we have. It was most exciting. I've seen such spectacular sights, and look forward to exploring more of this beautiful country," Lady D replied.

"But was it not uncomfortable?" the matron persisted, almost visibly shuddering at the thought of sleeping out of doors.

"Certainly we've had our little adventures. On one of our fishing trips we were caught in a torrential rainstorm and soaked to the skin. Arriving back at our camp, we were looking forward to our snug, dry tents only to find that they had leaked, and our bedding was drenched! But we soon had things dried by the fire, and the weather improved, as it does so readily here. We had some rather fine fishing the next day."

I liked her already for she seemed to me a down-to-earth, adventurous, and unpretentious person. When I was introduced to her, she said, "Did I not recently read your name in the newspaper, Miss McAllister?"

I had wanted no fanfare or press coverage at the opening of the Refuge, but its presence had soon become known, and a newspaper story had appeared a few weeks later. I was surprised that Lady D remembered it. I replied, "There was an article about the House of Refuge for Women, which I recently founded."

"Of course! A most worthwhile cause. But my, you seem terribly young to have undertaken such a great responsibility. What prompted you?"

"I grew up in a lovely, pastoral village in the Valley where everyone was decently clothed and fed. It wasn't until I came to the city that I saw how desperately poor and disadvantaged some people are, especially women. There was certainly a need for such a place, for we are already inundated with supplicants. Would Your Excellency honour us with your patronage?" I asked boldly.

I felt Rose stiffen beside me. I, too, wondered if I had overstepped the bounds of propriety by asking for money in this very social setting. Probably the normal channel for such requests was by letter.

"Yes, of course. I am most impressed, Miss McAllister, and I hope you will allow me to visit the Refuge some time?"

"I'd be delighted!"

"Now do tell me about your village, for you have reminded me of my own home in Ireland."

So I talked briefly of Todmorden and Moon Hall - hardly the Irish castle in which Lady D grew up! I drew Kate into the conversation, and Lady D was genuinely interested to hear how Kate's father had immigrated as a young man, and hacked a farm out of the wilderness.

On our way home, Rose said angrily, "I thought I would sink through the floor when you asked Lady Dufferin for money, Violet! How could you be so... so boorish!"

"She agreed quite readily," I countered.

"Of course she did! What did you expect her to say, with half of Ottawa listening?"

Kate and I exchanged amused glances. I replied, "Lady D does not strike me as the sort of person who does things merely for form's sake. She could as easily have put me in my place - charmingly, of course. But she's even interested enough to come and visit the Refuge. Which is more than you have been, Rose."

Lily hid a smile behind her gloved hand, and gave a smothered cough.

Rose practically snorted. "And not only that, but you monopolized Her Excellency! There were some people who didn't manage to get in more than a greeting!"

"That's all that some of them care to manage. They come to gawk and to partake of refreshments at the government's expense. Was there anything in particular that you wished to discuss with her, Rose?"

Sometimes I feel quite the devil for putting the wind up poor Rose, but she is so stuffy. She takes the social conventions much too seriously, and would do well to take lessons from Lady D. No doubt Rose was glad to see the back of me that day when her coachman dropped us at Lily's door.

Lily's dinner party was delightful. She and Augustus have such interesting friends - people of intellect with far-ranging interests and an appreciation for the arts. I think that Kate was a bit bedazzled, for they do seem a smart and clever crowd.

I was delighted that Daniel could come. He escorted me in to dinner, while Kate was paired with a law student who was working for Augustus at present. The conversation was lively and witty and stimulating. I knew I should miss times like this when I was once more ensconced in my solitary home.

After dinner, Lily's ensemble played for us - most impressively - and then others took their turn at singing or reciting. Kate and I gave them a sweet rendition of *Scarborough Fair*, for Kate has an angelic, if tentative, voice which fortunately overshadows my tolerable one.

Daniel held us entranced while he, with his melodious and seductive voice, recited the whole of *The Lady of Shalott*. With its lovely bucolic descriptions, I couldn't help but envision Moon Hall. And wasn't I like the Lady of Shalott, doomed to lead a lonely existence?

Kate and I shared the guest room. As we lay in bed that night, she said, "What an exciting life you lead, Violet, having interesting people like these to associate with! Adam is quite a nice young man," she said dreamily, referring to the law student with whom she'd spent a good part of the evening. I wondered if she was imagining what might have been if she hadn't already set her future course along another, completely different, path. Hastily she added, "He's much too clever for me, of course!"

"Stuff and nonsense! I think he rather fancied you, Kate."

"Poppycock! I think that Dr. Haywood rather fancies you, Violet."

"Nonsense! We're just good friends."

"He has such intense eyes, and they lingered on you for much of the evening," she persisted. "Especially when he was reciting that beautiful poem."

"You're imagining things!" I said with a laugh, hoping that I was right. I don't want anything to complicate or to destroy my easy companionship with Daniel. Surely he doesn't have any romantic notions about me? I, of course, don't have any such feelings about him.

Kate loved her visit to Ottawa. She talked about it all the way home on the train, as if she were trying to relive it all again before going back to her rather dull life on the farm. I said that we would do it again, but I suspect that once she is married, she will have no time to ramble off to the city with me. Then she will be under her husband's rule, obliged to set ample meals before him three times a day. Her days will be busy with polishing, scrubbing, washing, baking, preserving, gardening, milking, feeding, and mucking out. And later - or sooner - there will be children. And it made me feel infinitely sad. Where then will I find my spirited and gamesome friend?

It did make me think that country women are particularly isolated, with little intellectual stimulation such as one finds at Lily's dinner parties. So, what if I held weekly or biweekly get-togethers at Moon Hall, where local women could discuss issues - other than the latest gossip? Perhaps we could discuss literature or music or women's issues.

I asked Kate if she would be interested in such a club. She rather liked the idea of discussing and sharing books we had enjoyed. Who would we invite, we pondered. Ruth, of course; the doctor's wife, Mrs. Townsend, who has quite a library of books herself; the vicar's wife, Mrs. Moseby. Heather might be interested, since she isn't too far away by train.

And so we compiled a list, deciding to limit it to a dozen for the time being. We'd meet every two weeks in winter, and take turns hosting the afternoon meetings. And so the Fortnightly Club was born.

We had the first meeting here, at Moon Hall. As hostess, I was the one who gave a critique of a book I enjoyed. I chose *Wuthering Heights*, thinking that most would have read it, and a lively discussion would ensue, not only about the novel, but about the Bronte sisters. I was right!

Over tea I mentioned women's movements in the States which were agitating for women's rights, but many of the club members shied away from such radical thoughts, and so I didn't press the matter. For now it is enough that we have got together without discussing babies, ailments, and recipes!

November 29, 1872:

I was at the Refuge when Nancy Kelly went into premature labour. Lise ran to fetch Daniel, but he wasn't in so she left a message with the cleaning lady. Fortunately, there were enough willing and knowledgeable women to lend a hand. (It seems that I alone was ignorant of the process of childbirth!)

We made up a bed for Nancy in Marjorie and Lise's private sitting room, for which the girl seemed grateful. She was in great distress, and obviously terrified. I stood worriedly in the background as others wiped Nancy's brow and held her hands.

Nancy seemed to me a mere child herself, too pathetically young to be giving life to a new soul - and bearing the responsibilities of caring for it.

But I needn't have fretted, for the tiny babe was born dead. It was a girl. And I could only think how the child had been spared a difficult life, for that is all I could envision for it and Nancy.

As if reading my thoughts, Marjorie said to me, "She's better off this way, poor lamb. At least she has another chance at straightening out her own life before she is burdened with the care of children."

"I feel guilty to think that way," I admitted. "A life lost should be a sad event, not a blessing."

"But that is the case for many women. Some are so burdened by unwanted children that they even smother them at birth." I must have looked shocked, for Marjorie explained. "They say that they fell asleep while nursing and rolled over onto the child. Even the authorities look the other way, for how can they prove otherwise?"

"But surely there is some way to prevent a pregnancy in the first place!"

Marjorie laughed. "There is one sure way, but the men won't stand for it. Abstinence, it's called. And sure, there are other ways, but they're considered illegal and sinful. So is getting rid of the babe before it quickens, though you'll find all kinds of ways that women try to 'regulate' themselves. Just look at all the patent medicines out now that promise to do just that."

"And do they work?"

"Sometimes. But not often enough. There are many women who have a child nearly every year. If they don't die in childbirth, then they're worn out by the time they're 30. They'll try anything to prevent a pregnancy or end it, and who can blame them? Only those who think that women are useful only for breeding. And those who think that the pain and danger of childbirth are the just punishments women must bear for the sins of Eve."

"You sound bitter," I said, for Marjorie was no longer looking at me, but speaking from some past pain.

"I had seven children by the time I was twenty-eight. My husband discovered me trying to miscarry the eighth. We argued. He pushed me. I fell down the stairs, and that brought on a miscarriage. Then he threw me out of the house, calling me a murderess, and has never let me see my children since."

I was all the more horrified because she told me this without any emotion, as though she spoke from some long dead place. "But that's terrible, Marjorie! Surely you can see your children!"

She shook her head. "They packed up and left. No one knew where they went. One neighbour said to the States. I've never seen my children since. The eldest is already twenty-three and my baby, fifteen." She pressed her fingers to her forehead as if to squeeze back the tears that must surely threaten. But perhaps she had none left. She said, "You'll forgive me for lying about my widowhood."

I put my hand reassuringly upon her arm. "Have you never heard from any of them?"

"I wait, hoping that one day, one of them will care enough to find me. That's all I have left to live for."

I wanted to weep for her, for surely no one deserved such misery, and especially not Marjorie, who was so caring and kind. "You have another flock to tend," I told her. "Girls like Nancy need your help."

"I have a daughter her age," she said quietly.

That evening I asked Augustus if Marjorie had any recourse through the law, but he informed me that the father has exclusive rights to the children, and that what Marjorie's husband had done was within the bounds of the law.

I can't believe it! To think that wives can be discarded - for what? not wanting another mouth to feed? not being willing to risk another pregnancy? - and children stolen away from their mothers! If that is the law, then the law is truly an ass, and should be changed!

December 9, 1872:

The other day I found Lily weeping. Of course, she hadn't intended anyone to see her, but I blundered into her room without waiting for her response to my knock.

Lily is usually such a serene and composed person that I was instantly alarmed. I rushed to her side and asked her what was wrong, thinking that someone must have died.

She waved her handkerchief as if to dismiss the question or the seriousness of her grief, and said, "I thought I was with child. But things have proven otherwise."

For all that Lily and I converse, I realized that we never speak of personal things, of our fears and disappointments and heartaches. I had not realized how desperately Lily wanted a child.

"I'm so afraid that I might never be able to have one," she confided.

"Have you talked to a doctor?"

"No. It's not an easy thing to discuss with a man."

"Well, you've only been married three years. There's time enough," I said consolingly.

"You're right, of course. I'm just being silly. I shouldn't set my heart on it so much. Now, let's have some tea and you can tell me what you did today."

And then she was her calm self once again. I wonder how often she agonizes over this. How sad that Lily, who so desperately wants a child, should have trouble conceiving, while others try everything to get rid of their unwanted pregnancies.

December 22, 1872:

Of course, I was back in Ottawa for Rose's pre-Christmas ball. Rosecliff was beautiful, draped in evergreen boughs and garlands, festooned with red satin bows, and glowing with the soft light of scores of candles.

Rose was ecstatic that the Dufferins had accepted her invitation. Then she got all flustered because she wasn't really certain of the protocol. Should she have a throne for them? I assured her that special chairs would be appropriate, but no one expected her to provide thrones!

The Dufferins are gracious guests with an easy manner, who soon put everyone at ease. (But what a lot of sweaty armpits there were that night!)

Iris and Reginald came this time. Iris has the self-assured, blasé manner of an accomplished hostess. After a while, it seemed to me that she had rather effortlessly taken over Rose's role. She was also good at ignoring the daggered looks that Rose threw her way.

Daisy and Elliot couldn't come because Daisy was in bed with influenza. Which was just as well, I thought, for we wouldn't have to worry that Elliot - or even Daisy - would become offensively inebriated. Rose would die if one of the family should disgrace himself before the Dufferins.

However, with the Prime Minister present, it was more likely that he would be the focus of attention. He had already drunk enough wine at dinner to knock a lesser man under the table, yet he seemed hardly affected in wit or speech. I wondered if Lady Macdonald's well known disdain for such social functions is because she can't bear to watch her husband imbibe so freely. She never does attend balls or soirees with him.

Daniel looked quite splendid, and I wondered how I had ever thought him plain.

And now I have to admit, dear diary, that I am jealous! Of course there can never be anything between us, but my fickle heart will not understand, and sings with joy when he looks at me with those deep and knowing eyes. His strong, warm touch sends shivers of delight through me. And though I never allow myself to think beyond this, it is bliss to be held in his arms while we dance, to be the recipient of his smile, to bask in his admiration. So I revel in his friendship. It is all I can ever have of any man.

To discover that he shares such a friendship - perhaps more! - with another was devastating.

I knew as soon as I saw them together that there was something significant between them. There was such a tender, lovingly amused look in Daniel's eyes as he talked to her.

"Violet, I'd like you to meet Isobel Granger," he said by way of introduction. "She is a childhood friend from Montreal."

I thought he was going to say *sweetheart*. Certainly the way he looked at her made me think they might be sweethearts still.

Isobel is no great beauty, but she has a pleasing countenance and such understated elegance that she is attractive. With her intelligent blue eyes, her self assurance and sophistication, she has a presence that can't be ignored. I judged her to be about Daniel's age - twenty-seven. And I suddenly felt like a gawky schoolgirl.

"Isobel, this is Violet McAllister. I told you about the Refuge for Women which she started."

That he had discussed me with her while I knew nothing at all about her, was a blow!

"Yes, of course! I'm delighted to meet you, Miss McAllister," she said sincerely.

"Are you living in Ottawa now, Miss Granger?" I asked, hoping she would say no.

"Only while parliament is in session. My husband is an MP." A short, rotund, ruddy-faced, balding fellow who seemed to be in his mid-fifties joined them. Isobel said, "This is my husband, Charles. Charles, this is Miss McAllister, sister of our hostess."

"Delighted. Knew your father. Fine man. Enjoyed doing business with him. Sorry to hear of his death." And he was gone.

I couldn't believe that Isobel could be married to him. He was old enough to be her father, and about as interesting as a hibernating groundhog. With the intimate way that Isobel and Daniel exchanged glances - as lovers do, who need not speak to understand each other - I suspect that hers was an arranged marriage, a financial and business merger, and not a love match.

And even though I felt sorry for her, I see her as a threat to my friendship with Daniel. What if.... I daren't even think it, but what if they are even now having an affair? Surely Daniel, a bachelor, must have needs? I can more easily believe that Daniel has a long-standing relationship with a mistress than that he visits prostitutes. What if Daniel is only waiting for Charles to die so he can claim Isobel as his wife? I was not so naive to think that our present friendship would continue once he was married.

For I am in love with him. Never mind that it can never be consummated. A platonic love is as much a threat to a marriage as a physical betrayal.

I realize that I really know nothing about Daniel, other than that he grew up in Montreal and studied at McGill University. His mother and married sister still live there. His father died a few years ago.

But he and Isobel must have shared many things. They have past memories - as I have with Hugh - and I am jealous of even these.

What a capricious, treacherous heart I have! To think that I had been ready to run away with Neil only two years ago! And then I became obsessed with Hugh, my treasured childhood friend. But truth to tell, I love him still. How can I love two men so well?

But I realized even that evening that I couldn't allow my emotional vulnerability to jeopardize my friendships. They were too important to me - all that I have.

So I was charming to Isobel, trying to think of her as a friend, not a rival. And it was easier than I thought, for she is an intriguing person. (How could she be otherwise if she is the object of Daniel's adoration?) In fact, she is the type of person whom I would gladly have as a friend.

She was truly interested in the Refuge, and saddened by some of the stories I had to tell. She said, "We women will be powerless until we have the vote. That's something I keep pushing Charles to promote. Isn't that so, my dear?" she added as Charles joined us again.

"Ha! I'd be laughed out of parliament. What do you think, Redding? My wife's advocating that women be given the vote. Wants me to become the champion of women's rights!"

The opportunity could not have been more perfect. There was Horace Redding, about to be shredded by an unknown enemy. Me.

Horace Redding seemed to me aptly named. He has a round, shiny head with only a few tufts of hair above the ears, and a ruddy complexion. He resembled a large, pink pig in evening dress.

He guffawed. "Women don't need a vote, they need husbands! My wife can hardly decide between beef and pork for dinner, how could she possibly decide which issues are important?"

"Your own wife may have difficulty in choosing wisely," I replied smoothly, wondering if Horace even registered the insult, "but most of us are quite capable of making intelligent decisions."

"I don't wish to give offence, ladies, but women are not endowed with those attributes necessary in business and politics," Horace said.

"You mean like ruthlessness, pompousness, arrogance?" I asked sweetly.

Horace was not amused however. "Intelligence and good sense, my dear. Women are delightful but delicate and frivolous creatures who let emotions rule them. They need to be protected from the harsh realities of life."

I couldn't believe that Horace Redding had so easily delivered himself into my hands. I said, "And from evil, odious men, wouldn't you agree?"

"Indeed I would."

"Then surely your heart will be touched by the sad story of one of the poor young girls who came to our Refuge recently." I exchanged a glance with Daniel, who suppressed a grin. "Only seventeen, she was. A pretty, innocent young maid, who had been raped by her employer." I used that harsh word deliberately, and it rang beyond our stunned group to neighbouring guests who stopped their own conversations to listen. "He threatened her with disgrace and dismissal if she did not give in to his brutish demands. And poor Nancy..." I saw Horace Redding sweat. "... was too young and naive to know how to defend herself. And so he kept abusing her until she became so noticeably pregnant that the mistress of the house threw her out without a reference or even the wages owed her. So what justice is there for such vilely wronged girls, Mr. Redding? She has little hope of making a respectable marriage now that she is no longer 'pure'. What future for her but perhaps the streets? Or maybe she'll fling herself into the river rather than be further humiliated and abused by men."

"That's shocking!" Isobel said. "Do you know who the man was, Miss McAllister?"

"Who can say? Perhaps someone in this very room." My eyes bored into Horace Redding so that he had no doubt I knew of his guilt.

He blustered, "You can't believe everything you hear, Miss McAllister. Servants who leave in disgrace often lie."

"Indeed? How would you know, Mr. Redding?"

He must have realized he was putting his foot in his mouth. The story should have evoked his sympathy, had he nothing to hide. "People do tend to exaggerate or dramatize."

Bless Isobel for stepping in. She said, "Surely the girl's story is tragic enough. You would not want your own daughters to suffer such indignities. What you fail to realize, Mr. Redding, is that we women are dependent upon men. One day, your own daughters will be dependent upon their husbands. If those men are not honourable, your daughters, too, could be victims - in other ways than this poor child perhaps, but victims nonetheless."

Daniel said, "I'm sure Mr. Redding has sympathy for those less fortunate than he, and would be most happy to make a substantial donation to your Refuge, Miss McAllister."

I almost laughed out loud, to have two such staunch supporters! Horace, who was now an apoplectic shade of red, babbled, "Yes, of course. Delighted to do so. I'll send something around." He left us with obvious relief, and I wasn't completely satisfied to let him go so easily. But what could I hope to achieve, other than to expose him publicly, which would not help Nancy. Better to accept the hush money.

When Daniel danced with me, I said, "What an inspired idea you had. But it does make me feel like a blackmailer."

"Nonsense! Horace's conscience will be eased, but he'll always have great respect for you."

"Or fear of me!"

"Not a bad thing, I'd say. Perhaps that will prevent him from abusing other servant girls. And you will have some more money to help Nancy and others like her. It's the best of a bad situation."

"Perhaps.... Isobel was certainly wonderful in her indignation!"

"I think you'll find her a good ally."

Rather an ally than an enemy, I thought. She would be a formidable foe. I do like her, but I fear her power to take Daniel away from me.

I feel as if I am teetering on the edge of a precipice. I cannot allow Daniel to think of me as anything but a friend. (I dare not even kiss him for fear of infecting him!) So I must keep my own feelings well buried, and can hardly stop Daniel from choosing another woman with whom to spend his life.

But he comes to me in my dreams like a lover. I feel his lips teasing mine, his gentle hands stroking me, igniting indecent fires within me. And sometimes I wake with tears upon my face, for even in my dreams I know that he can never be mine.

Dear God, what have I done to deserve such punishment?

Chapter 17

The dew still shimmered on the grass as Kit ambled down to her garden. She felt ridiculously pleased with herself for being up and out so early. The sun was warm on her back and promised a pure, cloudless day.

Just in front of her, a startled family of groundhogs scurried into the tall grass. But one - a big granddaddy of a hog - stood his ground. He was wary, poised to run, yet there was belligerence in his stance.

"Shoo!" Kit said, stopping a few yards from him. "Oh, get lost, you silly creature!"

But still he stood there, and Kit began to wonder if groundhogs were dangerous. Did they ever attack people? Could they contract rabies? Undoubtedly.

How fast could they run, she wondered. Could she react quickly enough if it suddenly dashed toward her?

She noticed a potato-sized rock near her foot, and slowly bent down to pick it up. She was afraid she might alarm the groundhog into attacking, but it stood as if frozen.

"Showdown at the O.K. Corral, eh? Go on, get lost!" she shouted, hurling the rock at the animal. It was supposed to have landed in front of the creature, to scare it away, but Kit's aim had not been good. With a gasp of horror, she saw the rock bounce off the groundhog's head. It screamed and wobbled. Blood trickled down its fur. She had never thought to see such recognizable agony in an animal's face. It turned and staggered off into the meadow grass.

"Oh, God! What have I done?" She could imagine it hobbling back to its burrow, where it might linger for days before it finally succumbed to its injury.

Kit was too disconcerted to check on her garden. She spent the next couple of days trying to spot the wounded groundhog, to appease her guilty conscience, but she couldn't tell if it was one of the four or five that she saw. Surely she hadn't dealt it a fatal blow!

She remembered what Nick had said about shooting them, and wondered if she was being too squeamish. Probably the groundhog had only been stunned. She wished Nick were there to tell her how silly she was being.

When Kit did go to harvest vegetables, she was astounded by the size of the zucchini - as large as baseball bats some of them.

"Jeez! That's the biggest God-damn cucumber I've ever seen," Alan McGrath said, peering over the stone wall.

Kit laughed. "Must be the fertile soil here. I didn't know zucchini could grow this monstrous. Split it in half and you'd have a couple of canoes!"

"What is it? Zuke...?"

"You don't expect me to believe you've never heard of zucchini?"

"We don't eat that God-damn furren food round these here parts... But seriously, I haven't."

"It's summer squash."

"Does it taste like squash?"

"Not the kind I used to get as a kid."

"How do you prepare it?"

"Tastes great breaded and fried, or in ratatouille..."

Alan made his comical red-neck farmer face.

"I'll give you the recipe. And it makes terrific bread."

"Jeez, I'll stick to wheat for my bread."

"It's not that different from carrot cake. I'll bake you some."

"Just don't tell me what it is until I've eaten it!"

"Oh, get lost!" Kit said with a laugh.

She did bake a few loaves of zucchini bread, and took one over to the McGraths that afternoon, along with an armload of fresh zucchini.

Jean and Mary were busy in the kitchen. "We're putting up pickles," Jean explained, "but sit yourself down, if you don't mind talking while we work."

"Not at all." Kit liked the busy, homey kitchen, with its pungent smell of vinegar and dill. "I've brought you some zucchini bread." It suddenly struck her as presumptuous to be bringing home baking to a couple of women who practically spent their lives in the kitchen. She had been going to say that she brought it because Alan had never had any, but figured that might make things worse.

"Alan was telling us about that," Jean said. "We've never grown zucchini ourselves, but the ones I've seen in the store aren't anywhere near the size of those. All wrinkly they are too, in the supermarket."

"I threw the largest ones away - they were woody inside. But I have more than I can possibly eat or freeze or bake. So do help me with them."

"That's kind of you," Mary said, as if Kit had bestowed some great treasure upon them. She was still star-struck, judging by the gleam in her eyes, and it made Kit feel uncomfortable. Mary asked, "Have you been writing a new book?"

"I'm always doing that! But I have another project that I'm working on as well.... Did Alan or Stuart tell you that I found Violet McAllister's diary?"

"As a matter of fact I did," Stuart said, entering the room. To his mother he said, "Dad and Alan have gone off to the Co-op. They'll have their tea later."

The tea was already made, and Mary bustled about, pouring a large mugful for Stuart, and buttering a thick slice of fruit bread which she set in front of him. Kit accepted a cup of tea, and a small piece of the bread.

"Alan told me that you were knowledgeable about local history," Kit said to Jean.

Jean demurred. "I doubt if there's much I can tell you that Violet hasn't said better and truer in her own words."

"I was thinking about popular anecdotes. They might help me to understand how local people felt about the McAllisters."

"Well, they say when Violet got a notion into her head, there wasn't any way to dislodge it. Like the time she went to Ottawa in a blizzard. No one in their right mind would have gone farther than their outhouse on a day like that, but Violet said if the train was going then so was she. She'd promised her sister to be there for an important dinner party, and be there she would. Well, she drove herself to the village in the cutter, but it's a wonder that she and the horse didn't both disappear in a snowdrift, so they say. The train was late, but it came, and she went. The village folk thought her rather willful and eccentric."

Mary asked, "Is it true, Kit, that Violet waited all those years for that Spenlowe boy to come back for her?"

"There's nothing romantic about wasting your life pining for something you can't have," Stuart scoffed.

"You should know," Mary retorted sharply.

Kit said, "No, it wasn't true, though she let everybody, even her friends, think that." Not wanting to reveal anything more about Violet just yet, Kit quickly asked, "Is there a photograph of Violet anywhere?"

Jean paused in her work. "There must be one somewhere. She was a handsome woman by all accounts. I'll get in touch with the historical society and find out if they have one."

Kit sensed Stuart looking at her. Their eyes met briefly, but Kit quickly looked away.

She became acutely aware of his nearness. As if he were caressing her with his gaze, she felt her flesh tingle and burn. Remembering the sight of his strong, virile body half-clad brought a deeper blush to her cheeks. It was as if they were engaged in subtle foreplay right in front of his wife and mother!

Or was she suffering some sort of female vapours. It was too long since she'd had a man, she told herself firmly, and wondered how Violet had endured all those sterile, virginal years.

Kit had to admit that she had begun to think of Stuart as a modern Hugh. She had read Violet's diary so often that the people in it had become real to her. And she couldn't help but be smitten by the men that Violet had loved.

Jean was saying, "Violet started this Fortnightly Club. Half the women of Todmorden belonged to it in those days, but after Violet died, her sister in Kintyre kept the Club going, and it is still in existence there."

"Is it really? You know, Kate and Ruth were both members of it. Whatever happened to them... and to Hugh?"

"Grandma Ruth lived be to ninety-one. Pretty crusty she was, and she ruled this family until just a few years before her death. She got senile then, and kept seeing people from her past and not recognizing those around her, even her grandson - that's Duncan's father. Kept calling him Hugh."

Kit wasn't surprised to hear that Ruth had grown bitter and dictatorial. "How many children did she have?"

"Just the one. Pretty risky in those days, putting all your eggs in one basket. Kate had three of her children die, but the other seven survived her. She was fifty when she died."

So Violet's fears had been confirmed. Hard years of endless childbirth and drudgery coupled with hearbreaking sorrows had taken their toll.

"And Hugh?"

"They say he was a quiet, melancholy sort of man. Never had much to say, especially when his wife was around. Seems that she snatched the reins pretty early in their marriage. Hugh was only forty-eight when he died."

Had the heart gone out of him after Violet's death? Had Hugh found nothing to sustain him, nothing to fill the emptiness of his existence? Certainly Ruth wouldn't let him forget his treachery.

"Where is Violet buried? Not in the churchyard?"

"No, she saved the church some soul searching. She left a note to the vicar stating that she wanted to be buried on her land."

"But where? I haven't been able to find the headstone."

"She was quite specific about the spot. The headstone's probably fallen over. 'Twas leaning terribly last I saw it. Alan can show you some time."

"I can show you right now," Stuart said. "I've a few minutes to spare."

Mary threw her husband an enigmatic look. Jean shrugged and said, "As you please."

And Kit found herself ushered out the door, not at all sure she wanted Stuart to accompany her anywhere. She felt awkward with him, and neither of them spoke for several minutes.

"Let's follow the creek," Stuart suggested.

Kit struggled to find something to say to him, just to fill the uncomfortable silence. How unlike his brother he was! Alan could talk easily about everything; Stuart's thoughts were dealt out as if each cost him dearly.

As they passed within sight of the bungalow he was building, she said, "Your house is coming along well."

He grunted, and gave a rather disinterested glance at the structure - as if it had nothing to do with him. "I've got a brick layer starting next week. So the exterior should be done by September. It'll take me the winter at least to finish off the inside."

"Mary must be getting anxious to move into a home of her own."

"She's keen, all right."

Implying he wasn't. Kit wondered about their relationship. From the little she had seen so far, she inferred that they were not the happiest couple. But being on their own would surely help. As nice as Jean was, Kit could never imagine herself living as Mary did, constantly under her mother-in-law's rule. Mary and Stuart couldn't even have a decent argument without everyone knowing - and perhaps interfering. And how private could a bedroom be when it was next to your in-laws'?

Kit slipped on a wet rock and would have fallen had Stuart not grabbed her so quickly. His touch seared her flesh. Kit avoided looking at him as she righted herself and murmured her thanks. He seemed reluctant to release her.

They continued in silence, side by side, careful not to touch. The walk had never seemed so long.

Stuart took her past the house, right to the property boundary where a stone fence separated hers from the Bryce farm. It was at the farthest corner of the old orchard. He led her up through the tall meadow grass to a spot where the land levelled out. There, close to the stone wall, he swished his foot around, searching for the tombstone. A moment later he bent down and lifted a surprisingly ornate, lichen-encrusted limestone tablet, and leaned it against the wall.

Kit knelt down to read it, but it was badly deteriorated and the inscription was barely discernible. A trumpeting angel was carved into the arched top amid vines and curlicues. Almost reverently she ran her fingers over the etched letters.

Here lies Violet McAllister
1853 - 1879
Alone in Death as in Life

"How sad. She was only 26."

"Lots of people died young in those days."

"But not so horribly." Had Violet been going mad with syphilitic dementia? Or had she just been depressed by circumstances? Kit was determined to find out more about this once-dreaded disease.

"You talk as though it's important," Stuart said. "She's been dead over a hundred years. Nothing but mouldering bones under our feet."

Kit shuddered slightly at the thought. "It is important to me. I feel as if I know her." As if she were a friend.

Stuart shrugged and said, "Well, I'd best be getting back."

"Thank you for showing me this."

"Sure." He stared at her for an intense moment, and then walked away.

Hugh would not have been so callous. But she had to remember that Stuart was not Hugh, and perhaps nothing at all like his great-great-grandfather. She had to stop projecting her own romantic preconceptions onto people. As she had done with Nigel.

But Stuart was forgotten a moment later while Kit studied the headstone. She straightened up and looked around her.

"I can see why you liked this spot, Violet," she said. It was the highest point of the property, and overlooked the ravine and the valley beyond. Moon Hall looked impressive from this vantage point as well. "You could keep an eye on your entire domain from here, couldn't you."

Kit drifted back to the house, careful of nettles and groundhog holes. But she wouldn't have been surprised if a vindictive hog had bounded out and savaged her leg.

The Pughs were just pulling into her driveway when she reached the house.

"We won't come in," Cleo called from the car. "Just came by to drop off this invitation."

Kit went up to the car, and Cleo passed her a thick vellum envelope with her name beautifully inscribed on it. Cleo explained, "We always have a little 'do' for the neighbours at the end of summer. Of course, inviting literally everybody does have its little drawbacks, but then one can hardly leave out certain people, can one?" She must mean the Skuces, Kit thought. "And Rhett and I pride ourselves on being broad-minded. Now do be sure to mark the date on your calendar! Bye for now!"

They waved heartily as they drove away. Kit wondered if the 'do' was going to be as ostentatious as the wedding-like invitation.

Cleopatra and Everett Pugh request the pleasure of your presence at their third annual garden fete...

"I see you've received your invitation," Liz Meekin said, joining her.

"Oh hi, Liz! I really must hear all about this!"

"I'm not sure that I should tell you and spoil the surprise," Liz said with a laugh.

"Formal dress, is it?"

"You bet. We always look like poor cousins, but people rather expect that of us. Duncan McGrath shows up in a suit he hasn't been comfortable wearing in twenty years. Jack Skuce is in a Salvation Army hand-me-down that never did fit. Georgina Bryce must wear her mother's old Sunday-best dresses - flowery chiffon."

"I know what you mean. Poor girl."

"Myrtle Skuce always wears something too young - probably one of her daughters' cast-offs. It was a mini skirt and spangled top the first year! Cleo and Rhett look as though they've just come from the Henley Regatta - he, dapper in crisp white trousers and navy blazer, with a white silk ascot at his neck, and she, swishing around in something that whispers money, and a large picture hat. And then Leighton freaks them all out when he shows up barefoot and in jeans - he wears his best jeans, of course!" They laughed heartily.

With his flyaway, wispy red hair and scraggly beard, Leighton looked very much like an Ozark mountain man, and Kit could just imagine what sort of impression he must make on the Pughs. With surprise she realized that Cleo's definition of the undesirables one had to invite might very well include the "hippies".

"And I shall reveal no more," Liz said. "But I want to be with you when you arrive."

"To see the look on my face? Now you have intrigued me!"

"Anyway, I've come with another invitation - hardly so formal - from Leighton. He says he promised to take you to an opera this summer, and would you accompany him to *La Traviata* on Saturday night? He's persuaded Pete to go, too - thinks it'll be good therapy for him. And he's already bought your ticket."

"Then how can I possibly refuse? Tell him I'd be delighted. Is anyone else going?"

"Leighton's taken us all at least once - trying to instill some culture into us - but none of us is as keen on opera as he is. He'll pick you up at five - that'll give you time to dine before the performance. Leighton has this little French bistro that he fancies."

The 'little French bistro' turned out to be an expensive and wonderfully romantic restaurant in a restored Victorian mansion. The maitre d' winced only slightly at the outlandish trio before him - Kit in a stylish cocktail dress, Pete in an old Nehru jacket, and Leighton in his newest jeans, lumberjack shirt, and ripped running shoes - and conducted them to a very secluded table, presumably to keep them out of sight of the well-heeled guests.

The food was exquisite, and the company, delightful. Leighton was an intelligent and amusing companion, and Pete put his moroseness aside and joined in. He had questioned Kit about writing during most of the hour-long drive to Ottawa, and she had suggested that he establish a reputation for himself by writing short stories, or magazine articles on topics that he knew best, such as organic farming. The idea had seemed to excite him, and she noticed that he drank much less than usual. Having been an ardent Beatles fan, she could never look at Pete without thinking of John Lennon, and transferring some of that long-ago affection to him. And so Pete seemed like an old and valued friend already.

The National Arts Centre was only a block from the restaurant. It sprawled along the bank of the canal where its waterside cafe and cultural ambiance gave the area a European flavour.

Kit knew the story of 'The Lady of the Camellias', and was familiar with some of the melodies, but she had never heard the entire opera. From the opening bars of the poignant, haunting overture she was entranced by the powerful music.

Leighton was totally absorbed; he leaned into the music as if he could thus capture more of it. His right hand made small conducting motions, punctuating the air as the singer hit the anticipated notes. His face expressed fulfillment, and, above all, bliss.

"Well, what do you think?" Leighton asked her during intermission.

"I'm deeply moved. The soprano's voice is beautiful."

"Not bad," Leighton admitted, which Kit realized was high praise indeed. "She flubbed a line, but otherwise has done a creditable job."

At Kit's surprised expression, Pete laughed and explained, "Leighton knows every note and how best it should be executed." He looked around as he said, "Well, it's good to have a night out with the glitterati once in a while to reinforce just what's important. I wonder if those bejewelled women are enjoying the performance all the more for their costly trappings? Or are they a part of the performance?"

Kit sensed the envy beneath Pete's scorn. Sipping the drink that Pete had brought her, she glanced casually around the chattering press of people. They were clad in everything from shorts to shimmering floor-length gowns.

Her heart cartwheeled when she spotted Nick. He had already noticed her, and now smiled a gentle greeting. She was rivetted by those translucent blue eyes, like polished chips of aquamarine. Then Nick turned to a woman at his side, spoke some words to her, and the two of them approached.

"Hey, Nick!" Leighton said. "What a surprise to see you here! I guess all my training has not been in vain."

"Leighton, Pete, Kit - I'd like you to meet Christine Flint."

She was a stunning woman who looked as though she had been turned out by a Hollywood studio. She had a sleek, platinum bob that draped seductively across one eye, and flawless makeup that gave her the complexion of a wide-eyed doll. Kit suddenly recognized her. "Of course! You sometimes read the evening news on the local channel."

"That's right." Said rather smugly, Kit thought.

Christine exuded self-confidence like a cloying perfume. Although the elder by five or six years, Kit felt like an adolescent in her presence - and developed an immediate dislike of her. That was how Nigel's friends had made her feel.

The dimming of lights signalled patrons to resume their seats. "Let's meet after the performance," Leighton said to Nick. "We could go somewhere for a drink."

"Sure," Nick replied, glancing at Christine. She shrugged noncommittally - a coolly elegant shrug that implied she really didn't care to know his unorthodox friends, but would humour him if she must.

Kit could no longer lose herself in the music. Nick was too much in her thoughts. She knew she had no right to be jealous, and wondered why it bothered her so much to see Nick with another woman. Especially Christine. She was a greater danger than the dippy Cindy and her ilk.

Why a danger, Kit wondered. Hadn't she had her chance with Nick and thrown it away? Had she thought he would pursue her and woo her in some romantic, old-fashioned courting ritual? Or had she expected him to renounce all other women while having a close platonic relationship with her?

She was beginning to understand just how Violet had felt about Daniel.

The tragic conclusion and the evocative music moved her to tears, and she wished it were Nick at her side. But Nick was just a friend, like Leighton and Pete, and she would have to treat him as such. And expect nothing more from him.

They agreed to meet in the By Ward Market, an old section of downtown Ottawa that was slowly being revitalized. Trendy wine bars and glitzy singles clubs rubbed shoulders with warehouses and disreputable saloons. Expensive eateries, chain-store steakhouses, and sleazy diners were a stone's throw from each other. Mini-skirted prostitutes lingered on the sidewalks, drunks lay in the gutters and alleyways, and the glitterati strolled down the streets, feeling perhaps a bit daring.

Looking around at some beautifully restored buildings, Kit wondered which one of them had been Violet's Refuge. She could so easily picture how it might all have looked a hundred years ago when Violet and Tristan and Daniel had trodden these streets. She would have to come back here soon to explore on her own.

Christine had suggested they go to Brandy's. But Brandy's had a dress code - no jeans - and wouldn't allow Leighton and Pete in.

"Bloody ridiculous!" Leighton said. "We've just come from the NAC and from Armand's. They had no objections to our choice of clothes."

"Sorry, sir. Rules," the doorman said impatiently.

"Assholes!"

Nick suggested a wine bar closeby.

Kit was just as glad. She and Nigel had never been ones for nightclubs and discos, and judging by the glimpse she'd had of this place, she wouldn't bother with them. Through the thick smoke she could see desperate men and women strutting their stuff in fine feathers, gyrating suggestively to the throbbing, monotonous beat. A primitive mating game. This was the sort of place that Nick must frequent, she realized with distaste.

The wine bar seemed to be popular with couples and groups of people who wanted to talk. It had a '60s coffee-house atmosphere, with candles stuck in old wine bottles, dim lighting, and soft music. "Well this is a big improvement," Leighton said, deliberating over the extensive wine list. Kit was not surprised to discover that Leighton was something of a wine connoisseur. With glee he selected two bottles - a red and a white.

"Just as well those assholes wouldn't let us in," Leighton said. "I can do without hearing music tortured, and without seeing macho men with open shirts and gold necklaces coming on to airhead females."

"Nick and I met there," Christine said frostily.

"How unfortunate," Leighton said, unruffled. "That's the trouble with this generation - it's all icing and no substance. People are too concerned with how they look and dress and whether they impress people."

"It's important to make a favourable impression on people," Christine said. "That's the only way to get anywhere." Her look implied that Leighton would never make it.

"Ah, but where are you going? What noble ideals does this generation hope to achieve? Accumulating the biggest and the most, the fastest, from what I can see."

Including herself in Leighton's definition of "this generation", Christine was stung to reply, "And what did your generation achieve? They were just a bunch of disenchanted, drug-addicted idealists, sitting around whittling wood or making pottery."

"A revolution," Leighton said with quiet satisfaction. "Come now, Christine, you strike me as a relatively intelligent person. Don't tell me you are really so ignorant of how revolutionary the '60s were. As a simple example of just one of the drastic changes, look at morality - you and Nick would never have shacked up on the first date in those pre-60s eras." Christine was momentarily taken aback by his bluntness, but did not deny the accusation. "People didn't even kiss on the first date back then. You have us to thank for your freedoms, especially being a woman. Feminists fought hard to get you out of the kitchen. But I don't blame you for being envious of having missed out on the most exciting and turbulent decade this century. Your adolescence must have been terribly dull."

"Don't be ridiculous!" Christine spat. "That's one of the things I can't stand about your generation - your unfounded arrogance!"

Kit and Pete were enjoying the contretemps, but Nick looked concerned. Lightly he said, "Leighton pities anyone who missed Woodstock. I missed it too."

"But not in spirit," Leighton said, as if he were reminding Nick of all that he had abandonned.

Kit gave in to the urge to help Nick defray the volatile situation by questioning Leighton about Woodstock, although she really wasn't sure why. She'd rather liked seeing Christine put in her place so effortlessly by Leighton. Perhaps it was for that grateful smile that Nick bestowed upon her. Anyway, she was interested, and Leighton went on about that famous concert for about twenty minutes. It had obviously had a profound influence upon his life.

"I'd never really thought that man could live in love and peace until those few days. You could just feel it emanating from everyone around you. *Peace, man. Live and let live. Everybody's doing his own thing, and hey, man, it's cool.*"

Christine refrained from uttering snide comments, perhaps because she felt that she could never win an argument against Leighton, or perhaps she had just grown too bored to care. It was difficult to read anything from her self-contained expression. She said, "We really must get home to bed, Nick. I have a long day tomorrow."

Kit wondered if Christine had deliberately mentioned bed for her benefit - women seemed to sense potential rivals.

With a practiced smile Christine said, "I'm sure we'll meet again." At least she didn't lie and say how delighted she had been to make everyone's acquaintance.

But Kit could just imagine what she might be saying to Nick in private about his friends. And she found herself growing angry. Angry even at Nick, if he didn't defend his friends to this female.

There was silence for several minutes after they had gone. The bottles of wine were still half full, and Kit poured herself a generous glass of the white.

"You don't like her, do you?" Pete asked Leighton.

"I don't like people who are so full of themselves that they can't see beyond the narrow confines of their own skins. And her skin wasn't even natural - I wonder what she looks like in the mornings, without her warpaint. Poor Nick. I don't think he realizes just what he's gotten himself into this time. She won't be good for him."

Much of the gaiety had gone with Nick's desertion. Leighton grew quiet and pensive. Pete made a valiant effort to engage Kit in conversation, but they soon finished the wine and left.

It was a long and silent drive back to their world.

Chapter 18

January 7, 1873:

I gave Daniel one of my watercolour paintings for Christmas. It depicts Moon Hall set amid the summer-flowering gardens and the orchard, with the valley spreading away behind it. I wanted him to know something about my home (which he seems to find romantically pastoral), since I can't really invite him to come and see it for himself. He was delighted with the picture, and not only admired my artistry, but said that he was glad he could now visualize me in my home. He was most amused by my "signature", which is simply a violet painted in the corner.

Perhaps I was wrong to give him something that is to me, so intimate. Yet I wanted him to have some sense of where I live, the place I love. I wish I could invite him to come and walk the grounds with me, to take tea in the cozy back parlour, to share an intimate dinner. Sometimes I picture him sitting across the room, chatting about his day. It is so easy to imagine him here. A part of my life.

Tristan regards me with a kind of doggy sadness, as if he senses my own. I must not give in to these bouts of melancholy. Seeing me staring at him, he gets up and comes over to me, offering what comfort he can. He is already so tall, his head reaching to the top of the desk. I scratch his ears and am glad that I have him. That he invariably reminds me of Daniel makes him even dearer to my heart.

Daniel gave me a handsome, silver-topped walking stick for Christmas. With Tristan at my side and this heavy bludgeon in my hands, I shall indeed feel safe walking along the streets of the city!

Lily, Augustus, and I spent a delightful Christmas with Heather, Gordon, and little Emily. Then we all trooped up to Ottawa to stay at Lily's, for we were invited to Lady D's skating party on the 28th.

In the extensive grounds of Rideau Hall there is a huge toboggan slide, a curling rink under construction, and a skating pond. The Dufferins know how to enjoy winter.

There were lots of elegant couples and graceful young ladies gliding across the ice that afternoon. I have not had much practice skating, but managed to stay on my feet most of the time!

Daniel joined us later in the afternoon, and I was astonished at his expertise. He scooped me into his arms, as if we would waltz side-by-side, and whisked me across the ice.

"Where did you learn to skate like this?" I asked him.

"In Montreal. There are excellent rinks there, and not much else to do on a winter's day."

I didn't ask him if Isobel had been his partner then. It was enough that I had him to myself for a while and that Isobel was back in Montreal until parliament sat again in March.

"I feel as though I'm floating!" I said, marvelling at the sensation of sliding so effortlessly, secure in Daniel's arms. But even so, my ankles soon tired, and we decided to try the toboggan run.

This is a tall wooden structure, like a giant, snow-covered slide, set above the hill. It was a long climb to the top, but what a view of the city and the river nearby.

Daniel and I shared a toboggan. It was an exhilarating race to the bottom of the steep hill. Once we overturned and tumbled over and over in the soft snow. How we laughed!

Afterwards we all went inside for tea or mulled claret, and danced for an hour. What an absolutely perfect day!

March 8, 1873:

Whenever I get complacent or begin to doubt that I am truly afflicted by the dreaded syphilis - surely wishful thinking! - I'm jolted back to reality.

As soon as she entered the Refuge, I saw what I had so often feared I might one day confront in the mirror. The woman had festering sores on her face. Her hair was sparse and wispy, like that of an ancient crone, though she could have been little more than my age. She came in, shame-faced, bent, as if beaten down by life. But most appalling was the bundle she carried, wrapped in dirty linen and a moth-eaten blanket.

It was a baby, but a monstrously deformed little creature. It was tiny, but had an oversized, wizened head like an old man, and a neck that seemed too thin to hold it upon the body. It had a rasping way of breathing, as though it struggled for air. And when I got a closer look at it, I saw that it had twisted legs, as if it had been put together all wrong.

Other women backed away, but I had nothing to fear from her. I could only thank God that I had not yet the evidence of the pox so plainly upon my face. Marjorie cautioned me not to go near her, and sent Lise to fetch Daniel.

But I approached her and bade her welcome. She looked at me with startled eyes. Why? Because I did not shrink from her? How terrible it must be not only to suffer the ravages of the disease, but to be a social pariah as well. A modern leper.

"I'm Violet McAllister," I said. "And you're..."

"Mary," she replied. She looked down at the bundle in her arms. "My husband threw us out. Said he couldn't live with this monster I had given birth to!" Then she burst into tears and hugged the bundle to her breast.

"It's a pox runt," Marjorie whispered to me. "But ask her whose fault it is that she and the babe have it!" she said indignantly.

I knew what she meant. It was undoubtedly the husband who had infected his wife and doomed the child. But she bears the blame.

I offered her a bowl of soup, and fetched it myself, since the others seemed reluctant to go near her. And I do not blame them. They thought me brave, even foolish, but they cannot know that I am already doomed.

Daniel is a compassionate man. I had never seen him at work before, but I was impressed with how truly sympathetic he was to this poor, wretched creature. He told her it would be best for her and the babe to go to the hospital, until her lesions were healed. There she could be treated and properly cared for. Then he took her away.

He returned an hour later and drew me aside. "Mary's settled into the hospital. She is in a highly contagious stage of the disease, so it is best to keep her isolated. I'm afraid that the child may not live long. But perhaps that is for the best."

"Will she be cured?" I asked hopefully. Perhaps Gordon had been wrong, or maybe a new treatment had been discovered.

"Of her present symptoms, but not of the disease. Some will argue the point, but syphilis can lie dormant for years, and people aren't even aware they still have it. I had a patient once who suddenly went mad. Thought he was Wellington and that his French-Canadian servant was Napoleon. He almost beat the poor man to death before he was stopped. I discovered that he'd had the pox in his youth, and his madness was certainly symptomatic of latent syphilis."

Madness. I hadn't even thought of that possibility. That was even more frightening somehow than the physical manifestations. And surely Father had gone mad, too, seeing me no longer as his daughter but as a whore. I shuddered.

Daniel noticed and said, "It's a deservedly dreaded disease."

"Will Mary eventually go mad?" I asked.

"Possibly, but the disease behaves differently in different people. Some may never have more than a mild rash and years, even decades, later will begin to lose their mental faculties and deteriorate into paralytic imbeciles. Others suffer terribly from destructive lesions in bones and joints and organs.

"What worries me is that Mary will consider herself cured. If her husband doesn't take her back, what will she do? Too often the answer is prostitution. Then she will infect men who will sometimes infect their wives and breed syphilitic children with all kinds of physical and mental deformities."

What an apt way for a wronged woman to exact her revenge on men, I thought. Perhaps it was unworthy, but I couldn't help thinking that men who deceived their wives and took advantage of destitute women deserved all they got. But certainly their wives didn't. Nor their children!

"You're looking pale and tired, Violet," Daniel said. "Come, and I'll escort you home before I continue my rounds."

"That's not necessary," I replied. I was undoubtedly pale, shocked because Daniel had given me more horrible insights into what the future might hold in store for me - delusions, violent mania, paralysis, intellectual dementia. Will I one day be a blithering idiot, a grotesque parody of myself? Never will I allow things to get to that stage!

"It most certainly is. I may not be your doctor, but as a board member, I will remind you of our agreement."

"I've been here scarcely more than an hour," I protested, but in vain, for Daniel had already fetched my coat and was ushering me out the door.

I had to admit that it felt good to step out into the sunshine, which managed to banish dark and dreadful thoughts for a while. We'd had a thaw the previous week, so there were no great snow drifts left, but it was once again cold enough so that the roads hadn't yet dissolved into rivers of mud. A perfect day for a winter stroll. Tristan scampered along beside us, always happy to be outdoors. He was already so tall that I could easily stroke his head without bending down.

I told Daniel about Lady Dufferin's visit to the Refuge the previous week. She had sent a note, arranging the visit, but had arrived without fanfare and with a genuine interest in the place and the people. She'd spent quite a while talking to individuals, who, though somewhat awed and reluctant to complain to Her Excellency, did give her an inkling of what life was like for destitute women.

Upon leaving, she said to me, "You are quite a remarkable young woman, Miss McAllister. Do come to visit us at Rideau more often."

I recalled only too well my last visit - that wonderful skating party when I had felt myself melt into Daniel's arms. It was so hard to guard against the tender feelings that sometimes overwhelmed me. I strode along more briskly. And slipped on a patch of ice. I would have fallen had Daniel not been so quick to catch me.

"I can see that I will just have to teach you how to stay on your feet on the ice," he quipped.

I laughed. "I doubt that you will ever make a skater out of me. I'm much too tall and clumsy."

"Nonsense. I'm taller than you."

"But you learned how to skate when you were much shorter!" I countered with a grin. "You didn't have as far to fall then."

He chuckled. "True enough. But you are not one to give up easily, Violet. We'll make a champion skater out of you yet."

I thought his confidence in me misplaced. I am not as self-assured or dauntless as he thinks.

Daniel did not relinquish my arm, so we walked to Lily's arm in arm, like any married couple. Of course, he was just being chivalrous, preventing me from falling on the hazardous patches of black ice. But how happy and yet miserable I felt!

If only we could spend the rest of our lives like this.

April 18, 1873:

The Dufferins have had their first ball in their new ballroom. Although the magnificent room wasn't yet painted, it was prettily decorated with twists of tarlatan and bunches of roses. There was a crimson throne on a dais at one end of the room, and the band stationed at the other. There were over six hundred of us present, with supper provided for all!

But how disappointed I was that Daniel wasn't there. Surely he would have been invited. He must have been delayed by an emergency case, I thought.

It made me realize how little enjoyment there is for me, even in such a lavish entertainment, when I cannot share it with Daniel. In his company, a simple stroll or a brief conversation gives the greatest pleasure.

Of course I danced and conversed, but my heart was not in it.

Isobel Granger was there, and though I tried, I could not avoid her. "I haven't seen Daniel, have you, Miss McAllister? I know he was planning to be here. But a doctor's time is never his own, is it?"

It hurt that she knew Daniel's plans when I could only surmise them. She had done the same once before, quite deliberately, I'm certain, for I think she's trying to stake her claim to Daniel and perhaps considers me a threat.

She had come unannounced to the Refuge the previous week. I was surprised that she would just drop in without advising me of her plans first. But, as if reading my thoughts, she said, "Daniel told me you would be here this afternoon."

A simple statement perhaps, but one heavy with meaning. She did not elaborate, but left me to wonder when and where Daniel had told her this. I could not fail to grasp the implication of intimacy between them - one that excluded me.

But then she had been most interested and pleasant during the tour I gave her. I did not hesitate to point out the seamier side of life as represented there, but she was neither shocked nor squeamish. Before leaving, she made a most generous donation.

But why do I consider Isobel a rival? I can never marry Daniel. One day, she may be free to do so. In the meantime, why am I so jealous that Daniel has kept up an old friendship? Surely Isobel has a greater claim to him than I, who have known him less than two years. Daniel would undoubtedly think my attitude childish and unworthy.

I must not allow myself to become obsessed. And I must never, never allow Daniel to think that there can be anything more than friendship between us!

Chapter 19

"So glad you could make it to our little fete, dear," Cleo said to Kit, giving her an airy embrace and an approving look. Taking to heart what Liz had told her, Kit was wearing her Laura Ashley frock - surely designed for just such an occasion - and a straw bonnet.

Cleo was a sophisticated study in black and white from head to toe, and Rhett was sporting his yachting outfit. They looked sleek and fit and, with their matching silver hair fastidiously coifed, seemed remarkably young.

"Lovely," Rhett complimented Kit. "Like a fresh summer's day. And aren't we lucky to have such fine weather? Now do come and mingle."

A yellow marquee sprawled across the lawn with chairs and tables arranged beneath it. Long tables at either end offered wine and beer and plates of delectable munchies. But for those too busy to help themselves, waiters and waitresses in snappy uniforms circulated among the crowd offering the tempting tidbits.

"This is marvellous!" Kit said. And bizarre. She felt as though she had just stepped into a scene from *The Great Gatsby*. Nigel would love this.

The Pughs were pleased. "Yes, isn't it," Cleo said. "So good to see all the neighbours turn out for our little summer's end party. We're off to Europe next week for a month. We have this dear old friend who has a chateau in France, and we always spend a few weeks with him. And then we'll be back for just a week or two before going south for the winter."

"Who looks after the house? Myrtle Skuce?"

"Oh, no, dear! It's one thing to have her come to clean when we're at home, and quite another to leave her in charge," Cleo said meaningfully in a lowered voice. The Skuces were all over the place, but Myrtle and a small brute of a fellow that Kit realized must be the offensive husband, Jack, were sampling the wares at one of the tables.

Rhett said, "One mustn't tempt people to crime. They'd either have the place stripped bare, or else the whole brood of them would take up residence while we gone. That wouldn't do at all. We have a reputable agent from the town and some friends coming to check on the house periodically. Of course, our neighbours," he said, nodding his head in the direction of the commune, "do keep an eye on things, too."

Kit saw them picking their way across the stream, and was somewhat amused to see that they had made an effort to spruce themselves up. Of course she hadn't really expected Nick to be there, but was still disappointed at his absence. She was surprised to see Dianna, looking every inch the fortune-telling gypsy, and remembered guiltily that she had not yet visited her shop.

"I see it's as strange and wonderful as always," Dianna said as the group joined Kit. The Pughs had already wandered off to "mingle". "Excuse me while I shanghai one of those lovely waiters for a glass of wine."

"It's really against my principles to attend functions like this," Leighton admitted. "But I can't resist this one. Perhaps it's because I can see such potential for interesting developments. I mean, just look at the collection of characters. Who couldn't imagine something wonderfully dramatic happening?"

They all looked obediently at the various tableaux. Jean and Duncan McGrath were sitting at a table trying to make conversation with George Bryce, who kept eyeing his empty beer glass, probably wishing it were filled with whiskey. Georgina, with Arnie in tow, was standing shyly with Alan. Mary and Stuart were sipping white wine together, but not communicating. Myrtle and her husband were still sampling the goods - as if they hadn't eaten in days, or else were stocking up for the season. Some of their offspring loitered near the fountain, surreptitiously spraying each other with water when they figured no one was watching. Wayne was standing at the bar, chatting up an obviously disinterested waitress. Bonnie sat cross-legged on the grass with a glass of Coke in her hand, staring off toward the horizon. There were several people Kit had never met - farmers from down the road, a retired couple, and a professional couple who worked in town.

"I see what you mean," Kit said to Leighton. "But surely no one would dare be belligerent or create a scene. The Pughs wouldn't have it."

"Ah, but there's always the possibility. That's what intrigues me."

"Sounds like the stuff of opera to me," Kevin Fenwick teased. "You and Kit should collaborate on it."

"It would have to be a comic opera," Liz said. "Considering the cast."

"'Masters of Their Fetes', you could call it," Pete said to appreciative laughter.

"But I wonder how many of them really are... masters of their fates," Leighton mused.

Mandy said, "The Pughs certainly. I can't see anything daunting them."

"Except maybe the flies," Kit said. "I haven't seen Rhett with either a fly swatter or a can of RAID, but maybe we should get our refreshments before he breaks down and wages war!"

"We really should go mingle anyway," Mandy said.

"Must we?" Leighton said. "Then I need to fortify myself before heading into the fray."

They went to help themselves to drinks and canapés, and then obediently drifted apart.

Kit was waylaid by Myrtle, who grabbed her and practically thrust her into the arms of Jack Skuce. "Here she is, Jack, the lady what owns Moon Hall." To Kit she said, "This here's my husband, Jack."

Kit was grateful that he didn't offer his grimy hand to shake. He was no taller than she, but solidly built, and she sensed suppressed energy in him - the kind that could instantly be unleashed in a violent blow. His taut muscles were not the result of hard physical work, she guessed, but more a byproduct of continual anger.

Kit smiled politely and muttered an appropriate greeting. Jack ogled her assessingly from head to foot - much as Wayne had done the first time she'd seen him. There was something rude and invasive about his scrutiny, and Kit felt her cheeks burn with embarrassment and outrage.

Jack cocked a bushy eyebrow in admiration when he'd finished, and said, "So, yer the one that writes them sexy books, eh?"

"I wouldn't classify them as sexy," Kit retorted.

Myrtle nudged her husband, and whispered fiercely, "Love stories, I told you."

"Them ones that you and Bonnie drool over? Them ones that show women's tits ready to burst outa their dresses? I'd call that purty sexy now." His grin revealed broken and blackened teeth. "Make good money writin' that sorta stuff, do ya?"

"It's a living. Do excuse me, won't you?" Kit said graciously, and escaped with a sigh of relief. Behind her, she heard more fierce whisperings from Myrtle, and a growl in reply. She passed Wayne Skuce quickly, and went to join Alan, Georgina, and Arnie.

For all his bulk, Arnie seemed shrivelled up inside the overlarge suit he wore - undoubtedly one of his father's. He tittered at Kit's presence, and then pulled out the necklace she had given him from beneath his shirt.

"Arnie!" Georgina chided gently. "I said it had to stay out of sight today! You don't want to make Dad angry." To Kit she said, "Dad doesn't like Arnie to wear what he calls 'pansy' jewelry. But Arnie is never without his new possession. He just loves it, Kit!"

"I'm glad."

Alan said, "Hey, that zucchini bread of yours was pretty good, Kit."

"Well you can have more. I'm getting sick of eating zucchini. I've baked and frozen dozens of loaves, and I just don't know what to do with the rest."

"Oh, I could sell it for you at the farmers' market in town," Georgina said. "I go every Saturday morning with my produce."

"I will gladly give you all the zucchini you can handle, Georgina. I'll be happy just to think that it won't be going to waste. If I'm not down in the garden harvesting every day, they grow too large, and if I pick them, they rot in the fridge because I can't eat them all."

"How's the rest of the garden?" Alan asked.

"Just as you predicted," Kit said with a laugh. "Too large for me. Even with the raccoons stealing some, I eat corn on the cob every day, tomatoes at every meal. I've frozen the beans, and at least the potatoes and onions will keep. And it's all so much more tasty than the stuff from the store! But I feel like a pig, stuffing myself with this glut of food, just to keep it from going to waste. Still, I'm rather pleased with my first effort."

While she'd been talking, Kit had noticed Mary pulling on Stuart's arm and gesturing toward them. Sullenly he accompanied his wife. Beaming at them in greeting, Mary said, "Isn't this a lovely party! And what a beautiful dress, Kit! Just everybody's here. Oh, I do find these do-s exciting!"

"Sounds to me like you don't take your wife out enough, Stu," Alan said. Stuart glowered at his brother.

Mary jumped to her husband's defence. "Well, it's not often we get invited to something like this."

"Only once a year, in fact, eh, Mary?" Alan asked. "Not like all those parties you used to go to in the old days."

Mary glanced down at her glass, her face flushed. There was obviously some subtle family argument going on here, something that had started before they had arrived. Mary composed herself, and said brightly, "Aren't we lucky with the weather?"

Georgina had been looking anxiously toward her father, who now had Myrtle and Jack Skuce for company as well. Jack had brought him a couple of beers, which he had downed, and George's voice was beginning to rise above the hum of conversation.

"Perhaps we should take father home," Georgina whispered to Alan. "He had enough to drink before we even got here."

"Sure."

"... God-damn govermint's taxing us outa existence," they could clearly hear George say. "God-damn banks're screwing us with high interest rates. God-damn hippies're stealing my land!" His fist crashed on the table with the impact of a sledgehammer.

There was silence all around as people stopped in mid-sentence. It reminded Kit of that childhood game where everyone would freeze whenever the person who was "it" turned around. Whoever was caught moving was out.

"Look at this," he said, poking his cane into the thick carpet of grass. "Used to be part of my field. And there..." Pointing his cane to the southwest. "... All mine once. Cattle and sheep grazing. Now it all belongs to them!" The cane whirled round, stabbing the air in this direction and that, wherever George spied a "hippie".

A mortified Georgina was trying to coax him to get up. "Leave?" he bellowed. "Dammit, girl, I'll leave when I'm God-damn ready to. It'll be a cold day in hell before I let a God-damn chit of a female tell me what to do!"

Georgina blanched, and Kit felt sorry for her. Standing behind her, Arnie was continually rubbing his hands as though washing them. Alan and the McGraths seemed to be doing their utmost to calm George down, and suggest that it really was time to leave. But Jack Skuce was amused, and goading George into more indiscretions. Myrtle was elbowing her husband and shushing him. She reminded Kit of a squawking old hen flapping around.

The Pughs were stony-faced. Kit's friends appeared unperturbed by the venom aimed at them. In fact, Leighton seemed almost delighted that George had proven him right.

Between them, Alan and Duncan maneuvered George to his feet. He shrugged them off. "I'm not a complete God-damn useless cripple yet!"

Everyone watched his painful and unsteady progress across the yard. Georgina bade hasty farewells to friends and her hosts. Knowing what a shy and sensitive person she was, Kit was certain that Georgina would torment herself with mental replays of her family's disgrace. Kit resolved to visit her tomorrow.

With George's departure there was a general sigh of relief. The Pughs became excessively cheerful, as though they could thus erase the unpleasant scene from the afternoon. In response, people made an effort to assure them that they were having a marvellous time. Everything was in superlatives.

Kit excused herself from Mary and Stuart, after promising to give Mary the zucchini bread recipe. She was heading toward Liz and Kevin when Wayne Skuce intercepted her.

"Interestin' party, eh?"

"Yes, it is." She had intended to move on, but he was determined to detain her.

"I done a bit a work for them 'round here," he said, eyeing the place with a proprietorial air, as if he were responsible for its creation.

"Indeed?" She gave him a weak smile, and turned away, but Wayne put a restraining hand on her arm. The physical contact was an unpleasant jolt.

"Yer in a God-almighty hurry, little lady," Wayne said with a sneer. She realized that he was well on his way to being drunk. "It ain't considered neighbourly to go rushin' off like that."

"I really don't think we have anything to say to one another," Kit said, trying to disengage herself from his grip.

But his fingers tightened, digging painfully into her arm. "I got plenty to say to ya, little lady." His grimace sent shivers through her.

Leighton and Pete suddenly descended upon them and wrested Kit from Wayne's grasp. "Excuse us, Wayne. We just wanted to show Kit something," Leighton said, taking her arm and steering her away. Pete took her other arm, and they escorted her to the edge of the creek. Leighton said, "We'll stay here until he latches on to some other hapless female - God help her. He reminds me of a leach. Slimy creature!"

Kit burst into laughter. "You're priceless, the pair of you! And thank you."

"He's looking daggers at us right now," Pete said. "Oh... he's gone off to prey on another waitress."

"So I'm safe."

"For the time being," Leighton said. "I don't trust that guy."

"Do you know, I'm becoming more paranoid living here than I ever was in the city."

"Your senses are sharpened," Leighton said. "Things seem more intense."

"Or are."

Pete said, "People know each other too well in a small community. The crazies and the nasties can't hide in the anonymity of the crowd as they can in a city. There are lots of Waynes out there. You just can't easily identify them."

"That's not reassuring. But I intend to stay as far away from Wayne Skuce as I can."

The party gradually fizzled out. Kit noticed that Alan never returned, and wondered whether George Bryce proved to be difficult to handle, or whether Alan had just had enough. The rest of the McGraths left early; the Skuces seemed intent upon staying until they'd emptied the last bottle and finished the last shrimp roll.

Kit gladly accepted an invitation to a light supper at the commune. It was a relief to be there among friends, and not to have to go home right away to an empty house. By the time she left the farm, she was convinced that Wayne Skuce would be too drunk to be a threat to anyone but himself.

Still, it was with trepidation that she stepped out from her car. Oliver Twist bounded out of the darkness to greet her, and rubbed luxuriantly against her leg. Feeling suddenly much less alone, she picked up the cat and hastened inside.

Chapter 20

I love Moon Hall in all its moods. But now that spring is truly upon us, I feel invigorated to go ahead with my plans for a new garden. Jeremiah hates it, of course, but I am determined to make myself a "secret" garden down near the ravine.

I found the most marvellous statue when Lily and I went shopping in Montreal last month. It is a horned and cloven-footed, half-naked Pan, leaning against the trunk of a tree and playing his flute. He seems so cocksure, so sensual, and so pagan. Once I had purchased him, I decided that I needed a stone bench where I could sit and contemplate that intriguing fellow. These heavy objects should be arriving in a week or two, so I want all in readiness.

I told Jeremiah that we must have a flagstone path meandering through the perennial borders down to the secret garden.

"Well, it won't be much of a secret then, will it?" he mumbled.

"The idea is to tempt someone to follow the path, to find out where it leads," I replied. "And then to be pleasantly surprised to discover this shady nook beside the creek."

"You won't get no flowers growing there," he announced smugly.

"A few shade-loving plants - ferns, hostas, trilliums and other wildflowers. It's supposed to look natural, not formal."

"Foolishness!" he grumbled, undoubtedly thinking of the extra work this would cause him.

"We'll hire some strong lads to help out with the laying of the path, the clearing and levelling and so on. But you'll have to supervise them and mind they do it properly and just the way I want it."

He was somewhat mollified. I showed him where I wanted the new garden. There is a spot just before the ground drops sharply into the ravine, which can most easily be levelled. A few saplings will have to be cut down, and I want some evergreens planted to give additional screening, especially in winter, for I think the area could look just as lovely in the starkness of that season, with its backdrop of bare, black branches and soft, pristine snow.

I told Jeremiah we could hire his son, Josiah, who still doesn't have a steady job (although he did a lot of work helping to build the Skuce's pretty new house), and a couple of reliable boys from the village.

We were just tramping back from the ravine when Hugh came by with our order of milk and eggs.

How my spirits lift to see him! Usually one of his younger brothers brings our order, so I hadn't seen Hugh much all winter. Even when I visit Kate and Ruth, I might only catch a glimpse of him, for he is always busy, and now I hesitate to visit him in the barn as I so blithely used to.

He seemed glad to see me, though surprised at my outfit. "New fashion?" he asked, raising an eyebrow.

I have taken to wearing my riding breeches around the house, especially when I am working in the garden (or riding, of course). That is, without that ridiculous skirt over top! It is so much more comfortable and much less restrictive - and lighter! - than wide and sweeping gowns. I can understand why men wear trousers! But why shouldn't I have the freedom to choose comfort over style? And so I do, though I'm not yet so eccentric that I can't be forced into a dress most of the time!

Mrs. Skuce is quite scandalized, of course, though probably not surprised.

But I feel so free and unencumbered, striding around my estate in my breeches. What luxury! To Hugh I said, "I think it should be a new fashion. I don't think women can have any sense of equality with men until they can show that they have legs as well."

He laughed. "It seems to me that you are not plotting equality, but distraction. Seduction even."

"Nonsense! I have two legs, just as you have. What is so seductive about that?"

"Yours are more shapely than mine."

"Ha! You can tell that from these baggy trousers? I think it more likely that you men would see trousered women as a threat. We might start demanding other rights and equalities, too."

"I'm sure you will, Violet," he replied with a grin.

We had been strolling toward the house as we talked, and had reached the veranda. I said, "Will you come in for a cup of tea?"

"I won't come inside like this," he said, referring to his dirty work clothes.

"Then we'll have it out here on the porch," I decided. I asked Mrs. Skuce to bring out the tea, and so we sat side-by-side on the steps in the late afternoon sunshine. Tristan lay down on the porch behind us, his head poked in between us as if he were chaperoning, I thought with a chuckle. I told Hugh about my plans for the secret garden, and he agreed it would be a lovely spot.

"Gracious me! Look at the pair of you, sitting on the steps like a couple of urchins! As if we hadn't a chair for visitors to sit on!" Mrs. Skuce scolded as she brought out a tray.

"We're fine here, Mrs. Skuce," Hugh said. "Don't bother yourself now, for I don't intend to budge until I've had my tea, thanks all the same."

I took my cup and leaned against the veranda post so that I could see Hugh more clearly. It seemed to me he had something on his mind, but hadn't decided the time was right to speak it.

Mrs. Skuce brought out a bowl of potatoes, sat herself in her favourite rocking chair, and began peeling them. So now I had two chaperones!

We talked of Kate's impending wedding, for which I could feel no great joy, though I didn't let Hugh know that. And finally Hugh said, "We're going to have a baby, Ruth and I. And we were hoping you would be the Godmother, Violet."

I had been expecting that to happen almost since the day they were married, but it still came as a shock. It was such undeniable proof of their physical intimacy. I tried to sound delighted as I said, "Of course I shall! I'm honoured that you've asked me." But I couldn't help thinking that it could be me having Hugh's child, had things been different.

And yet, I no longer feel that same desperate heartache that I had once thought would never leave me. I feel a softer, gentler kind of affection for Hugh now. Now that Daniel has become my heart's desire.

I squeezed Hugh's hand as I smiled. Sincerely I said, "I am so happy for you! When is the baby due?"

"November."

"Ruth must be thrilled." As Hugh was, I could see.

"She is that. Already knitting the baby's wardrobe and planning to redecorate Kate's room as the nursery." He rose, having finished his tea and his errand.

"Give her my best, and tell her we'll get together soon for some sketching."

"I'll do that."

When he had gone down the road, Mrs. Skuce said, "I'm not sure Ruth's the best wife for Hugh."

"Why's that?" I asked in surprise. "He seems happy enough to me."

"Gives herself airs, she does, cause her father's a big landowner - but a farmer for all that - and she went to that Ladies Academy of yours. She's always been spoilt, used to getting her own way. Mind you, a baby will bring her back down to earth."

I always thought that Ruth's indulged and willful girlishness was what had charmed so many suitors, including Hugh. She liked to think of herself as an animated Dresden figurine - something precious and fragile and beautiful. But she was saved from shallowness by possessing intelligence and humour. So I just said to Mrs. Skuce, "I'm sure you're right. Once Kate is gone and the baby's here, Ruth will have little time to herself anyway."

I knew that wasn't what she had meant, but gave her no chance to protest for I announced that I had to get back to work in the garden.

How I love the long, late evenings when the sun is reluctant to set and the sky gradually fades from brilliant, lingering sunsets to shades of ever-deepening blue. I'm sitting at my desk, Tristan stretched out on the floor beside me as always, and I have decided that the Refuge gets along very well without me. So I intend to stay put for a few weeks at least, until I have completed my special garden. There are times, like now, when I have no wish to leave my beloved Moon Hall.

And I think it best not to see Daniel too often. I need to toughen my vulnerable heart.

June 22, 1873:

Kate was married yesterday. It was a lovely wedding, and the reception in the church hall in the evening was great fun. I even danced several times with Hugh, and realized I had none of those melting feelings in his arms that I had when I was in Daniel's. But I enjoyed myself nonetheless!

Heather, Gordon, Lily, and Augustus came as well, and stayed for the weekend, so Moon Hall has been quite lively for the past three days.

Mrs. Skuce was just beaming when she prepared breakfast this morning. She helped Betsy bring the many dishes into the dining room, which is rarely used these days, and said, "My, but it's good to have you girls home again! Miss Violet has the appetite of a bird and is no great challenge to cook for!"

Now they have all gone home and the place is silent once more. And I have to agree that their presence made it seem like Christmas.

I've resolved to have a yearly midsummer party, inviting my other sisters and their spouses as well. Though, truth to tell, their presence might put a damper on things. Rose would be critical, Iris, aloof, Daisy, silly, and Hazel, contemptuous. But perhaps they wouldn't choose to come anyway. I'd invite the McGraths and Kate, of course, and maybe a few others. Daniel, even. I'll have strings of Chinese lanterns throughout the gardens and.... Yes, I think I'd like to do that.

Everyone was impressed with my secret garden. Lily, who was with me when I purchased the pieces, was particularly interested in where I had placed them. She must have been skeptical, for she admitted that Pan seemed to belong in the wooded ravine. Mrs. Skuce thinks he is obscene and devilish in his half-man, half-goat nakedness.

I love to sit in that sylvan setting, especially early in the morning, with a mist hovering over the creek, or late in the evening, with the sun's fiery palette painting the sky. Pan seems to me to have just climbed out of the ravine and be heralding nightfall with his music. Silhouetted against the dying day, he strikes a primitive chord, conjuring up images of satyrs and nymphs and other pagan gods about to emerge for some nighttime revelry.

Only the mosquitoes destroy the romance of the place, so a douse in lavender water or some stronger, smellier stuff is called for!

The Blakes, Forresters, and I have agreed to rent a summerhouse in St. Andrews-by-the-Sea for the month of July. What fun that will be! First we had discussed spending a week or two with Iris at Seabreeze and then another week or two with Rose at her new cottage at Tadoussac. (That is where the Dufferins have also built a summerhome!) But then we decided that we intended to have fun instead, so a large cottage at St. Andrews was agreed upon.

Of course, I shall miss Moon Hall, but it can get impossibly hot here in July, and I do like the seaside. Betsy will go home to her family for three weeks, and the Skuces will have more time to enjoy their new home, although Jeremiah will still tend the gardens. He gets his break in the winter, when there is only wood to chop and fires to replenish.

The Fortnightly Club doesn't meet in the summer, when everyone is busy or away.

The Refuge will not miss me. Things are well in hand there. Marjorie and Lise persuaded me to hire Nancy Kelly, who proves to be a hard and dedicated worker. There is more than enough work to keep the three of them busy, they assured me, and so I agreed. That way, each will have a bit more time off, and certainly a break for well-deserved holidays. Anyway, the better weather has brought a decline in our popularity, so we breathe a little easier for the moment.

Daniel is going to Montreal for part of his holiday, and mentioned that the Grangers have invited him and his family to their summer home in the Laurentians. I shall not speculate on that!

Ottawa is pretty well dead in the summer heat. Those who can't afford to go away, close their shutters, pretending that they are away, and live in their back gardens!

Tristan and I walked once more to the secret garden, which seems even more mysterious in the moonlit darkness. Silvery strands of light slip through the leafy canopy, striking odd shadows as they slither to the ground. The mosquitoes are mostly gone for the night. Crickets chatter; nighthawks lament. Pan stands poised, as if waiting for us to leave.

Undoubtedly he and his cohorts will frolic in the ravine on sultry summer nights, glad of our absence.

Chapter 21

The kitchen door stood open, and the late summer evening sifted in through the screen door. Kit saw Georgina sitting at the scrubbed table, bent in concentration over some papers. When Kit knocked, Georgina quickly scooped them into a pile before turning toward the door.

"Oh, Kit. Come in."

"I didn't mean to disturb you."

"No, no. I wasn't doing anything important." Georgina's face twitched into and out of a smile.

"Ah, travel brochures!" Kit said, noticing them despite Georgina's efforts to conceal them. "Planning a trip?"

Georgina slumped back into her chair, resigned to share her guilty secret. "I'm forever planning a trip - in my mind. Do sit down, Kit. I guess this is the closest I'll ever get to Scotland, France, Italy." She picked up the glossy booklets with their enticing photos of misty castles, medieval towns, and Riviera beaches, and let them slide back onto the pile on the table. "I have such dreams."

"You should go," Kit said with compassion. "You should do something for yourself."

Georgina shook her head wearily. "I can't leave them for a day, let alone a few weeks. Sometimes I wonder why I bother - put them both in a home and go away, that's what I tell myself. But I couldn't. Besides, we don't have the money for travel." She laughed. "And I'd be hopeless on my own. I probably wouldn't leave my hotel room - I'd be too scared." Briskly she added, "But there's no harm in dreaming. And maybe one day...." She let the sentence drift off into the imagination.

Kit finished the thought in her own mind - that one day Georgina and her husband, undoubtedly Alan, would explore and enjoy the wonders of the old world, a world so alien to this rural backwater that even Kit could hardly believe it truly existed.

Georgina was no more liberated than Violet had been, Kit thought with surprise. Until her father had died.

"I haven't quite finished my chores, as you can see," Georgina said, indicating her mucky overalls. "Just taking a break."

"Well I won't keep you then. I was just wondering how things were today."

"Yes. After yesterday. I try not to let it bother me anymore. I can't bear to always feel guilt and shame for his disgraceful behaviour. But it's hard not to. Otherwise, the day's no different from any other. Thanks for your concern." She smiled. "I'm off to the barn. Come along for a chat, if you like."

Kit knew she was only being polite. "Thanks, but I'd best get home and do some work. I'll bring you a trunkful of zucchini on Friday. My contribution, meager though it is, to your travel fund. Bye!"

In the yard, Kit waved to Arnie who was coming from the direction of the creek. He raised a paw in salute and gurgled happily. Kit walked home along the gravel road.

She felt curiously restless that evening. She couldn't settle down to work on any of her books, nor to reading. Nick kept intruding into her thoughts. What was he doing tonight? Did he ever think of her? Or had his latest girlfriend banished any attraction he might have had for Kit? And why the hell did she care anyway? She wasn't in love with him!

Or was she just denying the obvious, as Violet had?

She turned on the late news, only to be confronted by Christine Flint as fill-in anchor woman. Kit tried to view her with detachment, but had to admit that she thoroughly disliked the girl. Because of Nick? Probably. Was he watching her now, admiring her cool competence, wishing she were already at home with him? And while she, Kit, didn't even know what "home" was to Nick, Christine was privy to his daily life, to all his endearing or irritating habits. Just as Kit had once been with Nigel.

Oh, damn all men to hell! Angrily she flicked off the TV, and felt better for having banished Christine from her home at least.

She picked up Violet's diary and again stepped back into a different world. Far from the romanticized ideal she had envisioned when she had first come here, she thought wryly.

She worked well into the night making notes of what she needed to research in order to write a fictionalized account of Violet's life. And of those other Victorian women in her circle - people like Kate and Ruth and Marjorie, and Violet's sisters, of course.

Jean McGrath called her the next morning. "Kit, I've been asking around about a picture of Violet, and I've discovered that Violet's great-niece is still living in Kintyre. She might very well have something for you."

Kit jotted down the name and address in excitement. Here was another tangible link with the past.

She telephoned Helen Talbot, who agreed to meet her at three that afternoon. So that gave her lots of time to get to the library in Kintyre where she could start her research.

Kit was astonished to discover an annotated reprint of Lady Dufferin's Canadian Journal, which gave details of her life as the Governor-General's wife. Just skimming through it, Kit could see that it would give her a different perspective on events. Here, for instance, was an account of the skating party at Rideau Hall that Violet had described!

But the library carried no books about syphilis. She would go to Ottawa soon and look for those in the National Library.

Realizing that she still had a couple of hours to kill, Kit decided this was a good opportunity to visit Dianna Webb's shop.

It was called Cobwebbs, and was located in a lovely old downtown building with an arcaded Victorian storefront. Several landscapes were displayed in the window, along with quilted crafts, lacy potpourris, and stained glass sun-catchers. The country atmosphere - the posh kind that Laura Ashley had helped popularize - was the dominant theme inside the shop as well. Here there were granny print tea cozies with matching placemats and tablecloths and frilly aprons, scented candles (hand-dipped), designer pottery, wood and soap-stone sculptures - in fact, any kind of expensive, hand-crafted item anyone could wish to give as a gift. And of course there were paintings - every inch of wall space was covered with one.

Dianna was serving a customer, so Kit browsed. She discovered it almost immediately. It seemed to jump off the wall, or call to her, or something equally bizarre. She examined it more closely. Yes, there was the violet in the corner. And there was Pan, the God that had frolicked in Violet's secret garden.

Kit took the painting down. It had obviously been recently reframed. "Where did you find this?" she asked as Dianna joined her.

"At a local auction. Good, isn't it? Is it by your ghost? I figured that was what the violet meant, since there was no signature."

"Yes, that was her trademark."

"She was quite a painter. Too bad that talented women weren't taken seriously in those days. With some formal training, she might have been a great artist."

"Well, I shall certainly take this for a start," Kit said, trying to contain her excitement. "I read about this, you know, and tried to imagine it. But it's almost eerie to see what the garden actually looked like."

"Especially through her eyes."

"Yes, you're right," Kit said, grateful that Dianna understood. "Have you come across any of her other paintings?"

"Only one so far. It's of Moon Hall. I kept it myself. I'll show you some time."

"Great!"

Kit continued to look around, surprised to see that several of the paintings were Dianna's - and that they were extremely good. There was one from the perspective of a farmhouse veranda, with an empty rocking chair looming large in the foreground, the ragged gingerbread of the veranda roofline framing the picture, and the distant barn and autumn fields being the focal point. All her paintings were of rustic scenes. And all her paintings had a cobweb somewhere.

"Is that your trademark?" Kit asked, pointing to a cobweb in the veranda corner.

"Sure. With a name like mine, why not?"

"Well, I'm impressed, and not just with the cobwebs."

"Don't sound so surprised."

"Did I? Sorry. It's just that I hadn't expected you to paint such pastoral scenes." Yet, why not? Hadn't Dianna spent years on the farm. She must have an appreciation of country life.

"Expecting indecipherable blobs? I do love the countryside, you know."

"I can see that. I'll take these two paintings as well," Kit said, choosing the veranda one, and another depicting an isolated stone farmhouse with a background of stormy sky. The cobweb here was strung between two foreground milkweed pods, caught in the last ray of sunshine. Kit also chose half a dozen items such as a tea cozy and candles.

"Well, you're my best customer so far today!"

"Business good, is it?"

"Oh yes. At this rate I'll have paid off the loan that the commune gave me by Christmas. I'm sure you were wondering how I managed this," Dianna said astutely.

Kit laughed. "I won't deny my curiosity."

"They bought out my share of the farm - using some obscure formula that Drew developed - and then they loaned me the rest. I've always wanted to have a shop like this."

Kit thought it suited her well. Today she was dressed in a patchwork print skirt and vest with a lace-edged white blouse - costly country chic. While she was wrapping Kit's purchases, she continued. "You don't know what a thrill it is for me to have made a success of this - on my own - after all those years of communal living and sharing. And, of course, we all know that Drew and Mandy are running the show, which is pretty hard to take at times." She looked to see Kit's reaction.

"Surely it's more..."

"Democratic?" Dianna interrupted. "Oh, sure, it started out that way. But Drew is a strong personality and doesn't like to be thwarted. He's convinced that his way is always the best. And we never forget that Drew financed the venture. He would have made a good lawyer - has great powers of persuasion. People have voted his way only to kick themselves afterwards for not sticking to their own inclinations.

"And Mandy relishes her role as the clucking mother hen, or Mother Superior, depending upon what is called for. Her attempts at peace keeping are more an exercise of power than a good-hearted gesture.

"It's not surprising that so many of us have left. But I can't deny that Drew has managed to make an enormous success of the farm - with our labour, of course, and that's why we're all entitled to a share.

"I'm not telling you this out of spite, Kit. For all their blemishes, they're still my friends. But I don't like to see what they're doing to Pete - ignoring his problems, allowing him to go on destroying himself. He should leave, but he hasn't the courage.

"That's one of the problems with that place - it insulates you from the real world. It's hard to climb out of that cocoon. People like Leighton and Kevin never will. They like to be coddled and protected and left to do their own thing, with no decisions to make and few responsibilities.

"Anyway, this is my reward," she said, a sweep of the arms indicating everything around her. "I've signed a lease for the apartment upstairs, and move in next week."

"Must be a spacious apartment," Kit said, gauging the size of the shop.

"It's marvellous - one of those huge Victorian flats with a fireplace in nearly every room. The merchants who built these places often lived above their shops with their large families. You'll have to come and visit."

"Yes, I will." Although she thought her judgments a bit harsh, Kit had been astonished by Dianna's forthright manner in discussing her friends - as if she had readily accepted Kit into that circle of intimates. "Have you had lunch?"

"No. It's my assistant's day off, so I usually just order in a sub or something. Care to join me?"

"Sure."

Kit picked up a small pizza from a nearby restaurant, and they sat in the sunny back room that had been outfitted with a table and chairs, a small fridge, and a microwave.

"I eat here a lot," Dianna explained. "Junk food mostly, but I love it. I do have to get back to the farm every once in a while just to get a good meal."

"I miss pizzas," Kit admitted. "And it's not often I feel like driving into town just to get one. I don't suppose Todmorden is ready for a pizza parlour?"

"Anytime you want to share a pizza, just come and see me. And next time we'll get a larger one. Neither one of us needs to be on a diet!"

They had a pleasant chat over their meal, and Kit promised to visit again soon.

Kit arrived just before 3:00 o'clock at the Talbots'. The house was astonishing - an enormous Queen Anne mansion with a tower and broad verandas sweeping into bandshell corners. It was set back on a large treed lot on a street of many such oversized properties. Plate glass windows were framed in elaborate stained glass so that the front hall - the size of a living room - was bathed in cranberry and sapphire and amber light. Surrounded by antique furnishings, Kit felt as though she had stepped back into the past.

But Helen Talbot herself dispelled that fanciful notion. Dressed in a youthful fuschia pantsuit which showed her athletic figure to advantage, her white hair stylishly cropped, her skin darkly tanned, she didn't look in the least Victorian. Nor her age, Kit thought, for surely she must be at least seventy.

She led Kit into a delightful drawing room whose wall of French windows gave onto the veranda. "What a beautiful place you have here," Kit said.

"Ah, yes. We love it. It's been home for almost half a century. So... you're living in Moon Hall?"

"Yes. And I'm charmed by it. You must think it rather odd to have a stranger prying into your family history, Mrs. Talbot, but I've become rather fascinated with your great-aunt, Violet. She sounds like a most interesting person."

"You mentioned you were doing research?"

"Yes, for a book set in Victorian times. It helps me to visualize things when I know more about real people who lived then." Kit had determined not to reveal the existence of the diary. She felt that Helen Talbot might well have a legitimate claim to it, and might object to Kit's using any of Violet's story in a book. After all, it exposed quite a family skeleton. One that no one else even knew existed.

"Are you a published author, Miss Spencer?"

"Yes, as a matter of fact, I've had seven books published - all quite successful. But they were set in 19th century England. I thought it was time to write a Canadian novel."

"I'm quite a voracious reader. A vice of mine, I'm afraid. I can't resist buying paperbacks. Historical fiction are among my favourites, but I'm certain I have nothing by you," Helen Talbot challenged.

"I write under a pseudonym - Victoria Penn."

Helen Talbot looked surprised. "Heavens! I've read every one of your books, and enjoyed them enormously. Well, well... this is a treat! You'll have to autograph your books for me before you leave."

"With pleasure.... So your grandmother was Violet's sister?" Kit tried not to inadvertently reveal what she already knew about the family.

"Yes, Heather, who married Gordon Forrester, the local doctor. My father was their second child, Jonathan, who also became a doctor, in partnership with his father."

"Do any of your family still live in your grandparents' house?"

"My younger brother bought the house from my grandmother's estate. I was already living here, and had no intention of moving, but I was glad that the house stayed in the family."

Kit, feeling that she needed to see it, managed to discover where it was.

"Of course, I've heard what happened to Violet..." she said, trying to lead the conversation.

"Yes, poor thing. They say she suffered some sort of brain storm. Of course, as children we were fascinated by her. It's not everyone who can claim such a gruesome story in their family history. But my grandmother was very fond of her sister Violet. She told me that Violet had been a bit daring and outrageous, but was a sensitive, caring person, much too good for this world. She said that Violet couldn't cope with all the tragedy and disappointments in her life. I think Grandmother always regretted that she hadn't been able to help her sister more, insisted she live with them or something. She thought that the loneliness of Moon Hall had contributed to Violet's unhappiness."

Would it make any difference if Helen Talbot knew the truth? Surely it was Heather who should have been told. And Violet had chosen not to. "Do you have any family photos?" Kit asked.

"As a matter of fact, I do. My grandmother knew that I was interested in the family history, so she left all her photographs to me. I'll go and get them. Would you like a cup of tea, dear?"

"That would be lovely, thank you."

Mrs. Talbot opened double mahogany doors that led into a library. Instead of glimpsing the rows of leather-bound volumes that she had expected, Kit saw an entire wall of paperbacks. How delightful!

Helen Talbot returned with a couple of very old albums. "You start looking through these while I make the tea."

Kit was grateful to be left alone with the pictures. There were many of family groups that were undoubtedly Heather and Gordon and their increasing number of children - photos of summer picnics on an expanse of lawn behind what must have been the Forrester house, and ones of summer holidays by the sea. St. Andrew's? Kit could see the children growing up, and as photography became easier, there were more and more informal snaps of family events and individuals.

Kit found her in the second album. For surely that was Violet. It was a studio portrait as large as the page, with an Ottawa photographer's stamp in the corner. The young woman gazed directly, challengingly at the camera as if defying it to capture her true essence. There was a hint of a mischievous smile on her face and in her bright and knowing eyes. She was what might have been termed "handsome" in those days - no great beauty, but with pleasing features that gave her an almost aristocratic dignity. And there was an arresting quality about her.

Kit could imagine this feisty young woman as the author of the diary, and stared back at the face with admiration and pity.

There was a great resemblance between Violet and Heather, although the latter had softer features and gazed more reticently into the camera. And there were other family groups. That one was surely Iris, for she was indeed a beauty, and yet, recognizably Violet's sibling. And that rather haughty matron must be Rose! And that charming couple could only be Lily and Augustus sitting on the veranda of their Sandy Hill home. Kit could almost recognize them all from Violet's descriptions.

She studied the pictures intently, looking for clues to personalities, absorbing the atmosphere, memorizing the settings and clothes. And she felt like a child that had discovered a treasure.

When Helen Talbot brought in the tea, she sat down beside Kit and began to explain the pictures, sometimes taking one out to check the facts on the back. She herself was enjoying showing off these old photos. And during it all, Kit kept asking questions, trying to ferret out what happened to the key players in Violet's story.

"My grandmother died in 1946. She was ninety-five, and hale and hearty until the last week of her life. She'd been married for sixty-six years and widowed for ten, and she'd had seven children - two of whom died of scarlet fever. But Grandmother had outlived all her siblings.

"... Lily and Augustus's son, Albert, became quite an influential lawyer and politician. They said he would have made an excellent Prime Minister. I remember him as always being very rational and level-headed and disciplined. And intimidatingly intelligent, although very kind to us lesser mortals.

"... Well, of course, the Thorndikes are cousins, but we never did see them much and have rather lost touch over the years. They're so terribly wealthy, aren't they?

"... Rosecliff was torn down to make way for the Supreme Court building. But Rose and Edwin were long gone by then. After Edwin's retirement from the government, they moved to Quebec City, and died there not many years later. One of their married children had stayed in Ottawa, one ended up in Montreal, another, in Victoria, B.C., and the others, in Quebec. But, you know, once my grandmother was dead, we didn't keep up family connections so much anymore. My Aunt Emily was the last one of us to make an effort to write to everyone at Christmas and try to host family reunions. Things fizzled out with the younger generations. I suppose it's rather sad, really. And yet, mostly we don't have much in common, except for some diluted genes."

Kit could see a resemblance between Helen Talbot and her grandmother and, thus, Violet. She said, "Would you mind if I had a copy made of Violet's portrait? I'd like to hang it in Moon Hall."

"Oh, I think we could arrange that."

"Thank you. I thought it would look right next to Violet's painting, which I discovered today."

"Did you indeed? Now I have several of Violet's paintings. Let me show you."

They were hanging in the library. There was one of Moon Hall, looking much as Kit imagined it would have in those days, with its lovely gardens and luscious orchard. Another was of the McAllister Mill with the tumbling falls and rapids in the foreground. The third was of men haying in the field beyond the ravine, similar to the one that hung in the McGraths' living room. Violet must have painted many of her favourite scenes over and over again, no doubt perfecting them as she experimented with colour and technique. Certainly the McGraths' was superior to this one.

Kit autographed all seven of her novels for Helen Talbot, then thanked her most sincerely for her hospitality.

"It was my pleasure, dear. There aren't many young people these days who are interested in the past, and willing to listen to an old woman's reminiscences. You really must let me know if there is any other way I can help you. I'll give you a call when I've had the photo reproduced."

On the way out of town, Kit drove past the old Forrester home, stopping outside it to get a good look. It was a large stone house in ample grounds, well maintained and relatively private, despite the encroachment of the commercial sector of the town.

Driving back to Moon Hall, Kit wondered if she would ever show Violet's diary to anyone else. Helen Talbot and her relatives might not appreciate knowing the truth. Neither would the McGraths, she was certain. Perhaps the actual story was best left buried.

Chapter 22

October 31, 1873:

Thank goodness I can write again, dear diary! And soon I shall try my hand at sketching and painting as well.

Before I explain, I must record that there is a virtual epidemic of babies to be born next spring, and I am to be Godmother to them all! Most exciting is that Lily is finally pregnant. She is ecstatic! Heather is expecting her second child, also in April. I suspect there must have been something in the sea air at St. Andrew's!

Kate is expecting in May, she informed me with quiet pleasure. She seems quite content, and who is to say that Angus isn't a most wonderful lover in private?

And now to explain.

It was one of those unnaturally, uncomfortably hot days in mid September, when autumn's cooling breath would have been more welcome. I was at the Refuge, the sleeves of my shirtwaist rolled up to my elbows as I was helping Marjorie with the baking. She makes the most scrumptious scones and Eccles cakes, which we regularly supply to several restaurants and tea rooms - an even more lucrative venture than our laundry service.

So we were all of us busily engaged, either in the kitchen or the washhouse.

Suddenly a man burst in through the front door. He was a large, brutish fellow, quite drunk, judging by his stagger, but with a most dangerous gleam in his eyes.

The woman beside me shrieked. She had come to us just the day before, her face badly bruised and cut from a beating by her husband. Obviously this man, for as he approached, she shrank back, whimpering.

"You stupid bitch!" he hissed. "Thought you could run away from me, did you?"

We'd all been too stunned by his precipitous arrival to do more than stare open-mouthed at him. Now I dusted the flour from my hands and stepped in front of him. Boldly, but with knots in my stomach, I said to him, "You're not welcome here, man. Go home and sober yourself up."

"Get outa my way, you snooty bitch," he growled. "I'm here to fetch back my wife!"

"I'm afraid not," I replied defiantly, maneuvering to block his way. "Your wife is under our protection, and has no wish to see you. Leave now or I will summon the police."

"Fuckin' hell!" he roared, shoving me aside so hard that I crashed against the table.

Then all hell seemed to break loose. He grabbed his wife who screamed that he would surely murder her. I tried to pull him off. Tristan was at my side, showing his fangs and growling threateningly - a frightening enough sound to raise the hackles of even a large and powerful man like that. But the bully was intent on his purpose, ignoring Tristan's warning.

As he viciously dragged his screaming wife toward the door, I tugged at him and even began kicking him. Cursing, he suddenly threw his wife to the floor and spun around to attack me. Tristan jumped at the brute, deflecting a blow that nevertheless caught me on the arm. My faithful dog fastened his large teeth on the man's wrist before the brute could strike again, causing him to drop the bloody knife in his hand with a howl of pain. And at the same time, Nancy Kelly struck him a resounding blow on the back of the head with a cast iron frying pan. He crumpled to the ground. Tristan stood over him, still growling.

"Make sure he stays down there," I said to Nancy. "Hit him again if necessary. Lise, would you fetch a police constable?"

"I'll fetch the doctor," one of women said, and dashed out the door.

"Doctor?" I queried. The others, I noticed, were all staring at me in horror.

Marjorie was at my side, offering me support.

I had been holding my right arm, instinctively, though it felt numbed by the blow. Now I looked down to see blood seeping between my fingers and trickling down my rolled-up sleeve. I have to admit I almost collapsed from the shock of seeing so much blood. I hadn't realized that the ruffian had slashed me with his knife.

Nancy handed the frying pan to someone else, and helped Marjorie escort me into the Matrons' sitting room, where they placed me on the couch. Marjorie fetched a roll of bandage, and wrapped it tightly about my wound, which I didn't dare examine. Then she made me drink a cup of very sweet tea.

"I dare say you're in shock," she told me, as she put a blanket over me, although I could hardly imagine why I needed one on such a sweltering day.

Tristan laid his large head on my lap, as if seeking reassurance. I stroked his head, telling him what a good boy he was. And truly, he might well have saved my life. I felt quite light-headed, afraid I would faint.

Through the window I could see the mesmerizing lines of laundry strung across our back yard, fluttering whitely against the blue sky.

The numbness was wearing off, and the pain was making me perspire.

Marjorie didn't tell me I'd been foolish to intervene and Daniel didn't comment either - bless him! - when he arrived. He looked at me gravely and asked me how I felt as he checked my pulse and listened to my heart.

"Giddy," I replied.

"I'm not surprised."

He unwrapped the bloody bandage carefully, which made the wound throb even more. I tried not to complain, but couldn't help wincing at times, as Daniel cut away my sleeve and examined the wound.

"It's quite deep. I want to clean it out before I stitch it," he said. "So I'm going to give you an anesthetic to put you to sleep for a little while. That way you won't feel anything." He smiled at me encouragingly and said, "You'll be fine."

"I'm sure you say that to all your patients," I quipped.

"Only when it's true," he replied. But his words seemed to belie his concern. It was only much later, when I was truly on the mend, that I discovered he had been worried about blood poisoning, erysipelas, gangrene, and tetanus.

"This chloroform will make you feel rather strange," he explained as he sprinkled some on a handkerchief and held it over my face.

When I regained consciousness, a clean, white bandage was snugly wrapped about my arm. I felt decidedly odd, as if I'd drunk far too much champagne, but in little pain as yet. Daniel scooped me into his arms and carried me out to a waiting carriage, which took us to Lily's.

"I've already sent word to your sister, so that she won't be so shocked upon seeing you like this," Daniel said. "Though I expect you'll have some explaining to do, once you're up to it."

"Have the police come....to take that fellow away?"

"They have. Marjorie told me what happened. Thank goodness for Tristan!"

"Yes. He's the best present I've ever had. I love him dearly.... At least that woman will now be safe from that brute of a husband. I couldn't just let him attack her like that. Drag her away. Did you see her face? He would have killed her," I was rambling on, my head resting on Daniel's shoulder.

He stroked my cheek in a most tender and affectionate gesture as he said, "I can't imagine you acting any other way, Violet. You were very brave. I recall you have a penchant for tackling bullies," he added, reminding me of our first meeting.

When we arrived at the Blakes' house, Daniel carried me up to my bedroom. I was still woozy and heard them talking through a sort of haze as they made me comfortable. Then I slept.

The pain was quite terrible for days, but Daniel had left me some chlorodyne to ease it. When he came to see me the following day, he brought a large bouquet of red roses, saying, "I thought these would cheer you up."

"They're beautiful! Do you do this for all your patients, Dr. Haywood?"

"Only the special ones," he replied with a smile.

Daniel has a very gentle touch, which nonetheless, couldn't prevent tears springing to my eyes as he changed my bloodied bandage.

"One day, we'll discover how to make bandages that don't stick," he said. "The wound looks good. No signs of infection. But you lost quite a lot of blood, so I want you to rest in bed for a couple of weeks."

"Don't worry! I have no intention of springing from my sickbed just yet." I did feel inordinately tired and found myself drifting off to sleep so easily. Perhaps from the effects of the medicine as well.

He cleaned the wound and the area around it with a strong smelling liquid which he called carbolic. Then he soaked a gauze pad with it, which he placed over the stitches, and rewrapped my arm.

"Your a model patient," he replied. "Wish I could say that of all of them!"

I felt quite pampered as Daniel came to see me daily to change my dressing, and often stayed for a brief chat as well.

One day I received a large bouquet of hothouse flowers with a note from Lady Dufferin! She wrote that she had read about my dreadful mishap in the paper, praised me for my courage, and said that she thought I might be cheered by these flowers from her conservatory. And she hoped I would be well enough to visit her again soon.

Rose was quite envious!

As soon as my arm began to pain me less, I was impatient to be out of bed. At first I managed only to get as far as the sitting room, where I sat and gazed out the window, realizing I was missing my beloved autumn at Moon Hall. How I would have liked to savour my secret garden, ablaze now with sensuous colours and fragrant with heady smells!

I was much happier when I could walk outside again, even though my arm was still in a sling. Daniel accompanied me and Tristan sometimes, as we wandered along the banks of the Rideau River, which runs quite close to the Blakes' house.

"I think you must be an exceptional doctor, Daniel," I said to him one such day. "Gordon told me I was lucky that I didn't develop an infection from the wound. He says it must have been the way you treated it." He'd also told me - when he and Heather had come to visit me - that I could have lost my arm, if not my life, were it not for Daniel's skill!

"I believe, as M. Pasteur and Dr. Lister do, in the germ theory. It's quite amazing what the use of antiseptic can do to prevent wounds from festering."

"Don't all doctors use it?"

"Would that they did! Any number of lives would be saved. But too many are reluctant to embrace new ideas, especially about poisonous, invisible organisms floating in the air around us."

"But surely not if the methods have been proven to work!"

"Even then. I'm doing some research into bacteriology and antisepsis myself. Oh, nothing too significant, but the topic fascinates me."

"Well, you'll have to tell Gordon, for he is most impressed, and wouldn't be if he knew about it himself!"

Daniel laughed. "I'll make a point of it."

Dear diary, how can I explain what even deeper feelings for Daniel grew in me then! Do I see him as my hero? Perhaps. Certainly I recognize in him a great skill and genuine caring for others, which I celebrate and admire. To have such a man as a friend is a privilege. To have him as a husband would be ecstasy.

And yet, we have our disagreements. At the October Board of Governors meeting, Daniel insisted that some sort of security be arranged for the Refuge.

"We'll hire a man. He can help out about the place and be there in case any other drunken husbands show up," Daniel said.

"We can't possibly have a man on the premises!" I retorted. "There might be all kinds of complications, with so many vulnerable women there. And where would he sleep? No, it just wouldn't work!"

"But Daniel is right, Violet," Lily said. "This sort of thing could happen again."

"We can manage on our own. We'll get a trained guard dog. And a gun. Surely no man will argue with a loaded weapon pointing him in the face."

"Not if you're the one holding it," Daniel said with a laugh, amused no doubt by my vehemence.

"But do you think that is wise?" Lily asked with a frown. "We know that you can handle a gun, Violet, but how many of the others can?"

Hugh had taught me how to shoot, though I'd never actually killed any of the rabbits and groundhogs that he regularly picked off. "I will. There's really not much to it. And as for target practice...well, I don't see how anyone could miss at such close range."

"And then I'll be defending you on a manslaughter charge!" Augustus said.

"We'd only use the gun to threaten intruders. Surely we'd never be called upon to use it!" I protested.

"Augustus is right," Daniel said. "There's too much potential for an accident. I'll agree to a guard dog and a few stout cudgels. For the moment. But any more dangerous incidents like this and more serious measures will have to be taken."

They all agreed and I was content. And determined that we would never need a man on the premises to 'guard' us!

I was amused to find myself mentioned in a newspaper column recently. It said:

> We are pleased to see Miss Violet McAllister striding the streets of Ottawa once again, her handsome wolfhound at her side. Miss McAllister, the founder and director of the House of Refuge for Women, was wounded during an altercation on the premises in September, but seems to have recuperated completely. The man who assaulted her is awaiting trial for attempted murder.

So here I sit, on this special anniversary, about to testify in a trial. I, who am myself something of a murderer.

November 12, 1873:

I had thought the trial of Gideon Jackson - for such is the name of my attacker - would be a simple, straightforward affair. But I was mistaken!

His barrister was actually able to evoke some sympathy for the man from the jury, pointing out that Gideon Jackson was just exercising his legal, marital rights in trying to fetch his wife back home. That he was drunk was unfortunate, since it clouded his judgement and caused him to lash out thoughtlessly at a woman who was attempting to keep him from removing his wife from the premises!

The prosecutor rightly pointed out that Gideon Jackson's use of a knife against a defenceless woman (me?!) was more than a thoughtless gesture. Other witnesses confirmed that the defendant would have struck me again had not Tristan and Nancy intervened.

But the judge and jury had been swayed, and the man was found guilty of the lesser charge of assault and given a prison sentence of only two years.

Of course I fumed. Augustus said, "If the victim hadn't been you, a prominent citizen, a 'lady' by all accounts and one who has the favour of the Dufferins, the fellow would had received an even shorter sentence."

"And if he'd slashed his wife, he would have had nothing more than a slap on the wrist!" I said, outraged. "If juries were composed of women, such barbarians wouldn't get off so lightly!"

The laws are so unfair to women! If married women were considered persons in their own right, rather than chattels of their husbands, they would surely suffer less abuse from men.

Strange to think that, as a spinster - what a horrid word! - I will have the same rights as any man when I reach the age of majority. Except of course, that I have no political say. Still, it makes the unmarried state much less loathsome to know that I have complete control of my life and my assets.

But I would gladly relinquish it all to be Daniel's wife.

Sir John A. Macdonald and his government have resigned as a result of the railroad scandal, and we now have a new Prime Minister, Alexander Mackenzie, who is certainly not as colourful a character as Sir John.

November 15, 1873:

Ruth gave birth to a healthy baby boy two days ago. What a proud father Hugh is! I couldn't help but feel envious - jealous, even - as I saw the little family.

Everybody is having babies and getting on with life, and I am forever the outsider. But I must not brood!

I sat alone with Ruth for a time, and was rather disturbed by her state of mind. She said, "I shall never again have a baby! It was horrid! The pain was unspeakable!"

I replied, "I've heard that you soon forget about it, and think only of the new baby."

"I'll never forget it! Never! Imagine it, Violet. For twenty hours I thought I was in hell, that the devil himself was inside me, ripping me apart to get out!" She shuddered. "I'm never going through that again! I wanted to die rather than suffer those tortures any longer!"

"Perhaps it will be better next time. It can't be so bad or women wouldn't have a dozen or more."

"Perhaps they are less sensitive than I! Perhaps they drop their young like the cows or the sheep! I don't care! All I know is that I am not a brood mare!"

I did not try to argue with her. After all, what do I know of childbirth?! "Well, you have a very handsome son. What will you name him?"

"Cameron." Which was her family name.

"May I hold him?"

She shrugged. "If you like."

I was surprised by her attitude. She didn't seem to be the proud mother I had expected from all her pre-birth preparations and excitement. She seemed indifferent to the baby. Almost hostile.

I met Kate arriving as I was leaving and had a brief chat with her. I did express my concern about Ruth's state of mind. She said, "Oh, that'll pass. Cameron was large for a first baby, but next time she'll find it easier. I'm more concerned that she takes so little interest in the baby. She's asked her mother to find a nurse for him."

"All my sisters have nurses or nannies for their children," I said.

"But Hugh can't afford that! Ruth still gets a yearly allowance from her father, you see, so she'll be paying the nurse from that."

I knew what Mrs. Skuce would make of that. She would say that Ruth was playing the lady of the manor again. It was bad enough that she - a farmer's wife - already had one servant!

I intended to keep my nose out of others' domestic affairs. My concern was that, unlike my sisters who had glowed with maternal joy after the births of their children, Ruth seemed bitter and unhappy.

I hope Kate is right - that this will soon pass.

December 21, 1873:

Such sorrow! My heart aches for Lily and Augustus, who are devastated by the loss of their unborn child.

Daniel, who attended Lily after her miscarriage, said that there should be no reason for her not to conceive another child in future. But at the moment, that is little consolation.

This time I nursed Lily, who had lost a great deal of blood and lay, pale and sad, in her bed for weeks. Once she was again on her feet, she spent long hours just sitting alone in the newly decorated nursery.

I felt so helpless, unable to reach her in her grief. It seemed I could do nothing to ease her pain, and neither one of us had the heart for distractions.

I didn't realize until now how much I had come to rely on Lily's quiet strength and equanimity. I feel rather lost myself, seeing her so forlorn.

Christmas will be a sad affair this year.

January 7, 1874:

Despite all, I had a lovely Christmas with the Forresters, thanks largely to my niece, Emily, who is a precocious and delightful two-year-old.

Lily and Augustus didn't join us this year.

But I went up to Ottawa a few days later and spent much of my time helping out at the Refuge. We have fewer guests at the moment, since many reconcile with their families during the

Christmas season, so there is more baking and washing for the rest of us to do.

Daniel found me there last Saturday afternoon. "Augustus tells me that you've been spending far too much time here lately," he said.

"So I've told her!" Marjorie said. "We can manage fine without her. But she won't listen."

Truth to tell, my arm, though it seems quite healed, still aches at times - such as when I am kneading dough. So I was glad of a respite.

"Fetch your coat," Daniel said. "I have the afternoon free, and I think you need another skating lesson."

"That's right. Put some colour into her cheeks," Marjorie said. She has taken a maternal attitude to me of late, which is rather endearing. "I keep telling her a young girl like her should be out having fun, not slaving away here every day."

"Lady Dufferin has a skating party on this afternoon," Daniel said to me. "She particularly asked after you last time we met."

Remembering the skating party last Christmas, my heart leapt with joy at the prospect of another such glorious afternoon in Daniel's company. He had a carriage waiting outside. As we drove to the Blakes', Daniel handed me a parcel, saying, "A belated Happy Christmas, Violet."

It was a first edition of Tennyson's poems. "It's wonderful! But where did you find this?"

"In Montreal."

"Thank you, Daniel. I shall treasure this." Leafing through it I saw *The Lady of Shalott*, which always reminds me of Daniel and his moving rendition of it.

At the Blakes', I changed quickly, leaving Daniel talking to Augustus and Lily in the parlour. They had declined to join us, but no one made any comment about a chaperone. Not that one was needed, of course, but convention dictated it. Still, I am the last to complain if such nonsense is overlooked!

Before we left, I gave Daniel the painting I had done especially for him. It was of Pan, emerging from the early morning mist that drifted still in the ravine. It had been difficult to capture the ephemeral quality of the mist, but I thought I had achieved a rather evocative rendering.

Daniel was most complimentary. And he said, "Your garden intrigues me, Violet."

"Then I shall just have to show it to you some time. I've already been planning a midsummer's eve party. Will you keep the day free?"

"I certainly will. I've heard too much about Moon Hall to miss such an occasion!"

"It might disappoint you, for it is merely an ordinary house, neither pretentious, like Rosecliff, nor elegant, like this place."

"It can hardly be ordinary if you have Greek gods frolicking in your gardens! I can just imagine what the neighbours must think."

I laughed, for Daniel was quite perceptively right. The neighbours - the entire village, no doubt - think me eccentric. So intimates Mrs. Skuce in her not-so-subtle way.

Lady Dufferin was most pleased to see me, saying that although I looked rather peaked, she was glad to see me so fully recovered. I did not hesitate to attribute my recovery to Daniel.

Lady D said, "I've heard of Dr. Haywood's skill." To him she said, "Perhaps you could do society an even greater service by imparting your expertise to young medical students."

"I'm afraid I am merely an able craftsman who enjoys his job, not a teacher," he replied.

Who had been extolling Daniel's virtues? And why had Lady D suggested Daniel teach medicine? Surely that was a most odd thing for her to say. Unless someone else had suggested it to her.

A rather ugly thought possessed me. Has Isobel Granger been planting such suggestions? What does she hope to achieve by it? Daniel's advancement?

Or Daniel's move back to Montreal, to teach at the university there?

Was I reading more into this than there was? Or was Isobel scheming to remove him from my reach?

I was roused from my disturbing thoughts by Lady D's insistence that I recount the incident with Gideon Jackson at the Refuge. Which I did, to a rather large and enthralled audience. Finally, Daniel and I escaped to the rink.

He was very patient as he showed me how to glide gracefully on an outside edge. After a while, we were skating quite harmoniously together, without my wobbles and jerky starts and stops. I said, "You make an excellent teacher," challenging him to comment on his previous denial and Lady D's curious remark.

"Only because you're an apt pupil. Generally I prefer to do, rather than teach." Which was all he said on the topic.

It was a marvellous afternoon - even if slightly clouded by the spectre of Isobel Granger. Would there not be endless, golden days like this if Daniel were mine?

Yet I am grateful for each and every one that I can steal.

Chapter 23

"It's become an annual event, this corn roast," Liz said to Kit over the phone. "We always have it on the Labour Day weekend, and some of our former members usually show up. Anyway, will you come? It's great fun."

"No need for further persuasion," Kit replied with a laugh. "I'd be delighted to come!"

"Great! We'll expect you about seven and don't eat first. Erick always whips up a few hundred hor d'oeuvres as well, just to make sure no one goes hungry."

Kit felt unaccountably excited about the invitation. Because she was expecting Nick to be there, she wondered? Certainly because she had no social life other than her frequent visits to the commune. They were her closest friends, those "hippies". Without them, her life would be pretty empty right now, she realized with surprise.

Kit felt too restless to get back to work. She spent a foolishly long time wondering what she should wear (jeans, of course, for such an informal outdoor event), and filing her neglected fingernails.

Christine would probably be there with Nick. So why was she acting as though this party at the commune was somehow different from any other evening she spent there? She hadn't seen Nick since that night at the NAC, and he hadn't visited the farm since he'd met Christine. She would probably disdain such bucolic entertainments. But surely Nick would come.

Climbing into her favourite window seat in the library, next to Ollie who was curled into a contented ball, Kit recalled the day that Nick had sat in the armchair and they had chatted easily, like old friends. How right his presence had seemed in this house.

She gazed out at the late afternoon. From here, there was a long verdant sweep of lawn to the road. Beyond the meadow on the other side of the road rose the rock-studded ridge, bristling with scrub pine and stunted oaks.

No cows grazed in the field. No chipmunks scurried up the tree trunks. No robins hopped about. No cars passed.

It was eerie how silent and empty the world outside her door was. It was the sort of silence that she had imagined during those cold war days of her childhood when everyone had feared THE BOMB. She had pictured a multitude of AFTER THE BOMB scenarios, but the one thing that they'd all had in common was this silence that stemmed from the absence of life.

Kit shook herself out of her reverie, but could do nothing to shake the feeling of being the only survivor on earth. "Well, Ollie, this is ridiculous," Kit said aloud. The cat's ears twitched, but he didn't crack an eye open to see what his mistress was on about. Kit jumped up, strongly tempted to phone someone - anyone - just to hear a human voice.

And then remembering that she was almost out of milk, she decided instead to go to the general store in the village.

Because the store did not carry a large - merely an expensively convenient - selection of foods, Kit always shopped in Kintyre, getting enough supplies for two or three weeks at a time. But the general store in Todmorden did come in handy for forgotten items and jugs of milk.

Once she was in the village, Kit felt herself relax, for here were children playing, young mothers pushing strollers, old men smoking pipes on front porches. She chided herself for her foolish imaginings.

Kit stopped the car beside the river and stepped out into the mellow afternoon sunshine. The water rushed over the low dam, but it was shallow at this time of year, and jutting rocks littered the cascading stream. On the far side stood the stone ruins of the McAllister mill.

Abandonned for nearly a century, roofless for decades, it was still impressive. On the west side it rose to its full four storey grandeur, although the cornice stones were balanced precariously at the summit. On the north side the wall had crumbled to only one or two storeys, but rose again on the east side.

Trees, lush and thick, grew out of the centre of the ruins, some rising above, their canopy of leaves giving the mill a living roof. Saplings and shrubs and thickets crowded around it. Birds, nesting in the crevices of the broken walls, flew busily back and forth.

Kit was glad that the picturesque ruins had been left, not razed by some developer or overly zealous local officials, who were usually only too ready to rid themselves of things no longer considered functional. The mill, like the railway station, was so much a part of the community's history, and helped to establish its unique identity.

The general store must once have been an attractive Victorian shop, but was now shabbily clad in aluminum siding. Its boomtown front made it seem taller and grander than it really was. There were haphazard displays of cheap toys, garden tools, kitchen ware, and gift items behind the dusty plate glass windows that flanked the recessed door. A bell tinkled when Kit walked in. Inside, it was disappointingly modern, yet rundown, with narrow aisles stretching far back into a recent addition. The dairy cooler was, of course, at the very back of the store.

The place had a fusty smell overlaid with the aroma of coffee (from the grinding machine) and the nauseating stench of butchered meat.

A few people nodded to Kit and she acknowledged their greetings. Although she didn't know anyone in the village, the villagers seemed to be aware of who she was.

Turning the corner at the end of the aisle, Kit almost collided with Wayne Skuce.

His annoyance gave way to a grin when he saw who it was, and his "G..." turned into "Gidday to you!" rather than "Goddamn!" He was dressed, as usual, in grimy jeans, jean jacket over a washed-out T-shirt, and fancy cowboy boots. Between his fingers he rolled a cigarette that he would suck on fiercely, eyes squinted, as if determined to extract every atom of smoke from its fiery depths. His fingers were stained umber from the intense and prolonged relationship he had with his cigarettes.

"Well, speak of the devil!" Myrtle Skuce said, catching up with her son. She handed Wayne another frozen dinner to carry. "Weren't we just talking aboutcha! When we were driving past your place not twenty minutes ago, I says to Wayne, she's sure got the old place looking good. Even them gardens ain't so overgrown anymore. And of course, our Byron does a good job of the lawn. No need for complaints there. But it must be right lonely, I says to Wayne. Such a big house for one person. And sure, I'd be happy to come for a chat, but I ain't one for putting myself forward now. I'll wait for her to call me, I says. And why don't you invite her to one of your parties, I says to him. Sure, the poor lady don't know many people round here. Betcha'd like to get out once in while, eh?" Myrtle asked, batting Kit with her elbow.

Kit was aghast at the suggestion. "I'm very busy," she hastily assured Myrtle. "Working on a new book. Peace and quiet is exactly what I need just now. And I'm not one for parties. But how kind of you to concern yourself about me," Kit added, regaining her aplomb.

In the periphery of her vision, she had been aware that Wayne hadn't taken his eyes off her, nor removed that lecherous smirk from his face. "We gotta party tomorrow night," he said. "If ya change yer mind. Up on the sixth line. The old Campbell place."

Myrtle knit her eyebrows. "You'd best not be trespassing."

His face contorted with anger. "Shit, Ma, the place is deserted! Nobody gives a good God-damn about the old house! Damn near fallin' down anyway." He grinned at Kit and added, "And the girls all think it's haunted. There'll be spirits aplenty there tomorrow night - one kind anyways. Whatcha drink, an' I'll be sure we have some. If ya wanna drop in."

"Oh, don't bother about that," Kit said dismissively. "I already have an engagement for tomorrow night. Do excuse me, won't you? I really must get back."

Her heart was thumping as she hurried to pick up some milk. Why did Wayne always make her feel so defensive? It was as if he awakened some atavistic fear within her.

She tried to put him out of her mind, but noticed his car pull out onto the road behind hers. He followed her back from the village (How else would he get home?), and she found herself casting nervous glances in her rear view mirror. A sigh of relief escaped her when she pulled into her driveway and he continued along the road. He tooted his horn at her, and then sent up a spray of gravel as he suddenly accelerated.

She was thankful to be home again, but when she was once more safely enshrouded in the silence of her domain, the reality of Myrtle's words struck home. God, it was a lonely place! At least when she was writing, her imagination was peopled with characters who became real to her, who filled the spaces of her mind, leaving no room for loneliness. But at other times she longed for someone to talk to, to laugh with, to make love to. Someone like Nick.

She tried to imagine Nigel here, but that evoked only images of him dominating the place, changing things, setting schedules.

Yet it was so easy to imagine Nick here, sharing candlelit dinners, comfortable evenings.... But of course, she didn't really know him, did she? All this was just her romanticizing again.

Kit knew all too well how Violet had felt. In fact, she was beginning to wonder if these were Violet's emotions she was absorbing from the atmosphere of Moon Hall. For how could she feel such yearning for Nick? She scoffed at the foolishness that Violet was somehow possessing her mind, even though she found herself caring as much for the people from Violet's past as for those around her.

And that was who she needed to write about. She pushed her other work aside and began pouring out her thoughts onto a clean sheet of paper, working late into the night. By the following evening, she was quite ready to return from the gloomy Victorian past, and to escape from the solitude of Moon Hall for a while.

Kit noticed several strange cars in the yard at the farm, but it was seeing Nick's Porsche that sent a tremor of apprehension through her.

Inside, people were milling about with drinks in their hands. There were exuberant conversations, spontaneous hugs, and laughter at remembered experiences. There was a sense of excitement in the air, as if this were a very special occasion indeed. Standing unnoticed at the open door, Kit suddenly felt very much out of place.

It was like a physical jolt, this sense of exclusion. The joyful people before her were close friends who had shared their daily lives for years. Her brief acquaintance with the inhabitants of Mole End Farm did not entitle her to claim the depths of friendship that these people shared. Her own isolation was suddenly magnified in comparison.

She would have turned then and left had not her eyes been caught by Nick's. He smiled at her across the room, and in that mesmerized moment of hesitation, Leighton came to her side, saying, "Kit! Come and meet some old friends."

He pulled her into the room via a table where drinks were set up, pressed a glass of white wine into her hand, and then introduced her to the nearest person.

"Dave, I'd like you to meet Kit Spencer. She's our writer friend we've told you about. Kit, this is Dave Schneider, one of our founding members. In fact, he was the only one who really knew what to do at the beginning, since he grew up on a farm. Oh, and this is Suzanne Avery, who left us many years ago. She's married and living in Vancouver, but comes back for this weekend every year - *sans* husband, I might add."

"Well, he'd be lost here," Suzanne said. "No, this is my weekend to revel in nostalgia."

Kit suddenly realized who Suzanne was - Nick's ex-lover. "Suzanne and I were a couple for years," she recalled him telling her. Kit found herself studying the woman more intently.

Suzanne was undeniably attractive, but in a freshly scrubbed and wholesome way - unlike the women Nick seemed to be dating lately. With her chin-length page boy cut, sparkling hazel eyes, and ready smile she seemed like the proverbial girl-next-door.

On the other hand, Christine, who was hard not to notice even in this crowded room, oozed glamour from every painted pore. She was in skin-tight leather pants that seemed to have been spray-painted on, and a cashmere sweater with a plunging neckline.

"Suzanne just couldn't survive without a career," Leighton continued. "She teaches public school - which has earned you my deepest admiration, Suzanne, even if I think you're crazy. I concede defeat around children. I've never been able to fathom them and have no desire to try."

Suzanne laughed delightedly. "Well, in about seven months I'm going to increase the population by one, and I'll make you an honourary uncle!"

"God forbid!" Giving Suzanne a hug, Leighton said, "I'm happy for you. Just don't expect me to babysit!"

Others who had overheard the exchange now crowded around Suzanne and added their congratulations. Kit took a long gulp of her wine and moved away. She made her way to the dining table which was laden from one long end to the other with a tempting and mystifying variety of finger foods. Kit chose something that turned out to be a delectably crisp mushroom roll.

A man, who eyed her quizzically, joined her at the table. "Fraser Brookes," he announced. "I'm with Dianna."

"Kit Spencer."

"Ah, yes, the writer! Dianna told me about you. I am pleased to meet you. And not only because I'm relieved not to be the only outsider here," he said.

"I know what you mean. I feel rather superfluous, too," Kit said.

"Nonsense, you two!" Dianna declared as she joined them. "There are lots of new friends here. Don't you think we get bored with our own company after a while? God! We lived here together for a least four years. Enjoy the food. As soon as all this 'tripping down memory lane' begins to pall, we'll get down to some real partying!" And grabbing a canapé, she swept away.

Kit chatted with Fraser, who informed her that he was head of the English department at the high school in Kintyre. He was divorced and had two children, whom he saw on Wednesday nights and alternate weekends. "Dianna swears she'll never be a step-mother," Fraser said shrugging, obviously wondering how he fit into her life. And now, glancing around the room, perhaps wondering if he even wanted to.

Kit noticed Nick standing with an arm around Suzanne. He pulled her close in a friendly, yet intimate, embrace - a sort of affirmation of all they had once shared. Kit felt a jab of envy.

She wondered if she could ever have such an easy friendship with Nigel, but feared not. It was sad that, despite all the good things they had shared, they were left with such bitter dregs.

And just as Kit wondered where Christine was, the woman was beside her, selecting a crab tart. Airily Christine said, as if to no one in particular, "This wasn't exactly what I'd envisioned the commune to be like, especially after having met some of the members."

Kit was tempted not to respond, but Fraser left to join a beckoning Dianna, and she felt compelled to say, "Oh? What were you expecting?"

Christine turned to face her, and, flourishing her tidbit, said, "Something much more primitive than this. Something less affluent and capitalistic. Lentil stew and soya beans, not salmon mousse and shrimp pate. I'm rather disappointed really."

"My dear girl, surely you don't think in stereotypes," Leighton said, topping up their glasses from the bottle of wine he carried.

Christine gave him a tight smile, but ignored his dig. "This looks like a pretty prosperous enterprise. I thought you people believed money was unimportant."

"We're not so naive that we think we can subsist without money altogether," Leighton said in that dismissive way that called into question the intelligence of the person to whom he responded. "Our success in this venture is merely a by-product, never intended for self-aggrandizement. But our biggest achievement is proving that organic farming can be profitable. Just think of the implications of that for the environment and for the farming industry, before you dismiss this as just a money-grubbing enterprise."

Kit thought that Leighton was perhaps a bit naive himself, if he hadn't realized that Drew did have grander ambitions, as Nick and Dianna had intimated. Or perhaps Leighton was just being defensive in the face of what he considered the enemy. It made her wonder why Leighton felt such enmity towards Christine.

Leighton went on. "And we haven't lost sight of all the other out-moded 'hippie' values we consider important -- such things as friendship, and loyalty, the good of the group taking precedence over the good of the individual. We spurn artifice, believing that the inner man - and woman, of course - is more important and interesting than the husk in which he dwells. Somewhat different from the aspirations of the 'Me Generation', wouldn't you say?"

Christine looked at Leighton with barely disguised contempt, and said, "Do excuse me."

"Aren't you being just a little hard on her?" Kit asked Leighton when Christine had moved away.

"I have no patience with people like that," he replied, pouring himself a glass of wine. "I've watched her on the news, looking for some intelligence behind those enormous, bruised-looking eyes. But all I see is this tart making love to the camera. I keep thinking she must have something going for her - other than her sex appeal - or she wouldn't be where she is now. But when I watch her, I'm convinced she's slept her way there. I don't want my news from a chick who looks as though she's trying to seduce me. Give me someone who actually appears to know what she's talking about - a professional journalist, not a shallow vamp."

Pete had joined them halfway through Leighton's speech. Watching Christine making her way towards Nick, he said, "Well, I can see what Nick's attraction is." Her tight leather pants glistened, so that her movements seemed sinuous, snake-like.

Leighton said, "Yes, but I thought even that would have become cloying by now."

Mandy requested everyone's attention, and when the talking had subsided, she said, "I hate to interrupt, but I think we should get started with the corn roast before it gets too dark. For those of you who've joined us for the first time, let me explain what we'll be doing. You can work in twos or threes - I've a sack here for each group. Go and pick four or five ears of corn each - or as many as you think you can eat - and bring them over to the fire on the east lawn. And, by the way, there's a magnificent sunset out there, so enjoy the evening!"

Leighton and Pete ushered Kit outside. The sunset was indeed spectacular - swirls of pink and mauve spiralling to a fiery orange vortex, as if the setting sun were sucking the colours down with it. Saffron light gilded the tips of the head-high rows of corn, which seemed to dance amid the bustling bodies that moved almost unseen among them. There was a shriek from somewhere, and a disembodied voice said reassuringly, "It's just a mouse."

It didn't take them long to pick the requisite number of ears, still warm from the sun. Someone had lit the bonfire, which was crackling gaily in the fast approaching darkness. Crude, hewn log benches were drawn up about the perimeter of the blaze. Nearby was a large plywood platform that Pete told Kit was for the dance after the feast. Someone had moved the bar out as well, so Pete brought them each a glass of cold white wine.

They were instructed by Mandy to gently peel back the corn husks and remove the silk. Then they were to rinse the ears in the buckets of water provided, replace the husks, and put the ears on the grill over the fire, where Erick, with long-handled prongs, would attempt to supervise their roasting. A pot of melted butter and numerous salt cellars were at the ready.

The corn was delicious, if messy to eat, and spiced with witty repartee. It was quite dark by the time they had finished, with a full moon rising white and pure over the treetops. Erick encouraged everyone to indulge in the gastronomic spread in the farmhouse. Leighton, who had set up the sound system earlier, excused himself to take charge of the music.

Pete said to Kit, "Leighton doesn't dance. He sees it as some sort of mindless gyration. He likes to smoke a joint and just listen to the music. And he always chooses the music carefully - every piece has some association for us, even though some of them are almost undanceable!"

A rousing, raunchy, rock-and-roll number propelled everyone to their feet. Kit danced with Pete who, she was glad to see, was taking it easy on the booze tonight. She was also glad to see that people didn't stay in couples, and so partners switched with every dance.

It wasn't long before Nick approached her for a dance. It turned out to be one of her favourite Moody Blues' songs - *Nights in White Satin*. Although Nick held her as though they were engaged in a formal waltz, his touch ignited latent fires within her. For the rapturous six minutes that they swayed together she felt her body melt towards his, felt herself gently being drawn closer until their bodies touched. He drew their clasped hands to his chest so that she was nestled against him.

And her senses were heightened so that she was acutely aware of the moon-kissed darkness that lay beyond the circle of firelight and into which the hauntingly beautiful music undulated to mingle with the shrilling of the crickets.

She didn't dare look into his eyes - that would have been too intimate an experience to have in the midst of all these people. And she didn't break the silence between them with inane chatter. The taste of his remembered kiss was on her lips, and she longed to turn her face to his. But she laid her head upon his shoulder, letting the voluptuous feelings wash through her, and hoped the music would never end.

And when he finally let her go it was as if with reluctance.

Leighton must have chosen the next tune to needle Christine - *Revolution* from the Beatles' white album. It was one of those undanceable ones that Pete had mentioned. So everyone just linked hands and rocked back and forth, singing along to the well known lyrics. Leighton followed that with four minutes of the Beatles' *All You Need Is Love.*

Nick and Christine left shortly after that, she, looking peeved.

And Kit danced with Nick many more times in her mind that night before falling into a troubled sleep.

Chapter 24

I have missed you, dear diary, but I've been afraid to write these last months, in case Daisy should discover me and insist upon reading you. She can be quite ruthless when necessary!

But I am way ahead of myself.

It's all quite tragic and terrible. Poor Elliot was killed in a fall from his horse in January. He had been drinking heavily, ridden recklessly, and broken his neck.

Of course, we all rushed to Daisy's side, for she was most distraught. But even worse was to come.

We met with Elliot's brothers after the funeral. The eldest, Andrew Caldwell, explained to us that Elliot had made many bad investments - and undoubtedly gambled far too heavily and disastrously, though Andrew did not allude to that. The upshot was that not only had all of Daisy's inheritance from Father disappeared, but she and Elliot were actually in debt!

It is unbelievable that Elliot could have lost such a fortune! And Daisy had had no inkling of this, nor of their debts.

Andrew said that their house must be sold to recompense the creditors. "Of course there is always a welcome for Daisy at our home," Andrew said. "But she will undoubtedly feel far more comfortable installed in her old family home."

"Daisy and the boys are most welcome to stay with me at Moon Hall," I said.

"The boys will be staying with me, Miss McAllister," Andrew said. "Elliot named me as their guardian."

"What?! That's ridiculous!" I countered. "Surely Daisy, as their mother, retains her guardianship."

Affably Andrew explained. "You don't understand, Miss McAllister. Daisy has no legal rights to her sons, nor has she ever had. It is only the father who has complete control of the children. And he has named me as their guardian in his will. It's all quite usual."

Incredulous, I looked to Augustus for a denial. He nodded his head in agreement, but with obvious regret.

Daisy was in shock. To lose not only her husband but also her home, her livelihood, and her children in one stupid and probably preventable accident was beyond her comprehension.

"But, Mr. Caldwell, you cannot be so heartless as to deny Daisy her children at this terrible time, when she has lost everything else," I appealed to him.

"I deny her nothing. She may see the boys whenever she wishes. It is far better for them, at this difficult time, to be part of a normal family - one with which they are most familiar, after all - to carry on in their school, surrounded by their friends. Next year, they will be installed there as boarding students, but for the time being they'll continue to go as day students and be a part of my own family."

An eight and a ten year old, torn from their mother and incarcerated for most of each year - was this what Elliot had envisioned for his sons?

Augustus, sensing my seething anger no doubt, intervened by asking, "Did Elliot make no provisions for the boys?"

"Fortunately, he did put a substantial sum in trust for them. It will guarantee them an education and perhaps give them a small start in their careers."

And so the law, in the form of Andrew Caldwell, snatched my nephews away. How scared and brave they were as they bid their mother a tearful farewell. I had extracted a promise from Andrew to allow the boys to visit Moon Hall this summer. But in snowy January, summer seemed too far away.

I was glad that the Blakes and Forresters were with us on the train back to Ottawa, for Daisy was still in shock, and I didn't know what to do. It wasn't until we reached Moon Hall that she gave in to her tears. Then she sobbed for days, and I still didn't know how to help her. No paltry words could ease the grief of her loss.

At first she wrote to the boys every day, and was cheered by their dutiful responses. I suggested that she accept Andrew's open invitation and go stay there to be near her children.

"I could not live under Andrew's roof," she replied testily. "His wife and I have never got on, and I know full well that he issued the invitation merely for form's sake."

"I wouldn't let that stand in my way if I were you," I replied.

"Well, you are not me, and you have no idea of how I feel!" she retorted. "I cannot possibly stay with a woman who thinks herself better than me!"

And so our relationship has developed, with Daisy growing ever more petulant and restless as her grief diminishes. She can't stand being cooped up at Moon Hall. She detests the tranquility and the lack of society in the country. Although she is still in mourning, of course, I can see that she longs for parties and balls. Visits to Kate or Ruth bore her, for she has no interest in them or their families. She found a Fortnightly Club meeting tedious as well.

She also drinks far too much sherry and port, and snaps at me when I suggest she should imbibe in moderation. (Heaven knows, I am no teetotaler, enjoying a glass of sherry before dinner myself.)

She finds fault with the redecorating I've done to the house, and wants to change everything - with my money, for she has none of her own!

The other day she said to me, "You really must sell this place, Violet, or get married. I still have a stake in this estate, and I want my money."

"I have no intention of doing either," I replied. "You know very well that it's mine for my lifetime."

"You're being very selfish, Violet! I can't believe my own sister would treat me so shabbily! You cannot imagine how terrible it is to have nothing of your own, to be completely dependent upon others for the very food you put into your mouth!"

Of course I could sympathize, for I could imagine it. At the Refuge, I saw all too readily what happened to women who had nothing of their own, and no relatives to care for them. I took Daisy there on one of my visits, but she could not see beyond the rags and despair to realize that she was no different from these women. Only luckier.

Sarcastically she said, "It's all very well to waste your money on those wretches, who have never known anything but poverty, but to help your sister is not noble enough, I suppose!"

I try to be understanding and forgiving, for she must surely be hurt and angry and despairing. But, by Jove, she can try the patience of a saint at times!

She has not been back to Toronto to see the boys, which I truly cannot understand. (Certainly, they know their nanny better than their mother, and yet...) But she finally had enough of Moon Hall, and took off to stay with Iris in Montreal. I am glad of the respite, but I do worry about her, for she seems to be in an hysterical, almost self-destructive mood.

In the meantime, I was glad that she was not present for the small 21st birthday celebration that Lily gave for me a few days ago. And how delighted I was that Daniel was there!

Well, I am now my own mistress, with the power to deal with and dispose of my property (not Moon Hall though) as I see fit. And to do whatever I damn well please!

May 10, 1874:

Heather had a baby boy in April, which they have named Jonathan, and Kate had a son a few days ago. My Godchildren.

It's a bad time for Lily, who would have had her own child by now.

June 22, 1874:

I feel bereft now that my house-guests have left. What a success the midsummer party was! I feel quite proud of myself for having contrived it all so well.

Lily and Heather and I shared our old room. Their husbands kipped down in Hazel and Daisy's old room. Rose and Edwin slept in Father's room. And Daniel had the other front bedroom to himself. It was just as well that my other sisters declined to attend. (Last August I converted the old guest room at the end of the hall into a modern bathroom, complete with an enormous tub and a flush toilet. It was a big hit! And what luxury not having to trot out to the outhouse anymore!)

I was so thrilled to show Moon Hall to Daniel! Luckily, I had some time alone with him.

He admired it all. When I showed him the library he seemed particularly impressed, saying, "This is what I'd like to have myself some day. Was your father a great reader?"

"I doubt that he had time to read much. He just enjoyed collecting books. As I do. I've given some of the most pedantic tomes to my scholarly brother-in-law, Tobias, but there are some very good collections and first editions here."

As Daniel browsed through the books, I sat in the window seat thinking how like one of my fantasies this was, having Daniel here. I would savour this memory, and perhaps embellish it, when I was once again alone.

As if reading my thoughts, Daniel said, "Do you never get lonely here, Violet?"

Dissembling, I said, "I keep busy. And when I want company, I visit the neighbours or go to Ottawa."

I don't know what he was leading up to, for we were interrupted by Mrs. Skuce, who needed advice about the food for the party. She was all a-dither with this great event, and had half the ladies of the village employed in helping her prepare and later serve the food.

With the French doors between the drawing room and parlour opened up, there was quite a large dancefloor. Most of the parlour furniture had been moved into the library, the hallway, and onto the veranda so that people could sit and rest there, while the dining room had been set up for a buffet supper. The house sparkled with candlelight, and the garden was bespangled with glowing jewels of lantern light. Moon Hall has never looked so gay.

Once I found Daniel in the library discussing something medical with Gordon and Dr. Townsend, but mostly he danced - often with me.

As the last light of the longest day died on the horizon, Daniel and I wandered in the garden, where others were also enjoying the sultry evening breezes. Smudge pots burned to deter the mosquitoes.

I was glad no one had discovered my secret garden, and we sat down on the cool stone bench. Music wafted out from the house, carried on the hot, scented breath of the summer night. But it seemed far away, as did the rustlings and murmurs of others strolling the grounds.

Daniel said, "Now I can truly picture this when I look at your painting, Violet."

"Do you think it too bizarre?"

"Well, Pan would seem to sit more naturally on a Greek hillside or in a lush Italian garden. And yet, you've created an odd type of garden here, where nothing seems ludicrous. Though logically I can't imagine Pan at home in the Canadian wilderness!" After a moment he said, "Of course, I couldn't imagine you here either, until now."

"And we all fit together, don't we - Pan, and Tristan, and Moon Hall, and I?" The big dog had joined us, and I reached down automatically to scratch his bristly head.

"Yes, you do."

I thought then that he was about to kiss me, for we gazed at each other, and time seemed suspended. It was like that fairy tale, Sleeping Beauty, where the prince must kiss the princess to release her from a spell. I'm sure I stopped breathing, waiting for his lips to touch mine.

But our spell was broken too rudely and abruptly.

"Leave me alone, Hugh! Just don't touch me!" I recognized Ruth's voice, and saw two shadowy figures approaching us. Ruth was bustling away from Hugh, but he pursued her.

"For God's sake, Ruth, I'm your husband!" he said in annoyance as he grabbed her arm.

I knew I had to speak, to alert them to our presence, before they said too many personal things that would embarrass us all. I certainly had no wish to overhear a marital spat.

Daniel rose with me, and we stepped out of the grove, Tristan trailing alongside us.

"And so I often paint this scene in different light - sunrise, sunset, summer, winter," I said to Daniel, as if we were in the middle of a conversation. "Oh, hello, you two. Daniel, I'd like you to meet my friends and neighbours, Ruth and Hugh McGrath."

After they had shaken hands - the two men that I love most in this world! - I said to Daniel, "Ruth paints as well, and we often go on sketching outings, up to the ridge or down to the river." And so I rambled on like a good hostess, my own moment of intimacy past.

Which was just as well, for I cannot allow Daniel to kiss me. I dare not poison him with my disease!

But how I crave the touch of his lips upon mine. How I ache to be crushed into his arms, to feel his hard body pressed against mine. How I long to tell him that I love him, and to hear him speak words of love to me.

Dear God, what have I done to deserve this punishment?

But if I were free to marry, I would have accepted Hugh's proposal. And we would have been happy, I think. What dissension is there between Ruth and Hugh? It saddens me to think of my dear, old friend unhappy.

But then I would never have met Daniel, to whom my very soul seems bound. He is my Heathcliffe.

What irony! Daniel was never destined to be mine, it seems. What capricious Fate has wrought this divine torture?

August 28, 1874:

I cannot believe Daisy! Elliot has been in his grave but half a year and already she has met and married another! He is a minor country squire from Wiltshire, and has taken Daisy back to England with him. So she leaves behind her poor sons, virtually orphaned now. With few qualms on her part, it seems to me!

They never did come to Moon Hall this summer, for Daisy was too preoccupied with her new *amour* in Montreal. She did go to see them before leaving, but what compensation is that to the poor boys?

Would she have behaved so precipitously had she not been impoverished by Elliot's profligacy? And if she had had her sons' welfare to consider?

Can I really blame her for snatching a new life while still young and attractive enough to do so? After all, what else is left to her?

October 31, 1874:

What terrible irony! Poor tragic Daisy.

What was she trying to prove? She has never been a good or avid horsewoman. What possessed her to participate in a fox hunt? I suppose it was an important part of the society she had married into.

I can't believe that she, too, has died in a fall from her horse.

And my poor, darling nephews! I really must go to see them. Perhaps Andrew Caldwell will agree to the boys having regular holidays with me or my sisters. I want to ensure that they know their mother's family. And know that we care for them. Poor orphaned mites!

Is Daisy's one of the restless souls that prowls the earth tonight on this All Hallows Eve?

I had a bruising ride today on Moondancer. Why? To tempt Fate to strike me down as well? But I know damn well that Fate has devised other cruel plans for me.

Yes, perhaps that is why I feel the need to punish myself, for there is a recklessness in me that dares me to defy Fate.

I need Daniel. My body cries out for his touch. I have dreams of his hands exploring my willing body and I burn with the need for fulfillment. I am in a fever. A rage.

Father, I hope you are roasting in hell! How could you have done this to me?

But there is no answer in this silent library. Tristan senses no ghosts, and so lies peacefully beside me.

But I am screaming inside. Is this the madness of the disease already claiming me?

Chapter 25

September 22, 1980

Dear Fran,

Your long and chatty letter was much appreciated. Sounds as though you're having a wonderful time. I might even come to visit you again!

No, I haven't heard from Nigel. I hope he hasn't discovered where I am, and yet sometimes - in irrational moments - I hate him for not having tried to find me. (I'm assuming that he's still the same Nigel - once he's determined to do something, he does it, and no obstacle is too great for him to overcome.) From this distance of half a year, our life together didn't seem so bad.

Strange how quickly those raging passions of anger and bitterness have mellowed to the point where I even question my right to experience them. Was Nigel really such a prig as I've painted him? Or have I blown things out of proportion and ascribed more faults to him than he deserved? Have I been unfair and inflexible and unreasonable in my case against him?

I just don't know anymore.

I feel full of contradictions. I have a love-hate relationship with this place. My apple crop was a disaster - the apples were diseased and wormy, so I let them all rot. (So much for my fruit stand!) Mice are invading my home, and, although the cat helps, I have to set traps in the kitchen cupboards. Neighbours have to come in every morning and dispose of the mangled bodies because I can't bear to look at them.

Alan came mostly, and teased her relentlessly about her squeamishness. But sometimes Stuart came in his place. Silently, save for a greeting, he would deal with the traps. His eyes spoke more than he did, and Kit was not comfortable with the smoldering longing in their depths. That made her think of Hugh, and it was dangerous, she knew, to transfer her rather tender feelings for him to Stuart.

The countryside is breathtakingly beautiful just now. The autumn colours are so intense - I've never seen the like. I go for drives just to sightsee, to try to drink in the vivid orange, the rich gold, the blood red of the leaves. And the smell - that old, dry, crinkly, musty, dense and heady fragrance of fall.

There is something about autumn that speaks to my soul. For no apparent reason, I get these feelings of poignancy rising in me, moving me to tears. As if some long-lamented, long-forgotten memory were awakened.

Violet's memories? Violet's yearning for her beloved autumn?

You'll think me crazy, but I feel almost haunted by this place and the people who once played out their lives here. I have this obsession to discover what happened to them. I've almost completed my final draft of the latest 'Victoria Penn', and then I intend to pursue my research on these compelling people and their time.

She had already mapped out the story and written some key scenes.

The house is big and empty and lonely at times, and peopled with ghosts at other times. I long for contact with real people.

She even missed the Pughs, who were still in Europe. Her commune friends had been busy with the harvest, and she'd seen little of them this past month. The other farmers were equally busy. Bonnie Skuce still came, but she was never very communicative, and Kit did not always have the patience to draw her out.

I went to visit Mom and Dad for a week, and found Launston Mills so normal and boring that I was desperate to get back to Moon Hall! (Mom calls me twice a week to check up on me, but she's still not happy with my living here alone. I'll have to find myself a lover!)

Maybe that's the problem. Maybe I've just been too long without a man.

But it was Nick she longed for, not Nigel. That a couple of sensual moments in Nick's arms could have affected her so profoundly, amazed her. She was convinced that he had felt something too - something magical, magnetic between them - and she had expected him to call her or visit. But he hadn't.

So had she imagined it all? Was she so caught up in Violet's emotional entanglements that she was projecting Violet's feelings for Daniel onto Nick, and claiming them as her own? Was she really such an emotional mess?

Kit became aware of a distant knocking, and was grateful for the interruption. Pete Sage came into the kitchen with a big grin on his face.

"I wanted you to be the first to know, Kit!" he said, flourishing a letter in his hand. "I did as you suggested - wrote an article about organic farming - and it's been accepted!"

"That's terrific! Which magazine?"

"*Rural Roots.* And they want more of the same. In fact, they thought an article all about the commune would be interesting."

"Great! I am pleased for you."

Shyly he said, "Thanks for giving me the idea. And by even suggesting it in the first place, you gave me the confidence to try it. Come to dinner tomorrow night. I'm going to order a celebration!"

"That's a wonderful idea. I'd be delighted to come." She almost asked if Nick would be there, but caught herself at the last minute.

Nevertheless, it was for Nick that she dressed with such care the following evening. Her heart sank when she didn't see his Porsche in the parking lot.

But she didn't brood long. She felt happy and comfortable being among her friends again. While they were savouring their aperitifs, she caught Teresa glowering at her.

She asked Leighton, who was sitting next to her, why.

"She and Pete had a bit of a thing going for a while after Pete's friend, Jackie, left. But Pete wasn't all that keen, and Teresa hasn't given up. Well, now she's jealous of you, because Pete's been singing your praises all day."

"Oh dear."

"They're completely incompatible, but Teresa just won't see it."

So that was the cause of the friction she had sensed between Pete and Teresa at other times.

"Hey, Nick!" Pete called out. "You made it!"

With all the conversations going on, Kit hadn't even heard him come in. He was alone.

"Christine sends her regrets. She has to work."

"Bullshit," Leighton whispered to Kit. "She just can't face another encounter with the '60s. Blinkered horses are much happier - they have nothing to distract them from their single-minded path."

Nick caught her eye, and smiled a private greeting. With his presence, she suddenly felt completely contented, and determined to enjoy every moment of the evening.

When Kevin mentioned how several of their animals had won ribbons at the Kintyre Agricultural Fair the previous week, Kit, thinking of the delicious prime rib roast she was relishing, replied, "I'm glad I haven't met your animals, or I might yet become a vegetarian."

"Actually, you have a good point there," Drew said. "I've been thinking that people are changing their eating habits - less cholesterol and fat, ergo less meat. We should devote more acreage to soya beans next year, for the vegetarians. And really start pushing the 'natural' aspect of our produce. I'll bet there are restaurants in Toronto and Ottawa and Montreal that would pay premium prices for organically grown vegetables. That's something we'll have to investigate."

"I think people are finally becoming more concerned about what they eat and how food is grown," Mandy said. "I think we could be onto something quite marketable."

"I've heard there might be a farm going up for sale on the next concession," Drew said. "Just a hundred acres."

Mandy said, " But that would give us plenty of of room for expansion!"

Kit could imagine that the two of them - Drew and Mandy - were accustomed to sparking ideas and opinions off each other. It almost seemed rehearsed, and yet Kit thought that they were just so attuned to one another that it came naturally. She could see how they might - as Dianna had accused - dominate the decision-making.

"I think we have more than enough to handle at the moment," Pete said somewhat sourly. "We'd have to hire hands if we expanded."

Drew shrugged. "And so we would, if necessary. I can't see that as an obstacle."

Kit asked, "How much land to you farm now?"

"A thousand acres," Drew replied.

"And we started with two hundred," Pete added, implying that they had already expanded too far beyond the original, simple commune, imputing a sort of rapaciousness to Drew's ambitions.

Remembering that this was Pete's celebration and sensing that tensions were mounting between Pete and Drew, Kit tried changing the subject. "I wish that there were magazines on the market for people like me. I mean, *Rural Roots* is all very well for farmers, but we city slickers who just want to putter around a small acreage could use information more tailored to our modest ambitions. You know the sort of thing - how to keep raccoons from stealing your corn, and how to identify nettles."

"And failing that, how to use burdock as an antidote," Nick added with a grin.

Was he deliberately reminding her of that sultry summer afternoon? Kit shivered at the remembered touch of his hands.

But she had no chance to talk to Nick alone. He left shortly after dinner, saying he had to get back.

To Christine, of course. Still, at least he had come and she had stayed away. Her presence would have spoiled everything.

When the rest of them had settled down on the couches with liqueurs, Drew said, "Kit, I've found out about Elliot and Daisy Caldwell. It was a bit of a surprise, really. It seems that their eldest son was my great-grandfather."

"So you're a descendent of the McAllisters. That's amazing!"

"It's almost spooky," Mandy said. "The McAllisters once owned some of the land that we've bought up."

"So what happened to your great-grandfather?" Kit wanted to know.

"He went into the law, as expected, and eventually became a judge. He had a reputation for being quite tough."

Heartless even? Kit wondered. Had the poor neglected and then orphaned boy turned his anger against the world by becoming a harsh and unyielding penalizer of its transgressors?

"And what about the other boy?" Kit asked.

"He went through law school too, but I gather he was a bit of a loose cannon. He drank himself to death quite young."

That he had become self-destructive didn't surprise Kit. But it was somewhat disconcerting that she felt such sadness for those unfortunate children - as if she had known them personally.

"I want to know more about Violet," Mandy said with determination.

"Yes, Kit, it seems to me you owe us a story," Drew reminded her.

So she told them about Violet's Refuge and some of the incidents there. Drew was obviously pleased to have such a remarkable relative.

Lying in bed later that night, Kit thought of how Nick had looked at her earlier, and knew that she hadn't been fantasizing about their mutual attraction.

She was still in a euphoric mood the next day despite the drizzle. She loved the mild autumn mornings when mist enshrouded the valley and blurred the outlines like an impressionist watercolour. Feeling restless and energetic, she went out for a walk as soon as the rain stopped.

She chuckled to think how sensibly dressed she was in her black rubber boots and roomy sou'wester. Nigel would be appalled to see how "native" she had gone.

Already her boots were glossy wet. In the still air, every blade of grass quivered with unshed drops.

Past the McGrath farm, the road was lined on both sides with maples whose branches arched and met over the road, forming a glorious, translucent canopy of gold and orange leaves. In stark contrast, the saturated bark glistened like coal. Water dripping from the leaves intoned a stacatto rhythm on the gravel and the withered grasses.

Kit walked toward the village along this awesome avenue, thinking that at this moment there could me no more beautiful spot on earth than this, and wondering who had had the vision to plant these trees here. She would not have been surprised if it had been Violet McAllister.

An approaching car slowed down, and Kit turned around to see Leighton rolling down his window. Kit could hear "Morning" from Grieg's "Peer Gynt Suite" drifting out, and thought how appropriate that gentle, pastoral melody was.

"Now that's a much more sensible way to spend the day," he said. "But I'm just off to the Co-op. I don't suppose you want a lift into the village?"

"No thanks. I'm just going to savour this."

He grinned and waved as he drove on.

And she did savour it - with every breath of the damp, fragrant air. A shaft of sunlight penetrated the mist and glinted off the burnished leaves, and then faded as the scudding clouds once again congregated and mingled.

Another car slowed as it approached. It was Wayne Skuce.

Kit nodded a greeting and kept walking. Wayne, driving alongside her, stuck his head out the window and said, "Hop in. I'll give ya a ride."

"No thanks. I'm just out for a walk."

"Suit yourself.... So, not workin' today, eh?"

"I enjoy exercise sometimes."

"I can think of better ways to exercise," he replied with a grin.

She chose to ignore the remark.

Keeping pace with her, he leaned on his elbow partway out the window as though in a tête-à-tête with her. The rumbling of his too-loud engine violated the peacefulness of the day; the faulty exhaust spewed out poisonous vapours. Kit wished he would drive off and leave her alone.

But Wayne seemed to be in no hurry. Kit challenged, "Are you not working today?"

"I'm my own boss. Don't need to work every day. And when I do, I make sure it's worth my while."

With the prices he charged, Kit wondered if he ever had any work. Or was he hinting at another line of business? Something illegal perhaps. She recalled Georgina telling her that Wayne had been suspected of theft once.

Realizing what an unsavoury character he was and just how alone they were on this stretch of backroad, she suddenly felt her skin crawl.

His ferrety nose twitched as if he scented her fear. He gave her a broken-toothed grin. No, it really was a leer. Yet how incongruous it seemed with his large, innocent cow eyes.

"I'm sure you must have better things to do than to waste time talking to me."

He chortled. "Well, I can think of better things to do than talk."

She stopped and turned angrily toward him. "I don't appreciate your insinuations!"

"Shit, it's only a bit of fun! Ain't ya got no sense of humour?"

She glared at him and said, "If you don't mind, I prefer to walk alone."

"It's gonna start pissin' down any minute. An' it's nearly a mile back to yer place. Yer gonna get soaked."

"I don't melt in the rain," she snapped, pulling up her hood as much to try to shield herself from Wayne's predatory gaze as in preparation for the rain. But she turned back, noticing the boiling black clouds closing in. A wind had sprung up; it tore the leaves off the trees, swirling and scattering them about.

Kit had hoped she was rid of Wayne, but he did a squealing three-point turn and crept up beside her again. Like a cat tormenting a mouse, he seemed to revel in her discomfort. "Ya might melt fast enough when the lightning hits," he said smugly as the first large drops pelted down.

Kit jumped when lightning crackled through the air closeby. She knew that the worst place to be was beneath these trees. She was almost prepared to throw herself into a ditch and wait out the storm rather than accept his offer of a ride.

Another bolt of lightning knifed down, uncomfortably close.

Surely she could handle Wayne. She would insist that he drive her straight home. She would make sure his hands didn't stray.

"Shit, but yer stubborn!" he said.

She would swallow her pride and accept the damned ride.

But just then she heard a car approaching from the village. She prayed it was Leighton.

He slowed down, and Kit said to Wayne, "I have a ride, thanks." When Leighton stopped beside her, she scrambled gratefully into the seat next to him. She heard Wayne shout "Fuckin' bitch!" before he swung around - narrowly missing Leighton's car - and shot toward the village.

To Leighton she said, "Am I glad to see you! That guy gives me the creeps!"

"I never could stand him myself, even though he's never preyed on me."

Kit was grateful for his understanding. "I don't know what it is about Wayne, but I disliked him from the moment I met him."

"Probably no different from the instant attraction some people have for each other."

"Instant revulsion in this case. He seems almost... evil. Do you think I'm over-reacting?"

Leighton pulled into her driveway, and let the car idle in neutral. The rain drummed hollowly on the roof. He plucked at his red beard as he considered her question. "I hope so: but I fear not. He's trouble. Did you hear that he and his friends were fined for partying in the old quarry down on the second line? It was a big, rowdy drunk. They had some girls with them, and it was bare buttocks in the moonlight when the cops arrived."

"Sounds like some debauched, bacchanalian scene."

"One of the girls claimed that Wayne had raped her, but she never pressed charges."

Kit shivered.

"Stay away from him, Kit. I wouldn't want to see you hurt."

She was touched by the concern in his warm blue eyes. "I'll avoid him like the plague."

But as she sat in the library later that evening, she resented the idea that she couldn't even take a stroll down the road without fear of being accosted by Wayne. At least he hadn't pestered her here. Surely he wouldn't dare start harassing her!

She felt suddenly nervous in the gloom. The electricity was off again - not an infrequent occurrence - and the oil lamps did not adequately dispel the darkness. Oliver Twist lay curled on a window seat, oblivious to the rain lashing the windows and the wind whispering through the cracks.

It was a wild autumn night - the sort that stripped the trees bare, leaving their skeletal remains shivering in the biting wind. And Kit did not feel absolutely safe and cozy in her nest.

Vividly she remembered her first encounter with Wayne, when he had stood cockily at the bottom of her stairs, and she, half naked at the top. How easily he had invaded her home then!

Of course, she'd taken precautions since then, always securing the doors as soon as she came in. But, like the ferret that he resembled, she almost expected him to pop out of a hole in the woodwork.

She laughed aloud at her foolishness. But before the echo even died down, she was alert to a peculiar noise. Ollie sprang up from his perch, yellow eyes riveted on the opening to the hallway.

Kit had become somewhat accustomed to the mice scurrying to and fro in the walls and ceilings - although their scramblings could be rather unnerving when she was lying in bed. But this high-pitched squeaking belonged to no mouse.

She could feel the hair on the back of her neck bristle. Was it the squeak of floorboards? Breathlessly she gawked at the dark cavity that was the entrance to the hallway, her eyes bulging almost as much as the cat's.

She screamed as a black shape swooped into the room, and flitted crazily about. It was a bat!

Realizing that her intruder was not human after all gave her a moment's relief. But she felt an instinctive horror of bats, and let out another shriek as it zigzagged around the room, sometimes flying directly toward her and then veering off at the last instant. It was this daredevil stuntwork that terrified so many people, she thought. And bats did get rabies - only last month she had read of a couple of children being attacked by a rabid bat. Bitten in the neck.

Oliver leapt for the prey, and Kit dashed from the room, flashlight in hand, and raced up the stairs. She locked herself into her bedroom, wondering what she should do now.

She could hardly call anyone at midnight, requesting help to round up a bat. But if she waited until morning, it might have found a hiding place, and if it wasn't routed, she would hardly spend another peaceful night.

At least it had taken her mind off Wayne, she reflected as she climbed into bed. She didn't even bother to get washed. There was no way she was opening that door until morning. She'd miss

Ollie's company, for he enjoyed stretching out at the foot of her bed, but he was no doubt relishing the hunt downstairs.

The cat woke her early with a peculiar mewling noise outside her door. Kit opened it a crack to find Ollie regarding her proudly with an offering of dead bat.

"Good cat," she said as he rubbed against her leg. And although she was sorry that the bat had been killed, she was pleased that she hadn't had to call one of the men in to rescue her. It was a great feeling of self-sufficiency. She patted the cat and gave him an extra helping of tuna at breakfast.

She did wonder how the bat had gotten in - was there a nest in her attic? - and was rather wary for the next few nights. But nothing else disturbed her.

Chapter 26

I have not written for well over a year, dear diary, for what is there to relate?

I am tormented by my love for Daniel, a love that I dare not express or reveal. So I've struggled to keep an emotional distance from him, while trying to maintain our friendship. How impossible that is!

And I never knew quite how Daniel considered me. There seemed more than mere friendship in our relationship - an innocent flirtation perhaps - but no blossoming romance. Or so I tried to deceive myself. For I never encouraged him or gave him cause to think of me romantically.

And yet.... My eyes must have betrayed me. He must have seen into my lonely, yearning soul.

And now I have crushed that tender, burgeoning blossom. I can hardly bear to write these words, dear diary.

It all happened at the most spectacular ball Ottawa - probably all of Canada! - has ever seen. Fifteen hundred of us were invited to the Governor-General's costume ball at Rideau Hall. It had been the talk of the city ever since invitations were sent out months ago.

It kept all kinds of tradesmen in brisk business - certainly a good thing, for we are in the depths of a depression and this event actually gave work to many who would otherwise be impoverished.

Still, as we alighted from the carriage and stepped into the glitter of Government House, I could not help thinking of the many hungry and desperate people I had seen, not only at the Refuge, but also in the streets.

From the entrance hall I caught a glimpse of the new Tent Room, which is decorated as a red and white striped marquee studded with shields bearing the arms of Britain, Canada, the provinces, and also the Dufferin family. A clever disguise for this indoor tennis court! The room was laid out for supper, and was dazzling with a massive gold centrepiece and the silver and crystal gleaming in the light from hundreds of candles.

The enormous, gilded ballroom also glittered with candles and gaslight, and was festooned with acres of pink and white flowers. But even more embellished were the people themselves. The silks and satins and velvets and ermines that swathed the illustrious guests would have kept many a less privileged family from cold and starvation this winter!

But I should not condemn, for I, too, had a costume specially made for this grand occasion. I went as the Lady of Shalott. After all, am I not like her, doomed to watch the world pass her by, never knowing the love of a man?

I had designed a simple white gown, like a long tunic, split at the sides almost to the hips to reveal a black underskirt. The tunic had wide sleeves ending at the elbows with a tight-sleeved black chemise beneath. The sleeves, neck, and skirt of the tunic were edged with embroidered gold ribbon, and I had a matching girdle at my waist which dangled down the front of my gown. My hair was left long and wavy, with the sides braided and drawn around to the back. On top I wore a white, veiled headdress. I think I succeeded in looking very (elegantly) medieval.

Lily and Augustus looked splendidly Greek as Orpheus and Eurydice, although Rose complained that Lily's diaphanous gown was rather too clinging to be quite proper. She herself was lost in her enormous hooped skirt and Elizabethan ruff, while Edwin seemed uncomfortable in his short padded breeches and hose. (For he has not the legs for them!)

Iris, who would on no account miss this event, was arrayed in a shockingly elaborate gown that nearly rivalled Lady D's. (The Dufferin household wore costumes of the court of James V of Scotland, with His Excellency as the king and Lady D as his consort.)

How wonderful the guests were! Eastern potentates hobnobbed with explorers and exotic princesses, while a multitude of characters had stepped out of the pages of popular novels or off the Shakespearean stage.

And when I saw Daniel I knew someone (Lily?) had betrayed my secret. Daniel was clad as a knight, his costume cleverly designed to look like chain mail - though it was grey wool - with a white tunic over top. But like the bold Sir Lancelot of Tennyson's poem, he wore a red cross and a crimson baldric across his chest.

What did he mean by it? Had not the Lady of Shalott been doomed by Lancelot, and gone, singing, to her death. (Like a madwoman?)

But I have to admit that he looked remarkably dashing.

He bowed deeply before me and said, "May I say how enchanting you look, milady?"

"You do me a great honour, Sir knight," I replied, gleefully joining in the game. "Have you slain any dragons lately, or gone on perilous quests for the Holy Grail?"

"I've merely rescued a few damsels in distress, nothing more."

"How chivalrous!"

But Isobel Granger must have known what Daniel intended to wear, for she came as Lancelot's lover, Queen Guinevere, with Charles, a rotund King Arthur. Her gown was ermine-trimmed scarlet satin with a sweeping train, over a gold petticoat, and a bejeweled gold chain at her waist. On her head she wore a red silk headdress with a long veil that draped almost to the floor, and topped with a simple, but effective gold coronet. I know she quite outshone me. But was there more to this little charade? Was she declaring that Charles, like King Arthur, was a cuckolded husband? That Daniel was already her lover?

Isobel is so charming, so adept at social witticisms, and makes me seem almost stupidly tongue-tied in her presence. Iris knows her, for it seems they move in the same circles in Montreal, and didn't fail to point out to me that Isobel is an excellent hostess, much sought after, who not only spends time and money on charitable works but also comes from a well respected and wealthy family. I hate her!!!

But I would not allow her, or my own raging jealousy, to spoil the evening. After the obligatory formal quadrilles, the band played waltzes, and Daniel is a divine dancer. In his arms I felt quite swept away as he whirled me about the room.

And in his arms I felt indeed like a damsel rescued from distress. At least for a time. He took me in to supper, although I could see that Isobel was trying to wrangle an invitation from him.

A small victory for me, I thought. But my own brother-in-law, Reginald Thorndike, brought Isobel in, who promptly seated herself on Daniel's other side. And although Daniel did his best to pay attention to me, Isobel expertly manipulated the conversation and had the attention and admiration of all within hearing. Would that I could say she is empty-headed and shallow, but she is not. She is thoughtful and well informed and has quite strong ideas which I find I share.

But I know that we can never be friends.

When Daniel danced with her, I saw how gracefully they moved together, as if from long practice. And I envisioned them together more intimately, though my mind balked at the prospect.

Poor Charles was neither an elegant nor competent dancer. He sweated profusely and breathed heavily from the exertion, so I was spared having to finish a lancer with him. I also danced with Hamlet - Daniel's brother, Jonathan - Mr. Macawber, Falstaff, the Count of Monte Cristo, and numerous others. But mostly with Sir Lancelot.

It must have been nearly 3:00 o'clock when Daniel suggested we walk through the conservatories, which were illuminated with Chinese lanterns. Other couples were strolling in and out, taking a break from the dancing, though the excitement of the evening precluded tiredness. That would come tomorrow.

Outside, large wet snowflakes were falling, but inside it was like a fragrant summer night. I was so caught up in the magical spell of the evening that I did not guard myself against my own treachery. I must have returned Daniel's probing look with my own emotions naked in my eyes, for, screened from others by the palms, he kissed me.

For a moment I was too deliciously shocked to react. His lips were warm and soft upon mine. But then I remembered.

With a groan wrenched from the depths of my wounded heart, I pushed him away and ran from the room. I tried to compose myself in the ladies' cloakroom, but decided I could not stay. I knew it was a terrible breach of protocol to depart before our Viceregal hosts, but at that moment I cared not whether I was ever again invited anywhere. And who would miss me in any case? I sent word to Lily that I was leaving, and hurried out the door, afraid Daniel might confront me, demanding to know what was wrong between us.

The Dufferins had engaged several of Ottawa's horse-drawn streetcars to ferry party-goers back and forth from the city, but I took one of the less conspicuous cabs idly waiting for the ball to end, and returned to the Blakes' silent house in the slumbering capital.

But I could not sleep. I stalked around the dark house like a caged animal, trying to sort through my confused emotions, staving off the tears of self pity that threatened. I stared out into the snow-bright night, watching the snowflakes drift down in the light from the streetlamps. And all I could see was Daniel twirling around the ballroom with Isobel in his arms.

It was nearly 5:00 AM when I heard Lily and Augustus return, but I dashed to my room. I could not talk to anyone tonight. And God only knew what I would say tomorrow!

We didn't rise until nearly noon, but I had hardly slept anyway. To Lily I explained that I had had a dreadful headache, and could not stay until the end of the ball. I did look pale and drawn, so she believed me, and, of course, did not admonish me about my rude departure. Although Rose undoubtedly will.

But Daniel came to see me late that afternoon. I had no chance to escape, for I had been passing the hall when he arrived.

I saw him alone in the parlour.

"How are you, Violet?" he asked, no doubt noticing my pallor.

"Tired," I replied. "As I expect most of Ottawa is today."

"Violet, did I somehow offend you last night?"

"No, Daniel. I had a wonderful time."

"Then why did you run away?"

He pinned me with his intense gaze. I could not lie to him, nor yet tell him the truth. And, God knows, I didn't want to hurt his pride or his feelings. If he loved me a tenth as much as I loved him, he would be devastated by my rejection.

"I love to be in your company, Daniel. You are one of my dearest friends. But there can never be more than that between us." I turned away from him, hugging myself. Steeling myself to go on as nonchalantly as possible. I walked to the fireplace, as if by putting more physical distance between us, it would somehow be easier to say the words.

I turned to him with determination, and smiled brightly, but not from my heart, which was breaking, bleeding. "I've determined never to marry, you see. I enjoy my freedom too much. So I'm not seeking a romantic attachment."

He will think that I love him too little, and he will do me a grave injustice and himself, unnecessary hurt. But it is better this way. If we allowed our tender feelings for each other to take their course, there could be only one outcome. I would have to tell him the truth. For I could never deceive him so terribly as to marry him, probably bear him diseased and defective children, and condemn him to a dreadful fate.

Of course, I've thought of that, dear diary, in the darkest and loneliest hours of the night. If I poisoned Daniel with my affliction then we would be irrevocably tied to each other in a most bizarre and horrendous fashion. But he would be mine. Yet I am no heartless vampire to doom my beloved so. And to give him cause to hate me.

"Do you not care for companionship, for children?" he asked.

"I am content to be an aunt, and have no desire for children of my own," I said, unable to look into his eyes as I voiced that lie. "As for companionship, will I not continue to have yours, Daniel?" Now I did look at him, entreating him not to deny me.

"Of course. But don't deny yourself the pleasures of married intimacy, Violet. We men aren't all such brutes as those you see and hear about at the Refuge, you know."

Did he think I had been distressed by the sordid side of marriage I had witnessed? "I know that. You mustn't think I've come to this decision without careful thought."

"Then I apologize for misreading the situation," he said ruefully. "Good day, Violet." And he was gone.

I was trembling, but didn't allow myself to weep until I reached my room. There I cried until I was empty inside. I feel like only a shell of a person, with my heart and soul wrenched out of me.

It's been a month since the ball, and I have secluded myself here at Moon Hall. And I fear for my sanity. Dark thoughts of suicide possess me, for I cannot deal with the pain and the hopelessness of my empty, doomed life.

So I have resolved to go away for a while. I've already written to Aunt Caroline to ask if she will accompany me on a 'Grand Tour' of Europe. She has been widowed many years now, and living quite modestly, so she will no doubt be eager to come along. But if not, I will find a companion or go by myself!

April 13, 1876:

I leave for Quebec tomorrow, from whence I take a steamship to England. Aunt Caroline is most grateful for my offer, and looks forward to our adventure.

The prospect has made even me lighter of heart.

I think that Lily is astute and knows more than I care to realize about Daniel and me. She speaks highly of him, and his brother, Jonathan, who is a close friend of the Blakes. So Lily is somewhat surprised and disappointed, I think, that Daniel and I are not yet engaged and that I am running off to Europe for six months. But she did not question my motives - bless her!

I saw Daniel, of course. I couldn't leave with our relationship in such turmoil.

I struggled to prepare myself for our meeting. There was almost too much between us now to re-establish that easy friendship we had, yet that was precisely what I was determined to do.

And I think I managed it. He came to tea with Lily and me, and I told him of my plans.

"Surely you've been to Europe, Daniel?" I said.

"My brother and I spent a summer there, before I went into medical school," he admitted.

"Then you must tell me all the best places to go!"

And so we spoke of Europe - romantic Europe, where I should have been going with Daniel and not my aunt!

Before he left, he said, "You'll be missed, Violet." His eyes searched mine, as if he were trying once more to break through my brittle shell to reach me. But he couldn't know that that shell was all that was left of me.

I deliberately misinterpreted his words. "Marjorie and the others do very well without me. They have it so well organized that the Refuge practically runs itself. But do look after them, Daniel."

"I will. Take care, Violet, and stay away from the Balkans!"

"Of course! I have no desire to get involved in a war!"

I smiled and waved. And wept inside.

October 31, 1876:

Europe was wonderful, dear diary! Long-dead knights still walk the battlements of great castles. Monks still chant in the echoing ruins of English abbeys. And pagan gods still rule Mediterranean temples.

I immersed myself in the history, marvelled at the cathedrals and palaces, and indulged in the rich and varied flavours of the food and wine.

And all the while I wished that Daniel were sharing it with me.

Aunt Caroline was a most adventuresome companion, though, and made no efforts to tame me this time!

Yet, I am glad to be home. I missed Moon Hall and my faithful Tristan, who stayed with the Blakes, but pined for me nonetheless. He is lying beside me now, as always, and is a great comfort to me in his devotion and unreserved affection.

I have managed to regain some equanimity. I suppose I have come to terms with my fate, and am not ready to abandon life just yet. There is still plenty to enjoy, even if so much is denied me.

Daniel admired the many sketches that I did - a visual record of my trip - some of which I will turn into proper paintings. How better to spend dismal winter days than reliving that exotic adventure in my imagination as I put paint to paper.

I think Daniel and I are truly friends again. I wrote to him often from abroad, sending postcards from every stop. (Only Lily received as many as he!) And I brought him a little gift, which delighted him. It is a small marble statue of Pan, so similar to my own garden god in posture and expression that I had to buy him.

Dear God, I hope our friendship is strong, for Isobel Granger is now a widow. And free to marry again.

Charles Granger had a fatal heart attack in Montreal in early summer, so no doubt Daniel has been comforting the grieving widow. At least Isobel will not be in Ottawa during the parliamentary sessions anymore. Or will that mean that Daniel will be in Montreal more often?

But I must not torment myself with things I cannot influence or change. And I cannot truly begrudge Daniel what happiness he may find with Isobel. She is still young enough to bear him children. He will be a good husband and father.

I love him too much to begrudge him that.

Chapter 27

"I've never been to an auction before," Kit confessed to Liz and Kevin as they stepped out of her BMW.

"Liz loves rooting around in other people's junk," Kevin teased.

"Because it's like a treasure hunt!' Liz retorted. "I've found some fine old pieces of furniture and silver and whatnot."

"But you have to have an eye for them," Kevin said to Kit. "Some of the things look appalling until they're cleaned or mended. Liz seems to be able to see beyond the neglect though."

"Maybe I should have become an antique dealer," Liz said, twining her arm in his. "Come on!"

They joined the other people who, having parked their cars on the front lawn of the farm, were gravitating toward the barn.

"First we'll scout around and see if there's anything worth bidding for," Liz explained.

"Is it like those Sotheby's auctions I've seen in movies where someone gives a meaningful look and suddenly finds himself the owner of a million dollar painting?" Kit asked.

"Not quite! When you register, you get a card with a number on it. If you want to bid, you raise the card to signal. But you do have to be careful not to get carried away trying to win the bid. I've seen real junk, like broken garden tools, sell for more than they would cost new!"

The farm was one of the ones in the valley that Kit could see distantly from Moon Hall. It was owned by McGraths, but Kit had not yet discovered how they were related to her own neighbours.

It was a beautiful autumn Saturday, but even in the mellow morning sunlight, the place had a forlorn air. The house, so similar to her neighbours' (it must have been the style of the day) had many of its windows boarded up. Kit wondered what the story was behind it.

Farm equipment was scattered about in the field beside the barn while the barn itself was lined with trestle tables spread with small things from the house - everything from chipped tea cups to toilet plungers. The larger furniture dominated the centre of the building, and even Kit could see that there were some good pieces of mahogany and oak.

But she found it all a bit depressing, for here, surely, was every item, from the most treasured to the cheapest utilitarian, that comprised a family's life and home. Exposed here for all to see and judge. And what did they reveal - that this family had once had the means to acquire some fine things, but had also had appalling taste (pumpkin-orange and lime-green striped curtains!) and perhaps little money of late, for there was nothing new. Even the black and white television was twenty years old.

Nonetheless, Kit joined those who were examining these relics of other peoples' lives.

Liz picked up a blackened spoon and turned it over. Quietly she said, "Look, Kit, there's the sterling silver hallmark. This just needs polishing."

"Look at the *M* on the handle!" Kit exclaimed. "This belonged to the McGraths. What I mean is, Violet gave an engraved set of silver cutlery to Hugh and Ruth as their wedding present. I saw the rest of this set at Jean's when I went to dinner. I wonder how this got here?"

Laughing, Kevin said, "I think she's hooked, Liz."

From behind her a voice said, "So you've discovered one of our family heirlooms, eh?" It was Alan. "I'll have to tell Mum, then you see if you can outbid her!"

Kit laughed. "Is she here?"

"You bet. She and Mary are just over there. Pop wouldn't come because this is his worst nightmare."

Kit and Alan moved away from the tables while Liz and Kevin continued browsing. "So who are these McGraths and what happened?"

"Distant cousins. It was one of Hugh's brothers who bought this farm. Charlie McGrath, the old man, just died and this is the estate sale. His son didn't want anything to do with the farm and moved out years ago. Now he just wants his inheritance. The farm is being sold, too, though it'll be hard to unload for a good price these days. Who can afford the outrageous interest on mortgages?"

Drew and the others, perhaps, Kit thought, wondering if this was the farm they had been talking about recently. "So how did this spoon from Hugh and Ruth's set get here?"

"Beats me! Maybe some jealous relative wanted to break up that expensive set to spite old Ruth. Slipped it into her pocket when she came to tea."

Kit chuckled. "I'm going to say 'hi' to your mother. Let me know if you find anything I could use!"

She went over and greeted Jean and Mary, who were examining a lace tablecloth. "This is quite nice," Jean said. "In want of a bit of repair, but it's hand-made."

Kit imagined some Victorian woman spending endless, painstaking hours creating that fanciful decoration. When? Between giving birth and milking the cows?

Mary said, "I can fix that alright! Have you found anything yet, Kit?"

She told them about the spoon, and Jean said, "There are a few pieces missing from our set. I'll have to have a good scout round."

"I have my eye on that bed," Mary said, and then blushed. It was a sleigh-back bed in gleaming walnut. "Furniture for the new house," she added hastily.

And Kit could only think of how odd that antique would look in that boringly modern bungalow.

She drifted off on her own, discovering a lovely cedar-lined pine blanket box that would look good at the foot of her cannonball bed, and a pretty antique oil lamp that might come in handy when the electricity went out.

She spied Myrtle Skuce but managed to avoid her, and felt slightly guilty for her evasion. But she wasn't so lucky with Wayne.

He must have been stalking her, she thought afterwards, for he was suddenly there, trying to squeeze through the same narrow space between the furniture and thickening crowds as she was. So Kit found herself thrust against him, his chest brushing hers, his face so close that she was sickened by his smoky, beery breath.

"Whoa there, little lady!" he said with that insulting grin as he grabbed her arms.

"Excuse me, Wayne," she said angrily as she struggled out of his grasp. He was strong, and even through the thickness of her jacket she could feel his fingers biting into her arms. But in her panic she managed to wrench herself free and shove past him.

"Pushy broad!" he called after her.

Kit's heart was pounding, although she couldn't understand the intensity of her fear. She was in the middle of a huge crowd of people, for God's sake! What could Wayne possibly have done to her here? But rational thought could not stop her shaking. She hated this game he seemed to have initiated, where he kept imposing himself upon her, taunting and threatening. Was he just trying to scare her, or did he have more sinister intentions?

Kit stepped out into the cool air, away from the warm and claustrophobic barn, where she felt she could breathe again. There were plenty of people outside, too, examining the machinery and tools.

Kit spotted it as soon as she rounded the corner of the barn. She gazed at it in disbelief and then awe. With excitement bubbling through her, she went over to touch it. It was the statue of Pan.

She would have recognized it even if she didn't have Violet's painting as proof. Pan looked as though he'd had a hard life and been long neglected. Bits of dirty, lichen-encrusted stone had worn away or broken off. But Kit knew she had to have it. She was desperate to have it.

But how on earth did it get here? If anyone would have had it, surely it would have been Hugh, she thought. But maybe Ruth had hated it. Maybe she had known of Hugh's tender feelings for Violet, and refused to have this somewhat lecherous remnant of Violet's life near her. Maybe Hugh had even arranged for his brother to buy it so that he could still see it and feel some connection with Violet. Or maybe she, Kit, was just letting her imagination run wild again!

When the auction finally started, Kit marvelled at the unintelligible speed with which the auctioneer gabbled and drove up the prices. Despite Liz's warning, Kit thought she might have paid too much for the chest, though the lamp was probably reasonable, and Pan was a steal. She was ecstatic.

"And how do you propose to get that ugly creature home?" Alan asked her.

"Well, I thought I might impose upon my kind neighbours to assist me," she quipped.

"Sorry, I don't have my crane handy."

"He can't weigh more than..."

"A ton or so. Likely break the springs in that fancy car of yours. But, hey, anything for a friend! But if this gives me a hernia, I expect daily visits in the hospital."

"It's a deal!"

Alan offered to take it in the truck, and he and Kevin, with Kit's brilliant idea to borrow a ramp, managed to get the statue on board (next to Mary's sleigh-back bed and dresser). Back at Moon Hall they also contrived to maneuver it into the secret garden for her.

It would need a plinth, she thought, after the others had gone. But she was thrilled to have restored Pan to his rightful spot. If Violet was watching her, Kit was certain she would be pleased.

.   .   .

The Pughs returned from Europe later that week, and Kit was glad to accept a luncheon invitation - even more glad to discover that they would be eating indoors this time. From snatches of their simultaneous soliloquies, she heard all about their trip and all about their plans for their winter in Florida. Despite their often infuriating manner, Kit knew she would miss them.

She went to visit her own parents again before their migration south. Except for a couple of weeks at Christmas, she wouldn't see them until spring either. With her brother and his family out of the country as well, it gave her a rather odd feeling of being left behind.

So Kit was somewhat forlorn when she returned home on a nippy October Saturday. Oliver Twist was happy to see her, as usual, and proudly brought her a field mouse that he had captured and mutilated. She tried to show her gratitude to the cat, while trying not to look at the corpse. Satisfied with her praise, Ollie sat down to enjoy his meal. Revolted by the crunching of bones as he tore into the carcass, Kit left him and went inside. She wasn't sure she could face his companionship for a while.

Perhaps she should go away somewhere. To Florida with her parents? But she didn't really like Florida and would be there for Christmas anyway. To Australia? It was so far, and she should be getting down to work on her new book - her completed one having already been sent off to her publisher. To England, which she loved and which always inspired her? But the idea of going anywhere by herself just now was depressing. She could easily understand Georgina's reluctance to travel alone.

Should she visit Nigel? See how they got on? Find out if seeing him rekindled the fire? She still had her key. The idea of his coming home to find her ensconced in the living room was not unappealing. She liked to surprise Nigel, to ruffle him out of his complacency.

But what if he had another woman living with him? What if he'd changed the locks? Did she really want to expose herself to such potential for humiliation?

A knock on the door roused her from her daydream. It was Nick.

"Hi! I've come with an invitation," he said. "Are you free for dinner?"

"I certainly am! And the invitation couldn't have come at a better time. I'm very poor company for myself today."

"Then come to the city with me for a night out."

She was stunned. "I thought... I mean..."

"Dinner at the farm?" he asked. "They don't even know I'm here. It's you I came to see."

She didn't know how to interpret that. When she didn't answer right away, he said, "Just dinner. No strings attached. Just friends. OK?"

"What about Christine?" Uttering that woman's name was like screeching nails across a blackboard.

"We're not living together, if that's what you've been thinking. We do see a fair bit of each other, but we're not inseparable. No reason for me not to take a friend to dinner. Now, are you going to keep me standing here at the door, or are you going to ask me in to make myself comfortable while you get changed?"

She laughed then. "You are being awfully high-handed!"

"Only because you're being contentious. I don't usually have such trouble extracting an answer to such an irresistible offer."

He was setting the mood with his banter, and she fell in with him. "Sounds to me as though you've gotten your own way for far too long... But it is rather irresistible."

Kit felt wonderfully light-hearted as she dressed. She had left Nick browsing through her books in the library. All thoughts of Nigel had evaporated.

"That was quick," Nick said when she reappeared fifteen minutes later.

"Too quick?" she asked, glancing critically at her favourite dress. She knew she looked terrific, and could see from his expression that he thought so too.

"Hardly. I'm impressed - by the speed and the results." He was standing by the portrait of Violet that Helen Talbot had given her. "Is this your ghost?" he asked.

"Yes."

"And her painting of the secret garden, I take it."

"Oh, Nick, I've got to show you something before we leave! Come on."

He followed her into the kitchen where she kicked off her high heels and slipped into her rubber boots.

"Oh, very chic," Nick teased.

She grabbed her trenchcoat off the rack and they stepped out into the chill of the late afternoon. Leading him toward the secret garden, she cautioned, "Watch out for the groundhog holes. There're all over the place."

"Softie!" he accused.

She threw him a grin.

Kit had lost no time in finding a pedestal for Pan. It resembled a short Doric column, which seemed a most appropriate spot for him to reside.

"Wow!" Nick exclaimed. "Where did you dig him up?"

"At a local auction. It seems you were right. Though I think Pan must have looked decidedly odd sitting in some farmer's field all these years."

Looking at her shrewdly, Nick said, "This ghost of yours has really gotten to you, hasn't she?"

"She's not a ghost to me. She seems as real as my best friend," Kit confessed. "I can visualize her sitting here, you see. She described it so often."

"Don't empathize with her too much, Kit. You get this sad look in your eyes whenever you talk about her."

"Don't worry, I'm not possessed! I don't feel as if her spirit is taking over my body or that I'm a reincarnation of her soul. Well... maybe only on dark and stormy nights!" Kit laughed.

"You really do need a night out in civilization!" Nick countered with a twinkle in his eyes. "Shall we go?" He extended his arm for her to take.

"Not until I change my boots!" she retorted, wrapping her arm about his.

"And I thought this was the new fashion."

There were no awkward silences between them in the car. They talked about the commune, about their university days, about their childhoods. The high-powered stereo system was turned low, and the old songs that played on the cassette reminded them even more of days past.

Nick was a competent driver, and Kit felt relaxed. As she looked at his hands gripping the wheel, she was tempted to reach out and touch him.

Here he was, offering her the friendship that she had wanted, and now she was starting to act like a silly schoolgirl! She really must get a grip on herself. Nick wasn't one for a permanent relationship, she reminded herself.

The maitre d' at Armands greeted him cordially. "Your table is ready, Mr. Radcliffe," he said, leading them to one near the fireplace where a cozy fire crackled.

When he had gone, Kit said, "You were pretty sure of yourself, booking a table before I'd even accepted!"

He grinned and said, "Actually I booked one last week too, but you weren't home, so I cancelled it and went to the farm."

She was pleasantly surprised by his honesty, and glad he wasn't playing games with her.

Her account of dinner here with Leighton and Pete made him laugh.

"I can imagine that Andre was not impressed with your escorts that night."

"You seem to be a valued customer."

"Well, they're better cooks than I am! But I won't be coming here so often anymore if I put my scheme into operation." He paused while the wine waiter brought and uncorked the Chateauneuf-du-Pape and poured him a taste. When their glasses were filled, Nick raised his and said, "Here's to friends!"

Their eyes met over the wine glasses. It was as if they had come to some understanding - friends for now. Sex could come later, or never, but it would not change the fact that they were friends first.

"I haven't been satisfied with my life lately," Nick told her. "At first it was exciting, gambling on the stock market with other people's money. I seem to have a knack for making money - even my own investments flourished! But I felt something was missing. I guess all those years at the farm had a more profound influence on me than I realized. But it wasn't until recently that I could pinpoint my discontent."

The waiter brought the shrimp cocktails.

After he'd had a few bites, Nick continued. "I realized I didn't want to be a stockbroker for the rest of my life. I want to do something worthwhile, other than make piles of money. After wracking my brains trying to think of what I was capable of doing and would enjoy doing, you gave me the idea. So simple! So obvious!"

"I did?"

He nodded as he chewed.

"Stop eating and tell me!" Kit said. "I can't stand the suspense!"

He finished the appetizer before he leaned back and said, "I'm going to publish a magazine for environmentally conscious big-city drop-outs like you, Kit, who don't know the first thing about how to buy or feed a woodstove, how to make organic pesticides and fertilizers, how to build cold frames or passive solar houses."

"Do you think there are enough people like me out there who'd want to know those things?"

"It's a gamble. But I do think so. Even urban people could get pointers from us on things like composting and growing better tomatoes and using herbs. And I think we could raise environmental awareness, too. That'll be part of our mission. I know most people think environmentalists are a bunch of crackpots, but they won't be able to scoff much longer. People are going to have to face the reality that we're polluting ourselves to death, and are going to have to start changing their own habits. We'll show them how to do it."

"It's certainly timely."

"I expect it will get off to a slow start. But I have a gut feeling about this. The way I have about a good investment. So I'm going to take a chance. I have a journalist friend with whom I've discussed this. I'm going to ask him to be the editor. I'm hopeless at writing anything more than a memo - my English grades were never impressive. I thought I'd ask Pete to become a staff writer - give him a chance to escape from the farm if he wants it or stay there and write part-time. I'll do the marketing. And I need you to help guide me through this."

"I have no experience in magazine publishing."

"But you have good ideas. You could advise us about story lines and writing styles. I might even be able to pay you as a consultant!" he said with a laugh. "But I'd certainly feel better about it if I had your support."

"You have it. I think it's a great idea! I only hope others do."

"My indefatigable arrogance tells me they will. Now you can start by helping me come up with a title."

They tucked into succulent plates of roast lamb, and discussed Nick's project while they ate. Kit was almost as excited as he. They finally settled on *Country Lanes* as the name of this revolutionary new magazine.

They savoured a rich and delicate lemon mousse, and lingered over coffee and liqueurs. It was late when they left the restaurant.

"I think we'd better take a walk before I drive you back. Make sure I'm not over the limit for driving. Will you be warm enough for a stroll along the canal?"

Armands was close to the Rideau Canal, which cut through the city and provided bicycle paths and parks along its banks. In the winter it became a popular seven-kilometre-long groomed skating rink.

It was a chilly night, but at least there was no wind. The walkways were pretty well deserted at this time of year. Kit's heels clicked slowly and rhythmically as they ambled, arm-in-arm, alongside the waterway. Light from the streetlamps shivered on the cold, black surface of the water.

"Of course, the sensible thing to do would be for you to stay at my place," Nick said. "I do have a spare bedroom."

"I didn't bring anything with me. I'd look like hell in the morning."

"I doubt that! But you don't mind waiting while I pack a bag? I really can't face coming back here again tonight. I'll stay at the farm. Anyway, I want to talk to Pete tomorrow."

"Sure."

Kit was surprised by Nick's place. She had expected something modern and flashy - a condo with the works. But it turned out to be the ground floor of a spacious, Edwardian house in the Glebe - an area of downtown Ottawa, close to the canal, that was being revitalized. He owned the house, Nick told her, and rented the second floor to a pleasant young couple who worked for the government. They skated to work in the wintertime.

It was a delightful place, in fact. Unlike Nigel's schizophrenic Victorian pad, this house retained the charm of the old woodwork, the marble fireplaces, the hardwood floors. The furniture was comfortable and serviceable, and not chosen to make a statement or an impression.

It would be so easy to stay here, Kit thought. It felt like home.

They were both more subdued on the drive back, but it was a comfortable silence that they shared. Kit lay back in her seat, listening to the music with her eyes closed. Nick's nearness was comforting.

"We'll have to do that again soon," Nick said, when he left her at her door. "Before I run out of money!"

"I'd like that. Thanks for a wonderful evening."

He made no attempt to kiss her this time, but just smiled his goodbye.

She listened for the ever-fainter whine of the engine as he drove away. In the crisp night air, she was sure she could hear the car turning down the concession road and then slowing down at the farm. Then silence. That tomb-like country silence.

Chapter 28

I hate November! Although it is not truly winter yet, it is a more desolate and gloomy time than winter itself. Everything is dead, but not decently buried beneath the snow. Rain is stingingly cold, the winds, brutal. The shrinking days are often grey and sinister.

But sometimes a day dawns warm and sunny, as if it had escaped from early fall. Indian Summer, we call it. A day that lets us pretend we are not fast descending into winter after all, though the threat can be caught in the sharp edge of the wind and the feeble sunlight.

It was on such a day that I invited Ruth to join me for a ride.

Kate had been to see me and confided that all was not well between Ruth and Hugh.

"Ruth moved into her own bedroom after Cameron was born, and hasn't been a true wife to Hugh since," Kate explained. "It's destroying their marriage, for Hugh is a virile man, and he wants more children."

"But Ruth doesn't?" I guessed, recalling what she had sworn to me.

"She's afraid, I think. Of course, it's not easy," Kate said. She was six months pregnant again herself. "I haven't forgotten, though the memory has been dulled by time, and I'm not looking forward to the actual birth. But we all have to do things that are difficult or painful. And what joy afterwards! But I think Ruth has lived too sheltered a life. She has always had everything done for her and expects things to be easy, effortless. She's not willing to make any sacrifices."

That is what Mrs. Skuce has always maintained. But I could not find it in my heart to blame Ruth for not wishing to repeat a terrible experience, and indeed, to risk her own life in the process.

"I've tried talking to her, Violet, but she just gets angry with me and tells me to mind my own business. But I worry about Hugh."

And I could understand his frustration and hurt. "So you want me to talk to her?"

"Yes."

Which is what I tried to do on this deceitful day that masqueraded as late summer.

We both rode hard, our horses enjoying the gallop as much as we. We went up the old logging road to the top of the ridge. There is a large beaver pond, where we stopped to rest our horses, and sat on a warm granite outcropping.

"What a glorious day!' Ruth said, taking off her hat and throwing her head back to feel the sun on her face.

"I missed riding Moondancer when I was away," I said.

"You are so lucky, Violet! Would that I could have gone to Europe with you! I can't imagine anything more wonderful than spending endless months touring the capitals."

"Perhaps you will someday," I said, but didn't really believe it myself. I know that Hugh is irrevocably tied to the farm.

Ruth scoffed. "I'll never get there, unless I go on my own! But I don't have your courage. Or money."

"It takes very little courage, Ruth."

"But not very little money," she added with a chuckle.

"True enough."

"Are you ever planning to marry, Violet?"

"No," I replied warily, not wishing her to begin probing me for explanations. Besides, I was the one who was supposed to be questioning her. Quickly I said. "Are you happy with Hugh?"

"Is that what this is about? Has Kate asked you to meddle in my marriage?"

I was somewhat taken aback by her quick perception and her bluntness, but I said, "She's concerned about both of you."

"I do love him, you know," she said defiantly. "I want to be allowed to love him in my own way. And I refuse to have any more children. There is only one way to ensure that, Violet. And if physical intimacy is all that Hugh wants of me, if he doesn't care for me or my needs, then he has deceived me, and doesn't truly love me."

"Isn't it pleasurable then?"

"Those few moments of fleeting pleasure are not worth the cost. Sure, it's easy enough for men. They don't have nine months of ever increasing discomfort, when you feel as if your body has been possessed by some foreign creature. And the birth...." She shuddered visibly. "I can't go through all that again, Violet! How can he expect that of me?" I could see that she was torn between

her love for Hugh and her terror of the consequences of the
physical closeness she probably craved as much as I longed for
intimacy with Daniel.

"But don't you fear for your marriage?"

"I do everything a good wife should. Everything but that.
In any case, he has a mistress now, so he no longer pesters me in
that way. Don't look so shocked, Violet. Hugh is a man. I'm glad
he's found someone to submit to his needs. He's been much more
cheerful lately."

Despite her words, I could see that Ruth was deeply
wounded. Was Hugh really betraying her? With whom?

Perhaps I'm not really surprised. Hugh is, as Kate had
said, a virile man.

"You can tell Kate that her brother, at least, is happy!" She
jumped up and mounted her horse, and rode off without waiting
for me.

I lingered, knowing I couldn't catch up with her. Besides,
there was nothing left to say.

April 15, 1877:

Isobel Granger has bought a house in Ottawa!

So she has begun her campaign to ensnare Daniel. For
what other reason would she settle here? She retains her mansion
in Montreal, and is by all accounts a very wealthy widow.

Because I cannot compete with her, I fear losing Daniel
altogether.

I have to admit that Isobel is clever in her campaign to win
Daniel from me, whom she must consider her greatest rival for his
affections. She actually invited me, along with the Blakes, to her
new home for dinner. Although she is still in mourning and does
not attend large functions, she often has small dinner parties.
With Daniel invited to as many as he can possibly attend.

Her house is in Upper Town - impressive, modern, and
substantial. It is much too large for one person. But I'm sure she
envisions Daniel sharing it with her. It's certainly large enough to
have part of it converted to a doctor's surgery.

The other guests that evening were Daniel's brother,
Jonathan, now a judge, and his wife, Charlotte, who seemed to be
an old friend of Isobel's from Montreal. For my benefit, no doubt,

there was an eager young man named Montgomery Fulton, who was about my age, but seemed to me infinitely younger than I.

Isobel said, "Montgomery has just joined the civil service, so I promised his mother that I would introduce him to all the most interesting people in Ottawa!" Obviously another old Montreal friend.

At dinner, Isobel did not seat Daniel at the end of the table opposite her - too blatant a declaration of her intentions perhaps - but instead, seated him on her right. She said, "Montgomery, will you do me the honour of taking the other end of the table? And Violet, I've put you next to Montgomery." And far from Daniel.

With the arrogance of youth, Montgomery babbled on and on to me about his position, leaving me to nod or grunt at appropriate times while my mind wandered. "Beautiful building, of course, but damnably cold to work in, I can tell you!" he said cheerfully between shovelsful of food, for he ate as enthusiastically as he talked.

Seeing an opportunity to change the topic and involve the rest of the diners, I asked, "Have you attended any of the entertainments at Rideau Hall?"

"Not yet, not yet! But I do hear that the Dufferins are keen on theatricals. The Earl's a descendent of that playwright, Sheridan, I'm told. I hear that he and his wife are both excellent actors and love nothing more than taking to the stage!"

"We've enjoyed their performances," said Lily.

"Daniel, have you mentioned the letter you received from Her Excellency?" Isobel prompted.

I bristled. Once again, she was privy to knowledge that I did not have.

"I wasn't aware that you knew about that, Isobel," Daniel said in surprise. I was grateful to him for not letting her get away with an intimation of secrecy between them.

"Actually, Lady Dufferin told me herself," Isobel confessed. "She thinks very highly of you, Daniel, and was most grateful for your assistance to His Excellency."

That story I had heard, but Montgomery had not, so Daniel related it.

"It happened last month, just after that ice storm we had. I chanced to be nearby when Dufferin stepped out of his sleigh downtown and slipped on the ice, falling heavily against a step. Some men had already helped him to his feet before I could reach him, but the Earl was so badly shaken and injured that he could not stand and fell again. I had him carried into a nearby shop where I examined him, determining that he had no broken bones, but was badly bruised, with some muscles torn. I bandaged him up and escorted him home. After that, his own doctor took over, and he's since made a full recovery. He was, in fact, luckier than some of my patients, who took bad tumbles on the ice and broke bones or cracked their heads open."

"Dufferin's a good chap," Jonathan Haywood said. "He's done more to pull this country together than all the politicians in Ottawa ever could."

"And his wife," I added. "After all, she's gone on these excursions with him, from one end of the country to the other, and to some of the remotest parts. I have a great deal of admiration for her, since even for the Viceregal couple, it can't always have been easy going."

"You're right there," Jonathan replied. "And those diplomatic journeys were crucial. I think they've succeeded in pacifying the disgruntled British Columbians who've been advocating secession from the Dominion. He - they've - certainly earned their keep."

"And they really are the most charming people," Isobel said. "I know a goodly number of Ottawa matrons who have more pretensions than the Countess, with far less reason."

"They've been good for the city as well as the country," Augustus said. "They've made us a little less provincial and given us a bit more self-confidence and pride."

"And they've shown us how to enjoy winter," Lily said. "I never thought I'd like tobogganing, but it was great fun. And both Violet and I have achieved some proficiency on skates."

"I can attest to that," Daniel said.

"Thanks to you," I couldn't resist adding. But I should have known that Isobel would best me.

She said, "Daniel is a good skater, isn't he? We spent a good part of our winters at the Rink in Montreal. Now we even have costume balls on the ice there, which Lady Dufferin particularly enjoys when she visits."

Feeling contentious, I said to her, "You must find Ottawa dull after Montreal."

"Not at all! I made so many friends here during my previous stays. It's a welcome change for me. I found I couldn't remain in Montreal just now."

I persisted. "But you intend to return there?"

She shrugged prettily. "Who knows? I've kept the house of course. But I rather like the freedom to do just as I please. If I do get bored here, I can just go back to Montreal for a while."

But not until she had caught Daniel, I was sure. Then she would lure him away from Ottawa as well, I could see it all now. And I don't really blame her.

But I can't help hating her.

Chapter 29

Kit glanced at the clock again. It was 11:40, only five minutes later than the last time she had looked.

She had gotten an early start this morning, arriving in Ottawa before nine, and had been well into the thick of her research at the National Library and Archives since then. Now she had a list of relevant books, most of which she would try to order through inter-library loan at the Kintyre Library, and a few which she had asked to see from the National's collection. These were being fetched from the stacks now, but it could be a while before they were available to her, and she did have to eat lunch.

The question was whether she should call Nick and invite him to join her.

What if he had another engagement? What if he didn't like his business day disrupted by personal calls? What if...?

To hell with her misgivings! He was her friend after all. She wouldn't have hesitated to call Leighton or Alan or any of the others.

Nick was delighted to hear from her, and arranged to meet her at Apricots.

Kit was early, and sipped a glass of white wine as she absorbed the atmosphere of the restaurant. It was decorated in apricot and cream, with green highlights - plants and picture frames and placemats. All very cute and co-ordinated. The clientele was equally well turned out - professionals and civil servants - affluent Yuppies.

When Nick entered the restaurant, Kit was struck anew by his easy good looks. He wore his business suit with a casualness which, though it made him look every inch the successful young executive, also suggested that he didn't take himself too seriously. And that endeared him to her even more. He returned several greetings from acquaintances, and then spotted her.

He smiled warmly at her. "This is a pleasant surprise. I'm glad you called me, Kit."

"Do you come here often?" Kit asked with amusement as Nick responded to more greetings.

"Ottawa is like a small town in some respects. But actually, I don't come here all that often. Mostly I brown bag it. Don't look so surprised. I'm rather an accomplished cook as well. We all used to take turns cooking before Erick took charge."

"A man of many talents."

"But very little time, I'm afraid. If I'd known you were coming, I'd have rescheduled my appointments, and then we could have had a leisurely lunch."

When they had given their orders to the waiter, Kit said, "I didn't decide to come until early this morning. My new book's starting to gel. But there's a lot of research I need to do."

"Are you going to stay in the city for a few days?"

Her attention focussed on Nick, Kit hadn't noticed Christine until she leaned over Nick, her platinum curtain of hair brushing his shoulder, and said coolly, "Dinner still on, Nick?"

He turned to her in surprise. "Hi, Christine. Sure. See you at seven."

She flashed him a smile and then walked off to a table across the room, with a fashionable, leather-jacketed young man in tow.

Wryly Kit said, "No, I'm not staying. I'll come up to the city every once in a while."

Not at all discomposed by Christine's presence, Nick said, "Great! Let me know when, and we'll make proper arrangements. Dinner too, if you're planning to stay all day. You and I have a lot to discuss."

She looked at him quizzically.

"About the magazine. Pete's agreed to be a staff writer..."

"I know. He and Leighton came to see me the other night. Pete was thrilled. He couldn't stop talking about it." They'd spent a pleasant evening chatting over a bottle of wine and lolling in front of the fire.

Nick asked, "What did Leighton think? He was pretty noncommittal when I told him on Sunday."

"Even his cynicism gave way to enthusiasm after a while. He thinks it has the potential to become a sop to Yuppies who want to feel noble by using biodegradable soap at the cottage, or composting their kitchen waste instead of chucking it into the garbage. But Pete and I convinced him that the three of us will make it more significant than that. We persuaded him to give us suggestions for story lines, too." Having gotten to know Leighton, Kit was not surprised that Nick valued his friend's opinion so highly.

While the waiter placed their meals in front of them, Kit noticed Christine playing up to her luncheon partner, apparently fully engrossed in him, although Kit had caught her glancing over from time to time to see Nick's reaction.

Nick followed her gaze. As if reading her thoughts he said, "I'm not the jealous type, so she's wasting her time. I don't believe in emotional blackmail."

Kit could imagine that Nick had never had difficulty getting whatever woman he fancied. But with his casual attitude toward them, he must have inspired jealousy in a few at least.

And although she could feel the twinges of it within herself, she didn't want a relationship with someone so... uninvolved.

Nigel had never been like that. Despite his self-possession, his nonchalance, he had been passionate in his lovemaking - and she used that term in the most liberal sense, as had the Victorians, to mean all aspects of courtship. She had felt as if he'd literally swept her off her feet. He had demanded devotion and given it.

And yet, gazing at the man who smiled so candidly at her, Kit wondered if perhaps a relationship less complicated by emotions would be all that bad. But wasn't she already enthralled by Nick? Didn't she think that Nick might fall in love with her, that things would be different - special - between them, as they had not been in his other relationships? Didn't all women want to believe that?

Kit felt curiously dissatisfied after parting from Nick. The thought that he was going to see - and sleep with? - Christine that evening was disturbing.

But back at the library, she quickly became engrossed in her research once again. Reading through hours of microfiche of old newspapers and magazines, she discovered the Ottawa of Violet's day, including references to her and the Refuge in articles.

They substantiated all that Violet herself had written about these incidents. Here, for instance, was the quote from the *Ottawa Citizen* that Violet had used in her diary. There was the account of the trial of Gideon Jackson. Here, a social tidbit about Lady Dufferin's skating parties, mentioning some of her guests, including Violet and Daniel. And there was a list of the guests who had attended the great costume ball at Rideau Hall - Miss Violet McAllister as the Lady of Shalott; Dr. Daniel Haywood as Sir Lancelot; Mrs. Charles Granger as Queen Guinevere. Just bare facts that couldn't even hint at the emotional turmoil that surrounded them.

Kit had been skeptical enough to wonder whether Violet had been prone to exaggeration or even whether she had invented most of the story in some weird, Freudian fantasy. But Kit was

convinced now that Violet's diary had not been the mad ramblings
of a frustrated virgin, but the simple truth.

Glancing out the tall windows that overlooked the Ottawa
River, Kit noticed that darkness was already settling in. It was
just about here that Rosecliff had stood, she had discovered, not
nearby at the Supreme Court site as Helen Talbot had thought.
Strange to think that people like Violet and Daniel, the Prime
Minister and the Earl and Countess of Dufferin had once partied
on this spot, where quiet and serious researchers now rubbed tired
eyes and rose from lonely contemplation to make their way home.

Kit had one more book she was determined to peruse
before calling it quits for the day. It was about syphilis.

It was quite dark when she left an hour later, and though
Kit hated driving in the dark, she hardly noticed. She was too
shocked by what she had discovered.

Violet could not have had syphilis. If her father had been
in the tertiary stage of the disease, as it appeared he must have
been, he was no longer contagious, and hadn't been for some years.
Daniel would undoubtedly have known that. What doctors then
didn't know was that syphilis was not hereditary, but congenital.
Once Violet's father had been past the contagious first and second
stages of the disease, he could still have bred healthy children.

If only Violet had told Daniel about her fears, or even her
brother-in-law, Gordon Forrester!

But Kit could understand Violet's reluctance to discuss it
with anyone. Syphilitics were considered lepers in those days. In
these modern days of antibiotics, it was too easy to forget how
dreaded the killer diseases like tuberculosis and diphtheria were.
And syphilis, she'd discovered, had been an insidious, horrible,
much feared and misunderstood pestilence that had a social
stigma as well. No well-bred young woman could possibly admit to
having a disease associated with depravity and vice.

And how could Violet explain her fear of having that
plague? Even in these modern, liberated times, women were loath
to reveal sexual abuse or incest.

Kit thought how different Violet's life could have been had
she not felt poisoned and doomed by syphilis. Happily married,
living to a ripe old age surrounded by children and grandchildren.
Not misunderstood and lonely and desperate.

Kit felt herself grow angry for Violet's sake, furious at how
unfair life had been for her. But this was surely the ultimate irony.
That it didn't have to be that way.

It wasn't until she'd left the lights of Kintyre far behind her that Kit took stock of her surroundings. It was a black night. The headlights of her car picked out the grey skeletons of trees reaching toward the deserted road. But aside from these lonely beacons piercing the thick night, Kit was engulfed by the darkness. She shuddered, and realized that she couldn't face going home to Moon Hall just yet. It was stupid, she knew, but it was as if she couldn't face Violet while she was still bristling with this shocking new information.

She should have stayed in the city for dinner, or even stopped in town. (A dose of Dianna Webb and a pizza would probably have been good for her.) But she was nearly in Todmorden, and the idea of driving the ten miles back to Kintyre didn't appeal to her either.

So Kit didn't hesitate to pull into the parking lot of the Wild Horse Inn, whose lights seemed more than welcoming tonight. She'd never been here before, but they did advertise a dining room. Anything was better than going back to that large, empty, dark house and slapping together a peanut butter sandwich.

The impulse to turn around and leave struck her as soon as she entered, but she told herself she was being foolish. And would forever regret that denial of instinct.

There was a strong stench of smoke and beer, and something more unpleasant - sweat? urine? Two older men clad in denim overalls, plaid hunting jackets, and baseball caps emblazoned with tractor ads were the only other occupants.

One of them raised a glass to Kit as she sat down, somewhat hesitantly, on a plastic-upholstered chair at one of the formica-topped tables. The waitress ambled over and laid a menu before her. She was a beefy girl with an oversized, aggressive bosom, frizzy bleached hair, pudgy be-ringed hands - one on each stubby finger - and an air of belligerence.

The plastic-coated menu was sticky. Kit couldn't believe they served many meals here, and wondered what was safe to eat. A hamburger?

She fought the urge to get up and leave; her writer's curiosity got the better of her. In its own disgusting way, the place was fascinating. She wondered what hapless travellers would stay in the run-down motel units adjoining the restaurant. She listened to the two old-timers lamenting life in their slow, slurred speech infested with swear words. She looked through the grimy windows at the circle of spilled light keeping the darkness at bay.

The hamburger that was set before her glistened with grease as though the bun had been deep-fried. Imagining what the conditions must be like in the kitchen, Kit suddenly lost her appetite.

She saw a couple of battered old cars and trucks drive up and half a dozen men alight. Wayne Skuce was the first one in the door.

"Well, well. If it ain't the famous lady writer," he said, coming over to her table. "Whatcha drinkin'?" She could smell the whiskey on him, and could tell by the glassy look in his eyes that he'd already had more than enough.

"Nothing thanks."

"Hey, now that ain't very friendly. Is it, lads?" He turned to the others, who had congregated about the bar and were too busy ordering drinks to pay any attention to him. He pulled out a chair and sat down at her table. "Two ryes, Betty."

"I said I didn't want anything," Kit stated firmly.

Wayne grinned at her. "Then I'll drink 'em both. But it ain't very neighbourly of ya. Jeez, ya hang around with them fuckin' freaks at the commune, but won't have a God-damn drink with me, eh?" His smirk suddenly disappeared. Kit shivered at the menacing look on his ugly, pinched face.

She pushed the plate away and rose. She gasped when Wayne grabbed her arm in a vice-like grip. "Ya ain't finished yer supper, little lady. Now I'd say that's downright insultin' to my good buddy, Bill, what owns this here place."

Kit wondered how she had gotten herself into this situation - alone in a sleazy bar with a bunch of drunks and a contentious creep trying to dominate her. She felt that no one would bat an eyelash if Wayne were to drag her out the door and rape her in the parking lot. His eyes challenged her to defy him - with that cocky confidence that she would lose, and regret trying.

Yet Kit realized that she needed to win this power struggle. Her heart hammering against her ribs, she demanded, "Let go of me this instant!"

"Do as the lady says," Alan McGrath ordered. Kit felt relief wash through her as she noticed Alan and Stuart at her side. She hadn't even seen them come in.

"Fuck off!"

Stuart grabbed Wayne and hoisted him out of the chair so quickly that the Coke spilled and the chair toppled over. Wayne had lost his grip on Kit's arm, and she rubbed the spot where he had most certainly bruised her. The drunken chatter was silenced as every eye was on Stuart and Wayne.

Stuart said. "If you weren't so pissed, I'd teach you how to treat a lady. Now get out of our way." He shoved Wayne backwards.

"You fuckin' bastard!" Fists clenched, Wayne started to go for Stuart, who was ready for him.

Although Alan's hands were perched lightly, protectively, on her shoulders, Kit could feel him tense in preparation for what could be an almighty brawl. The McGrath boys didn't stand much chance against six guys, even if the latter were pretty drunk.

Someone warned, "Watch it, the cops're comin'."

Wayne spat on the floor. "I'll get ya for this," he swore, glowering at Kit and the McGrath brothers.

They ushered her out the door just as the Provincial Police officer ambled in. Alan could feel her quaking, and said, "I'll drive your car, and Stu can follow in the truck."

"Thanks."

"Whatever possessed you to go into the Wild Horse?" Alan asked her as they started down the road.

"Hunger. All I wanted was a meal."

"I guess we forgot to warn you about that place. No self-respecting woman goes into that joint. There's not a week goes by that there isn't a fist fight in there. The cops keep a close eye on things."

"What were you doing there?"

"We noticed your car as we drove past, and decided to rescue you. Good thing, I'd say."

"Your timing couldn't have been better," Kit agreed. "Did he mean that about getting even with us?" She massaged her bruised arm. It felt singed where Wayne had gripped her.

"Don't fret yourself about that. He's been threatening people all his life. Can't remember how many times he's said that to me."

But you're a man, she wanted to say. *You'd win in a fair fight. No matter how independent I might consider myself, I'm powerless against creatures like Wayne Skuce.*

He looked over at her silent profile. "Don't let him worry you, Kit. He's pretty pissed. He'll have forgotten it by morning."

"Lucky him." She wouldn't forget.

Trying to lighten the atmosphere, Alan said, "Great car, this. Never thought I'd find myself driving one of these fancy jobs."

Kit laughed. "Alright, I promise not to brood."

"If you're really worried, I can stay the night at your place." He flashed her a wry grin. "On the couch."

She smiled. "I won't ask that of you. But thanks."

"Seriously, Kit... If you're worried...."

"I'll call you."

"Be sure you do."

It wasn't until they drove through the village and she saw the costumed children that she realized what night it was. "Oh, God, it's Halloween!"

"Yeah, I'd forgotten. Does that make things worse?"

"I know it shouldn't, but... when you think of what it means... The night the spirits are abroad...." Like Violet and her father. "I'm just being stupid!"

"Hey, if you feel uneasy, you can always stay at our place."

What she really wanted to do was to drive back to Ottawa and stay with Nick. But he was otherwise engaged. "I'll keep that in mind. Thanks, Alan... for everything."

Her house was shrouded in darkness, and Kit felt panic welling up inside her as they turned into the driveway. "I'm sure I left the outside lights on."

"Must have blown a fuse," Alan said. "I'll check it out for you, Kit."

She was thankful that Alan and Stuart, who had pulled in behind them, were with her. Unused to violence, or even the threat of it, she was still shaken by her encounter with Wayne. Of course she knew that he couldn't be lying in wait in the darkness of the carriage house, that he hadn't disabled the lights. And yet, she felt his sinister presence. He had imbued her with it, and she wondered how long she would be tainted.

When she got out of the car, Kit noticed a harvest moon on the horizon, like a giant pumpkin. At any other time she would have thought it strangely beautiful and poetic. But snatches of the Creedence Clearwater Revival song, 'Bad Moon Rising', popped into her thoughts, with its portend of doom.

Alan unlocked the door and ushered her inside. When he flicked the light switch by the kitchen door, the outside lights flooded the yard.

"I guess I'd forgotten to leave them on," Kit said. "So much for my memory!"

Seeing her perturbation, Alan said, "Sure could use a cold one, if you got one."

"Of course!"

"I'll tell Stu to come in."

The three of them sat rather awkwardly at the kitchen table, the men sipping beers and Kit downing something stronger. Alan finally said, "I haven't seen around this old place since you decorated. Mind showing me?"

"I've hardly decorated. The previous owners did a lot of work, and I haven't been inclined to change anything."

She took them through the different main floor rooms, turning on the lights and leaving them burning. "I know why you're doing this," she said to Alan. "And I appreciate it. Do you want to check the upstairs for me as well?"

He grinned. "Saw right through me, did you? I thought it would make you feel more comfortable to have the house frisked."

"You're right. It does. Can I leave the upstairs to you?"

She and Stuart returned to the kitchen to finish their drinks.

"A big house like this needs people. It feels terribly empty and silent at times," Kit said, and wondered why she had confided in Stuart. After all, he was the one who had delighted in his prediction that she wouldn't last here.

She saw compassion in his eyes, and then anger. "If that bastard gives you any more trouble, let me know," was his surprising reply.

"All clear," Alan said, joining them. "If you don't want us to stay, Kit, then we'd best be on our way. And if you feel the urge to call at three in the morning, just do it."

Kit couldn't settle to her writing. How many Halloween nights ago had Violet had her confrontation with her father and wished him dead? Kit had a vivid enough imagination to wonder if on this night at least, Moon Hall might truly be haunted.

But she was even more scared of Wayne Skuce.

She wandered about the rooms as if she were keeping horrors at bay by constantly establishing her presence. She longed to talk to someone, but didn't want to involve her commune friends in this sordid mess. She could imagine Liz insisting that she come to the farm to stay, but tomorrow would be no different, and she wasn't about to move in there. And Nick.... well, she was afraid that Christine might answer his phone. If her parents or Fran had been home she would have gone to visit them for a few days.

So she went to bed with a particularly boring book and a large brandy.

. . .

Kit woke with a start, her heart thumping. She hadn't remembered turning off her bedside lamp, but the high-riding moon cast a silvery light and strong shadows in her room. She gazed about wildly, wondering what had disturbed her.

Ollie sat bolt upright on her bed, his ears pricked up, his eyes staring at the doorway with that singularly uncanny knack cats have of appearing to see horrible things that others can't. Kit felt a primal rush of terror.

Suddenly remembering her fears of Wayne Skuce, she clenched a fist to her mouth to stifle a scream. As if he were in the house searching for her and she dared not alert him to her whereabouts.

She listened for the creak of floorboards.

Then she heard the sound again - the loud revving of car engines, and cowboy hoots. They seemed to be coming from the garden.

Although fairly confident that she was still alone in the house, she crept quietly from her bed. She grabbed the bedside flashlight, and tiptoed to the window. Her body tingled with fear. Childhood nightmares loomed large - creatures slithering out from the blackness under her bed, yawning closets hiding unspeakable monsters.

But they dissipated in the horror of what she saw on the lawn. Dangling from the branch of a tree was a body. A woman. Beneath her was a tombstone.

.   .   .

"It's just a dummy. A scarecrow," Alan said.

The policeman shook his head. "Just another Halloween prank, Miss. We get all kinds."

Kit hardly remembered calling the police.

"This one is particularly vicious," Alan said. "Well, you know the story of old Violet McAllister, Jim." He addressed the police officer. "And to bring her tombstone over here! You know who's behind this."

"So you say. But the lady didn't actually see anyone. Well, I'll be off then, Miss Spencer."

She nodded. Of course nothing could be done. Alan had already cut down the figure made with stuffed pantyhose and a tattered dress. He'd promised to return the tombstone to Violet's gravesite tomorrow.

Was this Wayne's revenge? Or was it just the beginning?

Kit put coffee on. "Will you stay for a while, Alan? You can sleep in the spare bedroom. I can't go back to sleep tonight. It's almost dawn, anyway. I didn't think I'd have to take you up on your offer to summon you at three in the morning. I'm rambling, aren't I?"

"Sit down and relax, Kit. You look awful."

"Thanks! I feel awful. I haven't even combed my hair yet."

"I meant that you look exhausted. And of course I'll stay - until it's time for the chores, anyway."

Kit fell asleep on the lumpy old sofa in the kitchen. She awoke to the smell of freshly brewing coffee. An afghan covered her, keeping off the early November chill, and a fire blazed in the hearth.

Mary McGrath was sitting in a chair beside it, knitting. She beamed at Kit. "I'll bet you could use some breakfast," she said.

Dazedly, Kit replied, "No, I'm not a big breakfast eater. Just some coffee for the moment. Thank you."

"Alan asked me to come and stay with you until you woke up. He had chores to do."

"That was thoughtful of you both, but I don't like to impose."

"Not at all! Heavens! I'm glad I can help. What a terrifying experience you must have had! Alan said the dummy looked pretty real, from a distance."

Kit would never forget the sight of it hanging there. For an awful moment she had thought it was real, until common sense had told her it couldn't be. And when she had stopped screaming, she had called Alan.

"I hope he doesn't do anything foolish," Kit muttered.

Mary shrugged. "You never know with Alan. He brought the thing home with him. Maybe he intends to return it to Wayne."

"As long as they don't get into a fight."

Mary started to say something, hesitated, but then plunged in. "How do you feel about Alan?"

Kit already dreaded the implications of the question. "I value his friendship. He's a nice guy." *Don't say it, Mary.*

But Mary didn't look up from her knitting to see the mute appeal. "He's sweet on you, you know. Of course, he hardly ever lets it show, but I can tell."

Kit wished Mary had kept these observations to herself. But if it was true, perhaps it was better to know, and to guard against giving Alan any hope that there could be more than friendship between them. She didn't want to hurt him.

Kit said, "We're just friends. I think Alan understands that quite well."

"Probably. But you can't help how you feel sometimes, can you? You can't always stop yourself from falling in love."

"I guess we all know what that's like." Trying to change the subject, Kit asked, "What are you knitting?"

"A baby outfit!" Mary's eyes shone.

"You're pregnant?"

"Three months!" Mary rubbed her belly reassuringly, although it barely showed. "I lost the others at four months. But it'll work out this time, I'm sure of it."

Behind the happy glow, Kit could sense Mary's uncertainty and desperation. She wondered if Mary expected this baby to salvage her marriage.

She hardly listened as Mary chatted on about the preparations she was making for the baby, hearing only that she hoped the bungalow might be ready in time - hearing particularly the longing behind those words.

Mary left a little while later, and Kit tried to put her mind to some work. She hadn't accomplished much when Georgina Bryce arrived later that afternoon.

"Alan told me what happened, Kit. How awful for you! He thought you might need some distraction today."

"He's right."

"And I brought you this," Georgina said, flourishing a rifle. "It's an extra one. You'll feel better for having it handy."

"I've always hated guns. They seem to take on a destructive life of their own."

"It'll make you feel less vulnerable - a gun will stop anyone. Evens out the odds a bit, don't you think?"

"I don't even know how to use one of these."

"I'll teach you."

Kit hadn't been outside since the previous evening. The tire ruts scarring the lawn and crushing shrubs and flowerbeds were a stark reminder of last night's rampage. After Wayne's hoodlums had strung up the dummy and positioned the gravestone, they had driven round and round the site, making sure they woke her up.

Perhaps Georgina was right. Having a rifle at hand might reassure her. Wasn't that what Rhett Pugh had been trying to tell her?

Georgina set up tin cans and Kit practiced hitting them.

"You've caught on quickly," Georgina said after a while. "Terrific aim."

"I keep seeing Wayne's face on the cans," Kit said. "God! Isn't that terrible of me? I've never hated - or feared - anyone as much as him. I know I should behave more rationally. Use some psychology on him. Outwit him. But my brain seems to seize up in his presence."

"Alan's worried about you."

Kit noted the wistfulness in her voice, and replied, "He's a good friend - a great guy. Although you know that better than I." She didn't want Georgina hurt by any mistaken notion that there was more to Kit's relationship with Alan than a platonic friendship. Yet what a mess! Georgina was so obviously in love with Alan; Alan was infatuated with Kit, it seemed; and Kit was irresistibly attracted to Nick. And all three of them were bound to be disappointed.

Georgina only smiled sadly.

Alan called her shortly after Georgina left, and Kit informed him about her target practice. She assured him that she didn't need him to sleep over, and that she would phone him at the slightest suspicion of trouble.

But there was none. Kit slept fitfully until dawn, when she finally allowed herself to succumb to exhaustion.

Chapter 30

I had intended to make the midsummer party an annual event at Moon Hall, but I didn't have the heart this year. Now I'm truly glad that I didn't.

Daniel came to see me today. I couldn't believe my eyes as he strolled into the garden, where I was working. He had his jacket slung over his shoulder and had loosened his collar, for it was a hot day, and his trousers were dusty from the road.

"Hello, Violet. I hope you don't mind my dropping in like this."

I'm sure my mouth was gaping in surprise, but I managed to say, "Not at all! Friends are always welcome!" I brushed the loose dirt from my hands and extricated myself from the perennial border, only then realizing that I was in my jodhpurs with my shirt sleeves rolled up almost to my shoulders, revealing unfashionably tanned arms. I also hate wearing hats, and I could feel that my face was sunburnt. "You'll have to excuse my casual attire," I said, shrugging ruefully.

"I think you look splendid. Trousers suit you."

"Tell that to my cook, Mrs. Skuce! She thinks they're much too risqué, and will be horrified that I've been seen by someone outside the village! Did you walk from the railway station?"

"Yes. It's a glorious day to be out in the country and I enjoyed my walk immensely." Staring out over the valley he said, "This is a beautiful spot you have here."

"I love it.... But you must be tired and parched! Come inside for some refreshment. I'll just wash the worst of this dirt off first."

He accompanied me to the pump, where he plied the handle while I rinsed in the cool water.

"Will you stay to dinner? Mrs. Skuce always makes something special on Saturdays."

"I'd be delighted."

"Then you have some cold lemonade in the parlour while I change into something more respectable."

"There's no need. I like you just the way you are."

"No, no, I must, or Mrs. Skuce will give me the evil eye, and probably even refuse to serve me!"

I don't know why I was prolonging things, because I was sure I knew why Daniel had come. I should have let him say his piece and leave. But I wanted him for every selfish, precious moment that I could have him to myself, with the dreaded words unspoken. Surely everything would change after that.

I changed quickly into one of my prettiest summer gowns, fixed my hair, and joined Daniel in the parlour looking rather more ladylike and refined. I poured us each a glass of sherry and sat on the chair opposite him.

"I have far too few people just stopping by to visit. The locals do sometimes, of course. But never anyone from the city. This is a treat!"

"Well, you haven't been to Ottawa for a long while," he said, studying me over the rim of his glass.

That was because I couldn't bear to witness my defeat. But I didn't want him to begin explaining his visit now, so I steered the conversation onto safer ground by telling him about my gardening. "I'll show you the fruits of my labours after dinner."

Betsy, a bit flustered, had hurriedly set the dining room table - which I never used when I ate by myself - while Mrs. Skuce had thrown more vegetables into the pot. Both did me proud, for the table looked lovely and the roast beef dinner was delicious and plentiful. Daniel and I shared a bottle of wine, and I never let the conversation stray from events and acquaintances in the city to more serious things.

The windows were open to the afternoon breezes and the fragrance of apple blossoms drifted in from the orchard. Except for the candlelight - which of course we didn't need at mid-day - this was just like living one of my fantasies. I wish it could have lasted forever.

After the mince pie, I poured us each a brandy, thinking that we surely needed it for what was to come, and suggested we amble down to the secret garden. On the way, I showed Daniel the new perennials I had coaxed into life from seeds, and took him on a detour through the orchard. We stopped at my favourite tree, where, leaning against the trunk, I said, "I still scramble up here, and look out over the valley from that branch. But not dressed like this!"

I knew I was beginning to sound desperate. Daniel had said that he had to catch the six o'clock train and it was now well past four. I took a deep gulp of my brandy, which burned its way down my throat to silence more inanities. As if sensing my disquiet, Tristan nuzzled my hand, reassuring me of his devotion, and I gratefully stroked his head.

When we were seated on the stone bench opposite Pan, I faced Daniel, knowing there was little left to say but what I dreaded most to hear. So I waited for him to speak.

"It's been a wonderful day, Violet. But I must be on my way soon." He put his empty glass down and took one of my hands between his. Mesmerizing me with that disturbingly acute look of his he said, "You're a good friend, Violet. So I thought you should be the first to know that Isobel and I are to be married."

Of course I had expected it, but the words cut me to the bone. And this was one wound that Daniel could not heal. I could say nothing at first. I just felt his warm hands clasping my cool one, letting the sensation soak through me, like the brandy.

As if needing to justify himself, he said, "We've loved each other since we were practically children. We'd intended to marry when I'd finished medical school, but her father had other plans for her."

So if he was in love with me at all, it was against his will. Just as I had not intended to fall in love with him. The gods are wicked and cruel!

He continued. "Now she is free to do as she wishes. I'm sure that is something that you can appreciate, Violet."

Meaning that I had said as much myself, and chosen not to love him. But how mistaken he was!

"Then I am truly happy for you, Daniel. I hope that we can continue to be friends." I spoke from desperation, of course.

"Certainly! You must visit us often. And Isobel wishes to help out at the Refuge. She thought a bazaar might be a good way to raise money for it."

So she was even planning to interfere in that! Would she allow Daniel nothing that did not involve her? God, it will be even worse than I had imagined!

"Well... I must be on my way. I've really enjoyed my visit, Violet. This is how I think of you, you know." He smiled warmly at me. "Mistress of this domain."

"The Lady of Shalott?" I couldn't resist saying.

"Just as mysterious as she."

"There is no great mystery," I mumbled, and quickly added, "Shall I ask Jeremiah to drive you to the village?"

"No, thanks, I'd rather walk. I need to clear my head. Undoubtedly there will be work waiting for me when I return!"

As if in a trance, I sauntered with him to the end of the drive and watched him stride away. From Moon Hall. From me. From my life.

Chapter 31

Liz came to see Kit the next morning.

"Are you alright?" Liz asked, watching Kit's pale face with concern. "Is there anything we can do to help?"

Kit shook her head. "Not unless you can cure my paranoia. Probably Wayne's had his bit of fun, and won't bother me anymore. Probably I'm overreacting - just a prank, the policeman said. But I can't help feeling that there was something more vicious and sinister in it than that.

"I've barricaded myself in here. I can't even get up the courage to go into my own garden! I keep a rifle beside my bed. I'm in a state of siege. But I don't know if my enemy will even strike.

"Once Wayne just walked into my house while I was up in the bath. Now my imagination keeps taking that scene one step farther - hearing his footsteps coming up the stairs. Remember the movie *Psycho*? I'm afraid to have a shower because then I wouldn't be able to hear the footsteps. God, I think I'm freaking out!"

"Maybe you should go away for a few days," Liz suggested.

"Maybe I should just admit defeat and move back to the city or home to my parents."

"Nonsense! Things won't seem so bad in a few days. Why don't you confront Wayne?"

Kit stared at her, aghast.

"Tell him you weren't impressed by his little escapade, and ask him what his problem is. He's really not the monster you think him to be. An unpleasant person, I grant you, but surely not a threat."

Kit felt annoyed that Liz viewed the situation so lightly. Unconsciously she rubbed her bruised arm. If Wayne had really grown up in an abusive home (and Kit didn't doubt it) then he'd learned only one way to resolve conflicts - with his fists.

Liz's attitude seemed to belittle Kit's fear, and she said no more.

Sensing the sudden coolness, Liz said, "Would you like one of us to come and stay with you?"

"No. I have to deal with this myself.... Do me a favour, Liz - don't tell Nick what happened."

"Why not?"

"I just don't want to talk about it anymore."

When Liz had gone, Kit felt bereft. She suddenly realized how alone she was. Oh, she could run to her parents of course. But they wouldn't always be there. And friends could only assuage the loneliness for a while. She wanted something more in her life.

Whenever Violet had felt lonely at Moon Hall, she had gone to Ottawa. Perhaps a couple of days doing research in the city would be both useful and therapeutic.

.   .   .

There weren't many tourists on Parliament Hill at this time of year. It was a dismal November day with a cold wind sweeping down the river valley and blustering on The Hill. Kit leaned against the wrought iron railing and peered down the steep slope thick with shrubs and trees. But now that they were winter-bare, crumbling remnants of the old stone path could be glimpsed. Lovers' Walk, Violet had called it. A green oasis in a barren lumbering town where the Prime Minister and Violet had liked to stroll.

Kit had already been through the By Ward Market, locating the Refuge, now occupied by an upmarket African art shop with creative window displays of colourful ethnic fabrics and ebony tribal masks. From there she had trudged to the Blake's tired old house in Sandy Hill, which looked as though it could do with a face-lift. Isobel Granger's house had disappeared to make way for a modern office tower, and Kit wasn't sure which place had been Daniel's old surgery, though she thought that it, too, might have been sacrificed to progress.

Kit had managed to get a tour of Rideau Hall, the Governor-General's (and the Queen's) official residence, which had changed much over the years. But the major additions made during the Dufferins' reign - the ballroom and the tent room - were still impressive. They must truly have awed the rustic Ottawans of the day. The toboggan slide, somewhat shorter now, and the skating rink were still there, too. Even today it seemed that the Dufferins were remembered as the most popular and flamboyant incumbents of Government House.

Kit pulled up the collar of her sheepskin coat against the nipping wind, and was glad that she had worn her leather boots. If only she didn't hate wearing hats, she would be quite snug. But there was nothing more to see here. She had finished at the library, too, so she might as well return to the hotel, which sprawled impressively on the opposite side of the canal from The Hill.

But it was unbearable to think of spending another lonely evening there, eating a solitary meal in the elegant and romantic dining room, envying those around her who were with friends or lovers. And her hotel room seemed even more desolate than Moon Hall.

For the past three days she had fought the temptation to call Nick. But why? Was she so afraid of getting hurt that she wasn't even willing to risk seeing him? She was being absurd, and had no right to feel sorry for herself!

Kit hurried into the hotel, and phoned Nick at the office. Just hearing his voice on the other end of the line gave her a thrill of pleasure. He invited her to dinner, and said he'd pick her up at seven. With three hours to prepare herself, she had an invigorating work-out in the Olympic-sized pool in the basement, and a long, hot soak in her tub. By the time Nick's Porsche pulled up outside the lobby doors, she was decidedly more cheerful.

A sharp, icy rain was whipping down the deserted streets of the city. Few people were out on foot tonight. Kit felt cozy and protected so close to Nick in the luxurious womb of the car. She wouldn't have cared if it were blizzarding outside or if they ever got to their destination.

But she asked, "So where are we going tonight?" They were driving along the canal and away from the downtown core.

"It's not a bad little place. Nice atmosphere. Food's tolerable. It's very quiet and conducive to good conversation," he replied with a grin.

Nick turned onto a sidestreet, and Kit suddenly realized where they were. Nick's place.

"Pizza?" she asked with a laugh.

"I assure you that my culinary skills go beyond ordering a pizza. Just wait and see!"

In the spacious, high-ceilinged living room, Nick had created an intimate dining area by the fireplace. A small table was set with white linen, an attractive stoneware dinner service, crystal wine goblets, and candles. The scene of the seduction, Kit thought wryly. But what the hell!

"And I suppose dinner is already cooked and that you don't need any help," she said.

"I never turn down offers of assistance," Nick replied.

But the dinner was ready and Kit merely helped him to carry it in.

"I'd say the food was more than tolerable," Kit declared, savouring the tender and delectable veal marsala. The wine was excellent, too, and the fire was reassuring against the icy clatter of the rain outside. "This restaurant rates at least five stars."

"I told you I'd have to stop dining at Armand's. I'm quitting my job at the end of next month. And we're planning to launch *Country Lanes* in March."

They talked about the magazine as they lingered over the meal. When Nick had poured them each a brandy he said, "Now tell me what you've been up to for the last three days. I thought I'd hear from you sooner."

He watched her across the flickering candle flame, but she replied without looking at him. "I've been doing research. And I didn't want to bother you."

He lifted her chin so that their eyes met. She could never look into those stunning blue eyes of his without that initial jolt to her senses that travelled down to settle in the pit of her stomach.

"Why don't you tell me about it," he urged.

"About what? The book?"

"No. The thing that's been bothering you. Your encounter with Wayne Skuce."

His name sounded like an obscenity. "I asked Liz not to tell you."

"She didn't. Leighton did. They're all concerned about you. So am I."

She looked at him over the rim of her glass, at his tender smile, thinking, *Don't do this to me, Nick. You're so easy to fall in love with.*

November had always seemed a deathly month to her - bitter, dreary, depressing. With the wind howling outside in the dark, inhospitable night, this island of warmth that Nick had created was wonderfully alluring.

"From this distance, I had begun to think it foolishness. Until you mentioned his name. And then this terror gripped me again. I just can't get over this feeling that something is going to happen."

He took one of her hands between his. "Stay with me tonight." His hands were warm and gentle, caressing, soothing.

His touch had such erotic power that she knew she couldn't resist the sexual magnetism that drew them together. Nor did she want to resist any longer.

.   .   .

She stayed with Nick for a week - a heady, exciting, delightful week. They spent cozy evenings locked away from the world in their private retreat. They enjoyed preparing meals together, snatching a kiss now and then, and sometimes forgetting about dinner altogether and improvising midnights snacks instead. They immersed themselves in the old-fashioned clawfoot tub, simmering in the warm water while the November night battered uselessly against the house. They lounged contentedly in front of the crackling fire, talking, touching, making love.

It was like the early days with Nigel - the tireless sexual energy, the intoxicating happiness. Except that Nick had not yet mentioned love.

And Kit was afraid she might outstay her welcome.

Knowing his carefree nature and lack of commitment to other women, she thought it best not to jeopardize their relationship by making demands that he could not meet. Their bond as lovers was fragile as yet.

When she told him that she was leaving, he made no attempt to stop her. Running his fingers absently through her hair he said, "Wait until Saturday and I'll stay at Moon Hall for the weekend - as long as you're not afraid of what the neighbours will say."

And although her heart ached at his easy acceptance of her leaving, she laughed at that suggestion. "I don't think any of them would be too surprised at what we crazy writers and you crazy hippies do."

"Well, I trust you'll have lots more research to do in the city," he murmured as his lips met hers.

．　　　．　　　．

Although it was a comfort to have Nick following her in his car, Kit wished she could have been with him. Already she felt him slipping away from her. Would he still see Christine? Or other women? It was a bitter thought that he probably would. He had made no secret of his womanizing.

And yet, hadn't he been with Suzanne for several years? Hadn't he made a commitment then? Perhaps these other women had held no interest for him aside from the purely physical. But was she any different from them in his eyes?

Kit tried to relax her white-knuckled grip on the steering wheel. How could she possibly settle down to her writing when she would constantly long to be with Nick? And wonder whom he was with.

He searched the house when they arrived to make certain that nothing had been tampered with. He stood for a while at the window, looking out at the naked tree where the dummy had twirled in the moonlight. "Have you thought of selling the house?" he asked her. "You must feel lost in here sometimes."

She was surprised by the suggestion. "I do. But I've come to love this place. Well, until recently. But I'll be damned if I'm going to let someone scare me out of my home!"

Nick raised his eyebrows as if impressed by her determination.

Moon Hall felt safe and comfortable while Nick was there. He had a presence that left a warm glow in his wake. When he returned to the city early Monday morning it seemed to Kit as if November had moved in with her. At least Nick had promised to be back on the weekend.

Work didn't go well that morning. She found herself daydreaming, remembering their lovemaking, the feel of his gentle hands, his naked skin against hers, the clean, masculine smell of his hard-muscled body. Just the thought of him made her feel weak and quivery.

She decided to have lunch in town with Dianna and do some research in the local library in the afternoon. And some shopping - the cupboards were pretty bare. And although darkness fell early and quickly, she made sure she would be home before then.

Still, it was dusk when she reached home. She saw them as soon as she pulled into her driveway. Like a tableau: Arnie Bryce holding the cat, towering over Wayne Skuce. She wanted nothing more than to turn the car around and go screeching off to the city. To Nick. But she felt compelled to confront the trespasser. Surely Wayne wouldn't try anything with Arnie there. And yet, Arnie was unpredictable. Kit wondered if he might scuttle away when he saw her.

She stopped the car beside the back porch where they stood, and with her heart in her mouth, got out.

"What do you want?" she asked Wayne.

"He hurt Ollie," Arnie said. "Hurt poor cat."

"Shut up, ya stupid idiot!" Wayne snapped. "Ya know dick-all! The God-damn cat got under my feet and I just pushed it outa the way."

The way he had Georgina's cat, all those years ago? Kit felt her blood run cold.

"What are you doing here?" Kit reiterated.

Wayne sneered. She noticed an angry bruise on his left cheek. "My old man says to tell ya that Bonnie won't be comin' here no more. Bet ya even forgot it was her day."

Kit was appalled to think that she had forgotten.

"Yeah, well, he says to tell ya that he won't have his daughter workin' for no God-damn bitch who's whorin' around with one o' them God-damn hippies." His smirk sent shivers down her spine that his spiteful words had not. "We seen ya." He spat on the ground. "And tell them God-damn goons o' yours ta lay off."

"What do you mean?"

"The McGraths won't always be around to help." With that enigmatic statement he turned and walked away.

It didn't even occur to Kit until later to wonder why Wayne had parked his car behind the carriage house, where it was effectively hidden. She shuddered to think what might have happened had Arnie not been there.

Ollie seemed to have suffered no permanent damage from his encounter with Wayne. When the man had gone, Arnie handed the cat over with a sheepish grin and then lurched off toward the ravine.

She wanted desperately to talk to Nick, but what could he do? How could he reassure her? And more than ever, she was afraid to hear a woman's voice in the background.

It didn't occur to her to inform anyone else, although she did wonder if Alan had been responsible for that bruise on Wayne's face, and if that was what Wayne had been referring to in his parting shot.

When Nick called her later that evening, she didn't mention the incident. When he was here on the weekend, maybe she would tell him that some neighbours did seem to take offence to their relationship. If it hadn't been Wayne delivering that message, she would have been amused.

It was past midnight when she was awakened by the telephone.

"I saw him stick it in ya," the voice hissed. "An' I'm gonna stick it in ya. Long and slow and hard." And then the line went dead.

Kit looked at the receiver in her hand as though it were alive, and smashed it down on the cradle. She let out a whimper.

Although the voice had been a gravelly whisper, she knew it was Wayne.

Was he out there now, trying to peer in, battering her sensibilities the way the wind battered the house? Only she was not so impervious.

Sleep eluded her.

Kit spent a restless day and fell asleep at her desk. When she awoke, the room was in darkness. She felt a scream bubbling up inside as she fumbled for the light switch on the lamp. Its rays did little to dispel the blackness beyond the circle of light on the desk. Envisioning Wayne's face suddenly appearing at the window, she steeled herself to close the drapes, and felt a measure of relief when they had shut out the night.

She listened for noises in the rest of the house, which she knew was in darkness and thus seemed hostile and threatening. How could she face going into the pitch black hallway with no light switch close to hand? And she couldn't find the damned flashlight.

She had locked the doors, but in her deep sleep, God knows what might have happened. She recalled what Wayne had once said about no lock stopping him if he was determined to break in. Had he somehow undermined the locks then, when he had installed them? Had he somehow gained access to the house?

Quietly she picked up the receiver, suddenly remembering the classic horror tale in which the babysitter gets a call from a psycho - from the upstairs extension.

There was no answer at Nick's.

This was ridiculous! She would go mad if she didn't stop this line of thought. She turned on every light in the library and then, with her heart clamouring in her chest, walked over to the gaping blackness of the hallway.

With the little light that spilled out of the library as her only guide, Kit groped her way along the wall to the switch, trying not to think of suddenly touching something - or someone - that shouldn't be there. She was so close to hysteria that she feared the slightest surprise might catapult her into madness.

The light came on with reassuring brightness.

From there it was easy to turn on the light to each room, and quickly close the curtains. By the time she got to the kitchen, she felt much more at ease.

It was only the strangeness of waking up at her desk at nine o'clock at night that had caused her panic. She was glad now that Nick had not been home. What had she intended to say to him, anyway? *I'm scared to leave my office. Come and rescue me?*

Kit had no appetite, and decided to settle for just a glass of milk for dinner. As she was sipping it, she heard Ollie meowing pitifully outside the back door, and realized that the poor cat had been out all day in the cold.

She flicked on the outdoor floodlights, but didn't notice until she opened the door leading into the driveshed that the lights hadn't come on.

Kit screamed as a hand reached out from the darkness, grabbing her cruelly by the hair, and yanking her outside.

"Did ya like my message, bitch?" he hissed as he pushed her up against a wall. "Long and slow and hard. Is that how ya like it?"

He hit her across the face when she screamed again. She struggled to lash out at him, to squirm out of his grip, but he was too strong.

"Did ya let the McGraths fuck ya too?"

He slammed her against the wall again, and Kit felt her head spinning. While she was momentarily weakened, he clamped his mouth on hers and shoved a hand under her sweater, viciously squeezing her breast.

And while her body rebelled, her mind latched onto an idea.

Using every nerve to steel herself against his revolting touch - the tongue that tried to thrust into her mouth, the coarse hands that pinched her nipples - she allowed herself to go limp. He chuckled triumphantly as he rubbed his hard crotch against her.

She suddenly shoved him hard and kneed him in the groin, not a crippling blow but enough to catch him off balance. She bolted toward the driveway as he doubled over.

But he was on her a moment later. She fought and kicked and resisted his attempt to push her to the ground. Her flailing arms deflected a full-fisted blow to her face, but it grazed her cheek and sent her reeling backwards. He grabbed her as she stumbled and, unbalanced, they fell to the ground.

Kit managed to twist her body so that he didn't land on top of her. As she tried to scramble to her feet, he whipped around to grab her legs, and felled her once more.

The sharp gravel bit into her hands and face, but she felt only the chilling bite of his words. "So ya like it rough, do ya?"

Her scream was strangled as he rolled her over and clamped his hand over her mouth. "Not so high and mighty now, are ya, ya fuckin' bitch!"

In the desperate darkness of the November night she couldn't see him. She could only make out his dark, menacing form, smell the whiskey and smoke on his breath, hot and sour on her face. But she knew it was Wayne.

He had her wrists clamped together in a vice-grip over her head. His other hand pressed smotheringly across her face. He rubbed himself against her as she squirmed beneath him. He chuckled and said, "Ya got the right idea, bitch! God-damn, I bet yer good!"

He took his hand from her mouth to fumble with her clothes, and Kit let out another futile scream. Who was there to hear her? Wayne belted her across the face and hissed, "Do that again an' I'll break yer jaw!"

But in that moment he relaxed his grip on her hands, and, using all her strength, she whipped them down, two-fisted, across the bridge of his nose. He howled in rage. Kit grabbed handfuls of gravel and hurled them into his face, and then, mercifully, she felt a rock beneath her fingers.

Before she could strike, his imprisoning hands were once more grabbing for her. She screamed again, and as he lashed out for her face, she struck him a stunning blow on the side of the head. As he slumped sideways, Kit wriggled out from beneath him.

Sobbing, gasping for breath, Kit struggled clumsily to her feet, the thin soles of her slippers skidding on the icy gravel. She could hear him groaning behind her and the scuffle of his feet as he roused himself from his stupor. "I'm gonna kill ya for that," he swore, and his voice was alarmingly close.

Propelled by terror, Kit finally got purchase and flew blindly ahead, toward the ravine. She heard herself whimpering as the noise of Wayne's pursuit drew closer. She knew she didn't have the strength to fight him anymore.

She struggled over the uneven ground that threatened to topple her, through the tangling, dried grasses that were once waist high and now lay battered and rimed and treacherous. She could just make out the darker shape of the trees along the creek, and a moment later she was sliding, tumbling down the slope toward the water. One foot caught wrenchingly on a rock.

She expected him to reach her at any second. She could hear his heavy breathing behind her, coming closer. Pain shot through her ankle when she put her weight on it, and she wanted to scream out in rage at some vindictive God who seemed to be thwarting her every effort to escape from Wayne.

She heard a thud, a grunt, and a curse, and thought that Wayne must have fallen. In that moment of respite, she wondered if she should try to hide in the darkness of the ravine. She groped for a weapon and her fingers closed on a heavy, knobby stick. But her pursuer was too frighteningly close, and so she stumbled on. Her progress was agonizingly slow, for she couldn't see the rocks and downed trees in the blackness, and had to grope her way inch by inch.

She couldn't hear Wayne anymore, and could see nothing in the darkness surrounding her. But she thought that at any moment Wayne would lunge for her, and her skin crawled in anticipation of a hand suddenly reaching out to grab her.

Kit slipped on a rock, and plunged through a thin rind of ice into the frigid water of the creek. She barely noticed that now, nor the throbbing of her ankle or the sting of sleet on her bruised face.

The McGrath's lights shone like a welcoming beacon in the darkness, and she focussed on them.

Realizing she was no longer in the shelter of the trees, but at the edge of the field near the road, Kit was once more wary. Maybe Wayne hadn't followed her along the ravine at all. He must have anticipated where she would go - instinctively. To the nearest neighbours.

Kit stopped, her body rigid with fear, alert. It was somewhat brighter out here in the open, and she could make out shapes - the bridge, fences, shrubs. Wayne couldn't be close. Unless he was lying in the grass ahead of her. Lying in wait. Waiting to pounce.

Stifling a cry of despair, Kit hobbled onward, ever faster, despite the numbness in her foot. She headed toward the blazing lights of the barn, which was closer than the house.

Ever closer. She could smell the musty animal smells now. Faster, faster. She was almost within the protective circle of light in the floodlit yard. Her head was filled with the ragged sounds of her harsh breathing. The icy air stung her lungs. Her chest ached, threatened to explode.

She couldn't glance behind her, couldn't bear to see if Wayne was almost upon her, about to drag her away from sanctuary. Almost within her grasp.

She tossed down the stick and clung for a moment to the rough, splintered boards of the barn wall. Gasping.

She surprised Stuart as she stumbled into the barn and collapsed in his arms. He was covered in blood from a calving.

There was a shriek a moment later as Mary and Alan entered. "Oh, my God! What's going on?" Mary asked.

Kit was clinging to Stuart, her own blood mingling with the cow's blood.

Chapter 32

My 25th birthday, and I feel desolate.

A thunderstorm rages outside, suiting my mood admirably. I watched it advancing across the valley, the roiling black clouds like a threatening mounted battalion, hooves striking thunder and lightning from the earth.

The Dufferins are soon to leave us, on their way back home after six years of holding the entire country, but especially Ottawa, in thrall. I have said my goodbyes. At least to them.

It has been eight months since Daniel and Isobel were married in Montreal. (Thank God they didn't invite me!) As I had expected, Daniel set up his surgery in his new Upper Town home, much farther from both the Refuge and the Blakes' than his bachelor flat in Lower Town had been. I think it has been harder for him to run his practice from there, since so many of his poor clients are now so distant, but he carries on. And they seem to know where to find him.

Daniel does come to the Refuge occasionally, even when his services aren't required, but I have to admit that I am not there much either. I have lost the heart for it. And it goes on splendidly without me.

Daniel, true to his word, has tried not to forget me, though I think that Isobel invites me reluctantly to her home. I am usually part of a large crowd, so Daniel and I have little opportunity to talk, and his position as host means I am fortunate to dance with him once in an evening. Sometimes he is even called out on a case, and then the evening loses all appeal to me.

Of course there have been no more skating lessons or toboggan rides. I did not even go to any of the skating parties at Rideau Hall this winter, but Lily did, and related that Isobel and Daniel were sometimes there.

Lily has never asked me about my relationship with Daniel, though I know she senses my unhappiness, and tries to provide interesting diversions for me. But I have spent most of my time here, at Moon Hall. Alone and brooding.

But I was at the Refuge last week when Daniel sought me out.

"Will you walk with me, Violet?" he asked.

"I was just about to be on my way, if you'll wait a moment," I replied, finishing up my checking of the accounts to realize that the Refuge was still financially healthy and almost self-sufficient.

We stepped out into the April sunshine which can be kind even while the air retains a nip of winter. But for me there was a decided chill in the air. Daniel was looking serious and I suspected that he had something unpleasant to relate.

After we had exchanged news and small-talk, he said, "I've accepted a professorship at McGill Medical School. It seems that my small experiments and my exceptional success with Listerism on patients has become known."

With lucky patients like me. But now I would lose Daniel altogether, for he would be moving back to Montreal. Had Isobel, through her many influential connections, wrangled this post for her husband to get him away from Ottawa and me?

"So, you'll give up your practice here," I stated. "You'll be sorely missed."

"It wasn't an easy decision to make, Violet," he said, fixing me with his intense gaze. I saw regret there. "I'll still have a private practice in Montreal, though a smaller one. And I'll have the opportunity to do more research, as well as ensure that a new generation of doctors is well versed in bacteriology."

"I thought you didn't like teaching," I couldn't help saying, somewhat accusingly.

"I'll manage. There are compensations. We all have to make concessions, don't we?" Daniel sounded as though he were trying to convince himself.

What concessions was Isobel making, I wondered, but didn't ask. It seemed to me that she has had everything her way so far.

I was angry. Angry that Daniel allowed himself to be so easily manipulated by his wife. Angry that he was deserting us - me. I said, "What about all the good you've done here? Doesn't it count for something? What about all your indigent patients? Who will treat them for free?"

"Some other idealistic young doctor starting out in his career," Daniel replied. He has an uncanny knack of reading my thoughts, for he said gently, "This is something I really want to do, Violet. My only regret is that I shall have to move away. My friendships here are very dear to me."

It was a close as he could come to stating his feelings for me, I suppose, and I relented. "I shall miss you, Daniel. More than I can say."

We were outside the Blakes' house when we stopped to face each other. Daniel said, "We'll make of point of keeping in touch. And you must visit us in Montreal. No doubt you will stay with your sister Iris occasionally."

But Montreal was foreign territory to me. I couldn't imagine going there often just to be near Daniel. He would be preoccupied with his new position and Isobel would undoubtedly have a full social schedule for them. I would be even more of an outsider in their lives than I was already. I don't want to become pathetic. But I said nothing. Let him believe this fantasy that our friendship can survive this upheaval. I am not so naive. After all, I have already lost the comfort and enjoyment of his frequent company.

They will move before summer. "Isobel will sell the Granger estate, and we will buy our own house closer to the university," Daniel said.

Was this Isobel's concession then, to give up her mansion in Westmount?

"And sell the house here, I suppose?"

"There's little point in keeping it," Daniel agreed.

"Then I will buy it," I said in a sudden impulsive fit of lunacy. "I rather fancy having my own place in the city. Now that Lily is expecting and the family, about to grow."

Of course that was just an excuse. I am desperately clinging to something that had been Daniel's. I will wander the too-large rooms, thinking that my beloved had sat there or slept here, breathed this air, touched these doors, gazed out those windows. And I will try to absorb any vestiges of him into my being. It is the closest I can ever get to him again.

Never mind that it had been Isobel who had bought the house, and that I am taking her leavings. Dust and wraiths.

Daniel was surprised at my words. And I was glad to be able to shock him a little. He seemed almost uncomfortable with my bizarre scheme, as if he knew my reasons and feared for my sanity.

Perhaps I am mad. Perhaps this pox is already corrupting my brain. But there is some pleasure and redemption in madness.

Chapter 33

"So you didn't actually see him then, Miss?" It was Detective Constable Jim Akers again.

The doctor had come to see her. (A doctor still making house calls? Unbelievable.) That old gentleman had patched her up and given her a strong sedative. He was with Mary now. There was something wrong with Mary.

"I told you it was too dark. But I know it was Wayne! He was short and wiry.... The things he said.... I recognized his voice.... He'd threatened me before, at the Wild Horse."

"Quite so, Miss. You and half the countryside. That's just his manner of speaking."

"You sound as though you're defending him, Jim," Alan accused.

"I'd like to nail the little shit just as much as you, Al. But we need a case that'll stand up in court. Let's just hope he left some evidence behind, and has no alibi. I didn't pass his car on my way out here, so he couldn't have been heading for town."

Wrapped in Jean's warm terry bathrobe and covered with a quilt, Kit had finally stopped shaking. She could feel the sedative taking effect, numbing her. Duncan sat silently in his well-worn armchair, his pipe shuffling furiously back and forth in his mouth. Kit had never seen Alan looking so serious. Jean and Stuart were upstairs with Mary and the doctor.

When the policeman had gone, Alan said, "I could kill that Skuce bastard."

"No, Alan!" Kit said. "You mustn't talk like that. You beat him up didn't you - after the Halloween episode?"

"He had it coming. I told him to stay away from you."

Which to a man like Wayne was a like a red rag to a bull. Wayne was a bully, a coward preying on those weaker than himself. He would take his revenge on Alan, not by hurting him, but the very person Alan had been trying to protect - Kit.

Alan blanched when the realization struck him. "Jeez! Kit... I never meant for him to take it out on you."

She managed a grim smile. "I know that."

Duncan said, "They're a bad lot, those Skuces. Trash, living in the trash they scavenge from the dump. More than once I seen them squabbling in the yard. Her, yelling abuse at him with words that made my ears burn. Him, up and ploughing her one in the face. The God-damn pair of them fair screaming at each other like two spitting cats, and hurling the rubbish at each other. They do say at least one of the kids always had a bruise or two, and not from banging into doors or falling out of trees. So Wayne's learned his lesson well."

Kit was shocked by those quietly spoken words. They conjured up sickening images of brutal beatings inflicted on helpless children. So much misery contained within the walls of that small, decrepit house on the corner.

Why had no one ever done anything about it, Kit wondered. Why hadn't the neighbours reported him? Why hadn't he been locked up, his children taken into protection? Why did people turn a blind eye to monsters like him who created new monsters by example?

Jean entered the room, tight-lipped, looking suddenly old. "She's losing the baby."

Duncan clamped his teeth so hard on his pipe that Kit thought the stem would break.

Jean said, "Doc Bailey had told her it might happen again, but she didn't believe him. She'll be inconsolable this time. I'm afraid she thinks it's your fault, Kit - seeing you in the barn, covered in blood."

Kit shuddered at the remembered stench of it, the thick, gooey, stickiness of it all over her face and hands, as if she had reached into the cow to snatch out the dead calf.

Jean continued. "It's nonsense, of course. Babies aren't lost that easily."

Jean hadn't said, *Seeing you in Stuart's arms*, but Kit wondered if that was what she'd meant. "I'm so sorry." It was not an apology, but an expression of sympathy.

Jean said, "This one just wasn't meant to be either. Like the others."

"Well, I won't stay long. May I use your phone?"

"No need for you to rush away. We've a spare room."

But Kit declined the offer.

She thought she was calm enough to call Nick now, but when she heard his voice at the other end of the line, she choked up.

"Kit? What's wrong?"

"Oh, God... Nick... Wayne...."

"What happened, Kit?

"He tried... to rape me."

"Christ! Are you alright."

She nodded, but could not force out the words.

"Where are you?"

"At the McGraths'."

"I'll get there as soon as I can."

Jean had returned upstairs, and Kit sat drowsily in the living room with the silent men. It was only a few minutes before Liz and Kevin arrived to take her to the farm. Nick had called them.

She could hardly keep her eyes open as they ushered her into the warm farmhouse, or acknowledge the solicitous greetings of the others. She was barely conscious of being tucked into a soft bed.

When she awoke, hours later, she felt disoriented in the dark. Sharp memories of her frantic struggle with Wayne flooded back. She flailed around in panic, trying to get out from under the confining comforter, to push back the suffocating, blinding darkness, sobbing and crying out as a man grabbed her.

"Kit! It's Nick!" He held her firmly, tenderly, until she stopped thrashing. "Shh, it's alright." He stroked her hair and cradled her in his arms as she wept.

When she awoke again it was noon, and Nick was sitting on the bed beside her, fully dressed, reading a book.

She tried not to dissolve into tears when he smiled at her.

"I feel terrible," she said, gingerly feeling her bruised face. She ached all over.

"What you need is a hot bath."

"You're right. Thanks for coming, Nick."

"Are you ready to talk about it? The police were here this morning, but I didn't let them wake you. They haven't found any evidence."

"No buttons? No bits of cloth caught on a thorn? No footprints?"

He shook his head. "The ground's frozen. They could see signs of a struggle on the gravel drive, all right." She noticed him clenching his teeth. "The grass around a groundhog hole was trampled, so they figured one of you must have fallen into that."

Wayne. That must have been when she'd heard the thud and the curse. "You see, those groundhogs are useful after all," she managed to jest. But by tripping up Wayne, those burrows had probably saved her.

Nick continued. "He'd taken all the lightbulbs out of the outside sockets, and they found your cat trapped under a crate." From whence had come the pitiful mewling that had been designed to lure her outside. "Seems he has an alibi, too. Playing poker with friends in town. Three of them swear he was there at the time of the assault. And it seems that he'd sprained his ankle, and claims he couldn't chase after anyone in that condition."

"From falling into the groundhog hole!" So that was why he hadn't followed her into the ravine, nor even stayed to ambush her at the bridge.

Nick said grimly, "His car was seen parked on a street in town."

"That's not possible! I know it was Wayne, Nick. I might not have seen him clearly, but I know it was him! He must have borrowed a friend's car. And that's why the cop didn't pass Wayne's car going into town. Wayne was driving a different car!"

"I don't doubt it. All cunningly, cold-bloodedly planned. I should have taken your fears more seriously. I shouldn't have let you come back here."

"It was my decision." But his concern slightly lifted the dark shadows from her mind.

"Tell me about it."

She snuggled into the comforting crook of his arm. It was easier to talk about it when she didn't have to look at him.

When she had finished he said, "Come back to the city with me, Kit. We'll come down to Moon Hall on the weekends, if you can face that place again. You just can't stay here by yourself until Wayne is in prison."

"He may never be," she said dejectedly.

"I could wring his scrawny, miserable neck...."

"No, Nick! Don't even think that."

He kissed her on the forehead and said, "I'll run you a bath and order up some coffee."

"Nick, promise me you won't do anything foolish."

He flashed her his teasing grin. "I never do anything foolish."

But she wasn't convinced.

Kit sipped strong, sweet coffee as she luxuriated in the bath. She washed the vestiges of cow's blood from her hair, feeling finally cleansed of the gore of the previous night.

Someone had fetched some of her clothes from Moon Hall. When she was dressed, she limped downstairs, surprised at the stiffness of her muscles and the soreness of her feet. She'd been shocked by her face in the mirror - her left cheek swollen, her lip cut, her forehead grazed. There was a lump on the back of her head, and her hands were scraped raw.

Nick was walking in the door just as she reached the kitchen. He was dabbing at his bloody mouth.

"Nick! What happened?" But she knew.

"I just had a talk with Wayne. I told him if he ever came near you again I'd cut off his balls. Excuse me while I get washed."

.   .   .

Moon Hall in the November twilight was a forbidding place. As she walked through the echoing rooms collecting some belongings, Kit knew that Nick had been right. She could no longer stay here alone. Not until she had healed.

Chapter 34

And so I am alone again on Midsummer's Eve. I'm glad I didn't try to repeat that one magical party, for to try to recapture it is impossible and would only taint the memory.

Tristan and I sat in the secret garden for the entire evening, I, sipping wine, with the bottle at my side to replenish my glass, just watching the light change from the brilliance of the sunset to the indigo shroud of the moon-gilded night.

The Blakes had a small party last week to bid farewell to Daniel and Isobel. Bless Lily for her thoughtfulness to me in arranging it all, and providing the most interesting company.

Yet the only truly memorable part of the evening occurred when I slipped out onto the front veranda for a breath of air. I was finding it difficult not to despair, for this was the last time I would see Daniel before his move. I needed a few moments to collect myself so that I could keep up my *joie de vivre* when I rejoined the others.

But then suddenly Daniel was beside me. He said, "I shall miss these times. Although we'll certainly come to visit my brother occasionally."

"But it won't be the same, will it? Don't you feel as though you've been part of the maturing of the capital? Less than a decade ago it still looked and behaved like a frontier town. Irish and French-Canadian lumbermen were still brawling in the streets and chucking each other over the falls! Now the city has some refinement and style. I rather feel as if we've helped it to grow up, Daniel. But for me it also seems as if something wonderful and exciting has come to an end."

"But a new era begins," he said, probably deliberately misinterpreting my sentiments. "The Depression is over, and the unemployment and poverty of the last few years has lessened. The demands made on the Refuge should be alleviated somewhat. There are theatres and Societies and Clubs and all kinds of signs of prosperity and culture. Even the aristocratic Dufferins are being replaced by royalty," Daniel said, referring to the fact that the new Governor-General was to be the Marquess of Lorne and his wife, H.R.H. Princess Louise, Queen Victoria's daughter, who will be arriving later this year. "So even the Queen must think that Ottawa has matured."

But how could I tell him that for me the life and soul of the city would be gone with his departure? I said despondently, "It just won't be the same without you here, Daniel."

He put his arm about my shoulder and gave it a reassuring squeeze. "I'll be here if ever you need me, Violet." I would have thrown myself into his arms then, had not some other revellers sought respite on the porch and ended our final private moment.

Tomorrow I go to claim my new house in the city. An empty victory.

Chapter 35

Moving in with Nick was like going from hell to paradise.

Although Wayne still pursued her in dreams, Kit always woke with Nick's arms around her. His tender lovemaking was gradually erasing the memory of Wayne's violation of her body.

They went to concerts and symphonies at the National Arts Centre, and out for the occasional meal. But mostly, they spent companionable evenings together. Although Kit spent her days at the library or alone in Nick's house, she was not afraid that Wayne would seek her there. That absence of fear was bliss.

It was only as they neared Moon Hall on Saturdays that she would tense up. She could not bring herself to open the kitchen door into the carriage house. Panic would suck the breath from her lungs. The blood would drain from her limbs, leaving her quaking. She remembered all too vividly that nightmarish instant when she had been snatched into a black hell, plunged into abject terror.

Nick never left her alone in the kitchen; so she would turn to him and find herself restored by his smile. She realized that he watched her constantly, ready to bestow a hug or to distract her in some way, and she was grateful for his vigilance and concern. So with Nick's help, that incapacitating fear gradually subsided, and she began to enjoy her home once again.

The only blight during those happy weeks was the assassination of John Lennon. Kit awoke to the news on the radio, and was as stunned and disbelieving as the rest of the world.

She spent the day listening to the radio, to the Beatles' songs - so poignant and melancholic now - and to the outpourings of grief from the callers. It was the end of an era, most of them felt. The death blow to the revolutionary '60s, to the hippie generation that sought only peace and love among mankind and for whom John Lennon had been a spokesman. Surely it was ironic, symbolic, that John should be felled by the bullets of a psychotic. It just showed what was wrong with the world; it was symptomatic of the decay of American society.

The DJs milked it for all it was worth, playing on the emotions of those fans who had seen John Lennon as a brilliant musician and a cult hero. That he should be so brutally cut down just as he had pulled his life back together and was making a musical comeback was so tragic.

Nick came home to find her sitting in the dark by the fire, the radio playing, Ollie on her lap, and tears trickling down her cheeks. They held each other for a long time.

The other shadow on their lives, Nick had managed to hide from her for a while. But with the problem escalating, he couldn't any longer. She heard about it when they were at the commune for dinner the following Saturday.

That evening was seared into her memory - that last time they were all together.

Pete, with his uncanny resemblance to John Lennon, played old songs on his guitar - Beatle tunes among them. The atmosphere was subdued, nostalgic. They mourned an old and valued "friend", an era, and a philosophy of life. It was as if they had suddenly awakened to find themselves no longer carefree, idealistic flower children, but reflections of their parents, approaching middle age. Life had gone on. The music had changed.

There was a fire blazing in the hearth. The lights were turned low; candles still flickered on the dining table. Their crystal goblets absorbed the glow of the fire and turned the last drops of wine to molten honey. They sat in companionable silence for a while, replete with another delectable meal. Safe within the circle of Nick's arm, Kit rested her head against his shoulder.

When she wasn't gazing into the mesmerizing flames, she looked at the faces of her friends. Leighton lay stretched out on the floor in front of the fire, supporting his head on his elbow. His pale, slender feet stuck out from the ragged hem of his threadbare jeans. His red beard and hair seemed ablaze in the dancing firelight. Pete perched on a chair nearby, strumming his guitar, his head bent in concentration so that his hair fell like a curtain across his face. Dianna sat cross-legged on the floor beside him, humming along absently. Her gypsy skirt was spread like a colourful teepee about her; a matching headband dangled to her shoulder. Liz was ensconced in Kevin's arms on the couch opposite, and Mandy and Drew were similarly entwined next to them. Teresa and Erick sat farthest from the fire, their faces almost in shadow.

Beyond them, through the window, Kit could see the anemic December moon - a soulless, lifeless, pock-marked rock basking in reflected glory.

"So what do you suppose the rest of this decade will bring?" Mandy said.

"It's an ominous beginning," Liz replied.

"Theoretically, of course, this is actually the last year of the '70s," Leighton said. "Not the first of the '80s."

"Then it's a hell of an ending to the '70s," Pete said, twanging a discordant phrase on his guitar to emphasize his point. "It was a good decade to drop out of anyway."

"I doubt things are going to improve much," Drew predicted.

Kevin said, "Maybe Nick's magazine will influence people. Maybe we can help make a difference in one small way."

"I'm certainly open to ideas for articles," Nick said.

"Maybe we can help dig up environmental horror stories - you know, like Love Canal," Liz said. "We'll alert people to the dangers of the pollutants they don't even realize they're being exposed to. They can't remain blind, deaf, and dumb much longer."

"Man is notoriously resistant to signs of his own destruction, especially when he's the cause of it," Leighton observed. "Probably because of his unmitigated egotism... Liqueurs, anyone?"

As Leighton offered the tray around, Teresa said, "Just now we have our own problem to deal with."

Drew explained to Nick, "We've had trouble again. One of the cattle was slashed. He'd gone for the jugular alright - the bastard probably wanted to make an impression with the buckets of blood that would have spewed out - but must have been interrupted, because it wasn't a fatal wound."

Nick looked at Kit's stupefied expression and said, "I didn't want to alarm you, but it seems that someone - undoubtedly Wayne - is causing problems. At first it was just minor mischief - tires were slashed, wire fences were cut."

As repayment for Nick's threat? Kit wondered.

"Wayne's getting bolder. Or crazier," Leighton said.

"Didn't the dog alert you?" Nick asked.

"You know old Molly," Mandy replied. "She barks at every chipmunk and raccoon that passes. We tend to ignore her."

"Have you informed the police?" Kit asked. "Can't anything be done?"

"No evidence, of course," Kevin said. "They're patrolling the area more frequently, but that won't stop anybody."

"It's terrifying not knowing what he'll do next. How far he'll go," Liz said, and looked shamefacedly at Kit. She had already apologized to Kit for not taking her fears more seriously.

"We should set a trap for him," Teresa suggested.

"A leg-hold trap?" Pete teased.

"Not a bad idea!" she shot back, unamused. "I don't enjoy being terrorized."

There was silence, and then Drew said, "We're doing patrols in shifts every night. Random inspections of the outbuildings, and, of course, we now check whenever the dog barks or the cattle bellow. That's about all we can do. Hopefully the bastard has had his thrills and will leave us in peace."

Although no one said anything, Kit wondered if they blamed her for these incidents. After all, they'd been living within shouting distance of the Skuces for eight years, and nothing like this had ever happened. For some unaccountable reason, she had aroused Wayne's malevolence, and he was lashing out, not only at her, but also at her friends.

"I like the idea of a trap," Mandy said. "We should be able to string up something that will set off an alarm." And they discussed possibilities for a while.

Before Nick and Kit left, Leighton had a quiet word with her. "I'm glad Nick's finally come to his senses. You two are good for each other."

It was the last thing he ever said to her.

Two days later, Leighton was dead.

Chapter 36

I am sinking into a black, endless well of despondency.

Lily is dead. My beloved, gentle, kind sister.

Her baby was born, a healthy boy she named Albert, but she sickened of childbed fever and died several days later.

I am glad that she had the joy of his birth. I have never seen her so happy as in the last months of her pregnancy, when she realized that all was going well. And how proud she was of her son!

But I can't help feeling that hers was a senseless, unnecessary death. Daniel agreed with me that it should never have happened.

"But Dr. Endicott assures me that he and the midwife used antiseptic methods when they attended her," Daniel said to me after the funeral.

"Then surely they have a misconception about what that means!" I said angrily. Hurt, disbelieving, needing to lash out, I wanted to accuse Daniel as well, screaming at him that she would never have died if he had stayed in Ottawa and attended her as her physician.

But I think that he felt some of that guilt himself. For someone accustomed to death, often sudden or even violent, Daniel seemed deeply moved by Lily's death.

Augustus is shattered. He carries on with things as if he is in a trance, just going through the physical motions while his mind and heart are elsewhere. And so he is rather helpless and befuddled, and I did what I could to help him. His cook/housekeeper is most efficient and oversees the nurse I hired for the baby, as well as the regular running of the house. Augustus thanked me most courteously for my help, but I cannot reach him in his despair. Only once did he break down and weep in front of me, hastily excusing himself from the room and not allowing me to share his grief.

It is just as well I now have my own accommodation in the city. My presence in his home seems to remind Augustus too readily of our many good times with Lily.

Kate, Hugh, and Ruth came to the funeral, for which I was grateful. And of course I appreciated that Daniel came. And that

Isobel didn't. She is expecting a child early in the new year and so, stayed in Montreal.

And yet, there was little comfort Daniel could give me. I was too desolate to take joy in his presence, and he was soon gone.

And I still feel as though I am in the midst of some dark and horrid nightmare from which I do not have the power to awake.

January 28, 1879:

Daniel has written to inform me of the birth of his daughter, whom he has named Lilian. I am touched that he seems to have done this in tribute to my Lily.

God, how I ache inside!

Chapter 37

Leighton's parents were frail and stooped. Stoney-faced, they gazed at the man in the coffin. As though he bore no resemblance to that little boy, Bob, who had been their son. Kit was rather surprised to discover Leighton's first, and once commonly used, name.

Leighton's two sisters were much older than he, matronly, bearing no likeness to him, save for their colouring. They were there with their portly husbands and adult children, all suitably sombre, but as if they didn't belong there. Leighton had been a stranger to them all.

Leighton's will stated that he wanted to be buried at Todmorden, and his family honoured the request. (Kit was surprised that Leighton had even made a will, but perhaps the disposal of his precious record collection had been the incentive. In a codicil he had left Kit a copy of *Traviata* in memory of their evening in Ottawa.) He had even specified which aria he wanted played at his funeral - sung by Maria Callas, of course.

They knew that he hadn't done that deliberately to torment them, but the only dry eyes in the chapel during that song were Leighton's family's. The music meant nothing to them; it didn't evoke memories of the son and brother.

The family declined to return to the farm after the simple service, which had consisted of a few words spoken in tribute by his friends. No clergy, for Leighton had been neither religious nor a hypocrite, but that had seemed to displease his parents. To Kit it seemed as if they had buried their son long ago.

Neighbours had come, but they, too, declined to return to Mole End Farm.

Kit was still shocked by the sight of devastation as they drove into the yard. Wayne had set the outbuildings ablaze, and, although the volunteer firefighters had responded quickly, the stored hay and straw had quickly fueled the fire. Only blackened ruins were left standing.

Leighton and Pete had caught Wayne dousing the barn with gasoline, and had cornered him. Wayne had grabbed a shovel and had swung at Leighton, who couldn't completely ward off the blow. The metal blade had caught him on the side of the head, and killed him instantly.

Wayne had been arrested en route to the American border.

They sat around in the kitchen lounge, quietly recalling happy memories of Leighton. The contrast with that pleasant evening - could it really have been only a few days ago? - was stark, unbearable.

Kit felt something of an outsider, as though she didn't have the right to feel the grief the others did. And yet she had come to think of Leighton as a special friend, and knew that he had accepted her into his exclusive circle of friends.

Pete said, "I saw the blow coming, like slow motion in a movie, and I knew what would happen. But I couldn't stop it! I feel so God-damned useless!"

"There's nothing you could have done," Nick assured him.

"That's right," Teresa said nastily. They'd all been drinking, but Teresa had consumed more wine than any of them. "It's you who could have prevented it, Nick. By not provoking Wayne in the first place. And that's all because of her!" she accused, glaring at Kit.

"That's enough!" Mandy ordered.

"It damn well isn't!' Teresa fumed, her eyes flashing, her freckles nearly invisible in her flushed face. "We never had problems like this before she came, did we?" she spat, impaling Kit with her eyes. "Leighton would still be alive if she hadn't started all this!" With that accusation flung brokenly at Kit, Teresa ran from the room sobbing.

Kit had turned pale at the scathing words. But how could she blame Teresa for voicing Kit's own thoughts? And yet, while they had been merely her private beliefs, there had always been the possibility that she was exaggerating her culpability. Now the idea had gained substance, reality, and seemed to quiver in the air.

"Stupid bitch!" Pete muttered.

"No, she's right, isn't she?" Kit said. "I've felt the same way."

"You can't blame yourself, Kit," Liz said.

"But I do! I keep thinking 'if only'...." She stopped, realizing that her plaintive remarks invited sympathy and reassurance, none of which she wanted from the others. But useless thoughts such as, *If only I hadn't stopped at the Wild Horse that Halloween night, if only I had accepted that damned drink from Wayne,* chased around in her mind.

"Nonsense," Mandy declared. "We all have a thousand 'if only's' in our lives. And if we had the benefit of hindsight, we would all have done things differently."

Kevin said, "You mustn't think that you could be responsible for, or somehow anticipate Wayne's behaviour, Kit. He's obviously a psychopath or a sociopath - unpredictable and dangerous. And you can breathe more easily now that he is behind bars."

But what terrible irony that her freedom should be gained through the death of her friend.

She noticed that Nick had grown strangely silent. Did he hold her accountable for Leighton's death, too?

Even back at Moon Hall, Nick said little, and Kit found it difficult to console him. "He was my best friend. More like a brother to me," was all he said about Leighton. She longed to wrap her arms around him and share his pain, but he said, "You go on to bed. I need to be alone."

But sleep eluded Kit, who felt that a rift had opened between her and Nick. She finally rose from her lonely bed and crept downstairs.

The floors were icy on her bare feet, but she welcomed the shock to her system. As if she needed some physical jolt to dispel the mental numbness caused by grief and guilt.

Nick had dozed off in the chair near the dying fire. Kit stoked it and added another log, and then stood for a while at the window, watching the wet snow melting like tears against the windowpanes. She draped a woolen afghan over Nick, and sat on the thick Persian rug beside him, hugging her drawn-up knees, her feet tucked beneath her capacious terry robe, and stared into the fluttering flames.

His touch on her hair was feather-light at first, and then he slid down onto the floor beside her, stroking her, looking at her as if he might never see her again. He made love to her fiercely, as if he could lose himself in her. When they went up to bed later, slipping in between the icy sheets, Nick was soon fast asleep, but Kit was even more wide awake. And worried.

She must have drifted off before dawn, and slept late. Nick had already finished breakfast when she, still groggy, joined him in the kitchen. As she poured herself a welcome mug of coffee, Nick said, "I'm going to the farm. Do you want to come?"

She hid her surprise. He had not left her alone for so many weeks that she had almost forgotten why. Now that he no longer needed to be her bodyguard, perhaps he wouldn't want her constant company. It shook her more than she thought possible.

Kit had no desire to face Teresa just yet. But it was Nick's question, rather than his assumption that they would go together, that made Kit say, "No, you go ahead. I think I'll have a hot bath and get some things done around here." *And you don't really want me to come, do you, Nick?*

He must have seen the bewilderment in her eyes. But he gave her a swift kiss and said, "See you later."

While she soaked in the tub, she tried to understand his motivation. Perhaps Nick needed to be alone with his oldest friends. Closing ranks and spending time together might help them all cope with their grief. And while that thought seemed logical, Kit couldn't help but feel hurt that she had been excluded.

Moon Hall was too empty without Nick. Kit could find nothing to keep her occupied, so she drifted fretfully from one unfinished task to another. By mid-afternoon Nick had still not returned, and Kit chided herself for feeling so hurt by his absence. He would hate to think that she was so possessive of him that she begrudged him time alone with his friends.

But damn him for making her need him so!

She put on her down parka and stepped out onto the snowy side veranda off the kitchen. There was no sign of Nick through the winter-bare trees.

Kit breathed deeply of the crisp, cold air. The sky was a dusty, faraway blue, as it is only in the depths of winter, when daylight is a pallid and feeble thing and cocooning darkness closes in early.

The frosted valley stretched away before her, the farmhouses huddled in the drifts amid clusters of sheltering trees. And if the scene was somewhat bleak and austere, it was also breathtakingly beautiful.

Kit felt a sudden lifting of her spirits, as if all this clean whiteness were washing the dark despair from her thoughts. The reality of her freedom from Wayne, from constant crippling fear, was finally sinking in.

Kit turned to the east, where the McGraths' fields crept up to meet the ridge. Scoured by glaciers millennia ago, this granite backbone jutted from the landscape and stretched for miles in either direction. Fir and scrub trees scraped a living at its rugged fringes, while fertile pockets of soil nurtured towering forests. Beaver ponds and swamps dotted the broad back of the ridge, and wild animals were plentiful. Kit had heard wolves howling, but the lonely sound had struck her as poignant, not menacing.

She noticed Alan walking up the driveway, and was glad of his company.

"Just came to see how you are," Alan said.

"Still in shock, I think. You've rescued me from sinister thoughts. Come in for a drink. I've had about enough fresh air for today. I really need something stronger to clear my head."

They sat at the kitchen table in front of the cavernous fireplace where half a treetrunk had been burning all day. Despite its vastness, the kitchen was a warm and welcoming place, mainly because of Kit's skillful arrangement of a jungle of plants, and her few but tasteful decorations.

Kit offered Alan a beer and took a sherry for herself. She seated herself at the end of the table, next to the fire and at right angles to Alan.

"Nick's at the commune," she explained. "They're all devastated."

"Jeez, I always knew that Wayne was a crazy bugger, but I never really thought it would come to this."

"It seems so senseless! But then, I guess death often is."

Alan gulped half his beer in one go, and then said, "I was talking to my friend, Jim Akers - you know, the OPP cop. One of that bunch of assholes that Wayne hangs around with has confessed that Wayne hadn't been playing poker with them the night you were attacked. He lied because he owed Wayne a couple of favours, and even loaned Wayne his car that night."

Kit shivered in remembered horror. The firelight played in her moon-pale hair and cast a sensuous glow on her face as she stared off into the shadows. She couldn't know how tragically beautiful she looked.

Alan gazed at her reverently for a moment - a look she did not see, nor was intended to see. Then he gave her a comforting, lopsided smile and covered her fidgeting fingers with one of his large, rough hands.

"He'll be behind bars for a long time, Kit," he reassured her. "And he's the one who's scared now. Scared shitless, I'd say."

She chuckled. Alan took his hand away from hers and said, "Well, best be getting back."

"Thanks for coming over, Alan. You always manage to cheer me up."

"Glad to oblige," he said in his self-mocking way.

When Alan had gone, Kit decided that perhaps a romantic dinner for two would lighten the atmosphere. Although she didn't have much fresh food in the house, there was meat and bread in the freezer and tins of vegetables and fruits in the cupboards. She busied herself preparing coq au vin with rice, beans, garlic bread, and peach crumble. With the kitchen permeated with delicious smells, and the soft strains of classical music from the radio filling the silent corners of the room, Kit felt comfortable, almost cheerful - and once more at home in Moon Hall.

Nick arrived back at dusk. "You've been busy," he said, surprised by the elaborate preparations.

Kit was pleased. The kitchen table was draped with a linen cloth and set with wine glasses and candles. Kit had been going to set the table in the formal dining room, but decided that the kitchen, with the blazing fire, was a more intimate and romantic setting tonight.

But the magic she had tried to create didn't last. Nick ate little, and said even less. He seemed too wrapped up in his own thoughts even to be aware of how strained the atmosphere was.

As they were finishing their wine, Nick said, "I won't be coming to Florida with you, Kit."

She had forgotten that she was booked to go to Florida soon, to spend Christmas with her parents. Nick had been planning to go along for part of the time. "If you don't want to go, Nick, I'll tell my parents we're not coming. I'm sure they'll understand."

"No. You go. You should be with them, and away from all this for a while. I need some time to myself, to get my head together. I'm going back to the city tomorrow, Kit." He looked at her regretfully.

Kit reached out to touch his cheek. "Nick...."

He took her hand from his face and kissed it tenderly. And then he let her go. "There's nothing you can do, Kit."

She was bursting with a thousand unspoken words, but could say nothing. She wanted to tell him how much she loved him, but she couldn't bear for him just look at her with that indulgent smile and those icy eyes and remain silent. That was too final. Leaving with thoughts and emotions unspoken gave her some hope.

Chapter 38

I have taken to striding about Ottawa in my trousers, riding boots, and a man's frock coat, with a great coat overtop when the temperature dictates. I have cropped my hair so that it reaches only to my shoulders, leaving it unbound, and go bareheaded except in winter when I wear a fur cap. My odd appearance has occasioned some comment in the local press as to my eccentricity, but I care not. I feel liberated!

Rose is mortified and has practically disowned me. Her conviction that I am crazy was strengthened when she saw my Ottawa home. It is virtually empty of furnishings save for a single bed upstairs and two armchairs and a table by the parlour fire. It suits me fine, for I invite no one. I have a cleaning lady who comes in once a fortnight, but I provide what meals I take myself. Often I eat at the Refuge where I spend most of my time when I do go to the city. Other times I buy bread, cheese, and wine at the market and that suffices to sustain me.

At least my physical needs. There is nothing to nourish or heal my soul.

After all, I cannot find a trace of Daniel within those walls. He did not live there sufficiently long to imbue the place with his personality. And I am not content to vainly seek ghostly comfort.

Baby Albert is thriving. Augustus cherishes the boy. The fact that Lily gave her life in exchange for his makes the child even dearer to him. He is slowly regaining his equanimity.

But I am not. I feel restless and destructive. And I fear that I am succumbing to madness.

June 21, 1879:

I cannot sleep. So I've taken to sitting out in the secret garden until the darkest hours of the night with a bottle of wine and my faithful Tristan at my side.

One moon-bright night we wandered along the ravine right to the McGraths' yard, where all reposed in stillness, the house, night-blind and empty looking. And I thought of Hugh, lying alone in his matrimonial bed, longing for his mistress perhaps, while Ruth tossed restlessly in her solitary room, perhaps craving the loving embrace of her husband.

       Are they any better off than I - these two I had once envied? Aren't they just as lonely and unfulfilled as I am?

Chapter 39

Kit disliked Florida at the best of times, but Christmas was the worst. Because there were only the three of them again this year, her parents had decided that it would be fun to do something different. But even they were disheartened, and longed for their traditional Christmas at home - a brisk, walk through the snow-bright night to the candlelight service at the church, a crackling fire and hot toddy awaiting them back home, the day-long aromas of roasting turkey with sage stuffing, a post-prandial stroll in the snowy dusk, admiring the Christmas lights.

"Well, we won't do this again," Kit's mother said as they sauntered barefoot along the beach after their turkey dinner. "Next year we'll stay home until the new year, as usual!"

They spoke on the phone to Richard and Fran and the girls, for whom it was midsummer. They were also nostalgic for their second missed Canadian Christmas.

Nigel had always thought Kit's need to be with her family at Christmas rather childish, annoyed sometimes that she wouldn't consider going off to the Caribbean or Mexico until Boxing Day. She wondered what he was doing this year, and imagined him sipping rum punches by an azure pool somewhere very un-Christmas-like.

She tried to call Nick but got only his answering machine, and wondered if he was staying at the commune. She didn't leave a message. If he didn't return her call, then she would be loath to phone him again. This way she still had the option of initiating a conversation. She did try Moon Hall, not really thinking he would be there, and only Ollie (or Violet) would have heard the shrill of the phone echoing through the empty house.

Kit downplayed her encounter with Wayne, though she was sure that her parents realized that, for they were deeply concerned. "I wasn't really hurt, just a bit bruised. And he is locked up now, and likely to be for a long time. Besides, I have Nick to look after me."

"That's all very well, dear," her mother replied. "But we have yet to meet this young man of yours."

"Well, you will when you get home, I promise," she replied, as much to reassure herself as her parents.

She forced herself to be cheerful so that her parents would never know how traumatized she had been by Wayne's brutal assault. It was only on her solitary beach walks or when she was in bed that she allowed herself to grieve for Leighton. And to worry about Nick.

So it was with trepidation and relief that she boarded the plane back to the frosty north. She hoped that Nick would be so anxious to see her that he would meet her at the airport, although they had made no such arrangement. She had driven there straight from Moon Hall, and had left her car in the long-term parking lot.

But Nick wasn't waiting. Was he expecting her or should she go home? She still had some of her things at Nick's. And she had a key.

There was an icy chill in the flat, and Kit knew immediately that no one had been there for days. Nick's resignation from the stock brokerage firm had become effective in the new year; so she had expected him to be here, working on the magazine. She wondered if he was at the farm or even at Moon Hall.

She hadn't realized until now just how much she had been counting on his being here, how desperately she wanted to see him and to be reconciled with him.

There was a note on the kitchen counter.

Kit,

Had to go to Toronto and Vancouver on business. Expect to be back about the 9th. Stay here if you like.

Nick

She crumpled the note in her fist. Well, he couldn't have made it much plainer.

Angrily she collected her belongings. Of course she had known she couldn't rely on Nick! How could she have been so foolish as to fall in love with him?

And when she had everything in a pile by the door, she collapsed onto the sofa by the empty grate and wept. When she had locked up, she dropped her key through the old-fashioned mail slot in the door.

She spent a lot of time crying over the next few days. Moon Hall once again became a refuge.

Blanketed in deep, unblemished snow, the place seemed truly cleansed. Kit locked herself in and felt secure in the firelit warmth, with the bleak winter frosting the panes and icy winds seeking to invade her sanctuary. Gales tore across the valley, swirling the snow and depositing it in great drifts. The nights were never so dark now, with the crisp snow reflecting the heavens. And when the moon was full, it skated across the lawns and spotlighted the naked black trees.

Kit talked to no one when she got back, except for Georgina, who had minded the cat and the plants. She couldn't face her commune friends just yet, and wasn't even sure how welcome she would be.

The ninth came and went with no word from Nick.

Kit immersed herself in her work, finding it ever more easy to empathize with Violet McAllister. She wrote sometimes until three or four in the morning, until exhaustion claimed her. That way she didn't have time to think of Nick or Wayne or Leighton or even Nigel. She became oblivious to everything around her, remembering only to feed the cat, if not herself.

That was why she was unaware of the blizzard until the electricity went off.

She panicked at first, for the late afternoon light was fading fast. She picked up the telephone receiver to call Georgina and ask if their electricity was also out, but the phone was dead. It was then that she looked out the window to discover a world transformed.

Through the driving snow, Kit could barely see beyond the veranda. The wind had sculpted four foot drifts in her driveway and piled it foot-high against her door. She couldn't even get her car out!

She was effectively trapped in her house with no electricity, phone, water, or heat, except for what wood she had left to burn.

How soon would the hydro crews have the power restored in this storm? In the city it never took more than a few hours.

Realizing that she could keep only one room warm, Kit built a fire in the kitchen grate. She hauled down lots of warm sweaters and blankets, and then pushed the comfortable couch into the kitchen in case she had to spend the night there. She found some candles that hadn't been chewed by mice, and collected every flashlight in the house. She didn't have a battery-operated radio, and so had no way of knowing how long the storm was slated to last. It felt strange to be so completely isolated from 20th century technology.

The wind howled and whined. It sucked on the chimney as if trying to deprive her of even the fire's meager warmth. And with the house already cooling down, Kit became aware of how little heat could be counted on from the fireplace.

She stood at the window, watching the last of the light fade, trying to discern something through the white curtain of snow. But her world ended a few feet from the house. To be thus alone and stranded suited her mood.

Remembering a story that Jean had told her, Kit wondered if it was in this kind of blizzard that Violet had set out on her journey to Ottawa over a century ago. If so, it was little wonder that the locals had marvelled at her foolhardiness.

The candles flickered uneasily - making Kit aware of how drafty the room was - but gave off only a feeble glow. They cast long, eerie shadows on the walls. She was loathe to use her flashlights more than necessary, so she could do little more than sit and think.

And during her hours of reflection, she wondered if she had been too quick to give up on Nick. What had he really done, aside from allow her the freedom to choose? *Stay here if you like.*

He didn't make claims on people - the "you're my girl" kind of attitude. He respected her as an individual on whom he wouldn't impose his own needs and desires.

But, damn it! She wanted him to need her, to desire her! She wanted him to be jealous if another man eyed her! She wanted him to feel as she did - desperately in love.

And if he didn't, then perhaps it was best to end the relationship now.

Kit jumped off the couch at the knock on the kitchen door, feeling her heart trying to leap from her chest. She suddenly envisioned Wayne Skuce standing out there, and was rivetted to to the spot, her body rigid, poised for flight, but spellbound. What if he'd gotten out of jail somehow? She felt a strangled scream clawing at the back of her throat.

The knocking persisted and a voice called, "Kit. Hey, Kit, It's me, Alan! C'mon! I'm freezing my ass off out here!"

She laughed then, released from her paralyzing fear, and was relieved to actually see his face when she opened the door a crack. "Just a minute, and I'll take off the chain."

Alan stepped in, accompanied by eddying snow and an icy blast of wind. His heavy parka was thick with flakes, which he shook off in a mini avalanche.

"How did you get here?" Kit asked.

"Snowmobile. I've come to fetch you over to our place. This storm isn't going to let up just yet, and the hydro could be out for days."

"Days?!"

"Sure. That's one hell of a blizzard out there, in case you haven't noticed. The road's drifted in, and it won't be ploughed till everything else in the county's done, and nothing but the major roads are being cleared until the storm actually stops. So the hydro crews can't even get out here. You can't stay in this place for days with that little bit of a flame there to keep you warm."

"I believe you."

"So get some things together. Mum's already making up the spare room."

With Alan holding the flashlight, Kit packed a small bag with her warmest things. Alan banked the fire, so it would burn more slowly and safely, and hopefully heat the house enough to keep the pipes from bursting.

"What about Ollie?"

"The cat'll be alright. Just leave him enough food for a few days. He'll probably curl up near the fire."

The wind outside nearly snatched her breath away. She was blinded by the sharp, driving snow. And she couldn't believe that she was sinking up to her knees in it. Winters in Toronto, or even Launston Mills, had never been like this!

With a powerful flashlight, Alan guided them to the snowmobile.

It wasn't far to the McGrath farm - only about a quarter of a mile - but Kit could see how easily one could become disoriented and lost in the sea of snow. Alan tried to follow his own tracks back, but already they had been swept away. They had to go slowly to avoid the ditches and trees and fences that suddenly loomed up whenever Alan lost the road. With her face going numb in the biting wind, and her hands beneath the thin leather gloves stiffening, Kit was relieved to see the faint lights emanating from the farmhouse - lights that they hadn't been able to see until they almost collided with the house. Alan pulled up by the back door, and she stumbled gratefully into the warmth of the kitchen.

Oil lamps burned and the wood stove radiated a cozy heat. Jean was pouring steaming mugs of tea.

She said, "Just in time! I'll bet you could use one of these." She handed Kit a cup.

"I sure can. And it's kind of you to invite me here."

"Well, we couldn't leave you at Moon Hall by yourself in this storm." Although she made it sound as if it were merely a neighbourly obligation, Kit had come to realize that that gruff, self-effacing generosity was just the local manner. And profuse thanks only occasioned a lot of embarrassment.

Kit and Alan followed Jean into the living room, where another small wood stove burned. Stuart and Duncan greeted her, but there was no dimpled smile from Mary. She glanced at Kit with hostility and then looked away.

Kit felt uneasy. She hadn't seen Mary since that fateful November night, and hadn't forgotten Jean's words. Did Mary still blame her for the miscarriage?

Mary suddenly rose and announced, "I'm going up to bed."

There was an awkward silence in the wake of Mary's rude desertion.

"I'm sure we'll all be ready for bed soon," Jean said. "Nothing better to do on a night like this than to hunker down under the blankets and hope that it's cleared by morning."

The storm seemed to have sapped their energy, for the conversation became spasmodic and desultory. Or perhaps it was just the tremendous heat pouring out of the wood stove that made them so tired. Fortunately, some of that heat drifted upstairs and took the chill off the bedrooms. But they couldn't close the doors or the rooms would soon have resembled refrigerators.

The guest room to which Jean led Kit was furnished with an antique four-poster bed, a wash-stand dressing table displaying a chipped but lovely porcelain bowl and matching jug, a pine wardrobe, and a rickety aluminum lawn chair. When Kit had changed into her flannel nightgown and terry dressing robe, she had a quick wash in the bathroom at the end of the hall. Jean had provided a pot of warm water for washing, and buckets of melting snow were used to flush the toilet. As Kit climbed between the icy sheets - having left on her heavy robe and thermal socks - she wished that bed-warming pans had not gone out of fashion, and could appreciate why they had been necessary.

Violet must have lived like this, Kit thought. Being cooked near the woodstove, and freezing anywhere else in the house. No wonder people had worn so many layers of clothes. No wonder they had not bathed often in winter.

Kit tried to curl herself into a ball to conserve her heat. The wind tore at the window, screaming to be let in. She was glad she wasn't alone at Moon Hall now. She wondered where Nick was. Was he thinking about her at all?

She longed to feel him lying beside her, to bask in their shared warmth. She ached to snuggle against his strong body, to feel his arms cradling her. To think that she might never again feel the tenderness of his touch, the heat of his passion, was too much to bear. She wondered if her tears would freeze on her cheeks.

Had Violet ached like this? Was it worse never to have known a man's love or to miss his every caress?

Kit heard the angry murmur of voices from the room next to hers, which was Mary and Stuart's, and although she could not hear the words, she felt like an unwilling eavesdropper. It was enough just to hear the tone and infer the content.

She slept fitfully, waking to feel the chill permeating her bones, the frostiness of the pillow beneath her cheeks. She heard someone pass her door, hesitating ever so slightly, as if pausing to look in, and go downstairs to load more wood into the stove. Whoever it was stayed near the fire, for she didn't hear him return.

It was still dark when she woke again, but she decided to dress and go downstairs to warm herself by the fire.

Stuart was sleeping in the armchair. He stirred when she approached.

"Sorry I woke you," she whispered, "but I just had to get warm."

"It is more comfortable down here," he agreed. "Do you want to sleep on the couch?"

"No, thanks. I don't think I can sleep anymore."

"How about a cup of coffee then?"

"Wonderful!"

He returned from the kitchen with a kettle of water, two mugs containing instant coffee, a sugar pot, and a milk jug. It didn't take the water long to boil on the top of the wood stove.

Kit sipped the steaming coffee gratefully, and finally stopped shivering.

Stuart gazed at her over the rim of his cup, and she realized that she hadn't really talked to him since she'd thrown herself into his bloody arms months ago. In her fear, she had clung to him fiercely, desperately, as if afraid that Wayne might yet tear her away. Perhaps it was little wonder that Mary, coming upon them so suddenly, had mistaken that embrace for passion.

And yet... She imagined what Mary must have seen - Stuart saturated in blood and slime, and she, contaminated with it as well, sobbing and hysterical - and thought that it must have looked more like a scene from a "B" horror flick than a love story.

"I'm sorry that Mary's got such a stupid notion into her head - blaming you for losing the baby," Stuart said, as if reading her thoughts.

Kit had been pleasantly surprised by Mary's show of spirit earlier, preferring that to her usual fawning adoration. In that moment of defiance, Kit's sympathy had been aroused.

In the early-morning intimacy, Kit was prompted to say, "Perhaps it was seeing us together like that which she can't forgive. She's misinterpreted that scene. You could set her mind at rest."

"If you're trying to save my marriage, Kit, forget it! There isn't much to save. Mary thought the baby would be the solution. But I'm just as glad she lost it. I don't want to be bound to her that way."

She knew he was right, and yet his words smacked of self-pity. "What will you do?"

He shrugged. "Nothing. We'll just drift on - and farther apart."

Kit wanted to shake him out of his lethargy. Why didn't he take himself in hand and do something with his life? If he hated the farm and his marriage so much, why didn't he leave instead of staying here feeling bitter and resentful?

Because he was weak, she suddenly realized. It wasn't so much loyalty and self-sacrifice that kept him on the farm. It was complacency and indifference and fear of failure anywhere else. He probably even liked playing the role of martyr.

She couldn't help feeling slightly contemptuous. Despite his earthy good looks, Kit wondered how she could ever have found him appealing. He was not Hugh, and never could be like him.

"Nick hasn't been here for a while," Stuart said. It was more a statement than a question, and for a moment Kit wondered if he'd been spying on her. But of course, everyone would recognize Nick's Porsche. It wasn't difficult to keep tabs on people out here.

Kit didn't want to admit to Stuart that her relationship with Nick was over, so she found herself making excuses. "He's been busy, and I've been working hard on a new book."

He stared at her with such intensity that she felt momentarily breathless. His desire was almost palpable.

In an intuitive flash, she realized how their relationship must seem to Stuart. Like an old-fashioned hero, he had jumped to defend her honour, ready to duel with Wayne that night at the Wild Horse. And when she had been desperate, hurt, frightened, wasn't it to him that she had run, flinging herself into his strong arms for protection?

He would never believe the horror that the memory of that embrace evoked in her.

"Kit...." he said, leaning forward and touching her hand.

Kit was relieved as she heard the stairs creak. Stuart quickly sat back, looking annoyed. Alan came into the room rubbing his hands. "Hey, that coffee looks good. I'm going to wrap myself around one of those before we start the chores. Couldn't sleep?" he asked Kit.

"Not long. I couldn't stay warm."

"Yeah, I know what you mean." He gave her a wicked grin. "They do say that two can keep warmer...."

"Shut up, Alan!" Stuart snapped, but Kit suppressed a smile. She found it hard to be offended by Alan's good-natured teasing. Stuart said, "And hurry up! It's time we were out in the barn."

It was still snowing, although the storm had abated somewhat. Peering out into the snow-bright darkness, Kit said, "Can you even find the barn?"

"We've seen worse than this," Alan said. "My grandfather told me that when he was a lad, they had real winters. Said he went into the village with his dad after a big storm once, and, as they drove along in the sleigh, they noticed what looked like a whiskey bottle sticking out of a snowbank. So his dad tried to pluck it out. Turned out to be an insulator on the top of a telegraph pole."

"A bit of a tall tale, I think," Kit said, laughing.

"He swore it was the truth."

"Then I have even more admiration for those hardy 19th century folk."

Duncan entered the room with a gruff "Morning", warmed himself for a moment by the fire, and then prepared to go outside. His sons followed.

Jean and Mary appeared a few minutes later, and began bustling about in the kitchen. Kit knew better than to offer her help.

Thoroughly toasted now, she moved away from the fire, feeling restless. Having worked so feverishly lately, she found that she couldn't relax. She hadn't even brought a book along to read. She skimmed through a few women's magazines that lay around, but none of the articles captured her interest.

She paced about, spending most of her time standing at the window, gazing out at the snowy morning. Longing for Nick. Remembering their evenings out in the city - a different world. It might as well be a thousand miles away right now.

Did this storm even affect them there, except to snarl the traffic?

God, what was she doing here, in the middle of nowhere, where life could suddenly regress a century and no one really cared?

And yet, it's where she needed to be to understand Violet McAllister.

But Violet wouldn't have let a mere storm keep her from Daniel. And she would not have given up so easily, assuming he didn't care about her simply because he hadn't contacted her. If she had been free to love Daniel, nothing would have stopped her, not even a determined Isobel Granger. And Violet would not have been afraid to open her heart to him, to let him know how deeply she loved him, even at the risk of rejection. After all, could that really be any worse than this anguished uncertainty?

If it had been possible then, Kit would have jumped into her car and taken off for the city. It was time to talk to Nick, to clear up any misunderstanding between them. Perhaps he felt that she had deserted him when he most needed her. Perhaps he needed consolation and reassurance. Damn this storm!

Jean summoned her to breakfast in the kitchen, and Kit was surprised by the food spread out on the table - sausages, bacon, eggs, pancakes, home fries, and toast. "How did you manage to conjure up all this?" she asked.

Jean chuckled. "On the concession where I grew up we didn't get electricity till '47. I learned to cook on a woodstove like this one."

"It's marvellous!" And the food was delicious.

The men tucked into heaping platefuls, and it was some time before anyone spoke.

"Reckon the ploughs'll be out soon," Alan said. "The snow's tapering off."

"You can plough the lane this afternoon then," Duncan said. They had a large shovel attached to the front of a tractor which they used to dig themselves out.

Kit said, "Could you do my driveway as well?"

"Sure, once I can get down the road," Alan replied. "But you're not in any hurry to go anywhere, are you? The highways'll still be a mess."

"I have to get to the city."

Alan shook his head. "You sure get strange notions."

Stuart looked hard at her, probing and reading her thoughts. A pained expression flitted across his face. He excused himself from the table with a curt "Have to see to the accounts."

Kit was relieved that he understood, yet sorry that she had wounded him. Although she had sensed a sexual attraction between them once, she had never encouraged him, and felt somewhat resentful that he was laying this guilt upon her. She hadn't asked for his attentions, and God knows, she had enough guilt to deal with already!

Kit insisted on helping to clean up, and dried dishes with Mary, despite the latter's coldness. Kit quizzed Jean about life without electricity, realizing that Violet's world would not have been all that different.

When Jean left the two women to finish up, Kit felt she needed to break the ice with Mary. She said, "I was sorry to hear about your miscarriage."

Mary snorted in disbelief.

Kit felt emboldened to say, "And I'm not after your husband."

An angry flush suffused Mary's cheeks. "Well, the damage is done, isn't it? He fancies himself in love with you."

"And it's easier to hate me than him."

Mary looked away. "Leave me alone, Kit."

"I'm not your enemy, Mary."

Mary turned on her then. "You think you're so much more sophisticated than us country bumpkins, don't you? I suppose you think that Stuart's not even good enough for you, don't you? And what good is he to me if he wants only you?"

Surprised as she was by this irrational outburst, Kit replied, "I think he wants a lot of things he knows he can never have."

"Bitch!" Mary hissed, and ran from the room.

"You've got Stu pegged, alright," Alan said to Kit from the doorway. She hadn't noticed him standing there. "He's one of those people who thinks that everyone else got a better deal out of life than he did. But he doesn't do anything to change it. Your basic whiner.

"It's Mary I feel sorry for," Alan continued. "She was one of the perennially cheerful ones - Pollyanna with a permanent smile. But Stu even managed to corrupt her."

Kit sat down at the table, "Well, it looks as though I've only made things worse."

"Couldn't be much worse, I'd say. Just feelings finally surfacing. Deep down she knows it isn't your fault."

"I'm beginning to think that a lot of people wish I'd never come here. I do myself sometimes."

"Don't you start getting Stu's disease. You know - self-pity."

Kit smiled gratefully at him. She was surprised that she had ever thought Stuart's solemn veneer hid a deep and sensitive soul, while Alan was flighty and carefree. It was unfortunate that Duncan didn't recognize the better man.

Chapter 40

August 22, 1879:

I went to the train station today to send a telegram to Marjorie. But what a surprise I had! There on the platform was Neil Spenlowe!

He was expensively dressed as a dandy, proclaiming to all the world - and especially to the citizens of Todmorden - that he was a successful man. There was a pretty woman on his arm, squeezed into the widest, most ostentatious silk gown imaginable, and lost beneath an enormous hat. The pair of them looked more suited to the stage than to Todmorden.

Neil and I stared in disbelief at one another, and then he said, "Why, Violet McAllister! What a surprise!" He cocked an eyebrow at my unconventional attire, so his comment was rather ambiguous.

I replied tartly, "Isn't it though? I'd rather expected to see you some eight or nine years ago, since you'd told me you would come back to marry me." I finally had a target on which to vent some of my inner rage. After all, it was because of Neil that I had lied and initiated the whole sordid downward spiral of my life. I felt vindictive and would spare Neil nothing.

His wife - if such she was - seemed petulantly shocked by my declaration. Neil laughed softly. "So you haven't forgotten our childhood infatuation?"

"I didn't realize you still considered yourself a child at twenty, Neil. You proclaimed undying love to me and then ran away - taking a substantial amount of my father's money with you. I realize now that your vows are worthless and that your kind of love can be bought and sold."

His handsome face darkened. "Don't tell me that you didn't find another suitor, Violet?" he said sarcastically. "With all your charms and... expectations?"

"Oh, more than expectations, Neil. My father is dead you see, and I am quite wealthy. But you showed me that men aren't to be trusted, especially with a woman's money. So I prefer my independence." Of course I spoke in retaliation, not in truth. But everybody else at the station heard our exchange, including Hugh, who was picking up some freight with his wagon. He regarded me with sadness and sympathy.

"You always were more than a match for any man, Violet," Neil said, turning away from me. He was insinuating that no man would want me, being so outspoken and unconventional.

But I wasn't about to let him go so easily. I still recalled how he had deserted and wounded me. "So why have you come back, Neil? To flaunt the wealth my father's money earned you? Or to show your mistress how far you've come from your squalid beginnings?"

The woman said huffily, "Come, Cornelius. I have seen enough of your precious village and its rude and crazy people! We're getting on the next train out of here!"

Hugh interceded then, whether to help me or to stop me making a scene, I'm not certain. He said, "Well, Neil, we never thought to see you again. Life must be treating you well."

I turned and marched away. As I mounted Moondancer I heard Neil in his smooth, self-satisfied voice tell Hugh about the brewery he owned in Toronto.

I rode home like a maniac, but I still felt wild and destructive. I even thought of taking my gun and going back to blast Neil's head off, but there's still a glimmer of sanity within me. Instead, I galloped down to the river, where I stripped naked and plunged into the fast, hectic water where it cascaded over a series of limestone shelves. I wanted the icy, rushing water either to cleanse me or to sweep me away.

But I sat there feeling merely cold and foolish, with tears running down my cheeks. Seeing Neil brought back all the horrible, ironic events that have so effectively ruined my life. I think that only Tristan's concerned barks kept me from rolling over and succumbing to the force of the water.

When I got back to Moon Hall, feeling drained and weary, Hugh was waiting for me. He seemed rather embarrassed, as if he, not Neil, were guilty of jilting me. Seeing my damp, dishevelled state, he began to look concerned.

I snapped, "Don't tell me about Neil! I have no wish to hear his excuses nor his great success story! I despise him and his ambitions!"

"I'm sorry, Violet. He's not worthy of you. He never has been."

"I know that now. But it's too late! If I had listened to my father, my life would have been completely different!" And yours as well, Hugh.

But I would never have met Daniel. Wasn't it all worth it in the end, just to know him?

Yet, wouldn't I have been blissfully ignorant and therefore content had I simply married Hugh and stayed away from Ottawa?

Daniel, I need you!

Chapter 41

As Alan had predicted, the roads were bad. Although the snow had stopped falling, winds blew treacherous drifts and white-outs across the icy highway. Kit drove slowly, despite her desperation to reach Nick, and almost aborted the journey several times. Radio reports continually warned people to stay off the highways unless absolutely necessary. She passed several abandonned cars in ditches, and twice nearly skidded off the road herself.

It took her well over two hours to do the fifty minute trip, and by the time she parked the BMW behind Nick's Porsche, her muscles had seized up from the tension of the harrowing drive.

And now what if Nick wasn't home, or was annoyed to see her? Or if Christine was here? Her heart hammered against her ribs, and her hands shook as much from apprehension as a reaction to the drive. She sat in the car for a few minutes to calm herself.

A snowplow rumbled by, blue lights flashing, tarnishing the snow mountains with a scraping of salty slush. The evening sky was aglow with the snowy reflections of streets lights, creating that bizarre nighttime brightness in which everything was clearly discernible. A couple of adventurous souls, well-bundled against the cold, plunged through the snow drifts.

Kit left Ollie and her suitcase in the car, and approached the house with trepidation.

She waded through the snow that had drifted onto the veranda. Her stomach knotted as she heard the muffled chiming of the doorbell.

Nick's face lit with that familiar, indulgent smile when he saw her. "Kit! Where have you been?" He ushered her inside.

"At home. Feeling sorry for myself... Missing you."

Her eyes searched his for reassurance. She saw both pleasure and pain there. He pulled her into his arms and said, "I didn't think you'd be back. You left your key."

"I didn't think you wanted me here. That note..."

"...was all wrong. I realized that after I'd left. I told you I wasn't a writer. I should have called you when I got back, but I couldn't. I haven't been fit company even for myself. And I thought you wanted to end things between us."

"I thought you blamed me for Leighton's death."

He moved away from her then. "God, no, Kit! I blame myself! I should have listened to you and stayed away from Wayne..."

"But if I'd never come, or if I'd accepted that damned drink from Wayne..."

"It's no good thinking like that."

"No it isn't," she replied quietly. "Leighton wouldn't blame you."

Nick ran his fingers agitatedly through his hair. "No, I suppose not. Damn it, I miss him!" He gathered her tightly in his arms.

Relief swept through her. She wasn't aware until now that she had been practically holding her breath, dreading his rejection. Tears stung her eyes. The strain of her arduous drive and these past uncertain weeks left her weak and trembling. She herself hadn't realized how desperately in love she was with Nick.

It was a long time before he let her go. His voice sounded choked as he said, "You must be boiling in that coat! Where are you coming from? Not Moon Hall? Not in that storm?"

"I couldn't wait any longer to talk to you."

Nick shook his head at her foolishness, but then said, "I'm glad you came. My own company's been driving me crazy."

He led her into the living room, which was uncharacteristically littered with papers, dirty plates, and half-finished drinks. "Sorry for the mess," he said. "I haven't been inclined to tidy up. Chaos suited my mood."

"I know what you mean. I have a feeling Moon Hall looks like this too. I haven't really noticed. How's the magazine coming?"

"We're just about ready to roll with the first issue, and we're doing the layout for the June one. I've signed up some more advertisers - that's why I wasn't here when you came back from Florida. So things are looking pretty good. As long as it sells.... You must be exhausted from your drive. How about a drink?"

"And a long, hot bath to ease my muscles. I feel as though I've run a marathon."

Nick sat on the floor by the tub, absently stroking Ollie on his lap, while Kit relaxed in the warm water. They drank wine and talked - a lot about Leighton, which was cathartic for Nick, who seemed visibly to relax.

He confessed that he had enjoyed Christmas with his own family. "My two sisters were home with their families, and everybody was cheerful. I felt like Scrooge at first, but the kids persuaded me to help them build a snowman and play with their new toys. It was like the old days, only with more people around. I guess I needed that. It helped me to forget for a while."

"Ours was just the opposite. The three of us felt disoriented and rather lost. It was almost a relief when Christmas was all over and we could go back to thinking it was just a holiday in the sun. And I missed you, Nick," she said, reaching out to him.

He clasped her hand in his and brought it to his lips. "I missed you too, Kit."

They whipped up some omelets for supper, and ate them by the fire. And when they made love, Kit felt for the first time that it wasn't just a physical communion between them.

.　　.　　.

They spent most of each week in the city, but retreated to Moon Hall for the weekends. Kit would leave early in the morning on alternate Fridays to work on her book or to putter around the house while the cleaning lady she had hired from the village did her biweekly cleaning, and Nick would arrive in the evening.

It was on those Fridays that Kit often had visitors. Alan came to tell her that Mary had left Stuart, and was living with her grandmother in town, and working as a cashier at the grocery store.

"Do you think she'll come back?" Kit asked him. A vacuum cleaner hummed far off in one of the sitting rooms.

"Not if she has any sense," Alan said. He was straddling a chair in the kitchen, watching her put the finishing touches on a pie. "Jeez, I didn't know you could cook, too."

"Don't tell me you've forgotten the zucchini bread?" she quipped.

"Never! Just never thought of you making ordinary things like apple pie."

"I'm just a 'down-home' girl."

"Ha! And my Aunt Fanny's a brain surgeon!"

"Is she?" Kit asked playfully.

He made a comical face. "Even if I had an Aunt Fanny, I can't imagine her being one."

They both laughed.

Kit slid the pie into the hot oven. She'd always intended to try the old brick bake oven, but had never gotten around to experimenting with it. She wiped her hands on her apron and asked, "And how's Stuart taking it?"

"He's his usual gloomy self, but I think he's relieved. Saved him from having to make a decision. Pop's pissed off about it - he's wondering when he's going to get his heir. Now he's on at me about when I'm going to get married. Mum's the one who really misses Mary. Said she was like a real daughter."

"Well, I admire Mary's courage." She'd shown a lot more strength of character than Kit had given her credit for. It couldn't be easy to leave the security of the farm when she had no career to fall back on. "And what about you? Are you ever going to get married?" she teased.

"Jeez, lay off, Kit! I haven't even got a steady girlfriend!"

"What about Georgina?"

Alan raised his eyebrows in astonishment, as though he'd never contemplated that possibility. "Georgie? She's like a kid sister to me." He frowned suddenly. "I'm worried about her, Kit. I think her old man's getting worse. Last time I saw her she was pretty glum."

"It must be a terrible strain on her, looking after those two. She should really get away by herself for a while."

"Will you talk to her, Kit? She might listen to you."

"Of course."

Kit wasted no time in doing just that once Alan had left and the pie was out of the oven.

She hated going to the Bryce farm, and was relieved that George wasn't in the kitchen. Arnie gave her a big grin and pulled his tiger medallion out from under his flannel shirt to show her that he still treasured it.

Kit was shocked to see how haggard Georgina had become. Her mop of frizzed hair was even more wildly untidy than usual. She was pale and nervous.

"You don't look well," Kit said with concern. "Come to the city with me - even if only for a few days. We have a spare bedroom. You and I will see the sights and do some shopping."

Georgina shook her head. "It's kind of you, Kit, but I can't just now. Things are not going well. We've got a mortgage coming due, and you've seen what the interest rates are. I can't afford to renew. I could barely keep us afloat before. Dad overextended himself during his expansion - the banks were only too willing to lend us the money then. I think we'll have to sell up..."

"Over my dead body!" George thundered from the doorway. He hobbled in, inflating himself to his full height before bellowing,

"You sell another inch of my land and I'll kill ya, do ya hear, ya ungrateful bitch! Always sneaking around behind my back. Do ya think I don't know what's going on? Didn't I run this farm fer forty years? And now ya've lost it all! Sabotaging it so's ya can go live in the God-damn town like that asshole brother of yers! And it's me yer blaming?"

"You talk to the bank manager then," Georgina said in exasperation.

"Don't take that tone of voice with me, my girl, or I'll show ya what's what." He raised his hand in a threatening gesture. "It was you what took that mortgage out five years ago. So ya just go and fix it up with the bank. Nobody's gonna throw me off my land! Nobody, do ya hear?"

As he left the room, Kit noticed Georgina quivering. She had her hands balled into fists. "I don't know what to do anymore, Kit," she muttered through clenched teeth.

"Perhaps I could lend you the money..."

"No. I wouldn't ask that of you. Why should you take less than the going rate? And I'm sure your money's tied up in investments. We can't keep going like this anyway. I can only hope that the interest rates will fall before our mortgage comes due next month. Then maybe we can limp along for another year or so."

"Well, if there's anything I can do.... Do reconsider my offer to get away to the city, even if only for a few days."

Georgina managed a half-hearted smile. "I'll think about it. Thanks, Kit."

But Kit was certain she wouldn't take her up on it, and wondered how else she could help Georgina. The girl was well on her way to a nervous breakdown.

She pondered the problem for a while, but came to no solution. And being caught up in her own affairs, it was too easy to forget the Bryces' problems.

The first issue of *Country Lanes* had appeared on the stands and sales, although not brisk, were encouraging. Subscriptions were already coming in, many of them from advance advertising that Nick had done in other journals.

Pete came to stay with them in the city while he looked for an apartment. The farm was a strange place without Leighton, he told them. Too much had changed; it was time to leave.

Drew had bought him out, and, flush with money, Pete savoured his new-found independence. Even as he donned his new clothes, he gained self-confidence. To Kit he admitted that he'd become unsure of himself these last few years, wondering what he was capable of doing, other than mucking out barns.

"I'd been feeling like some Dickensian urchin peeking in a window at a wonderfully lavish ball, longing to be part of the fun, but knowing I was to be left out in the cold," Pete told her. "The worst part was knowing I'd brought it upon myself - I was the bedraggled urchin by choice. And that made me angry, but not only at myself - at everyone. I'd been the victim of some elaborate hoax - urged to drop out of society, and then forced to watch all the others make comfortable lives for themselves. And I didn't finish my degree, so I have no qualifications, no career, no skills, and precious little work experience.

"My mother never tires of telling me how proud they all are of my successful younger brother. He's a lawyer. Avaricious little bugger - always was, even as a kid. I'd keep reassuring myself that none of them knew what was really important in life, and that I did. But after Jackie left, I didn't believe it anymore myself. It's easy to say money isn't important until you don't have any.

"So I was jealous of my brother. And of Nick, even while I felt he had betrayed us. Yet I wanted desperately to believe that I had made the right choice, that these last eight years hadn't been just a bad mistake. I really wanted to believe, like Leighton had, but I couldn't any more.

"I felt as though I'd lost control of my life. I didn't want to be dependent upon the commune for the rest of my life. And look what's happened to that place. At the beginning it felt as if we were all an important part of it and of the decision-making. But Drew had wrested control slowly over the years. So where did that leave me? At his beck and call."

Kit could feel his frustration and bitterness. She'd always been good - too good - at empathizing.

Pete said, "During the last few months I've come to realize that life isn't some sort of race in which I got a very late start. What I did eight years ago was the right decision for me at the time. Now it's time for a change." He shrugged. "It all seems so simple in the telling." Yet giving no indication of the emotional turmoil that that had engendered, was his implication.

"I know it can't have been easy, " Kit said. "It took me a long time to overcome my own rationalizations and inertia, and leave Nigel. Long before I actually left, I knew that it was pointless to stay."

She remembered the vague feeling of discontent, the irritability that had made her too quick to find fault and to take offence. She remembered the sleepless nights when she had watched the city lights from the attic windows, and had felt irrationally angry with Nigel for sleeping so peacefully. She, too, had suffered a sense of hopelessness. She hadn't healed either, until she had taken a decisive step - taken control of her life, rather than drifting along on the path that Nigel had mapped out for her.

With his hair cut fashionably short and his new square-rimmed spectacles, Pete no longer bore such a strong resemblance to John Lennon. It was just as well to let the past go, Kit thought.

She, too, noticed a change at the commune. Dianna was never there anymore - although Kit sometimes visited her at the shop - and Pete rarely came once he'd moved into his apartment. Erick had applied to a chef's school in Paris, and seemed confident that he'd be accepted. Teresa was moody and uncommunicative.

And Leighton had left a painful void.

Kit didn't even look forward to going there anymore, although she and Nick made a point of visiting every few weeks.

.　　.　　.

Kit usually picked up her weekend groceries on her way out of the city. But one Friday morning she decided to stop at the store in Kintyre, hoping, yet dreading, to talk to Mary.

It was an impulse she felt compelled to obey, although she really didn't know what she wanted to say to Mary, and was certain that Mary would resent her.

Kit found it hard to concentrate on the shopping as she maneuvered the cart haphazardly up and down the aisles, throwing in things that she probably wouldn't even use. When she caught a glimpse of Mary at one of the tills, she was tempted just to walk out of the store.

She pushed her cart up to the checkout.

Taking money from an elderly shopper, Mary casually glanced at her next customer and faltered when she saw Kit. Angry red blotched her face. She fumbled with the change, and turned even more crimson when the septuagenarian gently reminded her that another dollar was due to her.

Mary didn't look at Kit again as she began ringing through her items.

"Hello, Mary."

"I didn't think I'd see you here." It was an accusation. *How dare you intrude on my life. Did you come to gloat?*

"I was sorry to hear your news."

"Were you?" she said bitterly, stabbing at the keys as if pecking at Kit's face. "What do you know? You live in a dream world, like your books, where the beautiful and rich always get what they want. How can you have any idea how I feel?" Mary glared at Kit, the groceries on the conveyor forgotten.

Fortunately, the next two tills were vacant, and no one waited behind Kit.

Kit was stung to realize that Mary could so blithely dismiss the horrors that she had lived through in the past months as some sort of Gothic fiction. But then grief was usually selfish. She said, "I left someone I'd once loved, too. I know how hard it is. We weren't married, but we lived together for seven years. You don't just throw so much of your life away. And I still love him in a way. I suppose he'll always be a part of me. I just wanted you to know that I sympathize, and I admire your courage. I wish you well." Having voiced it, she realized that that was, quite simply, all she had wanted to say - to let Mary know that she understood and cared.

Her sincerity had reached Mary, whose eyes glistened with tears she would never shed in Kit's presence. Her hand shook as she finished totalling and bagging the groceries. The silence between them was strained, but there was nothing left to say.

Mary's "Goodbye, Kit," suggested a finality that she expected Kit to honour.

Kit, still disturbed by her encounter with Mary, was absently putting away her groceries when Bonnie Skuce called on her later that morning.

Kit hardly recognized her, smartly dressed as she was in one of the outfits that Kit had given her, her hair clean and shiny, even if raggedly cut. She looked radiant.

Bonnie said. "Pa told me never to set foot here again, but I reckon you won't tell him."

"I certainly won't! Well, I approve of your new look!"

Bonnie smiled happily. "I got a boyfriend, Kit! He's a real nice guy. Not like some of 'em - you know, the ones that are just interested in screwing around. He really cares about me." Which must be a novel experience for her, Kit thought. "He's a lot more mature than the boys at school."

"You mean he's not at school any more?"

"He's nineteen. Working to be a mechanic. Has his own car. He's waiting outside for me now."

"Why don't you ask him in?"

Bonnie shook her head. "We gotta be off. Listen, Kit, I'm sorry about what Wayne did... ya know. They wouldn't let me come and see you. Wayne beat me when... well, never mind. Just wanted ya to know. And to thank you for being a friend. I'm leaving home. Things are bad there. Pa's drunk most of the time, and exercising his fists too often. I can't stay there no more. Bye, Kit!"

Kit was touched and saddened. She had really given the girl so little, yet it must have seemed a lot to her. Kit couldn't believe that Wayne and Bonnie had sprung from the same loins.

She watched Bonnie climb into a rusty old chevy, and managed to catch a glimpse of a boy in a black leather jacket and straw-coloured shoulder-length hair. She hoped for Bonnie's sake that he truly was a nice guy.

On their way to the farm that night Kit and Nick noticed the "For Sale" sign on the Pughs' lawn. With the windows blinded by shutters, the place looked desolate already. But to think of that monstrosity without the Pughs coming back to fill it with their forceful, eccentric personalities....

"That's surprising," Kit said. "I wonder why they're selling."

"Maybe they've realized they'll never win the war against the dandelions and the horseflies," Nick said. "I'll bet they're moving into a big condo in Ottawa or Toronto. Harbourfront, maybe - or something like it."

"Yes, I can easily imagine them there. But you know, I'll miss them."

Kit asked Liz about it when they arrived.

"We were curious about that too, so Kevin called the real estate agent. Apparently Rhett died last month - had a heart attack on the golf course - and Cleo can't face coming back here without him."

Remembering how fit Rhett had looked the last time she'd seen him, Kit was surprised and sorry at the news. He and Cleo had seemed so invincible. And she couldn't even tell him how right he had been to warn her.

"Strange old birds that they were, I rather liked them," Kevin said.

"I think even Leighton sort of approved of them," Kit said, remembering that beautiful summer day of the garden fete.

The others seemed to be recalling the same thing, for there were wistful looks in the silence.

"Mandy and I have some more pleasant news to impart," Drew said. "Mandy's pregnant, and we're getting married."

"Usually it's the other way around," Nick said with a laugh. "But congratulations!"

"Why is everything suddenly falling apart?" Teresa cried dramatically, before rushing from the room.

Kit was momentarily shocked when she expected to hear a witty rejoinder from Leighton. It was always like that at the farm - expecting Leighton to appear or to say something, and then remembering.

"I'll see to Teresa," Erick said.

When he'd left the room, Liz said, "Do you think he'll take Teresa with him to Paris?"

"They have been getting pretty chummy lately," Mandy replied.

They all fell silent, undoubtedly wondering how four of them - Drew and Mandy, Liz and Kevin - could manage the farm.

Drew said, "We'll have to hire help. And I don't think we can afford to buy them both out. We'd have to get a loan. You know what the interest rates are at - over 18% last time I looked!"

"Maybe we can pay them out partially," Mandy said. "Ask them to hold off until the rates drop."

Thinking about all the changes, some of which she had surely precipitated, Kit couldn't sleep that night. Nick found her sitting by the window overlooking the valley. Even the full moon couldn't whitewash the dirty, melting March snow.

"Tell me what's bothering you," he said, sitting down beside her and drawing her into his arms.

"I feel like a jinx, Nick. Teresa was right. Everything seems to be falling apart. It has ever since I arrived."

"Do you think that people are leaving the commune just because you're here? Do you think that you caused the Skuces' problems?"

"No. But have I put romantic notions into Bonnie's head through my writing? Have I given her a false sense of reality?"

"Do you blame the girl for leaving?"

"God, no!"

"Maybe you gave her the courage to leave."

"I just hope she hasn't traded one hell for another," she said, envisioning Bonnie pregnant and abandonned by her boyfriend in some strange city.

Nick put his arms around her. "Not that long ago you convinced me not to feel guilty for circumstances beyond my control. Time you listened to that sage advice yourself."

As she snuggled against his chest she said, "I love you, Nick."

"I know."

Chapter 42

I know now that I am losing my mind. But it is the only thing I have left to lose.

Tristan and I were sitting in my secret bower as usual last week. The days grow shorter rapidly, and it was nearly dusk when it happened.

I didn't notice it at first, but Tristan's ears pricked up in alarm and he began to growl low and threateningly. And suddenly it charged up from the ravine - a malevolent fox, its teeth bared, an evil glint in its eyes, saliva frothing at its mouth.

I knew instantly what was wrong, and shouted to Tristan not to go near it. But the fox had no fear of us and advanced belligerently toward me. I tried backing up, but was hemmed in by the trees, effectively trapped, the snarling beast advancing with its flashing eyes and hideous sneer. Despite my desperate screams, Tristan attacked it and they fought viciously until the fox lay dead at Tristan's feet.

I was horrified. As a country girl, I know well the dangers of rabies, an excruciatingly deadly disease affecting humans as well as animals. And I knew that Tristan had just signed his own death warrant.

I threw myself to my knees and embraced my heroic friend, who wagged his tail happily at my outburst of affection. Resting my face against his shoulder, I wept, for I could see the deep bite marks on Tristan's flanks, which meant that he was doomed to a horrendous death.

"Stay!" I commanded as I walked away. Tail still wagging, but with a doubtful look in his eyes, Tristan watched me walk away. Back at the house, I sent Betsy to summon Hugh. "Tell him to bring his gun," I said.

I was sitting stroking Tristan's head when Hugh arrived. I didn't look at him as I said, "Tristan killed a rabid fox. And he's been bitten."

Hugh cursed and said, "Alright, Violet. Let me deal with it."

But I could not drag myself away from my good and faithful friend, who had twice saved my life. What sort of friend was I to now take his life in payment?

I spoke to him as I always did, as if he understood me. "You've been a devoted friend, Tristan, and I love you dearly. I don't know what I will do without you! I love you, old boy, and I'll never forget you!"

Hugh, grabbing me by the shoulders, pulled me away, suggesting I might want to absent myself.

I could not see for the tears streaming from my eyes, but walked blindly away, telling Tristan to "stay". When I heard the shot a moment later, I felt as though the bullet had pierced my own heart.

"I'm so sorry, Violet," Hugh said, embracing me.

I leaned my head against his shoulder, but I wasn't truly there. I had already passed over into the realm of madness.

We buried Tristan under my favourite tree in the apple orchard. I have fashioned a wooden cross for him with his name upon it.

Now I look down beside me to where Tristan has kept vigil these last seven years, and I can't believe that he, too, is gone.

I feel as if I doom all those I love.

Chapter 43

It was mid-April when Kit received a letter from Cleo.

My Dear Kit,

How kind of you to think of me in my hour of need. Your letter was much appreciated. So sorry to hear of the death of your friend and our erstwhile neighbour. I always knew the Skuces were a bad lot, but who would have thought they would resort to murder, and on our very doorstep! Rhett would have been intrigued to hear all that. How I do miss him.

Can you blame me for not wanting to live there anymore?! Anyway, without Rhett the place has no appeal for me - far too isolated for my tastes. I wonder how you can stand it, my dear! For the time being my friend in France has offered me a home with him, at his chateau. I've always loved that place, and Max is an old and dear friend. Now you mustn't have any naughty thoughts about us, although I'm sure people will talk. He lost his wife a few years ago, and we'll be good company for one another. And quite frankly, my dear, I find myself most suited to that kind of life.

I do wish you would find yourself a good man and settle down, so I needn't worry about you living amongst all those strange characters. If you're ever in France, you really must come to visit us. I know that Max would be delighted to have you as a guest....

Kit laughed. How typically Cleo! Anyway, she was glad that Cleo had found a niche for herself - and Kit could easily imagine her playing the *grande dame* at a French chateau. She would do it so well.

As Kit gazed out the rain-streaked window, she imagined a turretted, champagne-coloured castle sprawling amidst manicured grounds, and surrounded by sun-drenched vineyards. It might be rather fun to visit Cleo at that.

Kit detested the early spring when everything was muddy and grey and lifeless still. Pockets of dirty snow lay tucked in shady nooks, and although the ground had started to dry out, this past week of rain had turned it to porridge.

Mrs. Pridholm, the cleaning lady, stuck her head around the library door as if afraid to trespass any further and said. "Can I do in here now?"

"Of course! I have some things to do in the kitchen." Kit took her letter and her coffee with her, and finished them both in the kitchen.

She was startled a moment later by a loud banging on the door. And even more startled to see Arnie Bryce standing there alone and highly agitated. His face was contorted into what Kit at first thought was a hideous smile, but then realized was horror. He was panting and sobbing, and gurgled something unintelligible.

"Arnie, is something wrong?"

He nodded his head, his whole body rocking with the violent motion.

"Is someone hurt?"

"G'gina," he wailed. He was plucking at her arm, trying to get her to follow him.

Kit's mouth was dry with the fear that communicated itself from Arnie. She knew it was pointless to quiz him further on what had happened, but, aware that farming accidents frequently occurred, she envisioned something terrible.

"OK. Arnie, I'll come with you. Just a minute." She picked up the phone and called the McGraths. When Jean answered, Kit asked her to relay a message quickly to Alan, or anyone else who might help. Then she pulled on her jacket and wellies.

Arnie had been standing wringing his hands, rocking back and forth on his heels, with tears streaming unchecked down his face. Terror clutched Kit's heart, for she was sure now that something truly dreadful had happened. She hoped she had the nerve to face whatever horror awaited her.

Arnie wanted to pull her toward the ravine, but she put a firm hand on his arm and said, "We'll go by car. It's faster."

She stuffed his huge bulk into the front seat beside her. She was sure the drumming of her heart must be audible. During the short drive, she did realize that the rain had stopped, although dark clouds still threatened.

Kit pulled into the muddy yard between the house and the barn. Gazing toward the barn, Arnie let out an anguished yowl so eerie that it turned Kit's blood to ice.

The yard seemed uncannily quiet, and Kit experienced a moment of cowardice. Surely she could wait in the car until Alan arrived. But what if Georgina was badly injured, and needed immediate medical attention? Kit wouldn't even allow her mind to dwell on what could possibly have happened. At least Georgina hadn't been caught in a piece of machinery. Or was there something in the barn? A chainsaw even?

Arnie gave her no more time to think. He locked his bear paw around her arm and almost dragged her through the dark and forbidding opening to the barn.

Kit's "Georgina?" came out as a cracked squeak. She prayed to hear a response, but heard only the snuffling and shuffling of the cows. A chicken suddenly darted across their path, squawking and flapping as if chasing some phantom interloper. Tense as she was, Kit couldn't hold back a small shriek.

A moment later she gasped. And then screamed. And Arnie's whole soul screamed in protest.

Georgina hung from the rafters, her head lolling to one side, her face hideously bloated and purple.

Kit's shaking hands cupped her face, but her eyes seemed rivetted to the gruesome sight. The body swayed slightly. It dangled like a broken puppet. It wasn't Georgina. Surely not.

"Oh, my God," she whispered, backing away. "Oh, no!"

The noise of Arnie howling like a frightened child brought Kit back to her senses. He was knuckling his eyes as though he could erase that gruesome image from his sight. "Come away, Arnie," she said gently. "There's nothing we can do for her."

Kit suddenly remembered what George had threatened to do to Georgina the last time she'd visited. "Where's your father?" she demanded sharply. "Did he do this?"

Arnie looked at her curiously, as though he couldn't believe her stupidity, and Kit felt fear slither down her spine. He grabbed her arm and hauled her toward the house. Kit had no wish to go anywhere near a murderer, so she tried to pull away from Arnie. But he was determined she would see his father, and was deaf to her protests. She started to struggle uselessly. He dragged her along easily, and she couldn't get a purchase in the mud. She skidded and slipped behind him through the gooey muck.

"No, Arnie! I don't want to see him! Let go of me! Stop!"

He was strangely silent now, and seemed totally oblivious to her. He pulled her up the back steps and thrust her through the open door.

The stench of blood assailed her nostrils at the same moment that her eyes took in the scene. George Bryce lay sprawled on the floor in a pool of congealing blood. His eyes stared as if in disbelief. On the table beside him lay a wicked-looking carving knife, smeared with blood.

Kit heard herself scream. She turned and crashed into Arnie, who stood behind her, blocking the doorway.

For an insane moment, she thought that he was going to kill her, too.

As if too much horror had blinded him, his eyes took on a vacant look. He turned and scuttled back to the barn in his awkward, crab-like gait.

Alan and Stuart pulled into the yard. Kit, much to her embarrassment, felt herself sliding into darkness.

.   .   .

When Kit regained consciousness, she found herself stretched out in the back seat of her car. At first she thought it had all been a horrendous nightmare, but then she noticed the police car in the yard and an ambulance just pulling in.

Alan came grimly over to the car, his eyes burning with unshed tears. "Are you alright now, Kit?"

"I'm not sure I'll ever be alright again." She put her hands over her face, but the grisly images were imprinted upon her retina. "What happened?"

Alan rubbed his brow. In a tight voice he said, "Georgie left a note... *Sorry, Arnie, I just can't take any more.*" Alan turned away from her. He seemed to be gazing up to the heavens from whence a fine Scotch mist was descending.

"You mean, she killed her father and then herself?"

He nodded.

"Oh, God!"

They were silent for a few minutes, each thinking of what could - should - have been done to prevent this tragedy.

Alan said, "There was a letter from the bank saying they'd have to foreclose. I guess George must've flown into a rage. Georgie probably reached her breaking point...."

Kit could easily conjure up the scene - George screaming abuse. Georgina snatching up the knife and plunging it into her tormentor over and over again to stop his ceaseless carping. She wiped her eyes and said, "And then couldn't live with the horror of what she'd done in that moment of madness."

Kit watched the ambulance attendants carting the corpse from the barn.

"Poor Arnie," Kit said, feeling guilty that for an instant she had thought him responsible for this carnage. "What will happen to him?"

"He's sitting in the barn with his knees drawn up, clutching that medallion you gave him as though it were a talisman against evil. And he's grinning. I suppose he'll go into an institution of some kind."

They watched the other body being carried from the house. The last Bryce to leave this land.

Chapter 44

I detest November. For me it is the dead of winter. Soon we will descend softly and gently into the womb-like warmth of Christmas. In January it snows prettily or with exhilarating violence. February is full of surprises - glistening ice storms, fierce blizzards, or sudden thaws that give a taste of spring. And March brings the messy death throes of winter. But surely no time is as dismal and soul-destroying as November.

But I cannot survive another winter.

My heart is colder and deader than any melancholy November day.

Mrs. Skuce is scandalized that I don't attend church anymore (even though she belongs to the Scottish church and I, to the Anglican). But I can no longer believe in the God of my childhood. If He exists at all, why does He allow so much unnecessary suffering and sorrow? I feel no reverence for such a God. And to fear Him? What more can he do to me? And why should I worship a vindictive deity?

If I believe in anything, perhaps it is in the gods of the ancient Greeks - Pan and his cohorts - the arrogant, mischievous, scheming gods that toy with us mortals for their own enjoyment. Yes, that I can believe.

I have not seen Daniel since Lily's funeral last November. He writes to me occasionally, his letters full of impersonal events, the words barren of the sonorous richness and humorous affection in his voice. And what have I to relate but the dreariness of a useless existence? So I tell him of the Refuge and add tidbits of Ottawa gossip that I think will amuse him.

But this is a sterile relationship that brings me little comfort.

I have just penned this to him:

My Darling Daniel,

I cannot leave this world without telling you how much I have loved you.

Of course, the noble thing to do would be to say nothing, to allow you to continue thinking that I cared too little for you.

But I am not noble. Nor ever have been. I am merely a woman tormented and betrayed by forces beyond my power.

In truth, I have loved you for a long time. Loved you to distraction, to the very core of my being. I care more for you than life itself.

But I could never marry you, and for this deceit I beg your forgiveness.

You see, my darling Daniel, I have syphilis. Never mind how I contracted it, except to know that I was an unwilling victim. I was a child still, violated by someone I loved and trusted. Someone who has destroyed my life.

I wish I had had the courage to tell you this myself. But I didn't.

I tell you now, not to elicit pity, but to explain my actions. I can think of nothing more wonderful, no greater ecstasy, than to have been your wife. You once gave me the opportunity to express my love, and I had to disillusion you. You cannot imagine what that cost me!

Please do not think too harshly of me, my darling. If there is a heaven, then surely we will meet again. Please tell no one of my secret.

Farewell, my darling! Farewell!

Now that I have written it, I am not certain I will send it to him. What purpose would it serve? I will be gone, and Daniel will be left with what? Regrets? Pity? Horror even?

Perhaps it is best to leave things as they are. Let them all retain their misconceptions of me. Daniel, that I loved my freedom more than I loved him. Hugh, Kate, and the others, that I wasted my life waiting for that scoundrel, Neil. My sisters, that I am willfully, even spitefully unconventional. Only Lily came closest to understanding me, and even she did not know what was in my heart or what demons tormented my soul.

I have left the Refuge to the city of Ottawa with the proviso that Marjorie, Lise, and Nancy retain their positions as long as they wish. I have bequeathed them each a handsome legacy, so I wouldn't blame them for taking some ease and passing the responsibilities on to others.

I have provided for Betsy and the Skuces, and left legacies to my Godchildren. The remainder of my estate will be divided among my nieces and nephews.

My sisters will be able to sell Moon Hall, but at least I shall always be here, next to my beloved companion, Tristan. (The vicar will no doubt be relieved by my instructions for burial.) Perhaps my sinful spirit will be sentenced to forever walk this domain, but that will be no hardship to me. Indeed, I relish the thought that I might haunt Moon Hall forevermore.

I have said no goodbyes, and left no letters of explanation or regret. Let them make what they will of my death.

I am wearing my best black silk gown. For Mrs. Skuce. I don't want her to be embarrassed by any lack of dignity on my part. I know she'll appreciate this simple gesture.

I stare at the sealed letter to Daniel, looking at the way my pen formed the letters of his name, waiting to see if they would transform themselves into a vision of my beloved. But they are merely hieroglyphics whose substance and even meaning I seem to have lost.

That is how my life has become - empty, joyless, hopeless. Contentment has been usurped by rage and bitterness. So much that I fear that violent madness will soon possess me. I want to scream, to lash out, to destroy.

In this murderous fury I can think of nothing better to destroy than myself. While I still have the mental faculties and the power to make decisions and carry them out.

I hold the letter to Daniel in my hand, not sure if I should toss it into the fire or leave it with the others.

Oh, Daniel....

Chapter 45

Nick took Kit away for a week. They went first to St. Andrew's-by-the-Sea, where they stayed in a charming inn that had once been the summer home of Sir Charles Tupper - where Violet had been a guest at a picnic luncheon on the lawn on a long-forgotten summer's day.

Although the weather was chilly, Kit and Nick went for bracing walks through the quaint town, and the sea air was refreshing. It helped Kit to feel this connection with Violet, helped to cleanse her mind somewhat of the other horror, although she knew she would never be completely free of those grisly images.

Sometimes her mind would perversely focus on one, and she would feel her stomach tighten and threaten to rebel. By sheer force of will she concentrated on something tangible, and the revulsion would subside.

Even without thinking about recent events, there was enough lunacy and turmoil in the world to depress anyone. The new American president, Ronald Reagan, had been shot only a few weeks ago, there was unrest in Poland, the war between Iran and Iraq showed no signs of abating, and a deadly new disease named AIDS was starting to make the headlines.

Kit wondered if it was to be some new venereal scourge, something to replace the dreaded syphilis of previous centuries. When syphilis had first appeared, it had been a fearfully virulent, gruesome, and deadly pestilence, too. Over the centuries it had become a more subtle and insidious plague, and was even today, an elusive and not fully understood organism.

From St. Andrew's they travelled to Quebec City. With its 17th century architecture and European flavour, it was a different world from Todmorden. Here they spent days strolling the cobblestoned streets of the old walled city, and evenings lingering over exquisite meals in their fanciful, luxurious hotel which was perched on the cliffs overlooking the St. Lawrence.

The Dufferins had loved Quebec, and had fixed up the Citadel as another Viceregal residence. They were immortalized there as the builders of the Dufferin Terrace, which provided a magnificent promenade along the clifftop, and just outside the hotel.

Kit and Nick spent a few days in Montreal, too, where Kit tried to delve into Daniel Haywood's past. She discovered that he had been a much-respected lecturer at the University until his death in 1914. His daughter Lilian had also become a doctor - not an easy feat for a woman in those days. Isobel, a leading society hostess and do-gooder, judging by newspaper accounts, had died in 1901.

Kit wished she could have known Daniel's thoughts and feelings but no letters or diaries seemed to have survived him. Still, she was able to imagine an inner life for the man who was Daniel in her novel. But what had he truly thought of Violet's suicide? Had he felt at all guilty or responsible, regretting perhaps that he had not been around when she had most needed him?

The Thorndikes were still a prominent Montreal family, but there was no point in approaching them. Surely Kit knew more than they would about their McAllister heritage. They were so long enthroned in their Westmount castle that they probably didn't even remember an ancestor of such humble beginnings.

By the end of the week, Kit felt able to go home to Moon Hall, and needed to immerse herself in her work.

But the first thing that she did when they returned was to visit Georgina's grave.

The small cemetery was tucked in behind the Presbyterian church, hidden from all but the most observant eyes. It was bracketed by stands of trees, still naked, that would be lush and green in summer. Now, patches of sugary snow lay melting in the sun-dappled thickets. The tall trees swayed in the balmy breeze, their bony branches clicking. A bird warbled and trilled, calling for a mate. Or was it just rejoicing in the warming sunshine, at the signs of spring and the promise of summer?

A wrought iron gate, hinged on granite pillars, opened soundlessly onto the sunny glade.

The sight of the newly turned graves at the far end sent a wave of dizziness through Kit. Stupidly, she hadn't thought of George Bryce's grave at all. She hadn't expected George and Georgina to be buried so companionably side by side. It was horrid in a way. Even in death, Georgina could not escape her father.

But what did it matter to Georgina now, Kit wondered. She was beyond caring. At least they hadn't buried her in disgrace in some potter's field.

As Kit walked toward the graves, she noticed the many headstones of varying ages that bore the name Bryce or McGrath or Skuce. It made her realize - even more than the McGrath log cabin had - how deeply these people were rooted in the community.

Here was Hugh's grave, with Ruth next to him. And there rested Kate, who would be horrified to know what tragedy had befallen her descendants - though Kit could hardly believe that the boorish George could have been descended from her.

Leighton was not buried here, but in the non-denominational cemetery at the other end of the village.

When Kit reached the new graves, she struggled not to remember how she had last seen Georgina and her father.

Georgina had no headstone as yet, and George's was incomplete. It had been erected for Georgina's mother, but it was George's name that came first, with the date of his birth carved out but the date of death still blank. Georgina's mother was listed underneath as "his wife", as if she had owed her existence solely to him. His appendage and slave.

How absurdly peaceful it all was, almost belying the violent desperation of the woman who lay beneath the soil. Kit felt once again as she had when she'd finished reading Violet McAllister's diary - that so much raw emotion, such pain and despair, must surely leave something in the wake of their passing. Not this gentle country silence.

But there were no echoes of anguish. Not here. Only the sounds of life reawakening as spring seized hold of the countryside. The anguish reverberated only in the minds of those who had known Georgina.

Alan was beside her before Kit was aware of his presence. He had his hands shoved down hard into his jacket pockets. His expression was grim.

"What could I have done to save her?" he asked, staring at the grave.

"I don't know what any of us could have done, Alan. She had our friendship. But we're all of us alone, aren't we. The best we can hope for is someone to share things with to prevent that aloneness from becoming loneliness."

"Did I disappoint her? Did she expect too much of me?"

Kit could sense his guilt, but knew that she couldn't lie to him. "I think she loved you. But we can't be responsible for people falling in love with us," she said, thinking of Stuart.

Alan looked at her then, a wistful look that revealed more than he wanted to show or Kit wanted to see. It was gone before Kit was even certain she had seen it. Yet she knew. It was what she had often feared, what Mary had warned her about. Suddenly she felt tears welling up in her eyes - feeling the sorrow of so many broken hearts and broken dreams.

Whereas Alan had stoically kept his feelings a secret from her all this time, her tears were very nearly his undoing. He gripped her shoulder in a fierce, reassuring embrace. They stood together in silence while Kit composed herself. Then he turned and trudged away.

While she stood by the quiet grave in the gentle April sunshine, she recognized a bond between Georgina and Violet - two women, though quite different, who had sought the same way to alleviate the hopelessness of an unbearable life

After that it was easy to finish her novel. She dedicated the book to them both.

But now that Violet's story was finished, Kit felt as if she had lost another friend. Sometimes she just sat in the secret garden staring at the aged Pan, and trying to feel some connection with her ghost and muse. But she knew it was time to let Violet finally rest in peace. Perhaps Violet would be content now that her story had been told, even if no one knew it was true.

Kit attended Wayne Skuce's trial, but it lasted less than a week. With Pete as a witness, there was no doubt of Wayne's guilt - it became a matter of intent.

Facing that man who still terrorized her in dreams, she was suddenly, delightfully devoid of fear. That weasel was now himself nervous and fearful. And no longer the bogie man.

Wayne was found guilty of the lesser charge of manslaughter in the death of Leighton Pearse, and was sentenced to seven years in prison.

When Myrtle collapsed tearfully against her husband, he shrugged her away and was heard to mutter, "Stop yer God-damned snivellin', woman!"

In mid-May, someone tried to assassinate the Pope.

At the end of May, Nigel came to Moon Hall.

Kit and Nick were just finishing their lunch, having spent the morning preparing the vegetable garden. These normal, everyday chores were bringing her life back on an even keel.

Kit was helping Nick with the magazine now that she was between books, and had already researched and written a couple of articles. She was enjoying the change and the challenge, and felt she was doing something worthwhile. And it was keeping her too busy to brood.

But on the weekends they puttered around Moon Hall, fixing things, planning changes, and gardening.

"I wonder who that could be?" Kit said when she heard the knock on the front door. Only the Pughs had ever used that entrance, and for a moment Kit wondered it Cleo was here to visit.

She was flabbergasted when she saw Nigel standing there. And suddenly very conscious of her muddied jeans, sloppy shirt, and tangled hair.

As usual he was faultlessly clad. He smiled warmly, and betrayed no surprise at her appearance. He said only, "I hope I haven't arrived at an inconvenient time."

As if it were the most natural thing for him to be here at all. A weekend guest arrived early.

Kit found herself gobbling air, but managed to say, "Of course not. Please come in."

She wondered if he could see her trembling. All those suppressed emotions - the love and the anguish - were suddenly unleashed, and she was weak from their assault.

With a quick swivel of his head, Nigel took in the salient points of the hallway as he stepped inside.

Nick appeared from the kitchen. Nigel gave him a tight-lipped smile.

Kit said, "Nigel, this is Nick Radcliffe. Nick...you know Nigel," she finished lamely. "He was one of your students," Kit explained to Nigel's unspoken query.

"Ah... Well, Kat, this is quite some place you have here."

That nickname jarred. He had called her Kit Kat in the beginning, in some silly reference to a candy bar, and then had shortened it to his own pet name, saying it was much more logical for Kathryn anyway.

"Do come into the sitting room," Kit said. In her present grubby state, she hardly felt like entertaining there, but couldn't really see Nigel joining them at the intimacy of the kitchen table.

"Nick," she looked at him helplessly, "perhaps we could have some drinks. Scotch..."

Nigel said it at the same time as she did. He smiled and allowed her to finish.

"...on the rocks for Nigel. I'll have... whatever!" Turning to Nigel she said, "So... How did you find me?"

"I read about the murder-suicide next door to you. The article mentioned that you had been the first on the scene. You can imagine my surprise! Once I found the village, it was no trouble to discover exactly where you live."

That newspaper story had been at least six weeks ago.

Nick silently handed around the drinks, taking a large brandy for himself.

"We only spend the weekends here now," Kit said. "We're in Ottawa the rest of the week."

"I see."

Nick downed his brandy and said, "If you'll excuse me, I'll get back to the garden."

"Most certainly," Nigel said. He seemed more relaxed when Nick had gone.

Kit curbed her impulse to follow Nick. She wished he'd stayed to support her. As though it were a battle, and she wanted Nick on her side? Nick would never try to make her decisions for her, she realized.

Nigel's voice softened as he gazed into her eyes and said, "Well, Kat? How are you? That must have been quite a traumatic experience for you, finding those bodies."

He spoke of them as if they had never been real. Tartly she replied, "She was my friend, Nigel. Not just a body."

"Of course. I'm sorry, Kat." He rose from the chair and came to sit beside her. "I've missed you, Kat." When she didn't reply, he said, "In all my wild imaginings, I never pictured you in a place like this. It's so wonderfully old-fashioned and gloomy. Bleak House."

"Moon Hall. It even has a ghost," she said, and told him briefly about Violet McAllister. "You'll have to read my new book when it comes out. It might surprise you."

"So you've written something different?"

She looked into his grey eyes, and felt her animosity dissipate. "Oh, yes. I think you might even approve." She noticed that he had gone more grey at the temples.

"I shall look forward to that then." He took her hand in his and said, "Your parents were extremely unforthcoming about your whereabouts, as was Fran. I didn't know how to contact you."

"There wasn't any point, Nigel. There wasn't anything left to say."

He brushed back one of her vagrant locks. "Wasn't there? Do you remember Tintagel and Trebarwith Strand, and what was the name of that little pub?"

"The King's Head."

"Yes, of course!"

"Nigel..."

"Kat, isn't it time you stopped playing truant and came home? I've given you a year to get over... well, whatever it was that instigated this little rebellion."

Had he truly not realized that their relationship had disintegrated beyond repair?

He continued. "I'll even overlook... your friend..."

"I'm not one of your students anymore, Nigel. Not playing truant. I've made a new life for myself."

She looked sadly into his eyes, torn between her nostalgic memories of their good times together and her passion for Nick. Although he could be an insufferable, arrogant bastard, Nigel was faithful. But Nick had invaded her very soul, and could not be banished with happy memories of other days.

"Come now, Kat, that sounds like a rather melodramatic line from one of your books. Can you dismiss what we had so easily?"

Kit ran her hand down Nigel's cheek in a gentle caress. "In a way, I'll always love you, Nigel. We've shared so much. It's a pity we can't be friends. But it's all or nothing, isn't it? And I'm not coming back."

"I see. Well, I suppose there really is nothing left to say then." His manner was suddenly cold and dismissive. He rose.

"Nigel, don't hate me."

"Goodbye, Kat. I doubt that we'll see each other again."

So final.

Sadly she said, "Goodbye, Nigel." It hurt her to see him so wounded, but she had nothing to offer him, neither comfort nor hope.

She stood in the open doorway watching him stride down the driveway to his car. She wanted to run after him, to fling herself into his arms, to tell him - what? That she still loved him, but not enough to leave Nick?

How unfair it was that this man, with whom she had spent nearly a quarter of her life, and for whom she still felt such deep emotion, should be so ruthlessly and completely cut out of her life! As if he had died.

But she let him go.

As he pulled out of the driveway, Kit raised a hand in a half-hearted farewell. But Nigel didn't look back.

When he had gone, Kit poured herself another drink and flung herself restlessly onto the couch. It was all very well to say she couldn't leave Nick, but how committed was he?

Kit wondered if she made a foolish mistake in rejecting Nigel so completely. And yet, it hadn't been for Nick that she had left Nigel in the first place, but for herself.

She gulped her drink and then went out to find Nick. She was surprised that he wasn't in the garden, or anywhere on the property. He must have gone down to the farm. Apprehension gripped her. What if Nigel's presence had spurred Nick into a decision - to leave her?

Kit worked frantically, hardly conscious of what she was doing. Nick still hadn't shown up an hour later, and by then she was too exhausted with work and worry to continue.

It was a warm day, so she wandered down to the ravine, hoping to intercept Nick.

There was no sight of him. Kit scooped up a handful of clear, cold water and splashed her face and neck. She sat down on the fallen log that she had perched on last summer when sketching - that time that Nick had come by and compared her to the Lady of Shalott.

But he wasn't here now. Alan and Stuart weren't working in the field, and Arnie Bryce was no longer - and never had been - a threat.

She sat for a long time in the pleasant dappled shade. She rose wearily and turned toward the house.

And then she saw Nick coming from the direction of the farm. She waited for him, her heart pounding.

"Nigel's gone, has he?"

"A long time ago."

"Are you staying?"

"Of course. I love you, Nick."

He drew her into his arms. "I was afraid you'd go back to him, Kit." He hugged her tighter. "I remember telling you once that I wasn't a jealous man. Until now. I'd never had anything to be jealous of before." He kissed her brow, her lips. "I love you, Kit."

He pulled her down onto the grassy bank. "And I've wanted to do this ever since that day I saw you sitting so seductively on that log," he said, unbuttoning her shirt.

"Nick!"

"Don't worry. There's no one about. And, after all, this is our home."